One Bloody Shirt At A Time

A Deputy Ricos Tale

Elizabeth A. Garcia

Elizabeth A. Garcia

ISBN: 1470192845
ISBN 13: 9781470192846

A Few Words About
One Bloody Shirt At A Time

Margarita Ricos is not just any deputy. She's smart. She's courageous. She's a twenty-five-year-old Chicana with attitude who grew up on the edge of the United States in Terlingua, Texas. There, the peoples and cultures of two countries are blended, more than separated, by the once-fierce Rio Grande.

Terlingua is an unincorporated settlement built around a mercury mining ghost town of the same name. It lies in the southern part of Brewster County, the largest county in the largest state in the lower forty-eight. It has more square miles than inhabitants; and more mountains than you can count: tall, short, wide, narrow, jagged, rounded, naked, stunning mountains.

Margarita and her partner, Deputy Barney George, are entrusted with preserving the peace and upholding the law in a land where the flowers and people grow wild.

Crime in south Brewster County is seldom violent, and usually does not come in the form of murder or rape. Yet Norma Bates, a married, forty-five year old, mother of three, is found dead on her kitchen floor, lying in a pool of blood. There is a single stab wound in her chest.

Deputy Ricos is about to conduct an interview about the murder when she receives a call from the sheriff. He says he has a couple from Terlingua in his office claiming their fourteen-year-old daughter was raped. Since Margarita is young, and known to the girl, perhaps she can get her to open up. The deputy is stunned by the sheriff's news. Murder—and now rape—what is going on in Terlingua?

As the deputies work to solve both crimes, a sinister presence approaches Margarita in her home in the dark. Is it a murder suspect, or the unknown rapist, or a different kind of threat altogether?

Acknowledgements

First, I thank my daughter, Margarita Garcia, who is solely responsible for the creation of the cover of this novel. Not only is she talented, she is a joy and inspiration to me, and has been since the first time I saw her face. And no, the character of Deputy Ricos is not her, but is partly inspired by her indomitable spirit. She and her love, Amber, have been my first readers since that day in 2005 when I looked up from my laptop and declared, "I'm writing a story!" They gave me support every step of the way. Thank you for the millions of words you have read on my behalf, your astute observations and suggestions, and for reading the various versions of this novel over and over again until I finally got it right.

I'm grateful to my two beautiful and wise sisters who cheer me on and cover me daily with their prayers and love.

Lynne Smith, my mentor, teacher, and friend: I'm indebted to you for your constant encouragement and the many lessons you taught and continue to teach me.

Thanks to the staff of *The Big Bend Gazette* for having faith in my writing; enough to publish my short stories, so many of them I lost count.

I spent time with my friend, retired deputy Martin Willey of the Brewster County Sheriff's Office. I'm grateful to him for his explanation of protocol, for letting me study his weapon, and for answering endless questions. Mistakes and oversights are all mine, not his. My tale is not meant to be an instruction manual for law enforcement.

Thank you to all my friends who read this novel in various stages, and not only gave me ideas, but love and encouragement.

This novel is a work of fiction. All characters are therefore fictitious. Any resemblance to a person living or dead is a coincidence.

Thank you to the people of Terlingua for being who you are and for allowing me to be part of it for so many years. Yes, I moved some things around and took a few liberties, but I tried to describe the real Terlingua as best I could. It is truly an indescribable place.

In gratitude,

Beth Garcia
West Texas
March, 2012

For my parents, who taught me I could do anything.

Chapter 1

I cringed at the sound of shattering bone. Blood was everywhere. It spurted into the dust-filled air and spread across the front of his white western shirt.

Get up, for God's sake, get up!

Rivulets of red trickled away from him, gradually soaking into the dry, cracked ground.

Get up please get up you have to get up.

A bull's deadly hoof, backed by nearly a ton of force, had crashed its way through my husband's chest. Rodeo fans shrieked and tried to cover their children's eyes. Others fled the stands or stood frozen with shock. Some tried to climb into the arena but the bull, snorting and wild with panic, kept them back.

In slow motion, the clown sank to his knees, his mouth open in a silent scream. There was blood everywhere.

I jolted awake. The dream was always the same and I always woke with the same pounding heart and choking, powerless feeling of loss and grief. I didn't know if the accident had happened like I dreamed it because I hadn't been there. Worse than that, much worse, was that my last conversation with Kevin had been an angry one.

"I don't care if you ever come back from Amarillo," turned out to be my final words to the man I adored. Now I had to live with them.

I rose from the bed and sat on the edge of it. That the crunching of bone could have been heard was unlikely, even if the crowd hadn't been screaming. But the bull's foot had crushed Kevin's chest, that much was true and, I suxpposed, the only fact that mattered. It had been a gory scene—I had his clothes to prove it.

Kevin was a rodeo champion who won trophies, titles, money and other prizes. He could stay on a twisting, bucking bull past the required eight seconds. His dismounts were usually made in a smooth, fluid motion, gaining him extra points in the scoring of the ride. *Safe and smooth, Baby,* he'd say with a grin, and his rides had been, until that day, when his spur had become entangled in the strap. When he slid off the back of the bull, it bucked franticly, dragging him sideways a couple of seconds, then brought its hind legs crashing down. End of the ride, end of Kevin, and some days it seemed it would be the end of me.

I took his shirt out of the bottom drawer of the dresser and set it on my lap. At the funeral home, Kevin's things had been handed to me in a box. My mother tried to take it but I'd refused to let it go. The blood on his clothes was all I had left of him. It was a stiff, rust-colored stain, but it held his DNA and to me, right then, it was him.

Eventually I made a cup of hot tea, cooled it with a splash of Jack Daniels, and took it and the shirt onto my porch. I sat in a white wicker rocking chair and stared at a black hulk standing against a slightly lighter sky: Cimarron Mountain.

The stars were a dazzling display, oblivious to human misery and heartache. I pulled Kevin's denim jacket around me, snuggled down into it, and eventually fell asleep like that. I didn't hear the insistent ringing of both my cell phone and land line.

* * *

"Ricos!" Someone was shaking my arm and it was irritating as hell.

When I opened my eyes, a giant man dressed in a deputy sheriff uniform was leaning over me. It took a moment to register.

"Ricos, I've been calling and thought something had happened to you. Why are you sleeping on your porch?" His voice trailed away as he took in the bloody shirt on my lap. "You have to stop this, Margarita," he said gently.

"I couldn't sleep.... Why are you here? It's barely morning."

"Why is Kevin's shirt here? Why do you even have that shirt?"

I looked down at it. It was beautiful and had been perfectly starched and white before the bull ruined it. It was pure pima cotton with a ¼ inch white herringbone stripe and diamond-shaped, pearlized snaps up the front and on each pocket.

"I like this shirt," I said.

"Ricos, you've got to get a grip."

"Tell me how to do that."

He slumped his big self into the chair next to me and sighed.

"I had that dream again, Barney."

"Yeah, I thought so." He glanced over at my mountain. The golden-pink colors of sunrise were washing over its reddish spires and sheer rock faces. It was about as stunning as anything could ever be.

"I think I'm going to be all right, and then the dreams come and I realize I'm not."

"You're okay, Ricos. The dreams knock you off track, that's all. One day you'll stop having them. Time will take care of it if nothing else does. Meanwhile, you should stop handling that shirt."

"It's all I have of him, Barney."

"It's a bloody shirt, Ricos."

"But it's part of Kevin."

"The man you love is gone. It's been over a year."

"You can't tell me how long to be sad. Everyone says it's been more than a year like I should be over it already. That's crap."

Suddenly Barney shot out of the chair. "I came to get you 'cause there's been a murder. Norma Bates was stabbed last night and we've got to get over there right now." He frowned at his watch. "The sheriff should be arriving in about thirty minutes."

"Norma Bates murdered? Are you sure it was murder?"

"Well not one hundred percent until I see the scene, but people don't usually stab themselves in the heart, do they?"

Chapter 2

"What do you want me to do, Barney?" I pulled on a pair of latex gloves and swallowed the foul taste in my mouth. I was willing to do almost anything if I didn't have to look at the body again. I had already thrown up once.

Norma Bates was lying in a pool of blood in the middle of her filthy kitchen in a house that was incredibly hot—too hot for working or moving. Too hot even for being dead.

"Would you sweep?" Barney was lifting fingerprints from the area around the sink and didn't look up. "It looks like mostly trash but something useful might turn up."

The floor hadn't been swept or mopped in six months, at least. The dingy tiles were littered with bits of paper, spilled food that dried where it fell, and a few pieces of broken toys: an armless Shrek, a hairless, naked Barbie, and miniscule parts from Matchbox trucks and cars. I set the sad toys on a far corner of the counter. They didn't seem pertinent to the murder, only proof that children lived there.

I lifted a torn, partially crumpled photograph of a young Latino off the floor. His hair was black and shiny, and he had a been-at-the-beach-all-summer complexion. The smile on his lips was seductive—this man knew he was a knock-out—but his eyes were kind and somehow sad in spite of his movie star looks. The eyes, his best asset, were like gazing into an abyss full of stars.

"What are you looking at, Ricos?"

I matched the photo at the tear, and held it in front of Barney. "Do you know this man?"

He stood, slowly straightening his six-and-a-half-foot frame from a crouching position, swiped his face across his shirtsleeve, and frowned at the handsome man. "He's nice-looking. I've never seen him before. You don't know him?"

"I've never seen him, either."

"He could be your brother."

"I don't have a brother."

Barney sighed. "I'm just saying he looks like you."

"He's Mexican. I'm half Mexican. Other than that, I don't see a resemblance."

"You're a hard-headed pain-in-the-butt."

"What's your point?"

"Skip it. Maybe Norma and another woman were fighting over him."

"Or Norma was having an affair with him and he got sick of her and stabbed her," I suggested.

"You really think a woman as unattractive as Norma could get a good-looking man like that even once?"

"Good point."

I found a broom and dustpan in a closet. I had to fight a big gray spider for them, but I got to work, meticulously sweeping from the line of blood outward. I tried not to look at the dead woman. She had been stabbed in the heart and a big, bloody stain had spread across her chest.

The kitchen table had been shoved from the center of the room, where Norma now lay, to the far wall. One trapped chair had skidded along with it, and four other chairs were toppled and lay askew, dead in battle. Utensils, pots, and pans were scattered, maybe thrown in a fight—an attack or in self defense? Knowing Norma, I'd guess she started it, but guessing is unacceptable in crime scene investigation.

I had hated Norma Bates alive, but in death she was somehow pitiful. What a bitch she had been. Now she was a dead bitch, but since I was supposed to show respect for the victim, I kept my mouth shut. That wasn't hard since Barney wasn't saying much. He was sweating profusely and concentrating on lifting prints. His uniform looked like he'd taken a shower in it. Occasionally he'd straighten up, wipe his face, and curse with abandon.

On another day, at a different scene, I might have laughed out loud, but this one wasn't funny. The whole thing reminded me of Kevin and the bull and the bloodstain on his chest—the chest where I'd loved to lay my head.

I took a trembling breath of air that was stifling and smelled of stale blood and filth. The Bates family lived off the grid and had solar power, but not enough to run anything to cool the place. There was only an oscillating fan that half-heartedly pushed against the hot air.

Once the first pile of debris was swept up, I set the dustpan on the counter to examine the trash, using the pen from my pocket to move things around. There was dried macaroni, a few hairs, dust balls, scraps of paper, the crumpled photograph, some dried peas, and one earring. It was a gold hoop with a tiny heart in the center and I'd seen it before—and recently—on my mother. My heart went into my throat. *My mother did this? There's no way my mother could have done it!* I lifted the hoop with the pen and studied it. I was sure it was hers and it had been in the debris closest to the body.

Should I leave it and let it become part of the evidence? Yes, of course. But I could take it and match it for certain to the other one—if I could find the other one. To take it would be tampering with evidence in a murder investigation and maybe it wasn't even hers. Except I knew it was.

Sheriff Ben would flip if he ever found out I took it. I slipped it into my pocket, then took it out and started to put it back with the other trash in the dustpan. I glanced around like a shoplifter to see what Barney was doing but he wasn't watching me. I slipped the earring back into my pocket. I wanted to grill Mom myself, or that's what I told my conscience. Sweat poured off me as I swept up the rest of the kitchen.

Afterwards I stepped outside into the shade of a lean-to back porch. It wasn't much cooler, but the air smelled better and breathing was easier. I sighed and comforted myself with the breathtaking views in all directions, scenery that never failed me even when everything else did: hazy mountains with bare cliff faces of red-brown rock, boulder-strewn hills that appear to be gently rolling but are anything but gentle. In the Big Bend of Texas, nothing is as it appears. Bizarre shapes and show-off colors materialize as light floods the landscape. Things gleam for a while then darken, change shape, move, and eventually disappear as the sun cuts its path across the sky. By the time darkness settles, you wonder if the whole scene wasn't just a trick of your imagination.

Entire mountains come and go as if by magic, or hang suspended above the desert. Distances are deceiving. Is that strange rock formation fifteen miles away, or fifty? There are not many trees or shrubs to get in the way of the vistas, and on a clear day it's possible to see one hundred miles into Mexico.

And the senses lie. From the vantage point of the mountains, the desert looks like a desolate moonscape; from the desert, the mountains seem bare. Neither is true.

I looked around on the back porch, and then the rocky ground beside it. When that yielded nothing, I moved to the front of the house. There was a discarded cigarette butt and a crumpled, empty pack of Rojos brand, manufactured in Mexico. Maybe it meant nothing, and could have gotten there a hundred ways, but I put it into an evidence bag anyway.

The cloud of dust coming my way was most likely my boss, Sheriff Ben Duncan, and I told myself to go back inside but couldn't. He parked his Ford truck on the side of the road by the house and jumped down. When he noticed me watching he smiled and waved. I hurried towards him.

"How's it going, Deputy Ricos?" He extended his hand and we exchanged hellos as if there wasn't a dead body melting into the floor. Then he began to walk towards the house. I followed because it would've been wrong to stand by the road the rest of the day.

Sheriff Duncan is six feet tall. He's old, sixty-something, yet doesn't seem old. He has broad shoulders and stands erect which makes him seem younger, but he has an older man's tolerant attitude. His thick hair is wavy and completely white. He's been a lawman since he was twenty years old. I wonder if it wasn't his job more than age that turned his hair. I could almost feel mine going white when I thought of the close, hot smell of the blood in that dirty little kitchen.

When we got to the door, Sheriff Duncan paused, removed his hat, took out a handkerchief, and wiped his brow. "Hot as hell," he said as he replaced the hat. "Is Barney in here?"

"Yes sir, he's still fingerprinting. I just stepped out for some fresh air."

"It's hard isn't it, Margarita?"

"Yes, sir, especially when it's someone you know, dying violently like that. She was a mom, too."

I knew Norma's children would suffer because of her untimely death and I felt sorry for them. Although I had wished death on Norma many times, seeing it happen to her was another thing.

Sheriff Ben removed his sunglasses and wiped beads of sweat from beneath his eyes. I thought it was going to go badly for him in that kitchen. When he had stuffed the handkerchief back into his pocket he held the door open for me.

Our sheriff is a decent man and always treats me well. I'm one of only two women in the Sheriff's Office, and the only one in Terlingua. Marcy and I take a lot of hassle from the guys, all of it behind the sheriff's back. The male deputies think we can't possibly be as good as they are: only men should carry guns and hunt down criminals. (Like we all do so much of that!) To them we're either bitches or sex objects and sometimes both. The sheriff treats us as equals and deals with us fairly. He's soft-spoken and old-fashioned in many ways, which totally annoyed me at first. Now I've become more or less resigned to it. At least he isn't like the deputies.

I stood next to the sheriff and felt the earring in my pocket. While he observed the victim, I moved sideways to the dustpan and dropped in the gold hoop, then put the whole mess into an evidence bag. My mother would have to fend for herself. She is a grown woman and I'm a professional law enforcement officer. Surely she could explain how her earring got to the scene of a murder.

"Damn it's hot in here!" Barney's roar shook the house as he came down the narrow hallway from the bedrooms. He wiped his face on his uniform sleeve and might have continued cursing except that he saw our boss standing over the body.

"Yes, Deputy George, it certainly is that," commented the sheriff without looking up.

Barney removed the glove from his right hand and he and the sheriff greeted each other. Then my partner and I walked him through the Bates home. It was a mess, and there had been a violent struggle in the kitchen, but the house seemed more neglected than anything.

"Where's the rest of the family?" asked the sheriff. "I see signs of a family everywhere, but no family."

"We don't know where they are, sir."

"Maybe they went to that Baptist Church family retreat that started Saturday," Barney suggested. "A lot of people were going."

"They don't go to church," I said.

My partner glared at me. "How would you know that?"

"Because I know this family, Barney. Norma was very anti-organized religion."

Actually, Norma was anti-anything in which she wasn't the focal point, but I kept that to myself. She wouldn't have been able to sit still in a church and let God get all the credit.

"Maybe she stayed home and the rest of them went," Barney said overly patiently, as if I was mentally slow. He figured he was my superior because of his sex, an extra four years experience in law enforcement work, and his formidable size.

"Did you call Chuck?" Sheriff Ben asked Barney.

Chuck is our Justice of the Peace. Our J.P. serves as a judge for minor traffic violations and small claims court. He also marries people and pronounces bodies dead in lieu of a coroner, since we don't have one.

"Yes, sir," said Barney, "he'll be here any time. I notified the funeral home, too."

"Good," said the sheriff and pulled out his cell phone. He dialed, waited, and then said, "Guy? Sheriff Duncan." He was calling our constable. "I'd like for you to come to the scene of a murder." He listened. "Yes, a murder." He enunciated *murder* and rolled his eyes at me. "That's right, in Terlingua. Do you know where the Bates family lives?" Another pause. "Yes, that's the one. I want you to guard the crime scene while I speak with my deputies about the investigation."

Barney and I exchanged a glance.

Sheriff Ben listened a bit longer. "Thanks," he said, "we'll be waiting."

At that moment, our J.P. came through the door, preceded by his big paunch. He was an old guy and unlike our sheriff, looked it. The clipboard of papers he carried seemed too heavy for him in addition to the two-hundred-and-seventy-some pounds he hefted about. He was out of breath and perspiring profusely.

"Hot today," he said and tipped a blue Dallas Cowboys ball cap at me.

"Howdy, Chuck." Sheriff Ben stepped up to him, shook his hand, and then Barney and I followed suit.

When Chuck saw the body and the blood I think he considered bolting. "What time do you reckon she died?" he asked anybody. He did not touch or examine the body in any manner. Of course, there was no doubt about Norma's state. If anything, she looked deader than before.

Barney considered. "I'd guess between eight PM and midnight," he said, "judging from the blood and the amount of rigor."

Chuck glanced at the watch on his chubby wrist. "I'm pronouncing at nine-fifteen this morning, but I'm supposed to write the approximate time of death on here."

"Well, put nine-thirty last night then," said Barney impatiently. "I'm no expert on dead bodies."

The sheriff and I glanced at each other. I thought he looked amused. I sucked on my bottom lip.

"Do you have what you need from here, Barney?" Sheriff Ben asked after Chuck bowed out.

"Yes sir."

The sheriff was standing on the sink side of the body. I saw him looking at the various glasses and dishes that appeared to have been left there a while, judging from the greasy, room-temperature water that had started to stink.

"Let's wait outside," he suggested, and began moving towards the door.

The three of us sat together at the edge of the porch, our feet dangling over low-growing inkweed and dog cholla cactus. It was still stifling, but there was a slight breeze from time to time that felt cool when it brushed against my damp uniform. If you can be out of the sun then life is bearable in the desert. The sun is brutal.

To the left, about forty yards away, was a chain-link dog pen beneath a lopsided structure built for shade. Even the dogs looked miserable and barely barked at us.

"Did you have a look over there?" asked the sheriff, with a sweep of his hand in that direction.

"Yes," I said, "but I didn't see anything that seemed like it would have a bearing on the murder. Things that are scattered there are weathered, like they've been there a long time." I didn't think that surprised anyone.

At last the hearse arrived and Barney and the sheriff went back inside to oversee the proper handling of the corpse. Sheriff Ben is a stickler for respectful treatment of the dead.

While the men were inside I took the opportunity to call my mother, Stephanie Ricos. She pretended not to know anything about the murder. Or she really didn't know. I didn't know what to think.

"When was she murdered?" she asked.

"Mom, when was the last time you were at Norma's?"

"It's been at least six months I guess."

"You're sure?"

"Of course I'm sure."

"You realize that you'll be a suspect?"

"Why would I be a suspect?"

"You hated her. Everybody knows what she did to you."

"She did a lot of terrible things. A lot of people hated her."

"That's true, I guess."

"Are you at Norma's now?"

"Yes, we're waiting on the constable. He's going to guard the crime scene while we have a meeting with the sheriff."

"Guard it from what?"

"From anybody who thinks about messing with it."

"Well who would mess with a crime scene?"

"I don't know, Mom. Who commits murder in Terlingua?"

She didn't have an answer for that.

When the sheriff stepped back onto the porch he looked towards the layer upon layer of rugged mountains stretching to the west. "Wouldn't you think a man who lives seventeen miles away would be here by now?"

"Well, Sheriff," said Barney from behind him, "maybe he was doing something important."

"I'd like to know what."

"Maybe you wouldn't, sir."

The sheriff turned and gave Barney a look. I almost laughed out loud and had to suck on my lip again.

Chapter 3

We didn't argue when Sheriff Ben suggested we meet at any place with air-conditioning. He would probably have preferred a restaurant with a tall glass of iced tea, but we chose our office for the sake of privacy. As it was, news of the murder was spreading like a grass fire. We had ten messages asking about it when we returned to the office. It would only get worse if people overheard the local law discussing it. *We need to interview the deceased's husband* would become *Did you hear? Her husband did it.*

Our office is an outpost of the Brewster County Sheriff's Office, which is eighty miles away in Alpine, the county seat. The building is new and shared equally with Terlingua Fire and Emergency Medical Services. They occupy the front side; we bring up the rear.

Barney yanked a Dr. Pepper from the refrigerator and collapsed behind his acre of desk. I got a bottle of water for myself and a Coke for Sheriff Ben. Then we pulled up chairs in front of my partner.

The sheriff drank a couple of long swallows. "Deputy George, you look done in," he observed.

Barney wiped his face with a wet handkerchief, and sighed. "That Bates place is a depressing hell-hole even without a murder scene thrown in."

"Tell me what you got," our boss said.

Barney pressed the cold soda can against his neck. The hell hole had nearly killed him. "I got a hair off the victim that doesn't appear to be hers, and I scraped under her fingernails but I don't think that got us much. I lifted prints well, you saw the mess."

The sheriff nodded. "What else?"

Barney glanced at me. "Margarita swept the kitchen, the floor by both doors, and the front porch. We assume the killer came in the front because the back door was locked."

"I saw the evidence bags," said the sheriff, "did all that trash come off the floor?"

"Yes," I said, "except for a cigarette butt I picked up from the ground near the front porch and an empty pack of Rojos."

"What did you get from the kitchen?"

"Other than dried food and trash, I got a few hairs and one gold hoop earring."

I didn't mention my mother or my suspicions. I wasn't going to steal evidence on her behalf but I didn't intend to point the finger at her either.

"I noticed a photo in one of the bags," said the sheriff. "Who's the man?"

"I've never seen him before," I said.

Barney agreed without mentioning his looks or our flimsy theory that Norma had had an affair-gone-wrong with him.

"It appeared there'd been an awful struggle," said Sheriff Ben.

"Yes, we think so," said Barney. "Ms. Bates had a few marks on her face and arms, as if she was fighting someone off."

"Or attacked someone," I said. "She probably started it."

Both men looked at me.

Finally the sheriff said, "The coroner will give us more detail."

"I took some blood swabs," Barney added, "but I suspect it's all Norma's blood."

"Stabbing is personal," said Sheriff Ben, "and is usually a crime of passion. I believe we'll find that someone close to Norma killed her."

"We're probably looking for a man," said Barney, "since women aren't as prone to using knives."

I wondered where he got that tidbit, and hoped it was true.

"The struggle makes me wonder if someone went there to kill her and she fought back, or if there was a heated argument that escalated into violence," said the sheriff.

He mentioned that the autopsy would be performed in El Paso and would tell us such things as whether she had been raped, had sex recently, was pregnant, had been bruised internally, or if the killer had left a clue behind that we couldn't see.

"Shouldn't we be looking for her family?" I asked.

"I put the Alpine office on that," said the sheriff. "According to Norma's calendar, her husband was in San Antonio this weekend. He probably took the kids."

Barney and I exchanged a look. Neither of us had checked her calendar.

"Who are the obvious suspects?" asked the sheriff.

"Well, there's Stanner, Norma's husband, but he was in San Antonio," I said.

"That doesn't rule him out."

"Right."

"Who else? Did she have enemies?"

I froze, thinking of my mother.

"Well sir, my mother hated her."

And I think I found her earring at the scene. Not only that, I was going to steal it.

"Your mother?" The sheriff seemed surprised. "Why would your mother hate Norma Bates?"

"Maybe hate is too strong a word, but Mom and four members of the board of the medical non-profit she started had problems with both Norma and Lil Munch, another board member."

"What kind of problems?"

"Norma and Lil sued them individually and as a whole for mismanagement of the funds and other charges they dreamed up. The thing is, Sheriff, I don't think any of them would kill her. The suit went to mediation and the board got what they wanted. I don't know about the others, but Mom seemed to let it go after that."

"Barney will have to interview her, of course. I want you to make a list of those other board members. Find out where they were last evening. As soon as we locate Mr. Bates he'll have to be scrutinized, too. Meanwhile, talk to the deceased's friends and see if they know of any enemies you aren't aware of."

"She was not a very popular woman," said Barney, understating a fact.

"Why is that," the sheriff asked, "other than what she did to Ms. Ricos?"

"She had the reputation of starting trouble," said Barney. "She liked to get in peoples' faces and tell them what was wrong with them."

"We had a complaint once that she abandoned a German shepherd in the desert," I added. "Fortunately someone saw her and found the dog a home. She did mean things to her children, too. She'd buy a milkshake for herself but not for them."

"Usually those aren't the kinds of offenses that lead to murder," said the sheriff.

"That's true," said Barney, "but maybe she got in the wrong face."

The sheriff nodded and finished his Coke. "Who reported the murder?"

"Roger Lockey, one of Norma's neighbors. He says he went to speak with her about her dogs."

"Well, he's a suspect, too," said the sheriff, looking back and forth between us. "In fact, all the neighbors will have to be interviewed."

"Yes, sir," we agreed.

"Margarita, I'm going to let the constable go, so I'd like for you to go back to the crime scene and protect it until the Rangers show up. I can't release it until they have a look at it."

When Sheriff Ben got news of the murder that morning, he had notified the Texas Rangers. It's customary in small, rural sheriff's offices to use their services. They're the best criminal investigators in Texas.

"Barney, I'd like for you to interview Stephanie Ricos while her daughter protects our scene." He glanced over at me as if expecting a protest.

The Sheriff's radio crackled and at the same time the office phone rang. Barney grabbed the phone and the sheriff walked outside to answer the radio.

"Yeah, she's here," Barney said, "but she's busy." He wiggled his eyebrows at me. "We're working with the sheriff on a murder investigation." He listened a moment and then said, "Sure, she has your number. She'll call you later."

As he spoke he wrote *JIMMY JOE* on a message pad, drew a big heart around it, and shoved it at me. I crumpled the paper and threw it into the garbage.

When he hung up, Barney said, "That's no way to treat a fellow deputy."

"It'd be different if it was Sheriff's Office business."

"The poor ol' boy is nuts for you, Ricos. It wouldn't hurt you to have dinner with him and let him down gently."

"I tried that, Barn. He doesn't take no for an answer."

Barney sighed. "He's got it bad." Then he retrieved the note I had tossed, smoothed it out, and heavily outlined the heart, making it darker and bigger. He held it high, just out of my reach, easy for a towering hulk.

"Jimmy Joe is creepy," I said. "I should never have gone anywhere with him."

"Why did you?"

"I thought the invitation was a friendly gesture from a fellow deputy, like if you and I went out somewhere."

"You and I can't go out, Ricos. I'm married, in case you've forgotten."

I glared at him. "You know what I mean."

The door opened and the sheriff stepped inside. Barney winked at me and slowly crushed the heart-encircled note into a tiny ball.

Sheriff Ben sat. "Mr. Bates and the kids have been located in San Antonio, where he was visiting a publisher about his latest book."

Thomas Stanley Bates is a marginally successful author who makes a modest living from sci-fi novels and magazine articles. He is called "Stanner" by locals. Even if you don't want to use a nickname this community will give you one.

The family had been informed of the death by the San Antonio Police Department, the sheriff said. In addition to Norma's widower, the surviving family members included two sons, fourteen and eleven years old, and a daughter who was almost six.

After the meeting Sheriff Ben said he had to make a couple of phone calls and would meet me at the crime scene in twenty minutes. As soon as the door closed behind him, Barney said, "I wish you'd go talk to Old Man Lockey after the Rangers get there."

I agreed because I knew he and Barney didn't get along. Roger Lockey always described my partner as "that big, dumb deputy." Big, hell yes; dumb, no.

"You'd better call Shoots back or he'll be down here kicking ass and demanding to know why you haven't."

I rolled my eyes at him. Barney called our fellow deputy "Shoots" just to irritate me. His name is Jimmy Joe Blanks and I wasn't going to date him no matter what Barney thought, no matter what he nicknamed him.

I went to meet Sheriff Ben. When I arrived, he was dismissing the constable with his typical graciousness. Guy barely took the time to shake his hand before he leapt over the door of his convertible Jeep Renegade, started it, crammed it into reverse with a grinding sound, and nearly ran us down in his enthusiasm to get away from there.

Sheriff Ben cocked an eyebrow at me which made me laugh out loud.

"The Ranger should be here any time," he said, checking his watch. "I have to get back to Alpine."

I assured him I would be fine and he left me alone. Anyway, I had my memories and an overactive imagination for company.

For a while I looked around outside the house, hoping to discover something we'd overlooked. If there was anything it was probably inside, and I wasn't going there.

The dogs went wild in their pen as I approached. They had food and water but seemed lonely for human company.

"Hey guys." They whined and wagged their tails in response to my greeting. There were two German Shepherds and a Rottweiler/Lab mix. *Norma ran with the big dogs*, I thought, entertaining myself.

I stood there a while wondering about witnesses. There were no close neighbors but the road that passed the Bates house passed other houses, too. Someone might have seen something useful.

A nondescript white pickup skidded into the driveway, and when the dust settled a man in a straw cowboy hat was staring through the windshield at me. He grinned. I waved.

"I thought I'd never find this place," he said as he climbed out of the truck, "if this is even the place I'm supposed to be."

"Are you the Texas Ranger?"

"Yes."

"Then this is the place."

"It's in the middle of nowhere, huh? Well, it has to be the right place since a deputy is guarding it. What are the chances I'd pull up at the wrong house with a deputy standing on the porch?"

I thought he talked a lot for a Texas Ranger but then I didn't actually know any of them. He politely removed his hat and introduced himself as Frank James. He was a professional-looking man, older than me, with short-cropped, dust-colored hair. He wore perfectly pressed jeans, brown leather boots, and a white, crisp-looking dress shirt with a bolo tie.

"So, you want to show me the scene?" he asked.

No I sure didn't, but he was a Texas Ranger who had come to help us. I thought I should at least be nice to him.

When I opened the door, the heat and stench jumped out. Ranger James gave me a look that said he didn't want to go in, either. I followed him inside, wondering how many white shirts he went through in a week of crime scene investigations.

I gave him a rundown of the evidence we had, which he would take to his lab in Midland. Then I told him I had interviews to do, and we wished each other luck.

Chapter 4

Roger Lockey had reported the murder and was a suspect because of that, and the fact that he was first on the scene. He lived in a rock house less than a quarter-mile from the Bates place. Although he was known for his grumpiness, I thought it was just a front and he didn't scare me.

Mr. Lockey opened the door before I had a chance to knock, and greeted me: "I don't think they should send girls to do lawmen's work." Barney and his cronies would've loved that one, and would have mostly agreed with him.

Then, before I could respond, he added, "I didn't call no law." He moved to shut the door in my face.

"Good morning to you, too," I said, respectfully removing my hat. "May I speak with you a moment?"

"No call for being a smart-ass," he grumbled, but motioned me inside.

The décor was a jumble of hand-made furniture and funky decorations. There were old movie posters covering the walls—John Wayne and a young Clint Eastwood, and others, nameless to me, from back in the day. There were also oil paintings Mr. Lockey had done himself, and Mexican blankets that made their own frenzied color statement.

An evaporative cooler rumbled and complained its heart out in the window on one wall. Having spent much of the morning in the heat, I was grateful for its effort. I took a seat in a chair the old man indicated, after I removed a big gray cat. At first I tried to pet it, but it was grumpy like its owner, and stalked away.

"What did you want with me?" he asked, coming right to the point.

"I understand you reported the murder this morning."

"Yeah, I spoke with 911 and they notified that big dumb guy, whatshisname."

"Why were you at the Bates house?"

"I went to talk to her about her goddamned dogs."

"Did you speak with her?"

"How the hell could I? The woman was dead. Ain't that the point of this visit?"

"Did you touch her?"

"No. I was calling her name from the front porch. There was a light on and when she didn't answer I stepped up to the screen door and looked inside. That's when I saw her lyin' on the floor."

"Did you go inside at any time?"

"Hell no, I could see she was dead."

"What did you do?"

"I came back here and called 911 and they put me through to that idiot partner of yours. You can't be thinking that I killed her?"

"I'm not accusing you of anything. I just want to get the facts straight. What time did you discover the body?"

"I don't know exactly—maybe 7:15. That was when she always let her dogs out. They'd come over here and chase my cat and dig in my yard and shit everywhere. If I wanted dog shit in my yard I'd get my own damn dogs. I told her a hundred times."

"Did you see anything strange or someone you didn't know hanging around?"

"Well..." He rubbed his forehead with one wrinkled hand, "The strangest thing I seen was Norma lyin' there dead as a stone."

"You'd had problems with her dogs before?"

"Every time she let 'em loose I'd get into it with her 'cause she let 'em run wild and didn't watch 'em. She tried to tell me that my cat came to her yard but I know he didn't. He hates those dogs."

I knew for a fact that on at least two occasions Roger Lockey had gathered up the dogs' leavings and left them at Norma's house. She had reported it to us and I thought that was how Barney and the old man got into it the first time.

"Did you see or hear anything this morning that might give us a clue as to who killed her?" I asked.

"Nothing, I didn't go anywhere else until about an hour ago. I went over to the store."

"Were people talking about the murder?"

"Sure. There's the group that heard it over the scanner, and the folks that make things up. And the ones that talk without knowing much. You know how it is here."

I handed him my card with instructions to call if he thought of something else.

"Margarita Ricos," he read then looked up. "You seem too young to be a sheriff."

"I'm a deputy, not a sheriff."

"At least you're better looking than that big lug you work with. Where'd the sheriff get a big ol' boy like that and why would he want one?"

I nearly laughed. I wondered that too, from time to time, although I would never have said it quite that way.

"Margarita," Lockey said, mulling it over. "You named after the drink?" He chuckled at his clever self.

"How original," I mumbled, "like I never heard that one before."

He frowned absently and stuffed my card into his shirt pocket. "I like my tequila straight up with lime and salt."

"Yeah, me too," I agreed, and got away from there as quickly as I could without seeming unprofessional.

From Lockey's house it was a short trip to the Terlingua Ghost Town, once an abandoned cinnabar mining village. It's now home to several restaurants, a gift shop, an art gallery, a bed and breakfast, and homes recreated from abandoned rock structures. It sits high enough on the side of a broad mountain to have one of the area's best vistas; one that encompasses mountains, buttes, hills, odd rock formations, and miles and miles of Chihuahuan Desert.

There is a frame building that was constructed in the 1930s and housed a company store for the miners. Across the front of it is a long wooden porch, referred to by locals as "The Porch." If you say you're going to The Porch, you mean that one, even if you have your own porch, even if a neighbor has one you enjoy. The Porch is a popular gathering place for locals and tourists. Tall tales and current events are passed without concern about the veracity of either. News commentary from The Porch is about as reliable as any other source, and porch pundits abound.

I stopped there to see what people were saying about the murder. I knew they'd be talking about it based on what Roger Lockey had said, and because news travels faster than light in Terlingua, particularly bad news.

"Hey 'Rita, did you solve the murder yet?" asked a river guide, Larry Hinds, who is in his late-twenties, of medium height and athletic build. He has wavy dark hair that is longish—not quite to his shoulders. Larry lives in Terlingua year-round, one of few who do. We have seasonal tourism, fall and spring mostly, when our weather is pure heaven.

"Not yet," I admitted, "but I'm working on it."

My answer seemed to satisfy Larry. He dug around in the pocket of his shorts, brought out a cigarette, and went back to smoking, drinking a Lone Star, and ruminating.

I took a seat on the long, roughly-hewn bench among a variety of local folks who were talking, as I'd hoped, about the murder. There were a few smirks exchanged by those who thought a woman couldn't solve herself out of a paper bag but not one of them had the guts to say anything like that to my face.

After a round of jokes, Randy Moore, another young guide, sprang to his feet. "See y'all." He crushed a can he'd been holding and lobbed it successfully into an open trash can marked *Recycle*. "Hope you figure out that murder." He grinned, removed the tattered brown ball cap from his shaved-bald head, and bowed slightly towards me.

"It had to be Stanner," mused Jeff Smith, another local. Jeff is old. It seems like he's always been old. When I was a child he was old. He has wrinkles in his wrinkles and his graying hair is past shoulder-length and pulled back in a pony-tail. He's a mouthy know-it-all and needs a sign around his neck that says: *Shut Up People 'Cause I Know Everything*.

Everybody looked to me after Jeff's comment. "Stanner was in San Antonio," I said, and let it go at that.

"Well, I still think it was him only he had someone do it." Jeff seemed sure of his theory and when nobody agreed he added, "Well? Who had a better reason?"

Everybody looked at me again and one brave local, Harley, said what they all seemed to be thinking, "What about Margarita's mom, Stephanie Ricos?"

Larry came back into the conversation with, "She's a nice lady and all, but I've heard her make threats about Norma."

"I know Mom said things she shouldn't have," I said, "but I can't believe she would kill anyone. She's a doctor, and wants to heal people, not harm them."

"It's hard to imagine," said river guide Larry, "but maybe she'd had all she could take. That happens."

"Yeah, I know, and she's being questioned."

Another local called Rip said, "What about Old Man Lockey? He rants on about Norma. You should check him out, too." I assume Rip's nickname comes from the fact that he never wears long pants or shorts without a rip in the seat.

"What does he say?" I asked.

"Oh, mostly that he wants to shoot her and her dogs."

"Do you know him very well, Rip?"

"Nah, I try to avoid him. He's a mean old coot."

There were murmurs of agreement.

"Stanner has a girlfriend," someone else said. "Maybe he wanted to be free of Norma or the girlfriend wanted him to be."

"I always heard that—about him having a girlfriend," said Larry.

That talk wasn't helping me, so I rose and assured the guys I was on it and had work to do. A few of them graciously expressed their belief that I'd solve the mystery, *pronto*.

I called Barney and talked him into meeting me at the office to compare notes. He was just dumping his notepad, keys, and our mail on his desk when I came through the door and got right to the point.

"What about my mother?"

He sank into the chair behind his desk. "She says she hasn't thought much about Norma in a long time."

"Does she have an alibi?"

"Not really." He leaned back in the chair until it hit the wall. "She says she was reading and went to bed about ten or so. No way to prove or disprove that, but one thing does concern me." He lowered his eyes and studied a piece of junk mail.

"What's that?" I was anxious to know, yet dreaded hearing what he was going to say.

"She has a black eye—and not a very good story about how she got it."

"What does she say happened?"

"She says she ran into the bathroom door in the dark during the middle of the night, and she blushed when she lied to me."

"Assuming she's lying."

"Granted, assuming, but I don't think that's how she got that eye."

"What else?"

"Nothing else. She says she didn't do it and I don't have anything yet that says she did."

I thought about the earring but didn't mention it.

"What did the Texas Ranger have to say?"

"Wait a minute—let's talk about my mother."

"There's nothing else to say about your mother. She says she didn't do it and that will be that unless the evidence tells us something different. What about the Ranger?"

"I didn't stick around for his impressions. He said he would be in touch with Sheriff Duncan later."

"I hope we didn't miss something obvious."

"Me too, but we missed the calendar."

"Hey—anybody could have missed that. We don't have a lot of experience with crime scenes like that one."

"Or any crime scenes, period," I added.

I had been a deputy sheriff for three years and this was my first murder. My duties usually entailed warnings or citations for traffic violations, breaking up drunken disagreements at bars, serving legal documents, chaperoning dances and other large public gatherings, and occasionally investigating reports of domestic violence or petty crimes like theft or vandalism. Sometimes I served as bailiff in the circuit court in Alpine.

"I talked to Roger Lockey," I said.

"I know. I saw you there. After I spoke with your mother, I went to see some of Norma's other neighbors."

"Did anybody see anything?"

"Nothing. What did the old fart have to say? And who goes to see their neighbor at seven in the morning?"

"He says he went to bitch her out about her dogs and she was already dead on the floor. But I just thought of something, Barney. Were the dogs running loose when you got there?"

"No, they were in their pen."

He gave me a knowing look. "I bet that old jackass offed her."

"What do you two have against each other?"

"Did he trash me?"

"Not much."

"Doesn't he look like a murderer to you?"

"Well, not really, but I suppose it's possible. Why does he dislike you?"

"Maybe we should get a search warrant and go over there and look for the knife. I wonder why he didn't just shoot her, he has all those guns."

"Too noisy," I said.

Chapter 5

I called Miriam Vasquez, former president of the board of directors of the non-profit my mother started four years ago. It is called Doctores Fronterizos (Border Doctors). Volunteer physicians on a two-week rotating schedule, overseen by my mother, had been successfully treating illnesses, practicing preventive medicine, and safely delivering babies on both sides of the Rio Grande at no cost to the mostly-poor patients. It would be hard to guess how many lives had been saved and how much suffering alleviated before Norma and Lil decided my mother must be stealing from the organization.

When I told Miriam the reason for my call she seemed displeased to be a suspect but expressed no sadness over Norma's untimely death. That didn't surprise me, but she didn't say one word about being innocent either, which did.

She said she was going to be too busy until next week. I reminded her that we were talking about murder, not a social visit, and she caved before I had to start using big words like "subpoena." She agreed to meet me at my office in two hours.

I called Floy Graham, another former board member, and a retired nurse. She was home and had already been told about the murder by a friend of the J.P.'s wife. She told me in her deep south Texas accent, "Come on by, sweet gal."

The mouth-watering aroma of baking bread met me before she did. Flour was smudged across Floy's face and apron, and fine white powder had settled on her eyelashes. She looked like the same old Floy, as full of Texas Friendly as anyone I ever knew. I thought she was too polite to kill anyone, there being no hospitality in murder. Still, I had to talk to her.

Floy was dressed in red cotton drawstring pants and a red tank top. She wore huge dangly earrings that were also red, her favorite color.

"Come in, come in. Look at you, all dressed up in your uniform, so professional. Let's sit in the kitchen, do you mind?"

"Not at all, wherever you'd be most comfortable." I followed her down a hallway of highly polished Saltillo tile to a kitchen painted in different shades of yellow.

"I'm baking bread." Floy flicked one hand at the floury mess.

"Smells wonderful." I said, and took a seat where she indicated, at the less cluttered end of the table.

"How are you doing, honey?" Flo had that serious-sad look people got when they were trying to ask how I was getting along without Kevin. None of them wanted to hear the truth. It was too brutal for them.

"I'm doing okay, Floy, better."

"Would you like a piece of bread? I just took it out of the oven."

"I'd love that."

She sliced off a huge hunk of warm whole wheat bread and slid a butter dish and strawberry preserves my way.

"I have a few questions for you, Floy," I said between bites.

"What would you like to know?" She was attentive but didn't stop kneading.

"I want to know if you have any idea who could've killed Norma Bates."

Her expression was priceless. "Well, 'bout anybody, I reckon."

I laughed and nearly choked.

"That was mean. I shouldn't have said that. I know she had friends but I wasn't one of them." Floy suppressed a smile, and before I recovered, added, "It wasn't me that killed her. You were comin' to that, I bet. Now mind, I didn't care for her, but I felt sorry for her 'cause of her bein' flicted."

"Flicted?"

"You know—crazy as a coot. Af-flicted you Yankees would say." She put her hands on her hips and made a pasty white mess there, too.

"I was born in Texas, Floy, same as you."

"You were born in the wrong part of Texas to grow up talking right." It sounded like she said tawken.

I laughed. "Well, that's debatable but I didn't come to argue with you."

"That's good since ladies don't argue." Her hands went back into the bowl. "I guess we shouldn't be talking bad about poor ol' Norma. God bless 'er. She was lost as a goose in a snowstorm."

I nearly lost it again.

"Didya see her?" Floy asked.

"If you mean did I see her dead, yes, I did. I couldn't help but feel sorry for her—and especially the children. No matter how terrible she was with us, she was their mother."

"That's true, I reckon. That part's sad."

"Did you ever hear anyone say they wanted to harm her?"

"You were there, little deputy. Every person on our board, except for those chicken shits who bailed out, said they wanted to hurt her. As I recall, your mom had the most detailed fantasies, but all of us hated her. I'd be lyin' to say diff'rent."

"Right."

"If I were you, I'd check out Stanner." Her hands were like a couple of white doves rising from the bowl then pausing in mid-flight. "He doesn't seem like a killer, but that poor man had to live with her."

"We're going to be talking to him, too."

She separated the dough into two heavy ceramic bowls, covered them with red and white checked dishcloths, set them aside, then washed her hands and pulled up a chair close to me.

"I want to tell you 'bout somethin' I saw."

"What was that?"

"It was after the mediation in Alpine when I saw Norma and Miriam have it out in the parking lot of the grocery store. They were kickin' up dust."

"Do you know what happened?"

"What happened was Norma was comin' out and Miriam was goin' in, and Miriam said, *You bitch!* Norma said *I hope you're not talkin' to me,* in her high faloo-tin' way, like she was better'n anybody, you know."

"Right."

"So they were glarin' at each other and then Norma grabbed Miriam's hair and tugged at her. Miriam kicked her smack in her girlie goodies and said she'd kill 'er if she ever got the chance." Floy looked concerned. "I don't believe Miriam would really kill her, do you?"

"Who knows, Floy?"

"Well, the rest of us had our hearts in helping sick people but Norma—I don't know what she wanted—it was nothin' about helping people."

That was a fact I knew.

"Would you take some bread to your mother? She loves my bread."

"I'd be glad to, sure."

I watched her cover a fragrant, now-cool loaf in plastic wrap.

"You tell 'er not to admit nothin'," she said.

"I can't say something like that to anyone."

"Well, course not, little deputy. Take her the bread and tell 'er to call me."

"Yes, I will. Thank you, Floy."

"Call me if you think of something else you need." She smiled and gave me a hug.

* * *

I sat in my Explorer, called a few more people I had to interview, and then called Barney.

"Where are you, Ricos?"

"I just interviewed Floy Graham, former board member."

"Floy—is she that old gal, the Dixie Chick?"

I laughed. "Yep. Have you ever heard the expression 'she was lost as a goose in a snowstorm' or how about 'flicted', as in 'poor thang, she was 'flicted?'"

"Ricos, are you out drinking somewhere?"

"No, I'm just repeating some things I heard from Floy. She makes me think I don't speak English."

"Your English is fine. It's hers that's foreign, y'all. I don't know how you'd get anything from her. Talking to Floy is like trying to herd cats."

Barney got me started again. It felt so good to laugh.

"I think you better come back to the office," he said. "Are you drinking plenty of fluids? Maybe you're getting dehydrated."

"I'm coming back to meet Miriam. We have an appointment."

"Well you can't be laughing like that if you're conducting serious interviews about a murder."

"I know it. I'm hanging up now."

* * *

I took the back steps at my mother's house two at a time and charged in without knocking.

"Mom," I yelled, "where are you?"

"Table, come on in."

When I came around the corner into her spacious kitchen she was seated just past it in the dining room, pouring a glass of sweet tea over ice, as if she was expecting me. My mother makes the best iced tea in the known universe and I never turn it down, so she didn't bother to ask if I wanted a glass.

"Were you expecting me, Mom?"

I hugged her and took in the black eye when she looked up at me. It would have been a hard thing to miss. It was a sinister blue-black color covering an area about the size and shape of a fist. Her eye was bloodshot, and the entire area puffy. Mom's brown eyes usually twinkle, at least when she looks at me, but they looked dull, like she hadn't slept. Her hair is dark brown because she colors it to cover the gray, and it usually looks nice, but I don't think she had even combed it—not like my mom.

"I heard you in the driveway, but I've been listening for you. I knew you'd come once you talked to Barney."

I sat across from her. "So why do you have a black eye, anyway?"

"I already spoke with Barney about it. Stop asking me about the murder." She shoved a small plate of lime slices across the table to me but didn't meet my eyes.

"I asked you about your injured eye, not the murder."

"I ran into my bathroom door in the middle of the night. That's not a crime unless you know something I don't."

"There's no need to get an attitude, Mom. Barney told me you had a black eye which concerned me. You're my mother, unless you know something I don't."

She laughed and lightened up. "I'm sorry. I'm touchy about the subject of the murder. People are talking about me everywhere I go. I'm sure you've heard it was either me or Stanner."

"Yes, I've heard."

"Well?"

"Well what?"

"Do you think it was me?"

"You just said it wasn't."

"Don't you have any other leads?"

"I can't talk to you about the investigation, Mom. I just came by to see if you're okay. Later I'll bring some bread by that Floy asked me to give you."

"She does make the best bread. How is she?"

"She's fine, same ol' Floy. She wants you to call her."

"Does she think it was me?"

"She thinks anyone who knew Norma could have done it."

My mom laughed at that. "I won't be here later. I'm going to dinner with Annie and Sue Ellen and I'll probably be out late."

"I'll leave it on the counter." She was giving me the perfect opportunity to look for a matching earring. "Mom, when was the last time you were in Norma's house?"

"It's been a long time. I told you that already. I had no reason to go there. What makes you think I would?"

Because your earring was there, near the body, not knocked into a far corner but right there where I couldn't miss it.

"I was thinking maybe you'd run by to check on her kids or something." My mom worried about the children because Norma didn't believe in doctors and never took them to one, no matter how ill they were.

"You're thinking I ran by to stab her to get even with her for what she did to me."

"Of course I don't think that, Mom." Now I'd made her angry, and maybe for nothing.

I drank tea and covertly watched, trying to imagine her as a killer. That seemed a pointless exercise for a daughter who loved nearly everything about her mother. Instead of a stealthy villain with a knife, I pictured her playing hide-and-seek, chasing me through the house with childlike energy until we collapsed in giggles.

"I saw several kids at the clinic today," Mom said.

"Are they talking about the murder?"

"Of course."

"And?"

"They think it was a one-armed man," Mom said, "a space alien, or Dracula, pretty much in that order."

"I'll make a note of it."

* * *

I went into my cramped office that holds a small desk and chair, an ancient metal filing cabinet, and an aged, overstuffed chair older than me. It has a worn pink and purple flower pattern that's as hideous as it sounds, but it sits by a window that looks out at an exquisite cactus-and-boulder-covered hill that abuts our parking lot. I spend a lot of time in that chair, thinking and trying to figure things out.

I plopped down to check on my hill. The sight was a comfort for its stead-fastness as well as its beauty. I noted for the millionth time the three precari-ously-balanced boulders that hang in against all odds. A couple of turkey vultures cavorted on wind currents high above the steep rock face at the top of the hill, making black splotches against a bright cloudless blue. They made flying look effortless and joyous. Most days I longed to join them—except for meals. There is a trade-off for you.

Small, drought-tolerant ash, mesquite and catclaw acacia trees appear to grow straight out of stone. Agave, spiny ocotillo, and thick stands of prickly pear cactus claim the areas around and between the rocks. The gods of the Chihuahuan Desert have been generous with sticking, stabbing, biting growth, native grasses, and even wildflowers, less generous with rain. Things struggle to survive with-out moisture and have to adapt or die. It's a desert out there.

I had begun to doze when the sudden sound of the ringing telephone cata-pulted me from the chair in a panic.

"Deputy Ricos speaking."

"Deputy Ricos, Sheriff Ben." He hesitated as if he'd forgotten why he called, or didn't want to say. "I have a situation."

The way he said *a situation* made me feel chilled. "What's going on, sir?"

"I need you to come to Alpine."

"Okay."

"Margarita," he said and stopped like he couldn't go through with it. "I have a Terlingua couple sitting in my office and they say their daughter was raped."

My instant response was to scream *no way*, but we'd just had a murder. Instead of screaming I was speechless.

"The girl won't talk and the mother is too talkative. The father is too quiet."

"Who is the girl, Sheriff?"

"Mandy Robbins. Do you know her?"

"I know who she is but I don't know her well."

"She's only fourteen."

"Does she say who raped her?"

"She hasn't said one word, Margarita, but she brightened when I mentioned your name, so maybe she'd talk to you."

"What about Marcy?" In addition to being the other female deputy, Marcy is a nurse and a certified rape counselor.

"She's in El Paso for a seminar. She won't be back until Tuesday."

"Has Mandy had a rape kit done on her?"

"No. Her mother bathed her." I could hear the groan even though he didn't utter one.

"Well, there would still be signs of rape, most likely."

"I know that, Deputy, but her mother refuses to let me take her to the hospital."

The office door opened and closed and Miriam called my name.

"I'll be right there, have a seat," I called to her. To the sheriff I said, "I'm about to interview Miriam Vasquez about the murder. Should I reschedule?"

"Will it take long?"

"Ten minutes, tops."

"Go ahead then, but hoof it coming up here. Use your lights and siren." He didn't need to worry about that. One of the few perks of being a deputy is speeding.

I went to the front to greet Miriam. She hugged me and we told each other how great we looked. She is a slender, platinum-haired, blue-eyed woman in her mid-thirties. Soft-spoken, laid back, and somewhat frail, she seems like an easy pushover for a bulldozer like Norma. Miriam, more than any other board member, had defended my mother. She'd spent countless hours putting together evidence that backed up Mom's claim of innocence, and had stood up to Norma with the courage of a Revolutionary War foot soldier.

When we had settled in the outer office, me in Barney's chair and her in the one I usually occupied, I asked, "Why were you so reluctant to see me?"

"I'm sorry, you really threw me. I wasn't expecting to be a suspect, I guess."

"I'm interviewing everyone who knew Norma."

"Right, well I hadn't thought of that. It hurt me to think you'd believe I stabbed her."

"I don't think that, Miriam. I have to interview a lot of people I feel sure are innocent, but we have to start somewhere."

"So you're talking to all the former board members?"

"Yes."

"Even Lil?"

"Yes, even Lil."

"I was just wondering how you'd handle that."

"What do you mean?"

"I mean you didn't think much of Lil, either."

"I'm not looking forward to it. Maybe I can get Barney to do it."

"Oh, you should go yourself. It'll put her right on her ear."

"Miriam, other than talk among board members, have you ever heard anyone say they wanted to kill Norma?"

"No." She began fidgeting. "Look, Rita, the way I feel about Norma's murder is she had it coming. If I knew something I wouldn't tell you. I don't, but if I did—"

"You'd be aiding and abetting a criminal in a felony case and surely you don't condone murder."

She grinned at me. "Normally no, I don't. But Norma so had it coming. I'm glad her karma caught up with her quickly. Do you think someone will take out Lil too?"

"I hadn't thought about that."

"Rita, don't you think it was probably Stanner? I mean, he lived with her."

"We're investigating him."

"I hope he gets away with it. You can't tell me you didn't feel a murderous rage towards her for what she did."

"No, I can't tell you that, but I didn't kill her. It's one thing to feel like doing it and another to do it."

Miriam sighed. "It's a fine line we walk sometimes."

"You didn't kill her, did you?"

"No, I didn't."

"I want to talk to you about an incident between you and Norma in Alpine."

"Are you talking about the one where I kicked her in the crotch?"

"Was there another one?"

"No."

Miriam told me about it and it was more or less the same story Floy told me, minus the drawl and deep-south expressions.

After that I hurried her out. "I don't mean to rush you, but the sheriff needs to see me in Alpine on another case."

I left Barney a hastily scrawled note saying only that the sheriff needed my help.

When I came out of the office a red-tailed hawk was feasting on a small creature that she'd spread out on one of the boulders on my hill. She looked up from her bloody banquet, blinked at me, and decided I was untrustworthy. She grabbed her prize with sharp talons and swooped away with it as I headed for the Explorer.

State Highway 118 winds and climbs towards Alpine, straightens out for while, then winds and climbs again through the mountains standing between south and north Brewster County. We live in the largest county in Texas, covering 6,169 square miles of mostly rough and mountainous terrain. It is also the least populated county and surely the most beautiful. Alpine is the largest town, with a population about the same as the number of square miles in the county.

I drove as fast as I could, considering the road, with lights flashing and siren blaring, but traffic was sparse. After a short time I turned the siren off because it was annoying. I felt stressed enough without adding irritating noises.

First a murder, then a rape. Maybe it was the moon but it wasn't even full and there was no news about it falling or slipping out of position in the sky. There had to be something going on. Terlingua is the epitome of life in the slow lane and living there is enhanced by the natural surroundings, clean air, and long distance vistas that take your breath away. Crime is petty when it exists at all and usually our problems can be handled by a stern talk with the culprit and/or a brief stint of community service.

I had to slow, and eventually stop, for a travelling troupe of javelinas crossing the highway. Javelinas look like small wild boars but are not in the swine family at all. This group ranged in size from a big daddy of fifty pounds with well-developed tusks, to a tiny fellow of maybe seven pounds. They browse desert plants and are especially fond of prickly pear cactus.

I jumped when my satellite phone began bleeping to signal an incoming call.

"Why don't you ever return my calls?" barked Jimmy Joe Blanks.

I wanted to ream and belittle him, sling the truth at him, but my mother had ruined me with her admonitions to be nice to people. She used to tell me that I should dance with the nerds and the gangly, pimply boys that invited me because boys had feelings, too. It was irritating the things she'd said that I had taken to heart.

Jimmy Joe wasn't a nerd, nor was he gangly or pimply, but he was not my type and wouldn't take a hint. Truthfully, I didn't have a type. I wasn't looking for anyone and had a broken heart. I wasn't even sure I would have feelings again, except for an ever-present sadness that pressed down on me. It felt like the bull that crushed Kevin's chest had crushed mine, too.

Jimmy Joe was going on about wanting to see me—desperate, the poor man. I deeply resented my mother's calm voice which said to be kind. *Damn it, Mom, you couldn't have meant Jimmy Joe Blanks.* "Shoots." Thinking of Barney's nickname nearly made me laugh into the phone.

"Look Jimmy Joe, I'm flattered but it's barely been a year since my husband died and I'm not ready for another man in my life."

"I know, you've said that before but I felt we made a connection."

If he felt it, it was his connection. I felt nothing. He was a six foot tall deputy who was not unattractive but seemed too intense. Of all the deputies, he was the most sexist, told the filthiest jokes, and made the worst companion on the job and off. His hair was reddish-blond and he had green eyes that should have been an asset but were cold, like the eyes of a reptile.

"You're coming up here, aren't you? We could have a drink later."

Oh man, I wanted a drink, needed one badly. Drinking interested me, but not with a man I didn't like or trust.

I tried to get rid of Jimmy Joe by claiming overwork, depression, widowhood, a long list of things he seemed determined not to understand. At last I said I was expecting a call from the sheriff.

"The sheriff is busy," he said in an I-don't-believe-you voice.

I hung up on him. My mother doesn't know everything.

"It doesn't make sense to be nice to everyone," I said to a distant mountain.

Then, instead of stressing about violent crimes or obsessed deputies, I cheered myself with the promise of an upcoming drunk. I could almost smell the fragrance of rich gold tequila and the requisite slices of lime. The sliding down-my-throat part was best; the warm burning sensation that went from my mouth to my stomach to my brain and dulled it. *Everything will be all right* was its soothing message. Beer, tequila, bourbon, it didn't matter; all of it smoothed out the mangled pieces of my life and made broken things appear fixed; if not fixed, then acceptably broken.

I was kidding myself as much as Shoots Blanks was kidding himself. The thought occurred to me that maybe he was in as much pain as I was. That was scary and I flipped the siren back on. Better irritated than scared to death.

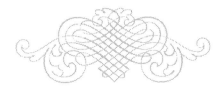

Chapter 6

Sheriff Ben was hovering at the door watching for me, something so out of the norm it filled me with dread. He held the door open but didn't smile. It was very un-Sheriff Ben-like.

"Deputy Ricos." He greeted me with a nod. He looked disheveled, and had been running his hands through his hair. Our sheriff always looks sharp and expects the same of his deputies.

My first instinct was to hug him and tell him everything would be okay. I'd go back to Terlingua to kick ass and take names all night if he'd just put his hair back in place and not look so sad and old.

He took me by the elbow. "These people, they're—odd," he whispered. "The girl seems afraid to speak. Come with me a minute."

He led me into an empty office. "What's going on in Terlingua?"

"I don't know, Sheriff. I'm wondering the same thing."

"We've never had so much trouble there before."

"Yes sir, I know. Barney and I don't like it, either."

"You've got to get through to the girl. She won't talk to me. You're young—and a woman. Maybe she'll talk to you."

"I'll try. Just let me speak with her."

"We're going to get to the truth of this," he hissed as if I was a suspect.

The sheriff offered me his chair and stood to the side of the family, his arms folded across his chest. Joe Robbins nodded at me, then stood and offered his hand. He seemed about to speak but his wife cut him off with her own greeting.

I tried to get a feel for the people seated in front of me. Julie Robbins, the mother, was like a brick wall between her daughter and the world. I couldn't blame her for protecting her child, but that wasn't going to help us. The first words out of her mouth were, "I don't want a scandal."

This was a rape, not a scandal. And why would someone live in Terlingua if she cared so much what others thought? Talking about people is the community's preferred form of entertainment. You could either live with it or move.

Julie Robbins looked like she'd borne the brunt of the rape. There were dark circles under her eyes and the brown hair hanging in her face was stringy and needed washing. She nervously picked at her hands.

Mandy's father hadn't spoken but he looked clean. His fists were tightly clenched and white from the strain of pressing against his thighs. I'd be angry too if my daughter had been raped. The mother was frantic and protective, the father stunned into silent fury by such a vile act against his daughter.

Mandy was pretty, with a sweet, innocent face. Her skin was flawless. Coffee-colored hair hung listlessly to her shoulders. She wore no makeup, earrings, or clips in her hair. She stared straight ahead with eyes that looked almost vacant.

I decided to start with her. "I'd like to hear what happened, Mandy, in your words."

"She hasn't spoken to anybody," interrupted Julie. "She refuses to speak."

"Is that true, Mandy?"

She shrugged. There was bruising around her neck and a red mark like a slap on one cheek. More than anything she looked sad, unbearably sad.

While I was thinking about what to say next, Sheriff Ben addressed the family. "I asked Margarita to come because she lives in Terlingua. She's young, and a woman. I thought Mandy would be more comfortable with her."

"Would you speak with Deputy Ricos, Mandy?" her mother asked gently. "You know Margarita."

The girl stared ahead.

"Would you let a nurse at the hospital examine you?" I asked.

"I bathed her," interrupted Julie. "I know that's the wrong thing to do but she was filthy and her clothes were torn and there was—stuff on her."

"Do you mean semen?"

She nodded and her eyes filled with tears. "Yes, that and dust, dirt, you know. She'd been thrown to the ground and there are big bruises on her thighs. I bathed her so I could get a good look at her."

The last thing in the world I'd want if I'd been raped was to have my mother bathe and look at me—and my mother is a doctor.

"We should never have let her attend that party, but it was chaperoned, and she was going to go home with her friend Brenda." She picked an imaginary something off her hand. "We don't know why, but she didn't do that."

"Were you raped at the party, Mandy?" I asked.

Still nothing from her and no expression I could read.

"If you won't talk to me I can't help you."

She shrugged and looked at her hands.

My intuition said to get her away from here, so I stood. "Mandy, would you go for a drive with me? We'll get a coke or something. You don't have to talk if you don't feel like it, but I'd like to talk to you."

Incredibly, Mandy stood. The sheriff brightened. The parents looked terrified.

"Where are you taking her?" demanded her mother.

"Please trust my deputy," said Sheriff Ben, endearing himself to me.

Mandy and I walked in silence to my Explorer. She grabbed my hand as if she was a little girl. It made my heart hurt so much I was terrified I'd cry since tears were always just below the surface. When I opened the door for her she sat, but seemed reluctant to let go of me. I stood holding her hand while she stared straight ahead.

"Everything is going to be all right, Mandy." I set her hand on her thigh and patted it. "I swear." Once I'd sworn it I couldn't take it back. How in the world could I make anything right for Mandy Robbins?

She didn't look at me or respond, except that her brown eyes filled with tears. Mine did too. I started the Explorer and had to ask her to put on the seatbelt. She did it without complaint, except she did it in the stiff, unemotional way a robot would.

I pulled away from the Sheriff's Office, wondering what to do.

"I can understand that you don't want to speak about it. It might be the hardest thing you ever do, but unless I know what happened, I can't help. Even if it was someone you love, you have to tell me."

She gave me a sideways look of teenaged disgust.

I took a different tack. "Mandy, don't you remember me from the soccer team?"

For a few years before Kevin died, I'd been a volunteer soccer coach for a girls' team. They played after school, without the approval or support of the school board and other management. They had no uniforms or fancy equipment, but they had a lot of fun and needed something constructive to do.

Mandy nodded and smiled at the dashboard. That was better than staring straight ahead like a zombie, so I persisted. "Would you like something to drink—a soda or milkshake?"

No response.

I pulled into a slot at Sonic. "When I came here as a teen, fries and vanilla coke were my favorites. I'm going to order that for you unless you stop me."

She didn't, so I ordered. Uncomfortable silence hung in the car like a curtain. I watched teenagers cutting up in the courtyard picnic area and thought about how fast a life can go from that kind of bliss to a landscape as bleak as the moon. I wanted Mandy to laugh and play again, and trust people. Yeah, I wanted global peace too, and for all the world to be loved and fed.

Our order came and after paying, I pulled onto Holland Avenue, a main thoroughfare that becomes Highway 90 as it leaves town to the east. I headed in that direction for lack of a better plan.

Mandy began nibbling the fries. "I love vanilla coke. How did you know that?"

"I love it too. It's so sweet it makes my teeth hurt, but that's never stopped me."

She made a sound that was almost a laugh. We passed motels, restaurants, and various stores. After the Dairy Queen was the university's agricultural center with classrooms, barns, riding stables, and a rodeo arena where Kevin had once practiced and competed. There was no way I could afford to start thinking about Kevin now.

After the Ag Center, the road runs parallel to train tracks, tops a rise, and then there are acres of green ranch land on one side and tracks and rolling hills on the other. I've always loved that piece of road.

"I don't know why," Mandy said, "but I like trains."

"I do too. They seem romantic and old fashioned."

I pulled into a deserted rest area. We got out with our sodas and sat at one of the shaded cement tables and looked at each other.

"I'm really, really sorry that Mr. Madison died," Mandy said suddenly.

"Thanks, Mandy."

Mr. Madison was Kevin. I never thought of him like that. Legally, I was Margarita Madison, but although I had taken Kevin to have and to hold, I never took his name.

"He was the best teacher in the high school everybody said, but I never got to have him. He was always nice to me, though."

"Let's talk about you," I said because I couldn't keep talking about Mr. Madison.

"I can't."

"You can trust me, Mandy."

"I know that, but I can't tell or I'll be killed."

"Is that what the rapist said?"

She gave me another disgusted look so I changed direction. "Will you tell me about your family?"

"What about them?"

"Are you a happy family? Do you have brothers or sisters?"

"I have a good family. What are you getting at?"

"Nothing, I just wondered about them."

"You're thinking my mom is weird."

Actually no, I was thinking about the sheriff's assessment of the Robbins as odd, and that the father was too quiet.

"I know she seems weird," Mandy continued, "but she just wants to protect me. She can't stand for bad things to happen."

"My mom is like that, too."

"Then you know."

"Yes, I know. What about your dad?"

She looked at me with eyes bright with sincerity. "My dad is the greatest man you could ever know. He's quiet—I guess you noticed but he's a lot of fun. He's especially quiet when my mom starts freaking."

"They sound a lot like my parents."

"I think if he knew who raped me, he'd kill him."

"I want you to tell me so I can put him away before your father gets into trouble."

"I know you're trying to help, but when he said he'd kill me, I believed him."

"Could you tell me what happened and leave out the names?"

Tears came then, and I had to bring a box of tissues from the vehicle. I held a hurting little girl while traffic passed, either going from Alpine to Marathon or vice versa. Some took the cut-off towards Fort Stockton. I tried not to think of the horror of her ordeal, but it was all I could think about.

Eventually the crying subsided.

"Mandy, was it boys from school who raped you?"

She nodded in the affirmative.

"You know them?"

"Yes." She shuddered from the crying, or the memory of rape, or both. She blew her nose and continued. "I went to a party last night. I was supposed to go home with my friend Brenda, but she left me because she was mad because I danced with a boy she likes." She wiped her eyes and blew her nose again. "So I accepted a ride with three boys I know. I can't tell you anything else."

"Can't you give me their names? I'll put them away so they can't hurt you again."

"I can't tell you. Don't you understand? He'll kill me." Her look was so forlorn I quit pressing her. We sat in silence until I asked her to tell me where she was raped. If I knew where, there might still be evidence that would lead me to the perps.

"I don't know where we were."

"Was it on school property?"

"No."

"Where was the party?"

"It was at Cindy's house."

"Cindy McAllister?"

"Yes."

"When you left there, where did you go?"

"At first we drove around. The boys were acting weird, and anyway, they were supposed to be taking me home."

I encouraged her to continue, but instead of speaking, Mandy leaned her head against me. I put my arms around her. "I'm so sorry, Mandy."

"He kept saying 'you want it, bitch. You made me do it.'" She spoke into my chest, her arms in a death grip around my waist. "Afterward, he asked the other boys if they wanted some, like I was a thing to share. That's when the others realized how much trouble they were in and they said no, they'd better get going, and the big one, he said he'd kill me."

"So only one of the three raped you?"

She nodded. "He forced the others to hold me down."

I smoothed her hair back from her face but couldn't think of one thing to say that would be a comfort after something like that. In the distance, a train whistle mourned, as if it understood. The train came around a hill, and was soon close enough to hear the clanking of the metal connections between the cars and the pounding wheels on the rails.

"I wish we could just hop on it," Mandy said above the noise, sounding as sorrowful as the whistle.

"Where would you go?"

"I don't know—anywhere but Terlingua."

I knew to the heartbeat how that felt. "It won't help to run away."

"How do you know?"

"Because I tried it. When you get somewhere, you'll see that your problems came with you."

She watched me with sad eyes.

"And the people who love and support you won't be there."

She didn't seem convinced, but said, "I guess I'd miss my family." Then she said in a sob, "The boy who raped me said if I told anybody he'd kill me and put my naked photos on the Internet."

"They took photos?" I couldn't believe something already so awful could get worse.

"One raped me, the others took turns holding me down and taking pictures of me."

"Can you describe where you were?"

"No, I felt lost."

"Did they take you far?"

"It seemed like it was. I remember one thing, though. Scary-looking old trucks and cars were there."

"You mean junkers?"

"Yes, partly covered by plants and stuff."

"How many?"

"I don't know, maybe five or six."

She pulled away enough to look into my face. I saw how white she was. "What if I'm pregnant?"

I felt like I'd been body-slammed by an elephant. "Did he use a condom?"

"I don't know."

"Will you let me take you to the hospital? They have a pill they can give you. If they won't, I'll find a doctor who will." *My mother, for one.*

Relief washed over her face and the color returned.

"Okay," she said, "I'd like to go."

Chapter 7

Mandy lay on an exam table while we waited for a nurse to examine her. I held her hand and dialed Sheriff Ben with the other to tell him where we were.

"Did she talk to you?" he asked.

"Some."

"I don't guess you can talk right now?"

"No sir."

"Her parents will demand to join you."

"I know, but can you talk them out of it? I'll bring her there when we're finished."

"They'll be furious with you."

"That's okay. It's the right thing, and Mandy wanted it. Please tell them that."

"Did she give you names?"

"No, but I'll figure it out, Sheriff."

"If her parents insist on coming I'll come, too."

I hoped Mandy would be examined before anyone could get in the way. As if in answer to that prayer, the nurse hustled towards us, and announced she was ready.

"I've gotta go, Sheriff Ben. They're going to do the exam."

"Good, I hope they can get something."

"I do, too."

The nurse, who was not Marcy, but was capable and kind, said there was tearing and trauma to the vagina. The perpetrator must have used a condom because there was no semen present. She made note of the many marks and bruises. I photographed them for the record, and promised a weeping Mandy that they would not be made public. When I mentioned using them in prosecution, she began to rally. I thought it wouldn't be long before she was ready to help us with her case.

Mandy's parents arrived, but the sheriff had held them off as long as he could and they missed the exam. Julie Robbins stormed into the room like an avenger just as her daughter was getting dressed. I felt sure she was going to hit me.

"Just what in the hell have you done?" she demanded in a snarl. "I told you we didn't want a scandal."

"Mandy wanted to come. Besides, it's protocol in a rape."

That was when she slapped me. My instinctive response was to slap her back. The second was to cry. It hurt and was insulting and damaged my pride. I was able to keep from doing either thing. My hand went to my face instead of hers, and I stepped away.

When the nurse opened the privacy curtain, Sheriff Ben was standing there. He'd heard everything. I watched him taking in the scene.

"It's against the law to assault an officer of the law," he said in his Serious Lawman voice. "There won't be a scandal if you'll calm down and be reasonable."

Our sheriff has a manner that makes people pay attention. He's large enough to be intimidating, but he's soft-spoken, gallant, and good-looking for an old man. Still, he means business—and he's armed.

Julie Robbins realized she had screwed up, but instead of apologizing to me, she apologized to the sheriff, and then went to her daughter's side. That was fine; it was where she belonged. Mandy let herself be hugged and baby-talked by her mom and I was relieved to see it.

I stood quietly by the sheriff. When he saw me looking at him, he nodded in approval. It made me feel like a superhero for a moment, until Julie Robbins opened her mouth to shoot me down.

"I don't want you going after whoever did this," she hissed at me.

I turned my back on her, which was as close as I could professionally get to a "screw you."

"We're going to do our jobs, Ms. Robbins," Sheriff Ben said. "Rape is a violent crime that is not tolerated as long as I'm the sheriff of Brewster County. It's a felony that we'll prosecute to the fullest extent of the law. I haven't spoken with Deputy Ricos about the details yet, but I will tell you this. If you try to stand in her way, I'll prosecute you, too." He paused and took a breath. "And if you ever touch her again you'll be seeing the inside of my jail. Is that clear?"

"Yes sir." She hung her head, attitude changed.

"Also, we'll need the clothing Mandy was wearing when she was raped. I'm going to send Deputy Ricos by to get it. I assume that won't be a problem."

"No sir."

The sheriff softened. "Your job is to take this young lady home and love and care for her the way only you can. If I were you, I'd keep her out of school a day or two until Deputy Ricos has the culprits in custody.

I stared at him in disbelief. He was putting a lot on me. Something in me stepped up then and I knew I could do it. I wanted to swagger like John Wayne, and declare that no sonofabitch was going to rape girls in Terlingua and get away with it while Deputy Ricos lived and breathed, but I held back.

* * *

All the way home I stressed about catching the rapists, except for when I was stressing about Jimmy Joe Blanks. He was angry that I wouldn't go for a drink with him and called me continuously on my cell phone until I lost service about five miles out of Alpine. After that, the satellite phone started. I didn't answer it and hoped it was him and not the sheriff or Barney. Either one of them would use the radio, but Jimmy Joe wouldn't dare. It was too public and Sheriff's Office policy was to have short, difficult-to-decipher conversations because of nosy people with police scanners. The sheriff would hear him broadcast his weirdness and would kick his ass. When I thought about the sheriff coming down on Jimmy Joe with both boots, I began to hope he would go ahead and use it.

When the calls stopped, I thought about abandoned trucks and cars. There were shells of vehicles here and there rusting into the desert. I could only think of one place in south Brewster County where there were five or six together. That was off South County Road, up a canyon at the base of a sandstone cliff.

I wanted to go then, but sunset was spreading its impressive range of red colors across the humps and bumps, buttes and mountains in the south of the county as I got closer to home. Absolute darkness would follow.

Barney radioed. "Unit Five to Unit Six. Call me."

I was glad to hear his voice, and called him on the satellite phone.

"How come you aren't answering your damn phones, Ricos?"

"Jimmy Joe Blanks is why."

"Ah, Shoots is still pursuing you hot and heavy."

"Did you call to harass me?"

"No, seems like it was about business, but you made me forget, thinking about Shoots. You could do worse than old Shoots."

"No I couldn't."

"I could name a hundred guys from down here that'd be worse. Most of them don't even work. At least Shoots is gainfully employed."

"Give it up, Barn, or I'm going to hang up."

"Okay, okay. I wanted to tell you about my interviews."

"Aren't you working tomorrow?"

"Yeah. Why?"

"Did you figure out the murder?"

"Not yet."

"Then can't it wait? Mandy Robbins was raped last night."

"Oh, man, in Terlingua or Alpine?"

"In Terlingua, by some boys in the high school."

"Oh, man," he repeated with sincere dismay. "It's only mid-September. School hasn't been in session but a few weeks. Do you know who did it?"

"I don't know yet." After that I had to tell him everything, including my ideas about catching the perps. By the time we hung up, I was pulling into my mother's driveway.

I entered the house through the back door, which she never locked, and left the bread on the counter. Even without lights, it was easy to move through the home I knew well.

With my penlight, I found the matching earring on her dresser—just one gold hoop with a tiny heart in the center. I checked her jewelry box, all the bathroom surfaces, and her nightstands—everywhere someone would leave an earring, but I only found the one. I left it where it was, feeling sick about looking through her things, and sick about what my find meant.

On the way out, I stopped in Mom's kitchen to peer outside. On the window shelf was a gold plated belt buckle that Kevin won the day he died. It came with a five thousand dollar purse. I had tried to bury him with it, but my mother had insisted I'd regret it; I should keep something that would've been important to him. Next, I'd tried leaving it on his headstone, but obviously she had retrieved it. I wondered what had happened to it and felt sure he hadn't come for it. If he could come back, he'd come for me, not a belt buckle.

Kevin was addicted to rodeo, danger, and an eight-second ride. At age twenty-six one small mistake ended his life. It seemed so unfair. Kevin had cheated death many times, but in a split-second, he'd run out of aces.

* * *

Sitting on my porch that night, watching my mountain in the dark, I got very drunk. When I ran out of tequila, I finished off Kevin's sipping whiskey. It wasn't like he'd ever sip it again. After that, I drank cold longnecks. I was on a roll, and the more I thought I should stop, the more I drank. What finally did stop me was a fuzzy thought that I had serious butt-kicking to do tomorrow and doing it hung over would be hell.

For a while I dozed in the rocking chair, but I woke up chilled, stumbled to bed, and more or less fell in and passed out, still dressed in shorts and a t-shirt.

I woke with a pounding heart. There was someone in my house. The hall nightlight was off and I had just replaced the bulb. It was dark, and I was alone and incapacitated by booze. Boots in the hall—had the rapists come for me? Would I be splayed naked, raped, and photographed? I was terrified.

I couldn't have lifted my Beretta 9MM even if I'd remembered it was on the dresser. I swore to myself that if I got out of this alive I would stop drinking. The cell phone crossed my mind—I could call Barney—but I didn't know where that was either, and thought I'd left it on the porch.

"Who's there?" I asked the dark.

There was no answer, but the footsteps halted. Then, about the time I started breathing again, they began to come towards me.

Chapter 8

Boots crept to the side of my bed and stopped. I couldn't detect movement, but sensed a presence. The anticipation of a next move was torture. I felt like a hooded prisoner waiting for the hangman to drop the trap door. I began screaming like a little girl but nothing came from The Thing in the Dark.

"Who's there?" I asked again in a pitiful voice. The room was spinning but I was sure there was a man by my bed—a man or a monster. From my prone position, he was huge, a looming evil that meant to do who-knew-what. Sober, I would've jumped up and fought him, but drunk and dizzy, I was helpless as a baby bird. "Speak to me," I demanded, sounding about as dangerous as one.

I sensed, more than saw, a hand coming towards me, so I rolled across the bed screaming and landed on the floor under a window. The room spun so much I couldn't stand, and while I struggled, the intruder ran back down the hall and out the front door. I heard it slam long before I was able to follow.

I made it as far as the porch, hung over the railing, and vomited. By then he was long gone. I wanted to call Barney or my father but was too ashamed. I couldn't let them see me smelling like a tequilería and so full of rage and sadness.

I sat in the wicker chair and cried and rocked myself. After a while, I became captivated by the big-star Texas night, and my misery eased itself to the shadows. Eventually I went back inside and checked my Beretta. With it ready to fire, I lay down in bed, shoved it under my pillow, and slept.

* * *

Getting up was hard, and I did it at six-thirty so I'd have time to get ready, slowly. I showered, dressed in blue jeans and a t-shirt, and then looked for a clue to the identity of the monster.

When the search turned up nothing, I sat at the kitchen table and drank hot tea and tried to eat dry toast. I wasn't sure there'd really been a monster.

I choked down a handful of ibuprofen and made it to work by nine o'clock. Barney was already there. When I saw him, I wanted to sob on his shoulder and admit how desolate my life had become and how hopeless I felt when I drank and how I couldn't stop. Instead I went into my office and sank into my favorite chair. Yesterday I'd been a superhero, or at least John Wayne. Today I was weeping in my office with my insides twisting like a desert willow in a high wind.

"Ricos!" Barney yelled.

"What?"

"Do you want to talk about it?"

"No."

Within seconds his extra-large frame filled the door to my office. He handed me a Dr. Pepper, his cure for everything. "Don't take this wrong, but you look like death warmed over."

"I feel like it, too."

"Did somebody hit you? There's a red mark on your cheek."

"Mandy's mother slapped me."

"Is that why you're crying?"

"No."

The Dr. Pepper tasted wonderful—cold and fizzy. Barney perched his big self on the edge on my desk, and looked at me the way my father did when I was little and did something wrong. It was a mixture of anger, humor, and affection.

"Spill it, Ricos."

I began crying again. "It's too lame for words."

"Spill it or I'll get it out of you the hard way."

I knew he'd never hurt me, but I spilled it anyway.

"Why didn't you call? Don't you trust me?"

"Sure I do, and I wanted to, but I didn't have my phone."

"What about afterward? You could've called me then." His big blue eyes were boring a hole into me.

"Stop it, Barney. What are you looking at?"

"Right now I'm looking at a tin star with a drunk pinned to it," he drawled in his best-yet imitation of John Wayne.

"Okay, John, give it a rest."

"You asked for that one, Ricos."

"Stop looking at me like that."

He shook his head slowly. "Ricos, Ricos, Ricos. We're the law in these here parts and if you're too drunk to kick butt I'll come kick it for you." He held his big fists up in a boxer pose.

I laughed and stopped crying and whining.

"Was your door locked?" he asked.

"No, I hardly ever lock my door."

"Will you start locking it?"

"It's locked now." That was too much like the horse and barn door story, and I wanted to cry again.

"Tell me about the man. Can you give a description?"

"Well, no, I never really saw a man. I heard boots walking towards me and they stopped by the bed."

"Did he touch you?"

"No, I rolled away to the floor."

"Who would come into your house like that?"

"I don't know. My friends would knock."

Barney thought about it. "Maybe some drunk came to the wrong house and when you started screaming, he left."

"Maybe, and maybe I imagined it."

"Do you think so?" His eyes were so sad I couldn't look at him. "Oh, Ricos," he said, and sighed.

I tried to change the subject. "What am I going to do about Jimmy Joe?"

"Do you want me to talk to him?"

"No. That'll make it worse."

"Have you told Shoots you're not interested?"

"Many times."

"And he continues to bug you?"

"Yes. He says we made a connection."

"That's what he's after, a connection. You know, your part with his part and—"

I held up my hands. "Stop right there. I know about sex."

Barney reddened. "Well, that's what old Shoots wants."

"Never gonna happen."

"He refuses to accept that you're not interested in him or his part. Maybe you should talk to the sheriff."

"That'd be like telling the teacher on him."

"Ricos, those Alpine deputies would tell on you first chance they had."

"I know, but I'm not like them. Maybe the kid that raped Mandy was in my house last night, trying to scare me."

"Why would he take a chance like that?"

"Maybe he heard I was talking to her."

He frowned, thoughtful. "I'm going to make a report."

"Please don't."

"Why not?"

"Sheriff Ben will see it."

"Oh."

"I'm going to quit drinking, Barney."

"I wish you would. Sheriff Ben doesn't have to see anything to know what's going on. He's like God."

"One of the local blabbermouths will tell him sooner or later."

"He only has to see you on a day like today. But that's not the reason."

"Then what is your reason?"

"You're going get yourself killed by some pervert because you're too drunk to stop him. Or worse, alcohol will kill you the slow way."

"I'm going to quit."

Barney left on another murder interview while I went in search of a crime scene.

* * *

Truck Heckart's place was about twenty minutes from our office, depending on road conditions. Today it was dusty and washboarded, but all the arroyo crossings were dry and had been for over a month.

According to the local Porch news commentators, Truck had come to Terlingua under suspicious circumstances. That would describe how we got a third of our population, but I gave newcomers the benefit of the doubt until they proved to be a problem.

Supposedly, Truck drowned his wife in a stock tank on his ranch and got away with it. His story was that she fell in, and although it was only chest deep, she panicked and drowned. Thirsty cattle discovered her floating body. I don't know how a tale can be more pure Texan than that.

According to Porch pundits, the good ol' boy system of justice in Hicksville, Texas didn't try too hard to find the facts, and accepted Truck's version at face value. They fumbled the investigation and passed the ball back and forth until they were so far out of bounds the game had to be called.

Whether Truck Heckart is a murderer or not I couldn't say, but his place could easily belong to one. He lives in a shack he constructed with scavenged wood. It was meant to be temporary, but time marched on, and the shack endures. It's situated at the edge of a shaded canyon where sunlight seldom touches it. That made the scene sinister, and although I didn't personally know Truck, and in spite of keeping an open mind, I approached with caution.

A battered old blue Chevy truck was parked near the house but no one came to the door when I knocked. The unofficial junkyard was located a short walk up the canyon. It seemed the perfect dark setting for violent crime.

The old trucks and cars had been shoved off the canyon edge and since then, rubbish of every kind had been thrown at the pile. I found boot prints in the sand, but not multiple sets. That made me think this couldn't be the place but it had to be because I didn't know another.

I winced at the nasty pile of stinking garbage. So far, in the southern part of the county, there are no zoning laws, both a good and bad thing. On the whole, we're people who don't want to be told what to do—and especially by a governing body eighty miles away. So technically, if a person wants to throw trash on their own land that's okay—except it isn't. I think there should be a prison sentence for leaving junk in the desert—the more junk, the longer the sentence. Under my new law, Truck would be looking at life.

I watched the ground for signs of a struggle: torn clothing, a condom—anything that could be evidence of rape. How evil to bring a girl to such a filthy, terrifying place on a dark night and rape her. I wanted to not think about it, but it's hard to look for a crime scene and not think about the crime.

I came upon a condom that looked too desiccated to have been used recently. I poked at it with a stick to be sure and left it. When a large raven flew over the canyon cawing loudly, I jumped. I tried to laugh at myself, but it wasn't funny.

Then I heard something behind me. The hairs on the back of my neck stood up as I peered over my shoulder. There was nothing there, and the sound stopped, but when I started moving again, so did something or someone else. My Beretta was in the vehicle, probably laughing its trigger off at me.

At that point my imagination took off, fueled by dozens of horror movies. I rounded one end of the pile, still seeing nothing, my heart galloping. The desire to run was as keen as the desire to demand justice for Mandy. Two seconds before I took off, I was grabbed from behind by strong arms that lifted me off the ground. Something akin to Sasquatch would eat me for dinner, or worse. A beard (fur?) tickled the back of my neck and the thing's breath smelled like it'd been eating burned rubber.

"Whaddayathinkyou'redoing?" It was human, and probably Truck.

Then something hard pressed against my backside. From experience I would say it wasn't a gun.

"Answer me!" he growled into my ear.

I started stuttering. "I—I'm looking for s-something. I'm a d-deputy sheriff." Yeah, that'd put the fear of God into him.

"You're no deputy. What are you looking for? Trouble?"

As suddenly as he grabbed me, he let me go. I turned to face him, even though what I wanted was to run as hard as I could.

He held up his hands. "I saw your vehicle and thought I'd have a little fun with you. No harm done."

"It wasn't fun for me. I should take you in for assault."

His eyes narrowed. "You're trespassing, and I didn't assault you."

I glared at him, but before I spoke he said, "If you're a deputy, then you know about trespass laws."

"You know I'm a deputy—you saw the vehicle."

"Yeah, so you know about the law."

"I didn't realize this was your property," I lied. "I thought it was a county dump."

"Well." He looked sheepish. "I won't prosecute if you won't."

He held out his hand. I saw the fleeting image of a woman floating face down in a metal stock tank, her dark hair fanned around her head. "I'm Truck Heckart."

I tried to shake the image and shook his hand. "I'm Margarita Ricos."

"For real what are you looking for?"

"I'm looking for evidence of a crime."

"It's no crime to throw trash on your own property."

"I'm aware of that, but why would you want to?" I didn't give him a chance to answer, although his response might have been interesting. "I'm looking for the scene of a rape."

"Look here—I never raped nobody! Maybe I gave you the wrong impression but—"

"No one is accusing you, but I think the crime happened somewhere around these old trucks."

"Why do you think that?"

"The victim indicated there were old truck bodies at the scene, but she doesn't know where she was."

"She wasn't here. I don't let people come back here, and when I see their lights I put a stop to it. Kids used to come partying and necking up on the rim, but I called a halt to that."

Partying and necking on the rim was how I knew about the truck graveyard, but that was before Truck moved there.

"I better not catch anyone shoving a vehicle off there, either," he said.

"I'm glad you put a stop to that."

"Damn right I stopped that shit."

"If you don't mind, I'd like to look around a little more."

"Knock yourself out. When you're done come up to the house for a beer."

"Thanks, but I'm working."

"Suit yourself." He scratched his head. "Hey—you married?"

"Yes sir."

"That figures." He wandered off in the direction of his house.

I went back to the Explorer and stuck my Beretta into the waistband of my jeans. It was another case of shutting the barn door after the horse escaped, but I didn't want to think about it. My head was killing me and the stench of rotting garbage made the nausea return.

I searched a while longer but came up with nada. Which meant there had to be another truck graveyard, but where? Mandy could be mistaken. She was under plenty of stress, but I couldn't believe she'd imagined the creepy old vehicles.

I drove to the Robbins' home, fearful that I smelled like a gutter drunk in spite of breath mints. Eating breath mints made me think of Truck's awful breath in my ear, but I dragged myself away from that nightmare in pursuit of a different one.

Julie Robbins came to the door and when she saw me, looked afraid. "I'm sorry I slapped you," she said before I said anything. I was glad to see that her hair was washed, and she looked less haunted.

"It's all right, Julie. I know you must be frantic and heartsick."

"You have no idea. Would you like to come in?"

"I'll only be a second. I came to get the clothes Mandy was wearing. The sheriff mentioned I'd be by to pick them up."

She hesitated, her nose wrinkled in disgust. "I put them in the trash. They're ruined."

"I need them."

"Whatever for?"

"I'd like to look at them."

Her expression said she thought I was insane, but she went to get them and came back with a stuffed plastic grocery bag.

"How's Mandy doing?"

"She's asleep now. I think she'll be okay—eventually. I'm taking her to see a counselor tomorrow."

"That's good. Will you tell her I said hello?" I turned to leave, then back to her. "Did you notice the car or truck that brought Mandy home Saturday night?"

"No. I heard it, but I didn't realize it would be Mandy until she came in the door."

I went back to my Explorer, opened the back, put on gloves, and took out the clothes. Everything was there: a short, tan, cotton skirt, a lightweight, embroidered blue blouse that was beautiful before it was ripped off her. Her bra and underpants were torn as well. The skirt was filthy, wrinkled, and stained with who-knew-what, but I thought semen would be one thing. All but one of the buttons was missing from the blouse. They would probably be at the scene.

As I was placing each item into an evidence bag, a small boy in a cowboy hat rode up on a bike and stared at me.

"Hello," I said. "Why aren't you in school?"

"Cause Mandy's hurt."

"Are you her brother?"

"Yes, I'm Michael but everybody calls me Little Tex. Are you the cops?"

"I'm Deputy Ricos."

"How come you ain't got a uniform or gun?"

"I didn't wear it today. I hope you're taking good care of Mandy."

He wrinkled his nose. "She fights with me."

"I guess older sisters can be difficult."

"Yeah." He looked around guiltily, then whispered, "I know something."

I squatted to his level. "What do you know?"

"You won't tell my mom?"

"No."

"I was 'sposed to be in bed but I wasn't. I was lookin' in the yard for my dog Buster and I saw some boys bring Mandy home."

"Do you know them?"

"I couldn't see them good enough, but I saw the truck."

"What kind was it?"

"It was high up and black, with big tires. And it was loud."

"That's a huge help, Little Tex. Anything else?"

"A boy said bad words. Should I tell you it anyway?"

"Yes, please do."

"He said, *Open your mouth and I'll kill you, bitch. Don't forget it. I ain't fucking kidding.*" Little Tex sighed and glanced around again. "I'm not allowed to say *bitch* or *fucking.*"

"Thank you for telling me."

"Mandy's scared. Are you scared too?"

"No, Little Tex, I'm going to put those boys in prison where they can never hurt Mandy again."

"That's good. I want her to be like she was before, even if she hits me."

Chapter 9

Some of the high school students drive to school, so I hoped the big black truck would be parked in the lot. There was a black truck, but it was a Nissan Frontier, not large.

The high school is small, one story, red brick, and not very old. The front doors open into a wide hall with classrooms down the right side and administrative offices on the left. It makes a backwards, upside down 'L' with more classrooms along the back, a science lab, a home-economics room, and between them, bathrooms. The science lab in the far corner was Kevin's room.

It was hard to face the superintendent, Dena Jablonski. She had pegged me as a troublemaker and heavy drinker early on in my school career. For a long time I had proved her wrong. Now I was proving her right. That hurt worse than my head.

I waited for her impatiently, almost tearful because of Kevin's room not being his anymore. I half-expected him to stride down the hall and take me into his arms.

"Margarita?" It was Jablonski and her look made me feel like a child caught playing hooky. No, worse than that: a child caught with pornography in the bathroom, or having sex on the playground—or in a classroom.

"Come on in," she said.

I followed, trying to put my imagination into neutral.

"What can I do for you?" She looked me up and down with distaste. I was wearing civilian clothes so I wouldn't be instantly recognizable on the school grounds, but I was clean and neat in spite of how I felt.

"You look like one of the kids," she said when I didn't respond. "It throws me." It could have been a compliment, but probably not, coming from her.

"I need some help," I said. How true that was. "Does one of the students drive a tall black truck with big tires?"

She thought about it. "That doesn't sound familiar."

"It might be any dark color."

"You mean a large truck or one that's been lifted?"

"Lifted, I think, but maybe it's only big."

"Nobody drives a truck like that to school. May I ask why you're looking for it?"

"No ma'am, this is Sheriff's Office business. I'm not at liberty to say."

"I don't like that."

Of course she didn't. She wanted to be current on the gossip, like everyone else in Terlingua. Especially when it involved students she could torture with her knowledge of their personal stuff. She was the first to trash bad parents, and maybe that could be forgiven, but she trashed her students, and that couldn't. Children needed her to step up and defend them, teach them how to survive in a cruel world, and teach them morality and decency.

I let out a breath I hadn't consciously held. "I'm sorry you don't like it, but I have the best interests of your students at heart."

"Well."

"Are there three high school boys that regularly hang out together?"

"There are lots of three and foursomes. They all hang out in groups."

"Do you have any students that are acting odd today, or have injuries—bruises or scratches?"

She gave one of her you're-an-idiot snickers. "Kids always have injuries, and they're all odd at that age."

I knew that was true, but I thought she should love them anyway. I stood. "I'm going to hang around and observe."

"Suit yourself."

I went into the hall during a class change, and saw a football player-sized boy in a corner, showing something to a smaller boy. I walked a few feet and saw it was photos. I could tell what kind they were by the reaction. But high school boys constantly pass inappropriate photos. Pick any day, something would be circulating.

I walked to the double glass doors and looked out at the parking lot, and past that, the dirt track and further away, the Chisos Mountains in Big Bend National Park. My mind, heart, and soul rested there for a brief moment.

I went outside, the better to worship them, and to think. I needed to find the truck. Maybe Barney would know it.

"I was just on my way to more interviews," he said when he answered his cell.

I described the truck. "I've seen that big boy driving it," he said.

"What big boy?"

In Texas, a *big boy* can be anywhere between a large newborn and an old man. Of course large men out of childhood are usually *big ol' boys*.

"That big kid that used to play football in Alpine. He got expelled last year and now he's going to school here. He's Judge Dooley's son and lives with the Sanchez family. I've seen him driving a dark blue Bronco that he's lifted to a ridiculous height. I think he goes to those monster truck rallies up by Presidio."

I wondered how Barney could possibly know all that. Then I thought that I might know it too, if I wasn't so focused on my own misery all the time.

"Thanks, Barney. That gives me a place to start."

"Any time, Ricos. You think he's your doer?"

"I don't know, but I suspect it."

"That would figure, him being the judge's son."

County Judge Everett B. Dooley heads up the county commission, the legal entity that runs county business and therefore employs the sheriff. Dooley is contentious even when his son is not the subject of an investigation.

I watched shadows chase sunlight across the mountains another few minutes, then got back into my vehicle and went by a convenience store to purchase a small bottle of orange juice. I was more driven by a pounding hangover than by thirst or a sudden need for a dose of vitamin C. While I was still sitting in the parking lot, my cell phone rang, startling me.

"Ricos," I practically yelled, thinking it was Jimmy Joe Blanks again.

"You're so funny," said my friend Austin with a snorting laugh. "I love how you say 'Ricos' like everybody knows who you are." His voice is nasal and a beat too slow. Austin was born with Down syndrome, but he never lets that get in his way.

"Austin!"

Hearing his voice gave me a lift. We'd been friends for four years and were close, like childhood buddies who'd always known each other. We met when I was attending college in Alpine. Austin was in college too, a fact that made him proud. He was taking one class at a time and putting his total attention on it. I was soon in awe of him and his flat refusal to be labeled retarded.

"You doin' hero work?" he asked. Austin is impressed by my law enforcement position, and believes in his heart that I'm a hero. His unwavering belief in me makes me aspire to be one, most days.

"Nah—I'm just interviewing people about a murder." I didn't mention the rape because it was somehow more awful.

"A murder?"

"Yeah, a woman was murdered the day before yesterday and we're interviewing people who might know something. What do you know that you're not telling me?"

"Gosh," he said. "I don't even live there."

"Are you coming to see me?" I changed the subject since he didn't get my little joke. Austin lives with his mother in Alpine.

"No, not today." He paused. "I have to get an operation, Margarita. I'm scared."

Austin was born with a heart defect, in addition to his other physical challenges. It seems unfair for so many problems to have been piled on him. There is nothing I can do about any of it, so I try to accept it as graciously as he does.

"Don't be scared, Austin. When will you have the surgery?"

"Will you come?" He sounded so small and frightened it pained me. "I want you to come."

"Yes, of course I'll come. Do you know the date?"

"No." He hesitated, worried that he couldn't remember the details. "My mother will call you later, okay?"

"Okay."

I wanted to ask him everything about the upcoming surgery, like what would be done and how long it would take and how long he'd have to be hospitalized, and the estimated recovery time, but I knew he'd be upset when he couldn't answer my questions. I didn't want to add to his fear and frustration.

"It's not tomorrow, is it?"

He laughed, sounding like himself again. "No! Not tomorrow, you big goof!" He paused. "I miss you." I could hear his heavy breathing and hoped he wasn't crying.

"I miss you too."

His wacky sense of humor was what I missed most, and his always-fresh view of current events, and his honest approach to our friendship—his honest approach to everything. All of us could learn a lot from the Austins of this world.

He and I spent hours riding horses, and lying on our backs looking at cloud formations, or watching approaching storms. We talked about our lives and what we believed, who we loved and liked and didn't like much. Austin probably knows me better than anyone. He had held me many times while I cried my heart out over Kevin's death.

Austin has a capacity for kindness and understanding that surpasses any I've ever known. It's one of his gifts. Another is his singing ability. He is blessed with an incredible voice and has an ear for music.

"I gotta go to class," Austin said. "I'm getting a C." He announced it as proudly as if he was telling me he'd made the dean's list.

"Good job, Austin! Have your mom call me soon, okay?"

"Okay. Bye, 'Rita."

I sat for a moment, worried about him and sad not to be able to see him right away. The life expectancy of people with Down syndrome is better than it used to be, but Austin still has a lot of physical problems and a heart that's already been repaired twice. He's only twenty-five years old.

I was still sitting there when another truck graveyard floated by in my memory. I didn't know if it was still there because I hadn't been there in ages. It fit Mandy's description: deserted, not far from the school, and would be scary at night.

A rough road starts just before the school property, crosses Terlingua Creek, and winds through a private ranch for several miles, until it passes an unpaved landing strip. Eventually it comes out on State Highway 170. That was the route I took, looking for a place I barely remembered.

Tracks were everywhere, crossing each other, so following any of them would be pointless. I bumped slowly across the rocks and wet gravel of the creek bed. Along the bank, yellow lemoncillo and bright white prickly poppies bloomed with abandon. Past the creek, I began looking for likely places to do violent crime. I thought it would be past the few houses that sat along the road. Perverts like privacy, and screaming girls attract attention.

On the other side of the houses, the road goes up a steep hill. I went slowly, looking for any hint that a vehicle had left the roadbed. Things that are disturbed in the desert tend to stay that way until a hard rain, high wind, or in most cases, the passage of time, changes them.

When the landing strip appeared on my left, I slowed to a crawl, thinking that anywhere along here would be a good place to pull off. Soon I found a flattened area where the berm had been run over, and a couple of small creosote bushes along with it. As I got out of the vehicle, I noticed a graveyard of ancient trucks and cars, five of them, rusting into the desert across the road. They appeared to be from the 1940s and 50s and were nearly hidden by wild growth.

From there it was a short walk to a bare area where the hardpan showed signs of a scuffle. It was more of a brawl than a scuffle. Mandy had fought hard— I found a ripped piece of a man's shirt to prove it.

I photographed the scene before I picked up the evidence: three blue buttons, a crumpled soda can, two cigarette butts, and the torn-off scrap of shirt. I walked back and forth in expanding circles looking for a condom, but didn't find one.

Chapter 10

Back at the high school, I asked again to see Mrs. Jablonski. When I inquired about the football player from Alpine High, she was unwilling to help and said I'd need a court order to get information about a student. We exchanged words and she finally softened, but insisted on speaking with the sheriff first. She sent me back to the outer office to sit, where a couple of elementary school students were fooling around, waiting for her, I presumed.

"Are you in trouble?" a small boy asked, his eyes wide.

"Probably," I said.

"Me, too." He crooked his arm around the neck of his friend. "We both are—for talking in class and being encouraged-able."

"I think you mean incorrigible."

"That's it. What'd you do?"

"I'm incorrigible, too."

"Way to go," the other boy said, and pushed his pal to the floor.

Old Lady Jablonski suddenly appeared. "Behave yourselves," she said in a stern voice. Typical Jablonski; she could appear and disappear like any witch.

"Come," she said to me, and both boys watched as if I was being marched to my death. I winked at them and followed her.

I could tell by her body language that things hadn't gone her way with Sheriff Ben. Her mouth was set in a grim line and she did her best to convey that having anything to do with the likes of me was beneath her. I persevered, like I had in school.

"His name is Wayne Dooley," Ms. Jablonski said after she tried to stare me down, "and he's a troublemaker. He was expelled from Alpine High. I only agreed to accept him here because his father is County Judge Dooley."

"Is Wayne a large boy?"

"He's the size of a grown man."

"Who hangs out with him?"

"Eddie Santos and Rick Florence are his buddies. They're only sophomores, but he likes younger kids because he can feel superior."

"Is Wayne a senior?"

"Yes. Here's a picture of him from last year."

The boy was wearing a football uniform from Alpine High, but he was holding the helmet so I could see his face clearly. He had sandy blond hair, brown eyes, and a surly, superior smirk on his face. He was the boy I'd seen passing photos.

"Is there anything else I should know?"

"That's hard to say since I don't know what you're doing, but be careful of Wayne. I believe he could be dangerous if cornered."

I stood and offered my hand. "Thank you, Ms. Jablonski. I appreciate your help. I'll tell you everything soon." *Right after every other living thing in Terlingua knows.*

She shook my hand and tried to smile.

Kids were in class, so I sat on the floor by the lockers, thinking. Someone had taken Kevin's place in the classroom, but I still thought of it as his. He taught earth science, physics, biology and geology. Kevin was smart, which I realize is debatable since he died bull riding. He was smart, but he loved danger.

A girl came out of a classroom and went into the bathroom. That gave me an idea. I moved to the soda machine, nearer the restrooms, and waited.

I had to wait through one whole class period, and a change of classes, but when things quieted down again, Wayne Dooley snuck down the hall and ducked into the bathroom. I waited until I heard the toilet flush, and then went in. He didn't look up at first, but when he did, he saw me in the mirror. "You're in the wrong one—the girls' is next door."

He was snorting cocaine and didn't seem at all concerned that I was watching. His backpack rested carelessly across the sinks, open. Inside was a bag of white powder and the edges of what I thought would be photos of Mandy. I had only hoped to catch him with the photos, but the God of Lawmen Everywhere smiled on me.

"You can't be in the boys' bathroom." He rubbed his nose vigorously. "What are you, some kind of pervert?"

I flipped my badge at him. "I'm Deputy Ricos and you're under arrest for possession of a controlled substance."

"You can't arrest me, you bitch!"

He came at me in a fury fueled by cocaine and general meanness. He outweighed me by at least sixty pounds. I would've tried to dodge him, except I remembered what he'd done to Mandy and feared for my life. When he reached for my throat, I grabbed his arm, pressed my knee against the side of his body, and flung him to the tiles. I'd never done that to such a large person and was shocked it worked. He started to rise, but I kicked him in the back of the knee and handcuffed him before he tried again.

"That's police brutality," he whined, and began verbally abusing me while I recited his rights.

"My father is your boss, you stupid bitch," he spit at me. "When he finds out you've treated me like this, you'll be history!"

"Your father approves of cocaine use at school?"

That quieted him for a few seconds. I wondered what his father would think about rape, but didn't mention it because I couldn't prove it yet.

I rifled through his backpack while he stewed. There was a small plastic bag with five joints, the photos of Mandy, more cocaine, and a wallet with his driver's license. He was eighteen as of three months ago. Things were looking up.

"Are you really eighteen?"

He sneered. "What do you think?"

"I think a boy eighteen would have better sense than to snort cocaine on school property right in front of a deputy sheriff."

"Fuck you. You're not even wearing a uniform."

"Let's go."

I grabbed him by the cuffs and had to shove him along, trickier than it sounds when the prisoner weighs one-hundred-and-eighty pounds and the deputy weighs a lot less, but I was determined. Size isn't everything.

Dena Jablonski came out of her office and did a double take when she saw us.

"Can she do this, Ms. Jablonski?" asked the prisoner in a whiny voice. "She's not even wearing a uniform."

"I guess she can."

"She came into the men's room without knocking."

Old Jablonski was trying not to, but she grinned in spite of herself. She looked at the carpet to hide it, but I saw, and so did Wayne because he mumbled, "Bitches."

Score one for the bitches, I thought, zero for the bad boys.

* * *

Barney looked up in surprise when I woman-handled Wayne Dooley through our door. He was still complaining and calling me names.

"I'd knock off the name-calling if I were you," said Barney.

"Why should I?"

"Do you realize that a small, unarmed woman dragged you in?" He came around his desk and took over. Moving a one hundred-and-eighty pound man is easy for him. "You should be saying 'yes ma'am' and 'no ma'am' to her."

He sat Wayne in a chair. "What's this you got here, Ricos?"

"This is Wayne Dooley. He was snorting cocaine in the boys' bathroom at school." I slung the backpack onto the desk and raised one eyebrow at Barn. "There's more of it in there, and a few joints, not to mention some interesting photographs."

Barney started going through the pack.

"Those aren't mine," Wayne claimed angrily.

"What's not yours?" Barney didn't look at him and instead, studied the photos.

"Those pictures aren't mine."

"You're admitting to the drugs?"

He shrugged. "I guess so."

"Where did these come from?" Barney held up the photos of Mandy Robbins naked and being held down against her will.

"Some guy passed them to me during class."

"What guy?"

"Just some guy."

"So a mysterious guy happened to come into your classroom and pass you photographs of a naked girl that looks like she's being held down against her will. Isn't she a classmate of yours?"

"I don't know her. She's in middle school."

"You don't know all the girls in your school?"

"I know some of them."

"Are you dating any of them?"

"Sometimes."

"Who?"

"That's none of your business."

Barney leaned towards him. "Everything about this is my business. You have illegal drugs on school property and photographs of a girl who's—what—maybe thirteen or fourteen? This girl is naked, obviously against her will. I'd guess she's been raped or is about to be."

"I'd like to know how you got those deep scratches on your neck," I said.

"I play sports."

"A girl didn't give them to you?"

"Fuck you."

"You'd better start giving us answers," growled Barney.

"I want my attorney."

"Of course, that's your right. Who's your attorney?"

"I—I don't know. I need to talk to my father."

"I'll have Sheriff Duncan call him while you wait in a holding cell," I said.

"You can't make me wait in there."

Instead of arguing, Barney moved him into it and clanged the door shut. Then he made a smart move. He said, "Take off your shirt. You have to wear a county shirt when you're in here."

The kid didn't know that wasn't true, and removed his shirt. He had painful-looking bruises all over his chest, and more fingernail drag marks.

Barney gave me a knowing look and turned back to him. "I guess we don't have a county shirt on hand. You can put yours back on. You want a soda or water?"

"I'd like a cold brew."

"Right, I'm as likely to get you a brew as you are to tell me the truth. Last chance for a soda." To me Barney said, "You call the boss since the boy's your prisoner."

I went into my office, but stood at the window. Everything was perfect out there. I don't know why I expected the whole world to crash and burn just because mine had.

"Ricos! Are you going to call the sheriff?"

"Yeah, yeah, I'm going."

I took my cell phone outside under the pretext of privacy and walked towards the closest boulder. After checking it to be sure it wasn't the one where the hawk ripped apart its prey, I climbed up and called Sheriff Ben.

I gave him my sketchy plan for proving that Wayne Dooley raped Mandy. I was sure the sheriff had his hands in his hair, but he never said he feared Everett Dooley, only that he would call him about his son. He also said he was coming for Wayne. He belonged in the county jail because of the seriousness of his crimes, and since Barney and I were busy with a murder and a rape. It seemed like he was talking about deputies from somewhere else.

I lay back against the warm stone and shut my eyes against everything. The world went away, along with my headache. I breathed deeply of air that smelled wonderful, a fragrant mixture of breeze fresh from the mountains, a million green growing things, honest dry dirt, and some flowering plant nearby. The day was heating up and I was lying on a rock in the sun like a lizard.

Had Wayne been in my house last night? I didn't think it was him, but it was hard to second guess criminals. Why was a vicious pervert like Wayne Dooley allowed to breathe this air? Or any pervert, for that matter? Only good people should be allowed in the desert. Things would be different if I made the rules.

I must have fallen asleep, because Barney snuck up on me. When I opened my eyes, big, startlingly blue ones were looking at me. My partner is no Mel Gibson, but he has the bluest blue eyes I've ever seen, and dark lashes. Women ask me about him all the time, but maybe that has more to do with their interest in his great size.

"Whaddaya think about working today, Ricos, or are you goin' to lie around all day bein' the Lizard Queen?"

I laughed and sat up.

"How'd you get up there, anyway?"

"I crawled."

He lifted me down. "What are you doing out here?"

"I was talking to the Sheriff and then I was just thinking. Don't you ever wonder why the desert smells so nice?"

"Well, I hadn't thought about it. I guess I take it for granted."

"I don't think we should allow bad people to live here."

He laughed and held the office door open for me while I removed the evidence bags from my vehicle. "We're trying to get rid of them, remember? But if you're including weirdoes, that might remove a large segment of our population."

"I'm talking about people with black hearts and dangerous pervs like—" I jerked my head towards the holding cell rather than speak his name.

"Let's put up a sign halfway between Alpine and Terlingua that says 'Perverts, Assholes, and Murderers: KEEP OUT.'"

"And people who leave trash in the desert."

He gave me a curious look. "I'll get right on that, Ricos. Speaking of murder, could we talk?"

"Yeah, how are your interviews coming along?"

"Let's go in your office."

He shut the door so our prisoner wouldn't hear anything. Then he sat in my favorite chair. With the furniture, Barney, and me, my office space was maxed. I set the bags of Mandy's clothes on my desk.

Barney barely glanced at them. "I don't want to know that sick story. Do you have semen evidence?"

"I think so."

"So he wasn't careful."

"I don't even know if he used a condom. I think he wanted to insult her. He figured she'd bathe, but he didn't think about her clothes, or doesn't care because he thinks his threats will keep her quiet."

"And they have so far."

"Yes, but I got a break."

I told him the story in condensed form.

"Looks like nobody's a match for you, Sherlock."

"Shut it, Watson. Save yourself."

He laughed at that weak threat.

"I spoke with Stanner," Barney said, "and I don't think he killed Norma. He seems sad and upset."

"He usually seems sad and upset."

"You know what I mean, worse than usual. I don't think he could get up the steam to kill somebody."

Stanner Bates was a serious man with a dry sense of humor. He was five years older than Norma, which made him fifty. He looked older, maybe because he lived with her, or because I was comparing him to my dad who had no gray hair. Stanner had a lot of it.

"I asked him the usual questions, and he doesn't have a clue about who could've killed Norma. He said he knew she made people mad, and he mentioned the mess with Doctores Fronterizos, and your mother in particular, but said he couldn't imagine any of them killing her. He did say one interesting thing."

"What was that?"

"Lil and Norma were no longer friendly."

"I wonder what happened."

He shrugged.

"Did you see the children, Barney?"

"They stood there in a corner as if they'd been painted into it."

"I feel bad for them."

"Yeah, me too. Kids can't help who their parents are or what they do."

"Yours come to mind," I said to aggravate him. He has two, a daughter almost two years old and a son who arrived a few weeks ago.

Barney's brows scrunched together suddenly. "You won't like this next part."

"What?"

"Read this." He handed me an evidence bag that held a run-over looking piece of lined paper. "Stanner found it stuck in a book Norma was reading and thought we should see it."

I recognized my mother's handwriting and felt suddenly cold. I took the paper from him and read it with dread. At the top was printed plainly in big letters, KILLING FOR HEALTH and then it read, *Norma has to be the first to go—figure out how.* On another line was written *Morton— drug dealer—many border health problems caused by drugs.* Below that was *William—Morton's partner in crime.* There was nothing more. The paper looked like it had been crumpled into a ball, as if to throw away.

"You should go over to the café and talk to Sylvia," I said. "She and Mom were writing a screenplay called 'Killing for Health.' It was one of their stupid ideas. Really, it was more of a game than anything."

"Couldn't you talk to her? She doesn't like me."

"Why wouldn't she like you? She likes everybody. You must have pissed her off."

"I'm afraid of her."

"Barney, you're bigger than John Wayne."

"He was only 6'4" and wore a size 11 boot, a little guy."

"I guess you wear a size bazillion."

"Only thirteen."

Locals call Barney "Roadblock", which should tell you what you need to know about his size.

"My point is that a one hundred pound English woman wouldn't have scared John Wayne for one second."

"That wasn't even his name."

"What does that have to do with anything? He was John Wayne to everyone."

"He was really Marion Morrison, Pilgrim."

"No wonder he changed it," I said, "but back to Sylvia. Why don't you hitch up your pants, hop on your big horse, and go dazzle her with your manliness?"

"I can't do that, she comes on to me."

"And that scares you? She's old enough to be your mother."

"So?"

"Okay, I'll go see her, but you'd better not tell any of those Alpine deputies that I threw up at a crime scene."

He tried to make his face an innocent blank, but a deep blush gave him away.

"You already told them? I can't believe it."

"Well, they're always asking about you."

"Great. So they're all a bunch of creeps."

"The next time you screw up it'll be our little secret. Come on Ricos, Sylvia likes you."

"Okay, but you owe me."

"Look, I'll do something for you. I'll talk to Shoots and make him stay away."

"Don't you dare. I want you to stay out of my personal life."

"I can tell him to leave you alone in a way that he'll get it."

"I don't want you to say one single thing to him."

"But what if he's the one that snuck into your house last night?"

"I don't think it was him and anyway, if he ever comes back, I'll have my partner." I patted my Beretta. "He's jealous and means business. His name is Bad—Bad Beretta."

"Guns are girls, Ricos."

"The hell you say. Mine is male. I think they're all male, just feel them and... never mind. Forget I said that."

He rolled his eyes at me.

"I have to go back to the school and ruin somebody else's day."

"Okay, we need to get out of this little office anyway before that little shit starts making up stuff about us."

"I don't think he's gonna have time to make problems for us."

"Do you want me to send those clothes to the crime lab?"

"The sheriff is coming for our prisoner, so you can give them to him. I'll put them into a couple of big brown envelopes so the perv won't see them."

"Good idea," Barney said with a John Wayne glint in his eye.

Chapter 11

I changed into my uniform and arrived at the high school at lunch time. One of my cousins, Manny Ricos, was cramming a backpack into his locker. He greeted me with a hug. We went outside at my request, and walked towards the track.

"Manny, do you know Wayne Dooley?"

"Everybody says you arrested him."

"So you know him?"

"Sure, how would I not know him?"

"You don't like him."

"Not much."

That was a relief because I didn't want any cousin of mine hanging with rapists and druggies.

"I assume you know Eddie Santos and Rick Florence?"

"Yeah, they're okay guys, but they've been hanging out with Wayne."

"Have you heard any talk I should know about? Not about drugs, but about a girl. Have you seen some photos of a naked girl being held down?"

He reddened in spite of being dark-skinned. "I saw them this morning. Kids are saying it was Mandy Robbins but I couldn't see a face. It seems like there was a light shining on her body, but her face was in the dark."

"What else are kids saying?"

"They think it's sick, and the girls are mad. Mandy's not at school today."

"I have reason to believe she was raped. Have you heard anything like that?"

He looked horrified. "No."

"Do you think Wayne is capable of raping a girl?"

"Well, he's mean and he talks dirty about girls—not dirty like the rest of us, but mean dirty talk. You know guys talk about sex and girls, right?"

"Sure, I know."

There was a covered area with benches at one end of the track and I indicated we should sit there. "Explain what you mean by mean dirty talk."

"Aw, do I have to say it?"

"I won't hold it against you."

"Well, he talks about kicking and biting girls to get them in the right mood. He says girls like it rough, and if you can't do it rough you're a pussy."

"What else?"

"Isn't that enough?"

"Yes, but I have the feeling you're not telling me everything."

Manny took a deep breath. "He says he wants to choke a bitch to death while taking her—his words. He claims killing a woman during sex would be better than sex."

"Good God."

"I warned you."

"You've heard him say these things?"

"Yes, but we mostly think he's full of shit. He's never done any of that, but the girls are afraid of him. You think he raped Mandy? She's not even in high school yet."

"She's in eighth grade, and I do think he raped her. He's in jail for having cocaine on campus, but I think that's the least of his crimes."

"Man, that's fucked up."

"What about Eddie and Rick? What do you think of them?"

"I don't think they'd rape anybody. God, I hope not."

"I'm going to have a talk with them."

"Kids might wonder why you're talking to me."

"Tell them you're my cousin and I love you and wanted to ask you how things were going. How are they going?"

"I'm fine, doing good this year."

"I'm glad to hear it."

"How are you, Margarita? I mean, the truth."

"I'm doing better."

"Mom wonders why you don't come see us and she thinks you're drinking a lot."

"I'll come by one of these days. Tell her I've stopped drinking."

He gave me a look that said he didn't believe me.

"I stopped this morning, Manny. I can't do it anymore."

"I'm gonna be on the basketball team this year. Will you come to some of the home games?"

"Sure, if you'll let me know when they are."

"I'd better go eat my lunch or else I won't get to. You know Jablonski."

I laughed and hugged him, then headed over to a lunch area near one side of the high school building. I sat myself down right between a couple of horrified tenth graders who were sitting at a table by themselves. It didn't look like they'd eaten much. Since I was wearing my uniform, they had no doubt about who I was, but would recognize me anyway. Eddie was a baby-faced but nice looking Mexican boy who was smaller than his friend by nearly a foot. Rick was tall and gangly, typical of a kid his age, and was just beginning to grow fuzz over his lip.

"Eddie Santos and Rick Florence," I said cheerfully. "Are you through with lunch? Let's take a walk."

"Where are we going?"

"Over there to the shelter by the track—unless you want to talk here. I've got nothing to hide from these kids."

"We'll go," said Eddie without enthusiasm. Rick said nothing but followed. When we sat I said, "Did you take photos of Mandy Robbins in the nude?"

"No, why would we?" said Rick, his first words. "Did she say we did?"

"I'm thinking you might do it if Wayne Dooley asked you to."

"We didn't."

"Eddie?"

"I didn't do it either."

"Okay, well that's that. If you decide you have anything to tell me, please call." I handed each of them a card after I wrote my personal cell phone number on the back. "I want you to think about something."

"What's that?"

"Wayne is eighteen and he's in a lot of trouble for raping Mandy." They watched me with huge eyes. "If you had any part in that, no matter how large or small, it would be to your advantage to come clean before Wayne gives his formal statement to the sheriff this afternoon."

Those two boys looked so terrified I thought it would be a matter of hours before I heard from one or both of them. If I didn't, I'd apply more pressure. I was sure at least one of them would cave before I had to get mean.

I called Sheriff Ben's cell phone before I moved my Explorer. He said he'd sent Deputy Blanks for the prisoner because he was too busy to come. Somehow I kept myself from groaning into the phone.

"We're sending Mandy Robbins' clothes to you," I said. "I want them sent to the crime lab but would you take them to the university's lab first and ask them if they can identify semen on any of it?"

"I'll do better than that. Marcy's back, I'll give them to her. She can identify semen several ways."

"I'm pretty sure it's there. I just want another opinion before I ask Judge Samuels not to grant bail for Wayne Dooley."

"I doubt if he'll go along with that. He believes children should be sent home in the care of their parents while evidence is gathered."

"It'll make a difference that Wayne is eighteen."

"He's eighteen? Are you sure?"

"Yes, sir."

"But you didn't arrest him for rape."

"I want you to do it when he gets there. Add rape to his charges."

"So you're sure?"

"Yes sir. Barney is emailing you photos. Plus you have the hospital report."

"I don't doubt that she was raped. I can't accuse Everett Dooley's son without knowing for sure it was him. He's already doing back flips that one of my deputies arrested his son for cocaine possession. Imagine what'll happen when I tell him he's raped a young girl."

"But Sheriff, that isn't your fault."

"Of course it's not, but that doesn't matter to Dooley. He'll want my badge for even suggesting such a thing."

I told the sheriff about my talk with Manny, and the vicious things Wayne said about girls, and what he fantasized doing.

"All that is sickening, Margarita, but we need definitive proof that this boy did it. I can't call Everett Dooley's son a rapist unless I'm damned sure."

"Can you buy me some time—just until tomorrow?"

"Yes. I'll ask the judge to delay bail as long as he can and I'll explain what we're doing."

"Show him the photos."

"I will. Everett Dooley is going to pressure the hell out of him but Judge Samuels won't care. Dooley has nothing to hold over him."

"I'm working on the witnesses. There are a couple of tenth graders who're in deep and are about to crumble. Take a look at the scratches on Wayne's neck. He has bruises and more scratches on his chest."

"I'll take note. The hearing will have to be in the late morning. There's no way to make it later because of the judge's schedule."

"Yes, sir, I'll figure out what to do by then. I may be bringing witnesses with me. I doubt if I can get Mandy, but she'd be the best one."

"Her testimony would make it stick."

"His semen will make it stick, but he'll get out on bail until we get the crime lab results and that could take weeks. He might kill her, Sheriff. Killing excites him as much as sex."

"I'm afraid that's probably true."

"I don't think you can afford to give her round-the-clock protection."

"You've got that right, Deputy Ricos."

I headed back to the airstrip, determined to find the condom. I couldn't believe a teenager would have bothered to carry it away. Most likely he tossed it, and maybe further than I realized. Starting where I left off, I expanded my search in ever-widening circles. My eyes flitted between the ground and the three-hundred-and-sixty-degree panorama. I was on a huge mesa with a view of part of the Chisos range to the south; Reed's Plateau, Needle and Castolon Peaks to the west; Willow Mountain and Indian Head to the east and many others, all stunners.

Delicate low-growing purple wildflowers bloomed along the edges of the landing strip, carpeting the berm in places, and showy ceniza displayed a dif ferent shade of purple on a nearby hillside. A cool breeze blew from the north, bringing a hint of autumn, in spite of the abundant sunshine. The pristine beauty of the area belied the heartless assault that took place there, but wild places don't hold onto those kinds of memories.

I turned my face to the sun. It was hard to pay attention to the grim business at hand on such a sparkling day. I nearly stepped on the condom. After bagging it, I called Sheriff Ben again.

"I've got the condom, Sheriff. I pray that Mandy's epithelials are still on it, because I'm pretty sure Wayne Dooley's semen is in it."

"That is most likely the case," he said, and sounded excited. "Good job, Margarita. Very good job. I'm impressed."

As he spoke, I swaggered around in the blazing sun, Pilgrim.

Sheriff Ben shot me out of the saddle in my glory moment. "Let me radio Deputy Blanks to wait for you at your office. I want him to bring me that condom."

Holy crap—Deputy Blanks. Who knew what Barney had said/done/told him?

Chapter 12

When I saw the Sheriff's Office cruiser in our lot, I didn't want to go in. I thought of calling Barney and asking him me to meet me somewhere so I could give him the evidence but if I did that, I would never live it down.

Both men looked at me when I came through the door. My radar said they'd been talking about me, and not about my impressive law enforcement abilities. Men don't give a rip if you can shoot the freckle off a nose at five hundred paces, flip a one hundred and eighty pound man to the ground, or find a solitary condom in one hundred acres of desert.

Barney turned scarlet, and Jimmy Joe's mouth hung open. He didn't even have the decency to blush. I smacked the evidence bag onto my partner's desk right in front of Deputy Blanks.

"This goes to the sheriff A.S.A.P.," I said, cold as Jablonski.

A two-day old used condom that's languished on the desert floor a couple of days is an unappetizing thing. He gaped at it and Barney seemed mute. I disappeared into my office where I stood at the window-with-a-view, arms crossed, mad at the world.

Who knows how long he'd been standing there looking at my backside when I turned around and caught Jimmy Joe Blanks gawking.

"I'm busy," I said with more attitude than a teen-aged girl.

"You don't look busy."

"I'm thinking. My mind is busy." I sat at the desk to hide myself.

"How come you don't like me?"

"I like you fine. I don't want to date you, that's all."

"I want you to give me a chance," Jimmy Joe said, and his reptile eyes flashed with emotion—or maybe only the thrill of the hunt. "I could make you happy."

"I can't be happy right now, Jimmy Joe."

"Sure you could if you'd let me in."

He sat in my overstuffed chair, which really irritated me. I wondered where big-talking Barney was hiding when I needed his help.

"I'm the perfect man for you." Jimmy Joe continued to talk about 'us' as if there was one. I thought about the rape, the murder, scary late-night footsteps, the condom, my mother—anything but Jimmy Joe Blanks.

Finally, my partner stepped up. "The sheriff is expecting you back pronto," he announced in a booming voice.

Jimmy Joe stood and leaned over my desk. I stood too, because I was going to smack him to the ground if he tried to kiss me. That would give the good ol' boy deputies something to talk about. I think Jimmy Joe sensed my plan, because he backed away saying, "I'll call you later. Think about what I've said."

"I will Jimmy Joe. Take care. Don't call me tonight, I won't be home."

"Where will you be?"

Barney stuck his head in the door again. "I wasn't kidding about the sheriff."

After Deputy Blanks left, Barney came in. "What are you going to do now?"

"I don't know, maybe shoot myself."

"And break Shoots' heart? How callous. I was talking about your case."

"I have about twenty-four hours to solve this rape."

"Well that gives you an hour for a late lunch with me and twenty minutes for interviewing Sylvia, and with four hours to sleep, that leaves a full nineteen hours and forty minutes. No problem for a sharp detective like you, Sherlock."

"Are you inviting me to lunch, Dr. Watson?"

* * *

After lunch we went our separate ways. I headed to Sylvia's Café.

Sylvia speaks with an English accent only slightly diminished by many years in the U.S., and knows everything going on in Terlingua. In addition to keeping her ear to the ground, she reads, and has time for friends. My mom and Sylvia have been friends since the day they met. They're tough, determined women who want to change everything bad about the world. They plotted for hours about ways to make money for my mom's border health project.

"Hey 'Rita!" Sylvia bounced towards me, but stopped just before reaching me. "Uh-oh, what's wrong?"

"Could I talk to you a minute, Sylvia?"

"Well, sure. Let's get some tea and go out on the porch where nobody will hear us and I can smoke."

The porch at Sylvia's Café is its best asset, not counting the food. It offers an unsurpassed view of the Chisos Mountains—the whole spread of them. You can see for miles into Mexico. Flowers of all varieties bloom from an eclectic combination of containers, few of which are flower pots.

Sylvia put her small hand on top of mine. "What's up, sweetheart? You don't look so good."

"I want you to tell me about *Killing for Health*. All of it."

"*Killing for Health?* Why? What about it? What does that have to do with anythi—?" She stopped mid-sentence and blinked at me.

"Just tell me about it, please."

"Does this have something to do with Norma's murder? You couldn't think we would actually kill anyone?"

"I want to hear about it in your words."

"Well, your mom and I are writing a screenplay. Some time ago, I was talking to her about helping the people in La Linda." She referred to a small village in Mexico, on the eastern side of the national park.

"I was nearly caught by Border Patrol when I came back," Sylvia continued. "The need there was great but they wanted to stop me. One child had terrible asthma and I took medicine that helped. They had no school supplies. You should've seen their faces when I brought out the paper and crayons. None of those kids had ever seen a doctor until I took your mother over there.

"I made the comment that I'd do anything to help those people and might have to kill for them. It was a joke, but we coined the phrase *killing for health*. If someone got in our way or disagreed with our mission, we would look at each other and say, *killing for health*. It was our way of saying we wouldn't be stopped and nobody better mess with us. As you know, we're really quite harmless."

She took a quick, shallow puff from her cigarette, as was her custom, and scooted back in the chair, her small face creased in concern. "You do know we would never actually kill anyone, don't you?"

"Yes, I know, but look at this." I handed her the evidence bag. "Just read it. Don't take it out of the bag. Here—turn it over."

She read it and started to laugh, then choked. "Where did you get this? Your mom threw it away. It doesn't mean anything!"

"Were you present when Mom wrote this?"

"Well sure, but we were kidding around, not kidding as much as daydreaming about who needed to die for the good of the health of people along the border. We were trying to get into writing, but your mom was bothered by something she heard in the community about her stealing money from the project. That's why she wrote that Norma was the first to go, because Norma started the gossip. I assure you it was harmless thoughts put on paper, and months ago. That's all it was."

"You don't have to convince me, but this paper was found by Stanner, and it makes Mom look guilty. Of course there's an explanation, but I'm afraid she'll become a serious suspect. Where were you yesterday morning?"

"I was here, like always, and opened at six. The Sunday morning breakfast crowd started coming about eight-thirty. We stayed busy until after lunch. I was cooking, so I couldn't have left even if I'd wanted to."

"Did you hear talk about the murder?"

"Well, sure, you know how it is. Everybody was talking about it."

"Any theories?"

"Some say it was Stanner, of course. He had to live with the woman so most folks think he had good reason. Then there's the stranger theory, and the picked someone up in a bar theory, the jealous lover theory, tons of theories, but none likely. Someone mentioned Doctores Fronterizos, but not your mother specifically."

"Well, if you hear anything at all you think might help, will you call me?"

"You know I will."

She patted my hand and took a delicate sip of iced tea. "Don't you worry, sweetie. Your momma is innocent and the real killer will turn up soon."

* * *

Later that afternoon, I called the sheriff. "I have two young men with me, Sheriff Ben, and I'd like for you to hear what they have to say."

Eddie Santos and Rick Florence had walked from school to my office and spilled their guts. They sobbed a horrific story that rang sad and true.

"I'm going to put my phone on the speaker function so we can hear each other," I said.

"I'm ready, Deputy Ricos. Good afternoon, boys."

They mumbled their hellos to the sheriff. I introduced them, and explained that they were fifteen and in high school with Wayne Dooley.

"What is it you'd like to tell me?" asked the sheriff.

The boys were speechless, so I got things started. "Sheriff, they were with Wayne when he raped Mandy."

"I want to hear it from them in their own words."

"Okay, Eddie, let's start with you," I suggested, since he was slightly more talkative.

"We didn't know he was going to rape her," Eddie said, then stalled.

"Keep talking. Tell the sheriff what you told me."

"Wayne said we were going to take her home and then when he went down the school road and pulled off towards the creek we just thought he was going to scare her, you know, take her where those old trucks are. It's spooky at night."

"Okay, keep going, Eddie," I prodded.

He began speaking rapidly in Spanish, which I understand, but the sheriff doesn't.

"Take your time," I told him in Spanish, "but please speak English."

"Oh, sorry. Wayne pulled onto the landing strip and when we got out he said we were going to give Mandy what she wanted. We thought he meant beer or drugs or maybe cigarettes. We didn't know he was talking about sex."

"Tell the truth Eddie," interrupted Rick, "we knew from the way he was talking before. We were just scared and we wanted it to be those other things."

"Okay. That's the truth Sheriff, we were so scared we 'bout pissed our pants. We didn't think he'd really do it, right Rick?"

"Right."

"But he was looking for a condom, and then he asked us to hold her down."

"And you did?"

They began to cry in unison. "Yes, we did."

"What happened next?" asked the sheriff.

"Mandy tried to run away, and he hit her hard, and she fell. She was crying and trying to kick him. That's when we held her because he said he'd kill all of us and leave us in the old truck graveyard."

Rick interrupted him again. "Tell the whole thing, Eddie."

"I didn't want to say it because Deputy Margarita is here."

"She's a big girl," Sheriff Ben said. "You can say what you need to."

Eddie took a deep breath. "He said he would cut our balls off and leave us in the old trucks to die in the dark."

They began crying again, and then Rick burst out, "We didn't want to do it!"

"You mean you didn't want to hold Mandy down?"

"Yes sir, we didn't want to. It's the most terrible thing we ever did."

"I want you boys to come up here tomorrow with your parents and make a formal statement."

"Our parents?"

"We can't take a formal statement from you without your parents or your attorney present. I guess your parents don't know about any of this?"

Both boys looked at the floor and Rick mumbled, "We didn't want to tell them."

"I can understand that, but they need to know. This is very serious."

"I'll help you tell them if you want," I said.

By the time the boys finished talking to the sheriff, we had a clear picture of the crimes against Mandy, and enough to charge Wayne Dooley with rape, assault, coercion, kidnapping, terroristic threats, possession of illegal substances; a long list of first degree felonies.

The sheriff told the boys he appreciated their honesty, but they participated in a serious crime and he'd discuss it with them further tomorrow. They were white-faced and still teary, but they agreed. Barney was out on a murder interview so I put the sign on the door that said we'd return and to call 911 in the case of an emergency, or the Alpine office. The dispatcher could always find us.

Then I took the boys home and helped them tell their parents the truth about Saturday night. They agreed to have their sons at the sheriff's office at eleven thirty the next morning.

After that, I went to see Mandy. When I laid out everything I'd discovered, she admitted that it was the truth. If the boys gave statements, so would she.

She hugged me, cried, and told me I was the most incredible woman she'd ever known. Man. It was one thing to impress Sheriff Ben, but it was really something to impress a teen-aged girl.

Chapter 13

"You call her," said Barney.

"You should do it. She hates me and you'd get her instant cooperation, you being such a big blued-eyed boy and all."

"I don't like her."

"Well, I don't either."

"We could arm wrestle for it."

"Oh sure, that'd be fair. Goliath meets Delilah and breaks her arm off at the elbow."

"Jeez, Ricos, you're confused. That was David and Goliath. Delilah was Sampson's curvy little squeeze."

"The Bible does not say it like that."

"If I re-wrote it in my own words, everybody would read it cover to cover."

"I'm sure."

"You call Lil and I'll give you an example."

"You're on."

There was a message on Lil's phone that advised she was visiting her cousin in Houston. She made the mistake of giving her cousin's number, which I wrote down.

"Let's hear it," I said.

"You didn't even speak with her."

"You said I had to call her, not speak with her. I called her. Pay up."

"Not so fast. Now you have to call her in Houston."

"You can't change the rules on a whim."

"Whim? You insult my integrity."

Eventually we called her together, using the speaker function of the phone on Barney's desk.

Barney identified himself to Lil's cousin and asked her politely if he could speak with Lil. She said yes and went to get her.

"Yes?" Lil said when she came to the phone. Rude as always, her specialty.

"Ms. Munch, I'm Deputy Barney George. Deputy Ricos and I are calling about the murder of Norma Barker-Bates."

"What does Deputy Ricos have to do with it?"

"She and I are investigating together."

"Well, really I—"

"When are you returning to Terlingua?" I asked, interrupting the whining I sensed was coming.

"I planned to return for Norma's funeral." She sniffed. "I understand it's being held up by your investigation."

"It's being held up by the crime lab, not our investigation. There has to be an autopsy because she was murdered," I said, with a strong intimation that she was an idiot. I hoped she got that.

"It's standard procedure," added Barney. "We'd like to interview you on the phone right now."

"What do you want to know?"

"Where were you this past Saturday evening?"

She sighed like we were holding up her life. "I was right here with my cousin."

"All day?"

"Well of course not. We went out to eat, but I was with my cousin who can testify to that. I've been here for several weeks."

I wondered what it'd be like to be around Lil for longer than a few hours. I imagined her cousin was taking heavy doses of Prozac by now.

"Ms. Munch, you were a close friend of Norma's?"

"Yes, she was one of my best friends. I miss her so much, you can't imagine."

"Do you know if she had enemies?" asked Barney. He held up his hand, knowing what her answer would be, and assuming I'd lose it. I tried to look sweet and innocent.

Lil hesitated a second, then proceeded. "Her worst enemy would be Stephanie Ricos, of course. We caught her stealing and she didn't take it well."

Barney held up his hand again and gave me a warning look. I wasn't going to say anything. I was hushed by rage and a burning sensation in my stomach.

Barney proceeded valiantly. "Isn't it true that Dr. Ricos also hated you?"

"Yes, of course. What's your point?"

"What was your position at the non-profit?"

"I was the Chief Financial Officer," she said as haughtily as if she was claiming to be Queen of England.

"Is that treasurer or what?" asked Barney, slapping her down.

I grinned at him.

"It's the position responsible for the money—keeping track of it, I mean."

"I don't mean to be critical," Barney said with a wink at me, "but how would Stephanie Ricos steal money if you'd been doing your job?"

I stood up and did a little happy dance.

Lil huffed and puffed. She was indignant and wanted Barney to know it. "Well, she wrote organization checks to pay her own bills and for all we know she pocketed all the cash donations and—"

"Well, Ms. Munch," interrupted Barney, "I believe she proved her innocence in court and you dropped your lawsuit, so I don't need to hear about that right now. What I need from you is names of people who might have wished to do harm to Ms. Bates."

Lil was speechless a moment. Barney and I high-fived each other across his desk.

"Well," she finally said, "There were other board members named in the suit. Perhaps one of them killed her. They all hated her."

"Do you know if she pulled a stunt like this anywhere else, before she moved to Terlingua?" I asked. "Maybe someone with an old grudge killed her."

"I highly doubt that."

"But you don't know for sure, one way or the other?"

"She never mentioned anything to me about something like that."

"Did you continue to be friends after the lawsuit?"

"Of course. Why do you ask?"

"I was just wondering about it."

Stanner had told Barney they weren't.

He came back into the conversation. "When you come back to town we'd like to see you in person. We'll make arrangements with you after the funeral."

"Well all right," she said as enthusiastically as if he'd said we were going to dig out her fingernails with an ice pick.

"Thank you for your cooperation, Ms. Munch. We'll see you soon." Barney cut the connection. "I don't look forward to seeing her in person, Ricos."

"Me either," I said, "Maude used to call her Lil Ass Munch, except to her face." Maude had been the board secretary.

Barney laughed at that moniker, but didn't say anything more.

Having to interview Lil Ass Munch in person was a good reason to get drunk.

* * *

La Kiva is a bar built on a high bank of Terlingua Creek. At the massive wooden door, a flight of steps descends, as if into a cave. It's an unusual place—a popular hangout for locals, a must-see for tourists. I chose La Kiva because my friend Phil was working. I'd already forgotten my promise to quit.

By the time I showered, dressed, and got to the bar, it was getting dark. From the parking lot I could hear strains of drinkin' and cheatin' songs. Phil usually played jazz or blues, but customers had a say. La Kiva often has live music, bands from everywhere, but my favorites are locals and part-time locals playing original tunes. Terlingua has more than its share of talented musicians.

I jumped down the steps two at a time. It had been a long day and the way I saw it, I'd earned it. I told myself that drinking at a bar was healthier than drinking alone.

"Hey Margarita," said Phil, a good-looking man in his early forties. Before my uncle sold his rafting company, Phil had been a river guide for him. Now his brown hair had streaks of gray and his face, though still tanned and handsome, showed a few creases around his eyes and mouth, probably from squinting and laughing day after day beneath the Big Bend sun.

I didn't think Phil liked it much that I'd become a regular drinker at his bar. I once told him, with the know-it-all conviction of a nine-year-old, that getting drunk was for dumb losers. That was when he'd been drinking, and long before I started.

"Hey Phil."

"The usual, Margarita?"

"Please." I hopped on a stool that was the wide stump of a redwood tree, the seat polished to a high sheen.

The 'usual' was a Corona and a shot of gold tequila, with lime.

After he served me, Phil leaned his tanned arms against the bar. "How are you coming on the murder investigation?" he asked.

I threw back the tequila, not bothering with salt or lime, and then sipped the beer. Phil immediately removed the shot glass and set it in the sink.

"Oh," I said, "it's slow, but she was just murdered Saturday night. Do you know anything I should know?"

"No, I was only wondering. I've been listening to speculations all evening and thought I might get some facts from you."

"She wasn't in here Saturday night was she?"

"No. Why?"

"I thought maybe she picked up someone."

"She never did that, or at least not here."

"There's always a first time."

"Want another shot?"

"Please."

As he was pouring it he said, "It feels weird to be serving liquor to a little girl who used to follow me around, constantly begging to go on river trips."

"I'm not a little girl anymore."

"Well, that much is evident."

"I still love to go on the river," I said, staring at his muscular arms.

"Maybe we could go sometime. I can still row."

"That much is evident," I said.

He laughed. "Seriously, would you go with me?"

"I don't think so, but thank you for asking."

"Is it because of my age?"

"No, it's not that." *It's because my heart is so heavy it would sink the raft before it moved two feet down the river.*

"What, then?"

"I'm just not ready yet, Phil. That's all I can say."

"It's only a river trip, no strings attached."

"You forget that I know how you guides are. I saw it all with my curious little eyes."

"Oh yeah, I guess you would think that."

We laughed, and he moved down the bar to serve another customer. Then someone played the Tennessee Waltz and I froze. Patsy Cline, though long gone, moved me to tears quicker than you can say eight-second ride. That was our song, only because it was playing in a rodeo arena the first time we saw each other.

With Kev and me it was practically love at first sight, even though I thought cowboys were redneck half-wits and he thought students in the law enforcement academy were overgrown kids still playing cops and robbers. Never assume, first rule of police work, good rule in general.

"Wanna dance?" I looked over to see Ethan Cooke, a guy from my high school class. He was attractive but there wasn't much to him. I dated him in high school. He was always more concerned about what I could do for him than what he could do for me. Sure, he might have grown up, but I didn't think he'd changed much. The local girls still talked.

"Hey, Ethan. How are you?"

"Come on, let's dance."

"No thanks."

I didn't think I would ever dance again. I loved to dance, and did a lot of it with Kevin, but like many of the things I did with him, it had been laid to rest when he was.

"Just one dance."

"No. Thank you, but no."

"How long are you going to mope around?"

"As long as it takes, I guess. Why don't you dance with somebody else?"

"'Cause you're the best looking girl in here, and besides, I like you. I've always liked you—more than you know."

"I like you, too, but I'm not in the mood to dance."

"Why don't you just wear black and cover your head?"

Phil, ever vigilant, walked up. "Move on, Ethan. Go on now."

"Thanks," I said to Phil.

"If I thought you were in the mood to dance, I'd be dancing with you myself. You remember that, don't you?"

"Of course, I'll never forget it." He had taught me to waltz when I was eight by letting me stand on his feet. He said he didn't like kids, but I was crazy about him, and he was patient and kind. He took me on trips when my parents allowed it. He taught me the basics of rowing a raft before I was strong enough to hold up the oars long enough to get anywhere. I had also laid with him and his customers in the sand to listen as he pointed out the constellations, satellites, and other marvels in the night sky.

He told gripping stories about the early settlers of the area, and knew the uses of every plant. He had an encyclopedic knowledge of the Big Bend. Girls loved him, of course. Phil was heartthrob handsome but tough enough that you knew he could handle any situation. Flooding rivers, wild animals, even collapsing canyon walls would be no problem for Phil. Oh man, did he swagger—better than John Wayne—and with much nicer legs.

"You could stand on my feet again if you wanted to."

"I waltz now, thanks to you, but I'll take a rain check on that."

As the liquor began to take effect it seemed to lift some of the pain, or erase it, or do whatever it did. I carried on ridiculous conversations with other drunks under the watchful eye of Phil. I felt safe with him there, which is why I drank in that bar. If anybody tried anything he was on it before I was.

As the bar emptied, Phil spent more time talking to me.

"Didn't you used to drink a lot?" I asked him.

"Yes, I did." He watched me warily. "I know what it's like to feel such heartache that nothing else matters and you don't care if you live or die. I lost a wife once, a long time ago."

I knew that—somewhere in the back of my alcohol-soaked brain I knew I'd heard his sad story. Phil was still my hero, I realized. Previously, I thought that Phil had thrown his life away, but that night I realized he was exactly where he could do the most good.

"How did you stop drinking?"

"First, I decided I wanted to. Then I started running and working out. I was nearly as compulsive about that as I was about drinking, but if you're concentrating on health it makes it easier not to drink. You can't drink if you're a serious runner, and running is a lot healthier than drinking."

"I was on the track team in high school. I used to love to run."

"My advice, since you're asking, would be to start running. Some people told me I was running away from my problems, but the truth is they left me. It seemed like it was just me and the wind out there and my problems came into perspective. They didn't seem so big anymore. When you're not drinking you can think clearly, and you'll be surprised at how your whole life will seem different."

"I'm going to try it."

"Run over here once in a while and let me know how you are, okay? And I still want to take you on the river."

"I guess I'm a little afraid of river guides, Phil."

"I'm a bartender now, not a river guide."

"Does that make it better?"

"Hell, no, I'm still a man."

I laughed and gave him a hug. I didn't know if running would work but I was determined to try it.

When I finally arrived home, I took a long, hot shower to wash away the day and sober me up. It only made me more relaxed, not particularly sober. I put on women's boxers, an oversized t-shirt, and then collapsed into my favorite chair on the porch. I often slept in it when I couldn't face the empty landscape of my bed.

Sheriff Duncan always told me that I must figure out a way to leave behind the violence, murder, and other terrible things people did to each other. He never said a word about using alcohol as an eraser, and I knew he wouldn't approve. I couldn't use the day I'd had as an excuse for drinking. Besides, it wasn't that.

Chapter 14

When my alarm went off a few hours later, I was in bad shape. I got up, took aspirin, and stood under a hot shower a long time. I wanted to eat, but I felt like my stomach was lodged in my throat. I finally toasted a bagel and ate it in tiny bites, dry. As painful as my body was, my heart was worse.

I was sitting on the edge of the bed, with my head in my hands, when Barney called. "Are you all right, Ricos?"

"I have the hangover from hell."

"I thought you might."

"How would you know?"

"A few people have mentioned that you closed up La Kiva."

"Already?"

"Already. Are you coming in?"

"Yeah, I'll be there in a few minutes."

"The sheriff called to tell you the bail hearing will be this afternoon at three instead of whatever you thought—something about the judge's schedule. He wants to meet with you and the witnesses half an hour before you see the judge. I rescheduled the families for you. You're damn lucky the sheriff won't be seeing you this morning."

"That's the truth."

"What's with you, Ricos? Are you trying to self-destruct?"

"I just had a little too much to drink."

"I'm worried about you. Sheriff Ben is bound to hear about it sooner or later."

"I'm going to quit drinking."

He had the decency not to tell me he'd heard that before. I finished getting ready for work thinking that somehow I had to get it together.

When I got to the office, Barney got me a cup of coffee, thinking it might help and I drank it hoping it would.

My partner wanted to update me about the murder investigation. I had the rape witnesses on my mind, and the meeting with the sheriff, and felt guilty for not being interested in finding the murderer.

"Norma's friends turned out to be a dead-end," he said. "They didn't seem close to her. No surprise there, I guess."

I thought being close to Norma would be like keeping a scorpion as a pet.

"They told me, in separate interviews, that they only saw her briefly when they dropped their children off at each other's houses. Neither hung out with her or knew her well. She told them Stephanie Ricos was stealing money that was meant to be used by Doctores Fronterizos, and that there was no doubt. They had proof."

I groaned.

"One of Norma's friends said she was a hard person to know."

"Yeah," I said, "that about sums it up if you don't want to use a lot of four and five-letter words."

Barney went off to interview Libby Thomas, Stanner's girlfriend, and I went into my office to finish my notes about the murder. Marian Williams, mother of my friend Austin, called to tell me about his upcoming operation. He was scheduled for surgery to repair a damaged valve in his heart to be done by a specialist he had seen for all of his adult life.

She gave me the details and said Austin wanted me to go with them, which I already knew. The surgery was two weeks away. The surgeon felt confident that all would go well because Austin was in vigorous health with the exception of his heart, which he promised to repair as good as new.

Austin is about an inch taller than me, compact and sturdy as a javelina, and although he has the typical features of a person with Down syndrome, he's handsome in his own way. He has clear green eyes that reflect the goodness and happiness in his soul, and blond hair as silky and fine as a baby's.

Many with Down syndrome have poor muscle tone, but Austin is an exception. He's muscular and strong because he's been active in sports since he was young.

"I'll go with you," I assured Austin when his mother put him on the phone.

"In your uniform," he insisted.

Austin believes my uniform holds magical powers. At times I believe it, too. I put it on and go from a normal, sometimes lazy and irresponsible woman, to a serious officer of the law, so responsible and mature I barely recognize myself. It's like Batman putting on his cape and mask or Superman changing into the "S" uniform. One minute you're one thing and the next, you're larger-than-life, expected to leap tall buildings in a single bound or save whole cities from the powers of evil; or maybe only stand close by a friend during heart surgery.

"With my uniform, if you insist," I said, even though lately the magical powers of the uniform were failing me. I didn't feel like a superhero.

I stood at the window in my office staring at the Chisos Mountains to the south. I needed to go there and walk, rest my head against them and feel the warmth of the sun stored in the stone. The thought of being in the mountains helped me believe I could give up drinking and maybe even the bloody clothes and self-pity. I had to do it. Somehow I had to find my way back to being me.

As if on cue, my cell phone rang and Sheriff Duncan said, "Deputy Ricos, I'm heading south. You head north and we'll meet at the picnic area."

"Right now?"

"Right now. I'm nearly there so step on it."

"You're talking about the picnic area at Elephant Mountain?"

"That's the one."

"I'll be there right away, sir."

This was probably the end of my job. What would I do now? As I picked up speed, I called Barney to tell him I was on my way to meet the sheriff but he already knew it. I thought that was a bad sign.

When I pulled into the roadside park, the sheriff was sitting on top of one of the cement picnic tables, looking at the mountain. It made my heart lurch to see him, and I dreaded what he was about to say.

"Good morning, Deputy Ricos." He patted the space next to him. "Have a seat."

"Good morning, Sheriff." I sat and looked up at the mountain, already becoming hazy in the late-summer sunshine. A cool breeze still stirred, but the air was warming steadily, typical of mid-September.

"I'm going to come right to the point," he said. "I expect you and my other deputies to uphold the law and keep the peace. I expect you to be an exemplary citizen, not just when you wear your uniform, but all the time. We had this conversation when I began training you, but perhaps you've forgotten it."

"I haven't forgotten it, sir."

"Well you're acting like you have and that's the same thing." He sighed and ran a hand through his hair. "I want you to pay close attention because I'm not going to have a conversation like this again. You can straighten up or we will no longer be working together. It's come to this—you may not stay out all night drinking in a bar and come to work looking like you do today. If you'd done it once or twice I wouldn't be concerned, but that's not the case, is it?"

"No sir."

"I don't know what you're thinking."

"I don't either, sir. It won't happen again."

"It had better not. I won't tolerate it. You're supposed to set a good example for others, not a bad one."

"Yes sir."

"I want you to stop hanging out in bars. Am I clear?"

"Yes sir."

"On a personal level, my heart hurts for you. I thank God that I haven't experienced losing someone I loved so much. But he's gone, Margarita, and destroying yourself isn't going to bring him back. Ask yourself this—would he be proud of you now?"

"No. He would be ashamed of me. He'd be shocked."

"For reasons no one can say, Kevin was taken from us, but you're still here. It seems to me like you should try to make something of your life. You have everything going for you. I think it's an insult to God to throw it all away."

"I don't believe in God anymore, Sheriff."

"Well, I think God still believes in you and whether you believe or not, I think you need to spend some time on your knees. Pray to the air, or the mountains, or to something you do believe in. I believe God is in all of it anyway."

I nodded but didn't speak.

"I know you don't want any advice from an old man but I can't keep myself from giving you some. If your life has lost its meaning, try helping someone else. Get involved in something good. And let Kevin go. He loved you very much and I believe you should honor that. Barney says you have the clothes he died in. Get rid of them, Margarita. Believing that a bloodstain is Kevin is like believing that a drop of water is the sea. You're kidding yourself and you're too smart for that."

"Everywhere I go, everything I do, reminds me of him."

"Of course it does. I'm not saying to forget him. I'm only saying you have to move on, for your own sake. Grieve for him, but let him go. Cry, scream, and roll on the ground, but then get up and look around you and see if you don't want to stay with the living. I know you don't want to live a kind of half-life like some of those people you deal with on a daily basis."

"No, I don't."

"I need you as a deputy in the southern part of the county. You and Barney are a reflection of my office. No matter what I think about you personally, professionally I can't tolerate the way you've been acting. If you could step back and look at yourself you wouldn't tolerate it either."

"No sir."

"You might try seeing this woman."

He handed me a card that had the name of a psychiatrist, Dr. J. Estrada in Alpine.

"She can help you sort things out if you have trouble doing it alone. She's good at what she does and I highly recommend her. She works with law enforcement all the time and understands what we do."

I put the card in my pocket.

"I'm impressed with the prompt, intelligent way you've handled this rape case, and I appreciate it. But this morning you don't look like my super-sharp deputy, you look worn out at age twenty-five. I can't bear it."

"I'm sorry, Sheriff Ben. I promise things are going to change."

He studied me the way he would a suspect, but finally said, "Don't you have a murder to solve, and an important hearing this afternoon?"

"Yes sir."

"You had better get with it, then." He stood and brushed off his uniform pants. I thought he was the finest example of a sheriff anyone would ever see.

I stood up and brushed off my pants. "Thank you for giving me another chance, Sheriff."

"Don't disappoint me," he said. "I'm old and I can't take it."

"You're not old."

"Your eyes are out of focus, my dear," he said. He slapped me gently on the back, then hugged me tightly. When he released me, he smiled. "Don't you ever tell a soul I'm a sheriff that would hug a deputy."

"No, sir, I won't."

I drove back towards Terlingua. When I got to the steep hill that we consider the halfway point between north Brewster County and south, I took note of the long stretch of highway in front of me. My head was killing me, my eyes burned, my muscles ached, and my heart hurt like hell, but I was sure I was going to get better.

Chapter 15

I went home, took a long, hot bath and fell asleep in the tub until the water got cold and woke me. After that I felt better and even ate something. I dressed in a uniform, my best leather boots, applied a little bit of make-up, and thought I looked acceptable. I wanted Sheriff Ben to beam at me and call me his sharp deputy, to be proud of me again. More importantly, I needed a way to feel proud of myself.

Barney looked up when I walked in and the admiring look on his face boosted my confidence. "Shoots is gonna have it bad today," he said under his breath.

I ignored that, went into my office, and sat in the overstuffed chair, careful not to crumple my uniform. I don't think I mentioned the yuccas on my hill. They were placed with care in perfect places and in exactly the right numbers. Too many would look crowded, and too few would just be sad. Looking at my hill made me think there was a god. Not an old, bearded man who sits in the sky looking down with a scowl to pass judgment, but a force far more powerful than that unimaginative image. All of Big Bend is landscaped to perfection, except where man has interfered. That should tell us something.

The hill yuccas are mostly Torreys. They produce huge flower clusters of lily white, bell-shaped blossoms, usually so heavy they bend the stalks trying to hold them up to the world. Yuccas are as much a part of the desert landscape as prickly pear cactus and creosote bush.

"Ricos," said Barney from the doorway to my office.

I looked up at him.

"What are you doing?"

"Nothing, looking at the yuccas."

"I can't believe you're not more anxious to solve this murder. Look how you jumped on the rape."

"It was a vicious attack on an innocent girl."

"Well, Norma Bates was innocent, too."

"I don't condone murder, but Norma was anything but innocent."

Yuccas illustrate how interconnected things are. Each species of yucca has a specific kind of moth that pollinates it. The yucca needs the moth to pollinate it and the moth needs the yucca to provide food and shelter for its young.

"You're not listening to me."

"I'm sorry Barney, what did you say?"

"I was saying that if we solve this murder it might shut some people up."

"We'll solve it, but probably not today. Today Judge Samuels is going to set bail on a drug possession charge. I have to convince His Grumpiness to add a charge of rape, convince the witnesses and the victim to speak in spite of their fear, and convince the judge to remand the prisoner to the county jail so he can't hurt any of them until he goes to the state prison. I'm sorry if I don't seem interested in the murder, but Norma's already dead. I agree that she deserves justice, but I think justice for a living child takes precedence over justice for a dead woman who did nothing but cause problems for people."

Barney took in a deep breath and let it out in a sigh. "I can't argue with that kind of logic." He looked perturbed and scratched his head. "You gotta give me somethin' I can sink my teeth into."

I laughed. "Go argue with someone else."

"Could we talk about the murder for five minutes? I don't know what to do next."

"Sure." I couldn't believe he was asking me.

"I've spoken with the people who were Norma's friends and all of her neighbors except Lockey. You covered that one. I spoke with Norma's ex-husband. He admits he hated her but I don't think he murdered her and he says he didn't. Stanner doesn't strike me as a killer and he had more reason to do it than anyone. I interviewed your mother and can't imagine she did it, even though she has that questionable black eye. You spoke with Sylvia, Miriam Vasquez, Ms. Dixie Chick, and Old Man Lockey. Am I missing anyone?"

"Stanner's girlfriend, Libby Thomas. What did you think of her?"

"She's pretty hot for fifty-something."

"I'm talking about the murder. I assume you spoke with her about that at some point during your visit?"

"Well sure, that's why I went."

"What do you think about her?"

"I don't think she killed Norma. Stanner moved here to be close to her but she says neither of them are the marrying kind and they would never have married even if Norma hadn't been in the picture. Soon after Stanner got here, Norma showed up with two little kids saying she was pregnant with his child. So he took her in. Libby thought he did an honorable thing, but he never quit seeing her. According to her, Stanner and Norma had an understanding in which Norma looked the other way."

"So Libby had no motive."

"That's what I'm saying. Neither Stanner nor Libby leads me to believe there was any love in the relationship between Norma and Stanner. He left for San Antonio on Thursday and spent Wednesday night with Libby, so what does that tell you? Listening to her, I think Stanner loved her more than he did Norma. Stanner and Norma were never legally married, did you know that?"

"Yeah, I knew that. They're common-law married."

"Libby says Stanner is kind and loving, and when Norma got on his nerves, he'd sit at a restaurant and sketch for hours, or he'd go to her place. In so many words, Libby said that Stanner didn't feel enough passion towards Norma to kill her. And anyway, she says he'd never have killed Norma because of his daughter, Vicky. According to her, Stanner would never do anything to hurt her or the other children."

"So we're back to nada."

"Seems like it, unless the crime lab turns up something."

"You didn't mention the other board members. Have you spoken with them?"

"They're on my plate for today. It's hard to think any of them did it."

I thought fleetingly of Maude, who had served as the board's secretary, calling Norma and Lil "The Barkers" and other colorful names. She was the one who had named Lil A. Munch "Lil Ass-Munch".

"I agree that none of them seem likely. Maybe a stranger killed her," I suggested.

"This is Terlingua, Ricos. Serial killers don't come here. Terrorists aren't interested in us. Serious crime doesn't happen here."

"You make that sound like it's a bad thing."

"Naw, I just mean to say that the stranger theory doesn't work for me. If she had picked up someone in a bar, then maybe, but I've talked to all the bars. Norma wasn't a bargoer and if she went, never went without Stanner. To think a stranger was creeping around in the desert at night and just happened upon Norma is—well, it's a stretch."

"Stranger things have happened."

"It is notable that someone struck while Stanner was conveniently out of town. That points back to him paying someone to do it. But tell me a motive."

"I can't think of one, other than the obvious, which somehow doesn't fit."

"Libby's alibi is the same as nearly everyone else's. She was at home alone and then she went to bed. That's my alibi too, except I have a witness, assuming my wife would vouch for me."

He sighed like he was single-handedly bearing the weight of the world.

"After today I'll help you, Barney. We'll figure this out. How hard can it be?"

"Damned hard," he said.

* * *

Getting a search warrant from Judge Samuels is like finding a matching organ donor. The ol' boy is impatient and cuts people off in the middle of their thoughts. It seems like he works against us. We're different parts of the same legal system but it doesn't feel like that. And, he makes it clear he doesn't think much of deputies.

Sheriff Ben looked at me with approval when I walked in, and then proceeded to wreck my day by saying I would be the one handling the judge. So he was throwing me to the mountain lions.

I tried to beg off but he insisted I knew more about the case. To make matters worse, Mandy was late and unresponsive to the sheriff's questioning. Eddie and Rick refused to enter the court when he mentioned that Wayne Dooley would be there. Mandy said she wouldn't go unless the boys did. None of the parents could budge their children. I felt like I was in a kayak heading full speed for a canyon wall.

Sheriff Ben said he would take the witnesses to the jury room in case they changed their minds. I didn't think he would get them that far, but I had to leave to go to the courthouse. I had no choice but to face the judge and tell him what I knew.

When Wayne Dooley's case was called, and the judge said it involved possession of an illegal substance, the district attorney, Ted Rogers, stood to correct him. He advised that the Sheriff's Office had also charged the prisoner with felony sexual assault and the People were asking him not to release the prisoner on bail due to the violent nature of the new charges. The judge looked straight at me as if I personally had set out to wreck his otherwise perfect day.

"Why wasn't I informed of this?" he boomed loudly, in case the criminals in a neighboring county were thinking of moving into Brewster.

"Sir, I spoke with your secretary and you have the paperwork in front of you."

I was thankful I wasn't the D.A. The look the judge shot him would have felled a lesser man. Judge A-hole shuffled angrily through papers until he found the offending documents right in front of him.

I was dismayed to see that Wayne's attorney was his father, Everett Dooley. That figured. Sheriff Ben came in, sat next to me, and whispered that the parents and kids were next door in the jury room, but they were still terrified to speak in front of Wayne. I'd already delivered the he-can't-hurt-you-in-court-and-besides-that-he's-handcuffed speech. Nobody had bought it.

Attorney Dooley objected to the county keeping his fine, upstanding football hero son in jail until the crime lab returned its findings. That could be four weeks, yada, yada, yada. I resented the assumption that a football hero would unequivocally be as lily white as a yucca bloom. Hadn't we had a lot of proof to the contrary? But in Texas, football is right up there with oil, cattle, and country music.

Eventually I was called to testify. When I said I had witnesses too afraid to come forward, Everett Dooley shot of out his chair as if a scorpion had stung him. "That's hearsay!"

"Judge," I said, "the victim and the two boys who were coerced into holding her down are so afraid of Wayne they refuse to come into the courtroom. If he could be removed they would testify."

Daddy Dooley said, "Will the judge please instruct the deputy to refrain from using inflammatory phrases like 'hold her down?' Also, I want to point out that my client has a right to hear the testimony presented against him."

"Judge, Wayne Dooley was in possession of photos of Mandy Robbins being held down at the scene by two boys who took turns doing that and taking photographs. They were threatened and humiliated by Wayne."

The judge scowled at me. "Yes, Deputy, I'm aware of the charges. You say three witnesses have spoken with you, and that might be true, but if they won't testify I can't hold this prisoner without bail based on one old condom you found in the desert which may or may not be relevant."

I glanced at the sheriff and wondered if he was going to let the lions devour me. It looked like he was. Then I had an idea.

"Judge Samuels, would you give me five minutes to speak with my witnesses?"

His brows scrunched together. He glared and was put out, but he granted me five. I hurried to the jury room, followed by the sheriff, and told the kids how we could enter without seeing Wayne. I promised I'd stand next to them and shoot him if he made a move. I explained again that me telling the judge that Wayne Dooley is a dangerous criminal was not the same as if they said it. It had to come from them or Wayne would be released on bail today, in a few minutes.

Mandy was weighing it all out. At last she stood. "I'll do it," she said. After that the boys had to do it too, or lose face to a girl.

I had them stand by the double doors to the courtroom while I went in and stood in front of the judge. "Your honor, I promised the witnesses they wouldn't have to see Wayne Dooley, so would you let them stand right here next to me and speak?"

It was fifty-fifty that he would either eat me alive or relent to this one small request.

"I object," said Everett Dooley.

The judge's eyes narrowed. "What could you possibly object to?" he growled, but didn't give him a chance to answer. "Bring in the witnesses," he ordered.

I opened the door and the sheriff and I, along with three sets of parents stood with our backs to the accused, making a wall between him and the single file of witnesses.

Judge Samuels glared down at Mandy, who seemed even younger than fourteen. His look softened, and with patience he said, "Young lady, I'd like to hear in your own words about the alleged rape. Were you raped?"

I was amazed to hear such kindness in his voice.

"Yes sir," she said, "I was raped by Wayne Dooley."

"Were you threatened by him?"

"He had a knife. And he said he would kill me if I told." She didn't weep or whine; she stood tall. I felt in awe of her.

"What gave you the courage to tell Deputy Ricos?" asked the judge.

"I didn't tell her. She figured it out on her own."

The judge's eyes shot at me in amazement, as if he'd just realized I was a vertebrate. "Well," he said. Then his attention turned to the boys and his eyes narrowed again. "And you boys, why are you here?"

Eddie Santos took a half-step towards the judge and bowed. Then he said in one big breath, "We're here to say that Mandy is telling the truth Wayne had a knife and he showed it to all of us and said he'd kill us if we told anyone anything I don't know if it's okay to say balls to a judge but he told Rick and me that if we didn't hold her down he'd cut off our balls and leave us to die in the old truck graveyard."

"Is that true, Rick?"

"Yes sir. It's the truth."

"Thank you. You may go out, but please don't leave the building."

Everett Dooley was on his feet. "Your Honor, this is some scheme these youngsters have cooked up to embarrass and discredit my son."

"Why would they do that?"

"I imagine the girl didn't want to admit to her parents that she had sex with some boy so she thought if she blamed an older boy, she could say it was rape." His voice trailed away at the look on the judge's face.

I hardly dared a glance at the sheriff. When I did he was biting his lip, and I looked away, afraid I would laugh out loud in court. Our judge does not like laughter in his courtroom, and possibly has stricken it from his life.

He looked down at the file on his desk and I thought he was finally seeing the photos. When he looked up he seemed sad. "I will not grant bail to the accused at this time."

Everett Dooley was speechless. Wayne looked less arrogant, more like a criminal in real trouble. The God of Lawmen Everywhere had smiled again. I stood as tall as I could. I felt like a Texas Ranger.

The prisoner was led away in his orange *BREWSTER COUNTY JAIL* jumpsuit. I thought fleetingly of Dena Jablonski and how I had scored another one for the bitches.

* * *

The sheriff and I were seated together in his office having a speaker phone conversation with Barney in Terlingua. We hadn't been there fifteen minutes when Deputy Blanks thought of a reason to interrupt us so he could gawk at me. I should have told the sheriff then about his unprofessional behavior, but I was too elated by the outcome of the hearing. From the point of view of Super Deputy, it was easy to overlook a lesser deputy's shortcomings.

After Jimmy Joe left, Everett Dooley walked in uninvited and verbally attacked me. "I have never seen such unprofessional behavior."

"What behavior is that?" the sheriff shot back.

"Trumping up evidence and trying to pin rape on my son."

"I know it must be hard," I said, "to accept that your son would commit such a vicious crime, but I'm doing the job I was hired for. Deputies are sworn to uphold the law and keep the peace. Surely you don't object to that. The law is still the law, even if the people we love have broken it."

That said, I thought of my mother, her black eye, her gold hoop earring on a dead woman's floor, smack in the middle of a crime scene. It's a hard mental fall from Super Deputy to Daughter of a Possible Murderer.

* * *

That evening I sat on my porch watching the gradually changing light on Cimarron Mountain, wondering for the hundredth time what cataclysmic thing had happened hundreds of millions of years ago to put the mountain there, and left it standing alone to face whatever life brought. Most people would never think to compare a bull's big hoof with fiery volcanoes, the shifting and colliding of the earth's plates, or the other immense pressures that forced huge mountains into the air, but in my head they were all born of the same incomprehensible power.

There was still about an hour of light before darkness set in. I was drinking an ice cold beer and thinking my usual dark thoughts, nothing new there. Halfway through the beer I got up, changed into shorts, tennis shoes, and socks. I did a few stretches, still watching the mountain. It was bathed in a muted, golden light.

I thought I should sit back down and at least finish the beer. It was a shame to waste a cold longneck. Running could wait until tomorrow. I could think about what Sheriff Ben had said then too, and Barney, my parents, most of my friends, and Phil. Phil had said to run. Running had given him back his life.

I didn't sit down with the beer, and instead poured it over the edge of my porch, put the bottle in the garbage, and took off at a slow jog up the dirt road in front of my house. This was something new.

I hadn't run much since my college days, but I remembered why I had loved it so much. It was a lot of things: the air in my face, the coolness caused by sweating, the steady movement of my legs. Running always felt like freedom.

I realized I was coming steadily closer to Cimarron Mountain. Why had I never thought to hike it, or even approach it on foot? Its grandness was humbling and the closer I got, the smaller and more humbled I felt. I could see its various bumps, ridges, valleys, canyons, and sharp spires more clearly than ever.

Arroyos were etched down its rocky sides, eroded over eons by the cascading water of torrential rains. There were trees growing in some of the narrow cuts, probably mesquite, cat claw acacia, or ash. Colossal boulders, some of them bigger than houses, littered the mountain from just beneath its bare jagged top, all the way to the bottom. Interspersed among those grew giant stands of prickly pear cactus, ocotillo, scrub mesquite, and various wildflowers and native grasses.

Sweat was running into my eyes. It burned and half-blinded me, but I didn't care. I hoped it was the alcohol and sadness leaving my body. My legs were beginning to tremble, so I turned before I reached the mountain and headed back.

I collapsed into my rocker and cried; it was sobbing more than crying. It seemed like running wasn't going to help. I wanted another beer. I went into the kitchen, looked at the rows of bottles stacked in the refrigerator, and shut the door on them. I ate a peanut butter and banana sandwich and drank nearly a quart of orange juice.

Exhausted, I took a shower and got in bed. In seconds I was asleep and slept the whole night for the first time in more than a year. That was running's first gift to me.

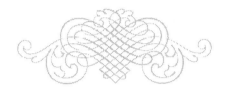

Chapter 16

Barney had gotten so little from Maude that he asked me to try. He thought she was hiding something; I thought she was just being Maude. She is an outspoken advocate of every human's right to health; outspoken about a lot of things, but can also be silent when she feels she should. Maude had served as the secretary of the board that ran Doctores Fronterizos during the time of the trouble with Norma and Lil. Like Miriam, she had staunchly defended my mother and the organization.

Maude is an attractive woman in her late thirties who is passionate about hiking, biking, and cats, in addition to our community's health and well-being. She is a writer, a good one, not to say she's famous. Yet.

When I stopped at her office, she was expecting me and opened the door before I knocked.

"Hi Margarita, come in!" She gave me a hug.

"Hi Maude. How's it going?"

"Great."

Flowers in colorful Mexican Talavera pottery bloomed in a variety of bright colors among the desert plants that dotted her yard. Two friendly cats greeted me as I entered, winding themselves around my legs. A smaller one peered from under the desk, reserving judgment about the visitor. I tried to coax her out, but she wasn't convinced.

Maude pulled a chair away from her desk, indicated I should sit, and plopped onto a footstool nearby and looked up at me. She swatted her unruly chestnut hair away from her face without lasting effect.

"This must be serious," she said, "You're wearing your uniform."

"I usually wear my uniform when I work."

"You look very professional."

"Thank you. As I said on the phone, I want to talk about Norma's murder."

"You're really trying to find out who iced the old barker?"

"Yes, it's my job."

"But you don't personally give a shit, right?"

"My personal feelings don't have any bearing. Besides, I believe that murder is wrong, Maude. There's a reason there's a law against it."

"You know what the good ol' boys of Texas say?"

"What's that?"

"Sometimes a sonofabitch just needs killin'."

I laughed. "Granted, and Norma was pushing her luck."

"They haven't hauled your mother off yet?"

"Well, not yet."

"Hey, I'm just messing with you. Steph would never kill anyone, no matter how many times she might have done it in her dreams. God knows, we all wanted to get rid of that barker. Your mom is a healer, not a murderer."

"I can't imagine my mom killing anyone."

"Nah, she never would. Hey you want something to drink? Juice? A soda?"

I declined her offer, and she asked, "What do you need from me?"

"I have to ask this for the record. Did you kill her?"

"No, I did not."

"Well, that's a relief."

"If I had, would you take me in?"

"Yes, Maude, I would. Where were you on Saturday evening?"

"I was home watching television with my husband. We went to bed about eleven or so. Neither of us snuck out to kill Norma."

"Maude, who do you think would've wanted Norma dead?"

"Anybody who knew her, I'd expect."

"Yeah, that's the general consensus."

"It's a crying shame this didn't happen before she got involved with our project. It would've saved us all that hell. I guess it sounds cold, and I know it's not polite to speak ill of the dead, but she was the biggest barking ass-munch I ever knew. If I had to guess, I'd say Stanner. Who'd blame him? And frankly, I hope he gets away with it. I've thought about it, and Miriam and I have talked about it, too. If it wasn't Stanner, then maybe it was someone from her past. I'd bet you a million dollars she's pulled this kind of stunt before. I believe she'd had practice, don't you?"

"Seems like it."

"Her killer might never be found." Maude thought for a moment. "If I were you, Miss Deputy Sheriff, I wouldn't lose a minute of sleep over it."

"I haven't, but I do have a job to do. The sheriff expects this murder to be solved."

"She needed killing and somebody had the guts to do it and that's what I have to say about it."

I had to laugh. "So that's your official statement?"

"Yes, that's it. Hey—if you figure out whodunit would you scoop me?"

"Sure, if you'll write the truth about Norma and what she tried to do to Mom and Doctores Fronterizos."

"You got it, whole truth and nothing but, and happy to do it."

Later I was seated in my overstuffed chair with my feet on the edge of the desk and a notepad in my lap. I was perusing my hill and wondering why our puzzle wasn't coming together. It felt like we only had some of the pieces. In contrast, things on the hill were in perfect order.

Barney ducked through the doorway and stood over me with his hands on his hips. "You're not fooling anybody with that notepad. Let me see what you've got."

I handed it to him. He read it. "That's pitiful."

"Yes, it is. What are we missing, Barney?"

He sat down on the edge of the desk. I hoped it would hold up. It was a cheap piece of county furniture that'd probably been around since my parents were babies.

"What'd you get from Maude?"

"Nothing. Her husband is her alibi. I don't think she's hiding anything. Her only suggestion, other than Stanner, is someone from Norma's past."

I asked about his interview with Ray Jasper, the only male board member. He was, in fact, still on the board of directors.

"Ray says your mother is innocent of the murder, just like she was innocent of the stealing and mismanagement. He made it sound like Norma stabbed herself to make Stephanie look bad."

I laughed. "He's a little sweet on Mom, I think."

"He thought Norma was 'mental' and never hated her, he claims. But like the others, he thinks we're wasting our time looking for the killer."

"She was mental, but that didn't stop me from hating her."

"Well maybe you're a lot more callous than sweet, sensitive Ray."

"Does he have an alibi?"

"Not a provable one. He was in bed. Sleeping, he says. Too bad he and your mother weren't together—they could vouch for each other."

"She better never hear you say something like that."

"Ray thinks Stanner did it. He says he's a good man but Norma slowly pushed him to it."

"Highly possible—that woman could have pushed the Pope into suicide at the altar of the Vatican."

"Your opinion."

"Granted. I don't know the Pope. He may be stronger-willed than I think."

Barney gave me an exasperated look. "What is it you're looking at out there? Are there naked men running around or what?"

"Sadly, no. In fact, there are no men. I'm watching a red-tail hawk hunting. She's made several strikes and has come up with nothing so far."

"Sounds a little like us," he said.

* * *

I went to re-interview Gabe Stanton, Norma's ex-husband. He didn't have an alibi for the day of the murder, and had admitted to Barney that he'd hated Norma. So had I, and I hadn't killed her, so maybe Gabe hadn't either. But he was a key suspect and the sheriff thought I should talk to him to see if he'd changed his story since his talk with Barney.

Gabe lives in one of the refurbished rock houses that are scattered over the hills of the Ghost Town. It's hard to grasp the fact that hardworking miners once lived in these native stone structures without plumbing, electricity, or any of the things we consider necessary. Most of the houses were built by the ancient art of stacking stones; fitting them together tightly so that no cement or other filler is needed.

Gabe's home is reached by a winding, rocky driveway but the reward is a knock-your-socks-off view of the area. He was expecting me and was sitting on a webbed lawn chair in front of his place, in the shade, drinking iced tea from a can. According to Barney's interview, Gabe was forty-two years old and a master carpenter by trade.

I greeted him as I jumped down from the Explorer. He stood and shook my hand, not smiling, but he didn't seem unfriendly. He invited me to call him Gabe. Then he offered me a cold drink, giving me the choice of Pepsi or iced tea. I chose the Pepsi since canned iced tea is a travesty. No way was he a Texan.

"Beautiful day," he said.

Gabe had dark brown hair that stuck out around the edges of a green ball cap and curled up in back. His face was angular, and though not unkind-looking, he had a hard look about him.

"Sure is," I agreed to his comment about the beautiful day. The air was so clear that seldom-seen Mexican mountains had come into view, as if they'd just popped up from the surrounding desert.

I took a seat, which he invited me to do with a wave of his hand.

"I'm sorry to have to bother you again, but I need to clarify a few things."

"No problem."

"When Deputy George spoke with you, you indicated you didn't have an alibi for the evening of the murder."

"Right, well, I was here alone. Am I a serious suspect?"

"He told me you said you didn't get along well with Norma."

"That's an understatement. I hated her!" He looked off in the distance. "But I didn't kill her."

Neither of us said anything for a moment, then he went on. "There was a time when I drank a lot and done drugs and I done some time—but I never killed nobody. I hit Norma once, and that's when she took our boy and said she wasn't coming back."

I thought doing time explained the hardened look—not to mention the toll that living with Norma had taken.

"You're Joey's father?"

"Right. She took him away and right after that I went to jail on a drug charge. While I was in, she divorced me. I was always in trouble back then, but I cleaned up my act since then, for Joey. And for me, too, I guess. I decided I didn't want to spend my life in different prisons while my son grew up with a crazy woman."

"How long have you lived here?"

"Three months. I came here 'cause of Joey. I want to be with him and he wants to be with me. He told his momma he wanted to live with me. I was living in Amarillo at the time and she said if I lived nearer, she'd let him see me more. So here I am."

He paused a moment, watching me. "Do you know Joey?"

"Yes. He's a fine boy. He looks a lot like you."

"I'm very proud of him."

"Do you like living here?"

"Yes and no. The pay sucks, but the place is beautiful. I like the peace and quiet. It's hard to stay sober, though. I attended Alcoholics Anonymous meetings when I was locked up and kept going when I got out." He sighed. "The loneliness makes it harder, and everybody here drinks, seems like."

I nodded. "Do you ever go to the AA meetings in Terlingua?"

"Yeah, some."

"Did you ever go to Norma's when you weren't picking up Joey?"

"Hell no! She was the last woman on earth I'd visit for any reason. I knew Joey was in San Antonio with Stanner. I was supposed to work the weekend, or he'da been with me. Anyway, I would never see her if it wasn't to pick up Joey."

"When was the last time you saw Norma?"

"Let's see, I guess that musta been last weekend when I picked up my son." He pushed his cap back. "I had to fight to get him and might not have except Stanner came in the room and said she had no reason to make him stay home. I never saw him stand up to her like that before."

We sat silently for a few moments, sipping from our cans, and watching turkey vultures soaring above.

"Gabe, do you have any idea who killed Norma?"

"No. That other deputy asked me that, too. I told him it coulda been anybody that knows her. She was a mean, calculating bitch. Everything was about her. She never considered anybody's feelings but her own. No—I said that wrong. It wasn't feelings she had as much as things she wanted."

"Can you explain what you mean?"

"It's like she was hollow inside." He touched his heart. "But she was smart and she figured things out and worked things around so she got what she wanted."

He stood suddenly, agitated. I tried to picture him stabbing Norma in the heart. He seemed like a man that could do it.

"I don't know what it is she wanted 'cept to make other people miserable."

"How old was Joey when you went to prison?"

"About eighteen months."

"And how long were you in?"

"Twenty months. I was sentenced to twenty-four months, but was released early. I kept my nose clean and never caused no trouble. When I got out, I was divorced and Norma and Joey were gone. Nobody knew where she'd gone. I found her through her brother, who lived in Houston at the time. She was in El Paso, homeless. That made two of us."

"What happened after that?"

"Norma went to a shelter for a while, then to live with her parents. They only took her in 'cause of the children. They sorta gave up on her long ago."

"Why is that?"

"She left home real young. Nobody could tell her a thing. She hitched to El Paso and went wild on the streets—caused all kinds of trouble and whatnot. The police sent her back to her parents twice, but they couldn't do nothin' with her. Each time she was sent home she'd just leave again and go back to living on the streets."

"I recall a story she told my mom that went like that. For a while she was with an alcoholic musician named Trent, right?"

"Right, and they had Ritchie."

"Did she ever marry Trent?"

"No. They lived together a while. I always thought she got with him just 'cause he had a place, you know? He was a good guy, trying to go straight but just couldn't. I know that feeling. He'd make good money playin' music and then blow most of it on alcohol and drugs. I'm sure Norma didn't help. She was into drugs and alcohol back then."

"But didn't she go back to school?"

"Yes. Norma was smart—it was heart she lacked. Eventually she got back into the drug scene again and that's when she met me. We were no good for each other, but since when does that ever stop people?"

No kidding.

"Barney told me you said Trent died in an auto accident."

"Yeah, a few years ago. Everybody thought he was prob'ly driving drunk, but actually a drunk hit him and killed him instantly. He'd finally gone straight and was starting to get somewhere with his music. Sucks, huh?"

"Yes, it does."

"I can't think about it or I'll be drinkin' again. I get to thinking, here I am not drinkin', going to AA, and tryin' to do right, and something else will kill me. Makes it all seem so futile."

We laughed. I wanted to ask him how he had given up drinking, the nitty gritty details. I didn't dare. He had said Alcoholics Anonymous, but how could a deputy go to AA in a town where nothing shared was kept secret for ten minutes?

After some small talk, Gabe asked, "Do you have any leads?"

"Nothing much."

"I guess you can't talk about what you know. Maybe Stanner had her killed. She had some money her parents left her. I bet she was surprised as hell they left her anything. I couldn't believe it when I heard, after the way she treated them all those years." He stepped into the house for more iced tea. "You want anything?"

"No, thanks." When he got settled again I said, "Norma told my mother she and her parents had come to terms, more or less, not long ago."

"Well, that would explain it." He took a long drink of the tea. "I hope that's true, for their sakes. They were good people and didn't deserve the hell Norma gave them." He took another long drink. "What about the life insurance angle?" he asked.

"What life insurance?"

"I'd forgotten about it, and it might not even be true. I just now thought about it. Norma mentioned a few months ago that she and Stanner had to get physicals 'cause they were buying a lot of life insurance."

"Did she say how much?"

"I think it was a million on each of them. They wanted to make sure their kids would be cared for and could go to college if something happened to one of them."

That seemed like a lot, and that alone didn't prove anything, but it was another lead that might go somewhere. I could hope.

Gabe watched me a long time, chewing on his lip, considering something. He finally spilled it. "Look, it might help you to know—well—the truth is, I was here, but I wasn't alone."

"That means you have an alibi."

"Yes, but I don't want to say her name. It's lonely here and I only just got to know her, and that was the first time we ever slept together. I was hopin' to do that again, and if I start talking about her I know she won't ever come back."

"Look, Gabe, I can make her understand that you need an alibi. You aren't talking for the sake of gossip. Surely she would understand."

"Maybe you could explain it to her."

"Of course. I'll leave no doubt in her mind."

"I'll call and ask her to come over."

Judy Rankin was a shy, soft-spoken woman about Gabe's age. I felt sure she wasn't someone he grabbed off the street to tell lies for him. She understood why her statement was important, and didn't hesitate to corroborate his story. I made sure she understood that the statement would not be public. She held

Gabe's hand as we were talking. No way would she hold his need for an alibi against him.

That afternoon I determined that Norma and Stanner Bates had been considering large life insurance policies but hadn't gotten around to buying them. I bet Stanner was kicking himself; except he seemed too laid back to kick himself over anything.

I also thought that a man who was going to kill his wife would have made sure the million-dollar life insurance policy was in place first.

Chapter 17

Thursday passed in a blur of interviews and regular duties. Things settled down at Big Bend High School. Mandy came by the office to thank me for keeping my promise that Wayne Dooley wouldn't be able to hurt her again. She brought me a plate of chocolate chip cookies she made herself, and presented them to me in the same serious, respectful way I would've been awarded a special commendation. I received them in the same manner. Her adoring look meant more to me than anything I could hang on the wall.

It had been four days since the murder, and no guilty persons had come forward or floated to the top of our investigation.

I had a close call in the afternoon when the sheriff instructed us, via Barney, to attend Norma's funeral the following day. She was being buried in the cemetery at the Terlingua Ghost Town and there would be a short graveside service. He expected us to show respect for the deceased on his behalf, since he couldn't attend. He was the boss, so Barney agreed without consulting me.

The sheriff pointed out that it wasn't unusual for a murderer to attend a victim's funeral. True, I told Barney, but that didn't mean I was going. I wouldn't go if it meant my job. I had a screeching fit about it. Kevin was buried in that cemetery and I wasn't going to go there with a bunch of other people and have them watch me fall apart.

Barney said calmly that the sheriff expected us to go, and he would pick me up if I fainted or anything. That was sweet, but I didn't want him there, either.

"You don't have to visit Kevin's grave," Barney said, his mouth full of my chocolate chip cookies.

"Yes, but I know it's there."

"Just walk in and don't look around. Stand close beside me. We'll swagger in and out, the coolest deputies you ever saw in the West."

I laughed at that but my final words: "I won't be there."

* * *

My partner was surprised and impressed when I showed up at the funeral in full dress uniform. Barney was standing tall—the only way for him to stand. He looked serious and professional, ready for any criminals that dared show their faces. When he saw me he grinned broadly.

The Ghost Town Cemetery has the same sweeping views as The Porch; all big sky, mountain ranges, and wide desert panoramas. It was comforting, in a way, to the living, probably not to the dead.

Some of the graves are marked only with piles of rocks, and have hand-painted, hand-lettered wooden markers. A few are ornate. Most are simple tributes to departed loved ones. Most have bright plastic or paper flowers, candles, photos or other small remembrances. There are simple graves from the mining days. Some are for children, even newborns. Reading the headstones is sad, not that I was going to.

I walked past a humble grave with a hand-made marker that reads: *Here in the arms of my beloved desert, I most assuredly rest in peace.* It eloquently expresses my own feelings about the desert.

There were others there besides Kevin that I had known in life, including a friend who fell to her death from a sheer cliff years ago, and an old, gentle cowboy-lawman I admired as a small child. He let me hold his gun once, showing me the importance of the safety and speaking quietly about the seriousness of his profession.

I didn't look around. Kevin would understand. Besides, he wasn't there in any real sense of the word. I had seen him briefly after the mortuary finished with him. The body of my blond cowboy was there, but whatever made Kevin who he was had gone.

Suddenly a big rough hand was laid against the back of my neck. I looked up into my father's handsome face. He smiled wistfully. "Mija."

Mija, pronounced 'mee-ha,' is a conjunction of two Spanish words, mi and hija meaning *my daughter*.

"Papi," I said automatically. It's pronounced 'poppy.'

He hugged me tightly. I laid my head against his chest, and wanted to stay like that. I didn't want to be at a funeral, and especially not there. I wanted him to lift me in his arms, the way he had when I was little and he'd taken me away from things that could hurt me. Tears sprang into my eyes. I couldn't have stopped them for anything.

"It's okay, Mija," he whispered to me in Spanish. "I'm here."

That made me cry harder. He was there for me. He hadn't known Norma, and wouldn't have liked her if he had. He was not a man to come to a funeral out of curiosity, and it was hard to believe he'd come under any circumstance. As far as I knew, the last time he'd been there was for Kevin's funeral and he had held me up then, too.

My father had been with Kevin the day he died. He and Kevin's best friend Mitch served as his crew that day, and were standing by when Kevin was trampled to death. It had been hard on them. Unlike me, who only dreamed the nightmare, my papi had seen it firsthand. He had been the one who came to tell me, driving like a maniac from Amarillo. Somehow he had kept himself together and been strong for me when I couldn't be.

He nudged me gently. Arriving in her look-at-me-I'm-the-queen way was Lily Munch, wearing an expensive-looking pantsuit and fashionable high-heeled boots. She looked hot and angry.

Let her sweat, I thought unkindly, wiping my teary face. She and Norma made my mom's life miserable for a number of months and they had done lasting harm to one of the few good organizations in our community. My opinion was that they deserved whatever bad things came to them. My professional opinion had to be different.

Lil Munch is fifty, with hair stiff-looking from repeated coloring. She is too tan. Her face looks leathery, though not very wrinkled. Her lips smile but her eyes don't. She perpetually looks down on everyone even though she's short.

Lil was widowed about two years ago. Her husband had been accidentally killed on a construction job in the Texas Panhandle. No matter what, I knew that had been a horrible thing for Lil. He was a civil engineer and left her well off, with a lot of assets and a large life insurance policy. In addition, Lil was suing the company for wrongful death. She would soon be a millionaire, if she wasn't already. I wasn't a millionaire or even close, but Kevin had left me life insurance money. That's how I know that money only makes the bills easier to pay. It doesn't fill the emptiness.

After the short, poorly-attended service, my father hugged me again and asked me to stop by his store later. Barney was talking to Lil so I assumed he was making arrangements to interview her. I sat on a stone bench by the cemetery entrance and watched the people leaving. I couldn't identify any murderers among them.

* * *

Lil had agreed to meet us at our office, so Barney and I went there to wait for her.

"What did you think about the funeral, Ricos?"

"It was okay, I guess. Hard."

"I feel proud of you for going."

"I didn't see anyone who seemed like the type to stab a woman in the heart," I said.

"I watched Gabe with his son and I swear I don't think he's the one. 'Course I know you can't tell about people by looking at them."

"Yeah," I said. "We're expecting someone with beady eyes and a snarly mouth, and claws for fingernails, and I know it won't be like that."

"Damn, Ricos, you got some kinda imagination in that head of yours."

"You should be glad you don't live in there—not that you'd fit."

At that moment Lil Munch Herself came slamming through the door.

"Ms. Munch—" began Barney.

I don't know where he was going with that because she interrupted him. "I don't have time for this."

"I suggest you make time for it," I said, unable to hold it back. Barney gave me a look that said he thought I should keep my big mouth shut but it was too late. When she sat in a chair next to me my skin crawled.

"This won't take long," said my partner, trying to be civil and professional.

I couldn't sit still. My feet were dying to kick her. I had disliked Lil Munch before she did anything to my mother. She treated people like they were her personal servants and never said please or thank you. Enough. I tried to make my face a blank.

"I can't imagine what I can add to what I've already said." Her snootiness seemed to be for my benefit, since she was looking Barney over in a spider-like way. It was creepy, but I didn't think he noticed, typical fly.

"Well, Ms. Munch, we've found that interviews in person are more productive. I'm going to record this conversation if you have no objection."

"Why would I object?" She looked back and forth between us, her nose turned up—we were lowly peasants in her little kingdom.

My partner was unperturbed, and asked her to state her name and the other required information. After she did that, he said, "I'd like for you to tell me again where you were on the day that Norma was murdered."

She sighed. "I was with my cousin Daphne Hendricks in Houston. I believe you've already spoken with her."

"Yes, I have. What did you do that day?"

Another you're-destroying-my-life sigh. "We had breakfast. Do you want to know what I ate?"

"That won't be necessary."

"After breakfast I read and wrote a few emails. We went shopping later and ate lunch at the mall. After that we went home and talked and rested. My cousin's husband returned later from playing golf, and made steaks on the grill."

"Was there any time when you weren't with your cousin or her husband?"

"Only when I was in the bathroom or lying on the bed in my room. What is it that you really want to know? Why don't you just ask me?"

I accepted her challenge. "Did you kill Norma Bates?"

She puffed up instantly, like one of those tiny sponges you drop in water and—poof—you have a little animal to play with in the tub. "Of course I didn't kill her. That's ridiculous! Norma was my dear friend and besides that, I was in Houston. I couldn't very well stab her from Houston, could I? Do you know how far it is from here to Houston?"

"Yes, ma'am, we're aware of the distance involved," said my partner, jumping in to keep me from going for her throat. He gave me a bare sideways glance. I scooted my butt back in the chair and tried to behave.

Suddenly the spider began putting heavy moves on the fly. She leaned towards Barney as if she was some sexy, irresistible babe about to offer herself to him.

"Deputy George, could we have a private talk without Deputy Ricos? I really can't say what I need to say in front of her."

Barney looked bitten. "I want to remind you that our conversation is being recorded so Deputy Ricos will eventually hear what you say. You understand that, right?"

"Yes, I understand. I'd just rather she weren't here while I speak."

I rose and said nothing. I didn't care if she put her hands in his pants. He was a big ol' boy and could defend himself.

As I was shutting my office door, I heard her say, "She scares me," so maybe Lil wasn't as clueless as I'd always assumed. She really had no reason to fear me. If I were ever going to hurt her or Norma, I would've done it when they were dragging my mother's reputation through the muck.

I sat in my comfortable chair, rested my boots on the desk, and contemplated my hill. I was becoming convinced that Norma had been murdered by a stranger—some weird derelict passing through—and yet that seemed so unlikely. Oh, we had weird derelicts in Terlingua, but not murderous ones—or not yet, anyway.

Suddenly there was a handsome blond man at my window.

"Kevin!" I jumped up and tried to figure out how to raise the glass. There didn't seem to be a way.

He put his hands against the window and I laid mine against his. He was wearing his dress-up clothes, including the Stetson he'd been buried in. I sat down hard and cried until there were no more tears left in me.

* * *

I plopped myself down in front of Barney. "What did she have to say?"

He stared at my red, puffy face. "Lil says she's afraid of you. She wanted to tell me that you seem more likely as a suspect than your mother—you being younger and stronger and more hot-headed and opinionated."

"What did you say?"

"I told her you had an alibi. She asked if you had a real alibi or was I just covering for you. I assured her that I'm a man of the highest integrity."

"What did she say to that?"

"She rolled those ol' fish eyes at me. I don't think I changed her mind any about your possible guilt, but then she suggested Miriam or Maude. They hated Norma too, she was quick to point out. She ranted about them but ended up back at Stephanie's doorstep. She said your mom threatened Norma to her face and in the community."

"I threatened her to her face, too, but I didn't kill her. I don't think I could drive a knife into someone, Barney."

"Well I wasn't accusing you, Ricos."

"I know, I'm just sayin'. So Norma's dead but nobody killed her."

"That would be about right."

"I think a stranger killed her. I know you said it's unlikely, but it could happen."

"Yeah, it could."

Barney regarded me silently.

"What I'm sayin' is that some sicko could've happened upon the house or Norma could have met somebody somewhere and told them where she lived, or someone could have followed her home. There's an endless variation of scenarios."

He nodded slightly. "Most likely it was someone from her past."

"Yeah, there's that, too. We have to stay open to all the possibilities."

"Right—there are sure a lot of them."

"What about the Texas Ranger? Did he add anything to our evidence?"

Barney frowned. "I don't think so. If he did, our sheriff hasn't said anything."

"I'd like to think we were capable of investigating a murder without any help from the Texas Rangers."

At that point my father walked in. He seemed anxious and didn't hug me with his usual enthusiasm.

"What's up?" I asked, and invited him to sit after he'd shaken hands with Barney.

My father was a real heart-stopper when he was younger. Even as his daughter, and even though he's old now, I know a good-looking man when I see one. Mom says the first time she saw him she thought he was a Marlboro Man. There was a cigarette commercial being filmed on a nearby cliff-top and the men were in and out of the bar where she was having a drink. When she asked my dad, she found out he didn't even speak English. He wasn't a model, but she fell in love with him anyway.

My father's skin is bronzed where the sun hits it and his eyes are nearly black, like his hair. I got his thick hair and dark eyes, but my skin is lighter than his, my mother's genes at work.

"I'm worried about your mother." He passed a worn cowboy hat from hand to hand as he spoke. "There's a lot of talk in the community about her murdering Norma."

"That doesn't make her guilty, Papi."

I didn't have to translate to Barney because he was raised in a Spanish-speaking neighborhood in south Texas. He spoke perfect Spanish and was paying close attention.

"That's not what worries me, Mija. I know she's not guilty. It's upsetting to her to be accused of this after all she went through before."

"We're trying to find the murderer as fast as we can," I said, although we were getting nowhere with that. I glanced at Barney, who was watching me.

"I'm not faulting you and Barney. I know you're working hard. I'm just worried about your mother. And I can't even say for sure that I saw her on Saturday evening. She needs an alibi and I feel like I'm letting her down. I can't lie about it, though."

"No, it wouldn't be right to lie. Mom doesn't want you to lie, either."

"Will you spend some time with her?" he asked.

"Sure, but maybe you would be more of a comfort."

My dad colored deeply, but said nothing.

"You comforted her for twenty years, Papi. Just because you're divorced doesn't mean you can't go see her and offer your support."

"I know that."

Barney said, "Listen, Sr. Ricos, we're going to find the killer. We don't even have the lab results yet. That might tell us things we don't know now."

"I'll try to be patient," he said with a wry smile.

After my father left, Barney said, "I think he still loves your mother."

"I know it, and she still loves him. They're the two hardest-headed people you'll ever know."

"So you come by it naturally."

I gave him a scathing look, but my looks are always wasted on him.

Chapter 18

Late that afternoon I went back to my mother's house. I couldn't decide what to say until I got there, but I was as nervous as if I was visiting Hannibal Lector instead of my own mostly-sweet mother. I walked in the back door without knocking and called to her.

"Living room," she yelled. "Come on in."

Mom was reclining in an easy chair, reading. She looked up. "Sit. I want to talk to you." She set the book aside and I saw it was a biography of Oscar Wilde by Richard Ellman, a book I had loaned her.

Her command to sit took me off guard, but my mother was always doing that to me. I'm terrified to tell her the truth and just as terrified to lie. The thought occurred that she should be doing the suspect interviews. If they lied, my mom would know.

"Did you come in here and take that gold belt buckle off my window shelf?"

I could feel myself flushing. "Yes Mom, I came to leave the bread and saw it."

"What did you do with it?"

"I put it with my things, like you wanted."

"Good. I was afraid you'd thrown it away."

"Did you want it, Mom, to remember Kevin by?"

"No Missy, I don't need it for that. I just didn't want you to do something you'd regret later. I don't need a belt buckle to remember him. Besides, bull riding skill was the least of the important things about Kevin."

My eyes filled with tears. She had that right. An Oscar Wilde quote came to mind: *I sometimes think that God, in creating man, somewhat overestimated his ability.* In creating Kevin, God had outdone himself.

"Still," she said, "he would've been proud of that buckle."

"I know, Mom. That's why I'm keeping it."

"How are you doing, sweetheart?"

"Not so great, most days."

"It'll get better with time. I hope you're not drinking too much. That isn't going to help at all and it's so bad for your health."

"Mom, I came here to ask you a few questions."

"Answer me about the drinking first."

"I'm trying to quit. I see that it doesn't help, except temporarily. I wake up muddled and still heart-broken, so I'm not going to do it anymore."

"If you have trouble with that, talk to your father. He gave it up, you know."

"Yes, I know. I'll talk to him."

"What did you want to ask me?"

"It's about Norma's murder."

"Get to the point," she said in her exasperating way.

"Did you do it?"

Her hand went to her heart. "Why would you ask me something like that?"

"Just answer the question with a simple yes or no."

"I already told Barney no."

"Now I'm the one asking you, Mom."

"I didn't murder her," she said softly.

"When was the last time you were in her house?"

"Margarita, I told Barney all this."

"I'm asking you—as your daughter. When was the last time you were in her house?"

"It's been over a year."

"I don't think that's true, Mom. I'd like to know the truth, please."

She picked up the book, as if putting it between us sheltered her from an attack. "What makes you think it's not true?"

"I swept up one of your earrings, one of the gold hoops with little hearts."

I waited to see how that would hit her, not feeling good about hitting her with anything.

"Well I must have left it there before," she said. "I haven't been there in a long time."

I wasn't going to call my mother a liar, but I didn't believe her. If she'd lost it long ago, the twin would not have been sitting on her dresser. Why would she still have it? A sickening dread washed over me. The thing that made me feel sure she was lying was that she hadn't looked me in the eyes. That wasn't like my mother.

I went by the post office, picked up the mail without looking at it, and went home feeling depressed and badly in need of a drink. I felt momentarily afraid to go in my house because of the longnecks in the fridge. Instead of monsters in the closet, I had them in my refrigerator.

I sat in the rocker to study Cimarron Mountain and talk myself out of starting on the beer. Once started, I wouldn't stop. Then I wouldn't run. I'd be disappointed in myself. Guilt would set in. Sooner or later Sheriff Ben would fire me. I'd feel physically awful tomorrow. My mental list of reasons not to drink began to grow, while some other part of me got on its knees and begged me to just go ahead and do it.

Flipping through my mail, I noticed a handwritten envelope stuck in with the bills and junk. It was a love letter from Jimmy Joe Blanks. I hadn't received anything so gushy since a boy left a letter in my locker in ninth grade. Jimmy Joe's letter had the same feel to it, but the locker letter had been left by a fourteen-year-old. Jimmy Joe was at least thirty. It was sad—and frightening.

I made myself change into running clothes. When I went into my bedroom I had the feeling someone had been there, looking through my things. I couldn't say what had been moved or why I thought that, except for the pillow. I had left it covered with the comforter when I made the bed, but it was now sitting on top of it.

When I sat, I noticed that the top dresser drawer was open slightly, but maybe I'd left it like that. I chided myself for not locking the doors. If I could remember to lock them I would know if someone had been in my house, but then an intruder would have to damage the door or the windows in order to get in, and I would have to remember to take the key. The things I owned of value were sentimental things; things nobody else would want. So why would anyone come into my house?

I lay back on the bed and vaguely remembered the late-night intruder, but wasn't one-hundred percent sure that had happened. I'd been drunk and sick so maybe what I'd perceived as threatening darkness had only been darkness, and I'd imagined the threatening part.

Okay! I yelled at myself in my head. *Just shut up and go run.* Incredibly, I rose from the bed, slammed out the front door and began to do it.

That evening I ran all the way to Cimarron and collapsed at its base, between a couple of eighteen-wheeler-sized boulders. I writhed on the ground, crying and screaming. I cursed a God that would take away a perfectly good man for no apparent reason. I cursed a bull that would dare put its foot on my husband when he was down. I even cursed a cowboy who just couldn't stay away from riding those bulls. What kind of idiot wants to ride on the back of a maniacal bull?

I yelled until I was hoarse, sobbed until I had hiccoughs, and eventually exhausted myself. I lay on my back and looked at the red-tinged sky with Cimarron Mountain looming over me. A purple and pink cotton-candy cloud appeared out of nowhere and hung near the summit, as if to shelter it. Maybe it showed up because of my out-of-control wailing fit. The mountain had survived volcanic upheavals, an ice age, the shifting of the earth, the dawn of man, and even violent thunderstorms, only to call a friend at the last minute, frightened by something at last. I laughed at that, sat up, and wiped my face on my shirt.

Then I ran home, ate a healthy dinner, showered, and went to bed. I had survived twenty-four hours without drinking. It was amazing.

Chapter 19

On Monday I decided to get up early to run. I thought it would be easier in the cool part of the day rather than in its final heat, but didn't know if I would sleep as well. Since there was only one way to find out, I was up about dawn, sitting on the side of my bed, contemplating the floor. My legs were sore and complained at the thought of moving.

The morning was still cool when I started walking at a brisk pace. There was a slight breeze, and the sun had not come over the mountains in the east. Being up early has its rewards. The sky is usually rose-colored with streaks of gold and turns the landscape various shades of red, pink, and purple. I love that time of day; it's the getting up I hate.

I headed towards the highway instead of in the usual direction, looking for a change of scenery. I passed a few vehicles before I cut into an arroyo for an off-pavement run. They waved and I waved back.

When I started back I stopped at my father's convenience store. He looked up from book work, pleased to see me.

"Mija, que pasa?"

"I've been running," I answered in Spanish.

"You're not going to wear those shorts in public?"

"I already did, Papi. They're running shorts."

"If you were younger, I'd forbid you to wear them."

"You did that, as I recall."

"Yes, but you snuck them out of the house and wore them anyway."

"You know about that?"

"I know about a lot of things."

I thought it best to leave that alone. "Papi, how did you quit drinking?"

My father never spoke about his out-of-control drinking and I only knew about it because of things my mom had said.

"Your mother told me she wouldn't marry me if I kept drinking like I was, so I was determined to quit. I found if I didn't start, I was okay. It had become more of a habit than anything. I would meet some guys after work and we drank beer. I usually drank too much. I thought the prospect of going home to your mother was more enticing than hanging out with a bunch of smelly guys, so I gave it up."

"You didn't go to AA meetings or anything like that?"

"No, Mija, but if you need to go, you should do it."

"I will."

"You'll never get over the pain if you don't face it. You'll stay bewildered and bitter and hurting. I don't want that for you."

"I know." I moved to him and hugged myself close against him.

After a while I asked, "Papi, would you like to have Kevin's truck? If you would, I'll sign the title over to you."

"What brings this on, Mija?"

"It's been sitting for more than a year. I'm never going to use it, and I thought you might like to have it." I had already given the horse and horse trailer to Mitch.

"But you might need it."

"For?"

"I don't know—lots of things. Trucks are useful to have."

"That's why I want you to have it. I'll never drive it. If you want to, you could trade it in for something different. Either way, Kevin would be pleased for you have it. And besides, I want you to."

"Well, thank you. I'd love to have it. Won't it upset you if I drive it?"

"No. I don't want to, but that doesn't mean you can't. Will you come and get it, because I'm not going to drive it over here for you. I hope you understand."

"I do."

"Will you come soon? I—I'm trying to get rid of the last of the things." I didn't mention the bloody clothes that I was still unable to part with. I would give them up, but it wouldn't be today.

"I think that's healthy," he said.

I hugged him again and started to run on, but in a second I turned around. "I don't want to forget him, Papi."

"You won't Mija." His eyes were bright with tears. "You won't."

* * *

"Listen," Sheriff Duncan said after the usual phone pleasantries, "I've just spoken with your mother and she's agreed to let us take a cheek swab for DNA. Barney's also going to take her fingerprints, and a few hair samples. We'll see if anything matches evidence from the crime scene."

I didn't know what to say, so I stayed quiet, waiting to hear what he would say next.

"If it was anyone else under suspicion, you know we would've already done this."

When I didn't speak, he said, "We have to run this investigation like any other."

"That's what we're doing, Sheriff."

"Your personal involvement may cloud your instincts. Hell, Margarita, even I don't think she had anything to do with the murder, but this must be handled like any other murder investigation. Try to understand that."

"But the evidence against her is circumstantial."

"Yes, but it's all we have. If nothing matches we have to look elsewhere. If it does, we'll have to look more closely at her."

"I know you're right. What about the Bates family members?"

"We've already submitted samples of their hair and besides, the hair you found at the scene is dyed, and none of them dye their hair."

My mom colors her graying hair. Flipping through our suspects in my mind, I couldn't think of any who dyed their hair, except Lil, and she was the wrong color.

When we hung up, I walked into the main office for a bottle of water. What I really needed was reassurance. I collapsed into Barney's visitor chair.

He stopped typing and looked at me. "Did he mention anything about me taking a cheek swab from your mother?"

"Yeah, I'm freaking out."

"It's routine, try not to worry."

He went back to his work and I went back into my office and turned on my computer and stared at it. Soon Barney came in and dropped his oversized self into my overstuffed chair. Fortunately for me, I wasn't seated in it.

"You worried about your mom?"

"A little, I guess."

"The evidence can't say she did it unless she did."

"There's something I haven't mentioned to you."

"What's that?"

"That earring I found at the scene belongs to my mother."

"Are you sure?"

"Very sure."

"And you were going to tell me about this, when?"

"I'm telling you now."

"You should have told the sheriff."

"I can't tell him now. He'll say I was withholding information. The crime lab will tell him soon enough."

"They didn't get anything from it, Ricos. The sheriff just faxed some of our reports. Didn't he tell you?"

"He might have. I was too busy freaking out to listen. So what do we have?"

"Most of the fingerprints match the ones I took from family members, but there are three that aren't theirs, and aren't in the system. The hairs we found are from four different donors. The earring you say is your mother's didn't turn up anything so it's possible it's been a while since she wore it. According to the autopsy, the victim was stabbed with a sharp, smooth-bladed knife, like we thought. She was healthy, not pregnant, and no recent sex. There were no drugs or alcohol in her bloodstream. What we have so far is *nada*, just like we had before."

"So if Mom's hair is there it's going to look bad for her."

"Yes, although she might have a plausible explanation." Barney stood and stretched. "I'm going to go get swabs, fingerprints, and hairs from Sylvia and your mother. I'll be back after that."

"Okay."

"It's gonna be all right, Ricos. This is strictly routine."

After Barney left I called Stanner to ask him about the dogs.

"They couldn't have been out," he said.

"How can you be sure?"

"Norma never let them out on the weekend. She always loaded them up and took them to run by the creek or along the river. I spoke with her Saturday afternoon, and she said it wouldn't be as much fun without the kids, but she was going anyway. It was a ritual with her. Ever since she got those dogs she's taken them to run on Saturdays and Sundays. Does it matter about the dogs?"

"I don't know. Roger Lockey reported Norma's death and said he had gone to talk to her about them."

"That can't be right. She only let them out on weekdays, when she thought people would be gone, and there'd be less for the dogs to get into. And she was having so many complaints from Lockey that she'd almost quit letting them run loose. She nearly always took them somewhere, or she and the kids walked them on a leash."

"When I interviewed Mr. Lockey he seemed very perturbed about the dogs."

"That's old stuff," said Stanner. "Maybe he and Norma got into it about something else, but it wouldn't have been the dogs."

"Were the feelings between Norma and Lockey so heated that he could've been the one that killed her, in your opinion?"

"I don't think so. He was fond of our kids so no, that doesn't seem likely. I don't believe he would've killed the kids' mother."

Her ex said he wouldn't have killed her because she was the mother of his son. Libby Thomas said Stanner wouldn't have killed her because of his youngest daughter, Vicky, and most people agreed. Libby loved Stanner, so she wouldn't have killed Norma, either, because of Vicky. My mother was concerned about any motherless child. Stanner didn't think Lockey would've killed her because of the kids. What was the deal with that?

The point was the dogs had not been running loose, as Old Man Lockey said. Even if Norma had set them free at night, they wouldn't have been back in their pen when Barney arrived at the scene of the murder. I wondered if Roger Lockey was the last to see Norma Bates alive, or if it had been my mother.

After speaking with Stanner I settled myself in my chair but I didn't look at the hill. I was afraid I would see Kevin. And I was terrified I would never see him again.

* * *

When Kevin came home from the roping I was standing in our kitchen naked. I wasn't even wearing an apron. I pretended to be busy cooking, but my hands were shaking in anticipation. He stopped just inside the house and dropped his new leather chaps to the floor. Then he shut the door without taking his eyes off me, his look so full of lust it was a wonder my legs held.

"Guess it's a good thing Mitch didn't come in with me," he said as he walked towards me. By the time he reached the kitchen, he had left a trail along the floor: boots, socks, jeans, and his denim shirt.

"Nice way to greet a man," he said softly, cupping my breasts in his hands. He was standing behind me, and laid his face against my neck, nuzzling me. I put my hands over his in a gesture of encouragement, but didn't say a word.

We began kissing and he pinned me against the counter, pressing against me. The hard edge pained my back, and after a few moments, I escaped and ran to the bedroom just ahead of him. After a few minutes of being chased, I landed on the bed. Kevin crawled towards me, laughing softly, his blond hair falling across his eyes. We were both naked and teasing each other. I laughed and backed up, my legs apart, exposing myself to him.

"Oh, Baby," he said in a hoarse voice.

The next thing I knew his mouth was on mine, the taste of him familiar and welcome. His lean body pressed against me and I moved suggestively beneath him. His smell was his alone, a faint mixture of cologne and Kevin—an aphrodisiac.

He moved enough to get his hand between us and massaged one hard nipple gently but insistently, groaning when he touched me. I was the one that should've been groaning, but I was breathless with anticipation, unable to make a sound. We'd been teasing each other too long. Every nerve ending was revved, demanding attention. All of them wanted it at once, right now.

I ran my hand along his chest, hard with muscle and tanned from riding bare-chested in the sun.

"Kevin, Kevin, Kevin," I moaned.

"What Baby?"

"Keep touching me."

"There's no chance in hell I'm going to stop." He leaned back and looked at me, his eyes glittering. "I can't stop, Margarita." He began to gently bite my neck and I was gone. "Baby, Baby," he whispered into my ear.

He eased two big fingers into me gently, then more insistently. I gasped and wound my legs around him. I brought my hips up against his hand, grinding against it.

"Please," I moaned, "please, Kev."

He continued to move his fingers and I wanted to beg some more but couldn't.

Suddenly he raised himself off the bed, lifting me with him, and set me near the edge. I lay back. He looked down at me, his faced flushed and his nostrils flared a little. He ran his hands under my bottom and lifted it towards him slowly, making me wait. I licked my lips. He was lifting me towards him, so slowly—

"Wake up, Ricos!"

Why was Barney there? I woke up so angry I wanted to kill him. It was rare to see Kevin in a dream I wanted to have, and he ruined it. Despair was a crushing weight on my chest but I was so aroused I suddenly wanted Barney. The temptation was raw and I could barely resist. Barney was a man and that was what I wanted. I would wrap my legs around his big frame and—I looked up at him, shocked speechless by my lust.

I'd never seen him so red in the face. "I had to wake you, Ricos. You were making sounds like you were having sex and anyone might come in our office any time."

He turned and left me to my misery. Within a few minutes he was gone. I heard the door shut and then the start of his Explorer.

* * *

I needed to drink but was afraid to drink alone. I was afraid to go out where I might see a man. I had to do something or lose my mind. I thought long and hard about Phil and his barely-veiled offers. A woman could do worse than Phil. I mentally flipped through the men I knew, wondering about them, rating them, wanting Kevin.

Sheriff Ben told me clearly not to hang out in bars. Maybe a fast ride in my Mustang would help. It's midnight blue, beautiful, a gift from Kevin, bought with rodeo winnings. I love it and its willingness to go as fast as I want, but of course it makes me miss the man who gave it to me.

I put a six pack of longnecks in a cooler and drove towards the Rio Grande, breaking nearly every traffic law in the state of Texas, except I was wearing a seatbelt and didn't drive through a red light. But that's only because there isn't one. I was speeding, drinking while driving, had an open container, was weaving over the center line, and incorrectly passing other vehicles. If I had stopped me I would've taken me to a holding cell to cool off. That gave me a halfhearted laugh.

I flew through the resort town of Lajitas to a promontory above the river. It's a place where a low wall built of native rock follows Highway 170 for several hundred feet. It is dedicated to the memory of a local man, and intended to be a rest stop, a place to admire the Rio Grande. I parked in a pullout, got a fresh beer out of the cooler, and sat on the wall to drink it.

I could smell the river the minute I got out of the car. It had an earthy, damp smell that I associated with trips into Mexico and rafting and canoeing adventures. It was a smell I had loved since my childhood, and I found it oddly comforting.

I watched three Mexican cowboys ford the river in the last of the dying light. The ropes tied to their saddles reminded me of Kevin. Everything about them reminded me of him, except for their coloring. *A cowboy is a cowboy*, I thought cheerlessly.

Soon I was sitting in the dark, which suited me fine. It was better if no one saw me drinking, or saw me at all.

The cowboys tied their horses to low-growing mesquite bushes along the bank and walked up a grassy hill below me. They sat at a table in a picnic area belonging to the resort. It was dimly lit by solar path lights. I knew a lot of guys from the other side, but none of these were familiar. It was a still night and I could hear everything they said. None of it interested me until they mentioned a dangerous man, Chapo Rodriguez. He was a troublemaker and small-time criminal well-known to Barney and me.

Chapo stole his neighbor's goats whenever he wanted to kill and grill one. He shot peoples' dogs and cats as an act of vengeance, and vandalized property. He had served time for stealing building supplies from a construction site, more than once. Chapo was a reason we were constantly breaking up bar fights.

He hated it that I wouldn't go out with him; and wondered why, even after I told him. He was the kind of man to laugh in your face if you called him an asshole, but might shoot you in the back later. Well, that was my opinion—and Barney's.

"Did you see those alligator boots?" asked one of the cowboys.

"Man, I know those boots cost around eight hundred. With the belt he must have laid down over one thousand dollars. What do you make of that?"

"He said he had a job doing something for some old gringa."

"Maybe he's fucking her."

"There's no woman alive would pay Chapo to fuck her, not a woman in her right mind anyway."

That was the truest thing I'd heard all day. The men nearly died laughing about it, slapping each other and getting hysterical.

"Say Chico, if Chapo can get a thousand, you could get a hell of a lot more."

They were teasing the youngest, best-looking of the threesome and I thought he could get a thousand if Chapo could get a dollar.

Then another one of them spoke. "He said he was buying a new truck and he put ten thousand down."

"Shit! That's a lot of damn fucking."

"Well maybe he knows to do things you never heard of."

Their conversation lapsed into gutter talk. If they'd had any idea a woman was listening they would have toned it down or quit talking. Mexican men don't talk like that around respectable women.

Yes, ten thousand dollars was a lot of money to make having sex; especially for a crass, homely man like Chapo Rodriguez. He was doing something illegal; I would've bet a month's salary on it.

Eventually the men moved on, headed in the direction of the Lajitas Trading Post. When they disappeared into the darkness, I started my Mustang and drove towards home.

I only had two beers, I consoled my throbbing conscience on the way. *Playing with fire*, it reminded me.

When I passed La Kiva, I felt as drawn as a moth to a yucca. I drove by, went home, and thankfully, slept. I did not have another dream of Kevin.

Chapter 20

I ran an extra-long time the next morning to put off facing Barney. He'd hurried out of the office after the dream incident, before I'd found the courage to rise from the chair, and I hadn't seen him again.

He was seated at his desk drinking coffee. As I came in I started to blurt an apology but he held up his huge hands. "Stop right there, Ricos. Nobody can help what they dream."

Again I started to speak, but he interrupted. "I assume you were having a really good one." His mouth curled and trembled like he was trying not to laugh.

"Yeah," I said, and disappeared into my office and turned on the computer.

I avoided the chair as if it was possessed, and stood at the window instead. I longed to see Kevin, and at the same time, didn't. Anyway, he never showed up at my window again.

I thought if I slept in that chair once more, maybe I could finish the dream. But I would have to get rid of Barney first and lock up the office, and anyway it didn't seem possible. Kevin was gone and dreaming wasn't going to cut it.

My hill was resplendent. I watched a pair of lively cactus wrens picking insects out of a yucca. They are noisy birds anyway, but suddenly they began to scold and complain a notch or two above their normal level. They began swooping and diving at something on the ground. I thought a cat, but instead a lone coyote slunk away from the hill and disappeared into the desert.

When I checked my email, I had fifteen from Jimmy Joe Blanks, all begging me to let him into my life. He could satisfy me, he could make me happy, he would do whatever it took—blah, blah, blah. His letters ranged from verbose, flowery expressions of undying love to borderline pornography.

I forwarded them to Sheriff Ben with a note. "This man is stalking me, Sheriff. I have repeatedly told him I don't want to date him. His behavior is unprofessional, but more than that, I think he's crazy and he scares me." I copied Barney so he would understand my actions.

After a while I walked back into the front office and sat across the desk from Barney. He looked at me, a little wary.

"Barney, I just sent you a copy of fifteen emails from Jimmy Joe, and a letter I sent to the sheriff."

"Did you say *fifteen?*"

"Yes, fifteen. Jimmy Joe is stalking me. He calls non-stop, writes love letters, and now emails. And wait 'til you read them. It's freaking me out."

"You did the right thing. All this time I thought he was an okay guy because he's a fellow deputy."

"You can't assume somebody is okay because of their job."

"No kidding."

"I overheard something last night about Chapo Rodriguez," I said.

"What's he up to now?"

"He's doing something illegal."

"Seems like we can assume that, since we're talking Chapo."

"He's come into a lot of money suddenly. His friends said he was doing some kind of special work for an old gringa."

"My guess is he's gotten involved in drugs," Barney said. "It was bound to happen."

"Possibly."

"What are you thinking, Ricos?"

"What if he did a murder for hire?"

"You're thinking he did Norma?"

"Maybe. I've been wondering about that empty pack of Rojos I found at the scene. He smokes them."

"Him and millions of other Mexican guys."

"In Mexico, yes, but in Terlingua, no."

"When did you become an expert on what Mexican men smoke?"

"I observe people. I grew up surrounded by Mexican men, and even my father says American brands taste better. Most of the smokers I know smoke Marlboros or Camels and other macho brands, not Mexican cigarettes."

"That pack could've gotten there a lot of different ways—like on the wind for one."

"Right, but you know what Sheriff Ben says. There's no such thing as a coincidence in a murder investigation."

"Yes, but in real life there are coincidences." He paused, watching me. "You're stuck on Chapo, aren't you?"

"Not stuck on him, but I think he's worth considering. He's a callous guy and a callous guy stabbed Norma in the heart, and how many around here can you imagine doing that?"

"You have a point. But we can't make him guilty just because we don't like him."

I gave him a look. "Everyone suspects that Stanner had Norma snuffed. Who would he get to do something like that?"

"Chapo."

"Right. I'm going to check around, that's all I'm sayin'. Chapo doing Norma makes sense. He would have gone in, stabbed her, and gotten out of there. It looked like she struggled, but Chapo wouldn't have given her much of a chance."

I shivered at the thought of waking up to Chapo in my house; Chapo with a knife.

"The other thing about drugs," I said, "is that you don't get rich suddenly. As far as we know, he's not been involved before, so you can't tell me he jumped in and has already made a huge success out of it. For one thing, how would Chapo make a huge success out of anything?"

"Well, if he offed Norma that was a success."

"Oh no, it wasn't. I mean, if he killed her, we'll get him. I don't think getting the needle in Huntsville is an indication of a successful life. Not exactly a thing to make your mama proud."

"You're a trip, Ricos. Knock yourself out. Just be careful around him. Don't forget you've had trouble with him before."

"How would I forget that?"

"If he sees you sneaking around he's going to think you want him. Be careful, that's all I'm saying."

"I'm just going to take a look at his truck when I have a chance."

"Well okay, but you know what they say about Mexican men."

"What's that?"

"Admiring their big ol' pimped out trucks is like admiring their dicks. But I don't guess we should talk about that today."

"Good plan," I said, and felt my face burn.

I stopped at my dad's to see what he knew about Chapo. My father usually knows everything happening in our community. People confide in him because he's trustworthy, listens intently, and doesn't interrupt. He taught me early that if I want to know something, I should let others talk. Listening is an art and it pays: his motto.

He hugged me and we established that we were both doing fine. "Have you heard anything about Chapo getting involved in the drug trade?" I asked.

"No, Mija. Who would trust him to carry drugs? He can't keep his mouth shut, and is always bragging. He looks for trouble and would hardly be a blend-into-the-wall mule. He would want to start at the top and anyway, somebody would have shut him up by now. I wouldn't give him a week in the drug business." He paused to study me, and frowned a little. "Why are you asking?"

"He's come into money, and I was just wondering about it, that's all. I figure he's doing something illegal and I'd like to know what."

"You should stay away from him."

"I plan to."

"Didn't you already have some personal problems with him?"

"Yes. Don't worry."

"You tell me not to worry and then you wear shorts like you had on yesterday. Chapo Rodriguez is the best reason I can think of not to dress like that, Mija."

"Okay, Papi. I get it." There is no point to arguing with my father. It would only annoy both of us and he always wins.

"You look very nice in your uniform, properly covered."

"I'll wear it day and night."

He gave me a look that made me change the subject. "Who do you know that smokes Rojos?"

His answer was: "Chapo. Most guys smoke American brands but he likes Rojos. He's asked me to carry them in my store but I can't. Anyway, even if I could get them, it wouldn't be worth it for one man who isn't dependable. What do Rojos have to do with anything?"

"I'm just thinking, Papi. When I have something more concrete I'll tell you. Right now I don't know much."

"Just remember what I told you."

"Right, listen and don't talk."

"Talking is trouble." He paused, frowning. "So are those shorts."

I thought how much I loved my quiet, intelligent father. He had only a fifth grade education, but had taught himself more things than most people would learn in a lifetime. The only thing that really stumped him was English—and my mother.

I hugged him again and told him to have a good day.

"Don't wear those shorts again," he called after me.

I drove by the Big Bend Motor Inn Café, where Chapo worked as a dishwasher, and sometimes as a cook's assistant. He was the biggest reason I never ate there. Sitting next to the building, where employees usually park, was a new, red, king-cab, Ford truck. It had to be his. It was large and showy and had a serape draped over the seat and at least one saint hung on a chain from the rearview mirror. Most of the Mexicans I know drive like crazy people and expect their saints to protect them.

I pulled in behind the truck and wrote down the tag number and the name of the dealer, Odessa Ford in Odessa, Texas.

My cell phone rang. When I answered the sheriff said, "I want you to know that I just called Jimmy Joe Blanks into my office. He's so delusional he thinks you're only a few steps away from marrying him."

"I don't even want to talk to him."

"The point of my call is to tell you I fired him. I agree that he's stalking you. But just because he lost his job doesn't mean he'll quit, so I want you to be careful. If you have one speck of trouble from him, call me or get Barney involved. Is that clear?"

"Yes, Sheriff. Thank you."

Then I took a deep breath and went inside the store/restaurant to purchase a bottle of water. To the cashier, I said loudly, "Whose red truck is that out there? Is it yours?" She looked totally not like the big red truck type and gave me a look that said I must be nuts.

Yes lady, if you only knew.

Chapo spoke marginal English but he'd heard *red truck* and stepped into view. I could see him from the corner of my eye. I felt sure I was going to regret this.

"I think you're talking about Chapo's truck," the cashier said.

"Oh well, it sure is beautiful." I was counting in my head, one-two-three-four and before I reached five Chapo stepped through the swinging door from the kitchen.

"Es mi troca," he said without smiling or saying hello. Yes, I already knew it was his truck. I tried to smile.

Chapo is short and stocky, slightly taller than me but much heavier, with a barrel chest and the beginning of a beer gut. He has a pock-marked face and is light-skinned with black eyes that dart, like a feral creature. I know it's hard to tell about a person by looking at them, but Chapo is the evil stranger, the man you don't want to meet in a dark alley; a man you want to keep away from your children.

He jerked his head towards the side door. "You me go look," he said, attempting English.

What Barney had said about Mexican men showing off their trucks gave me pause, but I thought that applied to all men, not just Mexicans. Anyway, the thought made me not want to go.

Chapo held a soda can in one hand while the fingers of the other sensually touched the vehicle as he spoke about it.

I tried to seem interested. "It's beautiful, Chapo," I said after a while, in Spanish, "but I couldn't afford a truck like this on my pay."

"I work side jobs," he said with a shrug.

"Could you get me some work?"

He puffed out his chest. "You wouldn't want to do the things I do."

Without doubt.

I looked off at the mountains until I realized that Chapo was looking at me. "You're much more beautiful than this truck and your lines make a man—"

"What is your side job?" I interrupted.

"Oh, nothing interesting." Then he crumpled the soda can and threw it to the ground. "I gotta go back to work. I'll take you for a ride sometime," he said over his shoulder when he got to the door.

Not in this lifetime.

When he was gone I picked up the can and put it into an evidence bag. I knew several things. One was exactly where he'd bought the truck. Also, he said he had gotten a reduced interest rate because he'd made a large down-payment, and even told me it had been ten thousand dollars. I also knew that whatever he was doing in his spare time was something dark. But I would've assumed that.

I decided to get some clarification from Roger Lockey about the dogs and the real reason he had gone to see Norma. Maybe he was having an affair with her. But the autopsy had shown no recent sex. Maybe that's what the fight was about. Can an old man even do sex? *Get your head away from sex*, said the one sane woman who tries to live in my head.

The road to Lockey's took me past the Bates house. As I approached, I saw there was a truck in the driveway and as I got closer, I could see it was not just any truck. It was the small, blue Ford Ranger pickup that belongs to my father.

I pulled into the driveway behind it and sat gripping the steering wheel, stunned. Were both of my parents involved in the murder of Norma Bates? Was my father the killer and my mother covering for him, or was it the other way around? My head was a jumble of scenarios, none of them good, and none of them complimentary to my parents. How could they've had anything to do with it? I was raised by these people.

There was no sign of a human. The police tape we had strung over the doors and windows was mostly gone, or sagging and blowing in the slight breeze. There wasn't any over the door, and no way to tell if it'd been removed by a person or the persistent winds that blow most nights. Surely neither of my parents would remove tape from a crime scene, but that paled in the face of murder.

I was so freaked out looking at my father's familiar truck next to that cramped, hot, stinking house that I nearly called Barney. I reined in my galloping imagination and told myself that my parents had not become raving, murdering lunatics. But one of them might have made a terrible mistake.

I was forced out of the Explorer, thinking about my friend Austin and how, in his eyes, I was one of the superheroes. My heart was beating too fast, my stomach felt queasy, and my legs appeared to be commanded by someone else's will—hardly a superhero response.

I was nearly to the porch when I heard sobbing. For one horrible, fear-filled moment I thought it would be Norma's ghost waiting for me. I rounded the house, my heart full of dread. Sitting at the edge of the porch was my mother.

"Mom!"

When she looked up, an expression of horror passed over her tear-streaked face. "Go away."

"Mom, what's going on? Why are you crying?" I jumped up next to her.

"How did you know I was here?" She looked frightened, as if I'd found her by using my fearsome psychic powers.

"Mom, what are you doing here?"

She looked off at the mountains to the west—or in that direction anyway. "I've done a terrible thing, Margarita."

Those words made my heart stop its galloping. In fact it stopped altogether. I don't know how I found the strength to do it, I felt like a pile of Jell-O, but I put my hand on her arm. She began to cry again and leaned against me. I put my arms around her and she sobbed against my chest as if her heart was broken.

I began to cry, too, and I wasn't even sure what we were crying about. A terrible thing—she said she'd done a terrible thing. I thought about all the times she'd held me like this when somebody hurt my feelings, or I'd been injured or life had otherwise bitten me in the butt—taking away Kevin, for instance.

"Mom, you have to stop crying so I can stop crying." I wiped my face on the sleeve of my uniform, forgetting it was my uniform, forgetting everything except the terrible thing. "What is it? You can trust me."

"I can't tell you."

"Mom, you're on Norma's back porch."

"It's not hers now," she said with attitude.

"Why are you here, is my point."

"I can't tell you. You're the last person I want to tell."

"Well Mom, you've got to tell somebody."

"Oh no, I don't."

"Mom, you're in Dad's truck, sitting on Norma's porch crying. You need to tell me what you've done so I can help you. I assume Dad's not here?"

"Of course not! I borrowed his truck so I wouldn't be recognized. Everyone knows that truck of mine."

"Why are you being so secretive? Tell me, Mom, so I can help you."

"I came to look for something, but I looked in the window and I saw the blood on the floor. Blood doesn't bother me but it's all black and—"

"What did you want to look for?"

"Margarita, that's what I don't want to tell you."

"Did you leave something here?"

"No. It's—it's that she had something of mine."

"What could she have had that's yours?"

My mother sighed as if she was losing patience with me. She took a deep, shuddering breath. "Norma had letters and photos that were none of her business. The truth is she was blackmailing me."

I had fifty questions at once, and not one would come off my tongue. My mother had killed Norma because of blackmail? It seemed too small-town Murder She Wrote.

"Don't look at me like that. You haven't even heard the worst part yet."

"You're going to tell me you're the one who killed her."

My mother gave me the angry-amused-disgusted look she used to give me when I talked back to her. She reared back like she was going to slap me. My mother had never hit me.

"For heaven's sake Margarita, I'm not a criminal."

The thing was she didn't say it like she meant it.

My hands went to my head. I think I was going to tear my hair out. Maybe I was going to slap myself. I felt like I'd gone insane.

"Mom, start at the beginning. What could Norma possibly have found to blackmail you with?"

"That's none of your business."

Man.

"What does anything you did have to do with Norma?"

"Stop asking me questions."

"It's my job. I'm trying to find a murderer. Often blackmail is the reason for murder. You do the math."

"I didn't murder her."

"I'm trying to make sense of blackmail and murder and you being here in Dad's truck sitting on Norma's porch crying."

My mother made no move to enlighten me.

"Mom, if Norma had pornographic photos of you or whatever, why didn't she come forward with them during the lawsuit? She tried to discredit you every possible way, why not use them then?"

"Who said anything about pornography? What an imagination you have."

No kidding.

"We can sit here all day, but I can't tell you the details. You're my daughter and I love you, and it has to do with that."

"It has to do with me being your daughter?" My head had begun to pound.

"She wanted me to admit that I'd stolen money from Doctores Fronterizos and step down from my position. She wanted me to say publicly that I was in the wrong and she was right all along."

"What were you going to do?"

"I don't know, but I wasn't going to bow to her demands."

"Mom, this just makes things look worse. It's more circumstantial evidence against you. People go to prison all the time on crap like this."

"You aren't going to tell anyone. My point in coming over here was to get the things she stole. Nobody has to know."

"Mom, I have a professional obligation to tell what I know, not to mention a moral one."

"This can't stay between you and me, as mother and daughter?"

"I don't see how—but even if I never said anything, don't you suppose that half of Terlingua has seen my Explorer here, and Dad's truck? I'm surprised nobody has stopped to see what's going on. You know how this place is."

"I don't want everyone to know about this."

"Mom, would you tell Barney? You say you can't tell me, would you tell him?"

"He would just tell you."

"How am I going to save you if you won't tell me what's going on?"

"You'll have to let me fry, I guess."

"It's a lethal injection now, but it still isn't pleasant. Mom, I can't stand by and let you get the needle for something you didn't do. I would try to help you even if you were guilty."

"My life isn't your responsibility."

Arguing with her was like arguing with my father.

I went back to the office and relayed all the facts to Barney. We sat quietly for a minute, pondering what to do next until the phone rang. Barney answered it and for a long time he listened, looking shocked, and glancing at me occasionally.

"What?" I mouthed, but he only shook his head.

"Okay." he said. "Yes, I'll explain it to her. There won't be any problems."

When he got off the phone he cleared his throat. "That was the sheriff. The lab says the hair is a match for your mother's."

I couldn't speak. My mind was racing. I stood, unable to be still.

"There are plausible explanations for how it could've gotten there, Ricos. Besides her having gone there as the murderer, I mean."

I interrupted. "It could have come in on me when I entered the crime scene."

"Yes. It could have. The sheriff said that, too."

Barney hesitated. "He has to get a warrant to search your mom's house and yard. It's routine when crime scene DNA matches. He says it's nothing to worry about and hopes you won't. He's calling your mom now to explain it to her."

"Are you and I going to execute the warrant?"

"No, you're too closely tied to the—uh—suspect. He's bringing it down tomorrow, with a deputy from Alpine and the three of us will do it. It'll be nothin', Ricos. Don't look so worried."

"I'm not worried. I know my mom is innocent."

I didn't know any such thing and I was really starting to sweat.

* * *

That evening I ran, ate a good dinner, and didn't drink. It seemed like running took me to another place, the way alcohol had, but with positive side effects. Sleep came easier, I cried less, and the bloody clothes stayed in the drawer. I knew they were there, but I didn't hold them.

I woke with a panicky pounding heart and thought a light had been shining on me. I was naked, but my Beretta was tucked under the pillow. He was a lot more protection than a nightgown. I got up and peered out the window into the darkness, but didn't see anything.

When I lay back down I thought about Chapo and how dangerous he was. He was the type to sneak around in the dark, or watch a woman sleeping. Had he been the one in my house before?

I locked my house so anyone breaking in would have to make a lot of noise. Before, I'd blamed Mandy's rapist. Barney had thought it was a drunk stumbling into the wrong house. I thought we'd both been wrong. It had likely been Chapo Rodriguez.

Chapter 21

The next morning I walked outside to look around. The area below the window was disturbed. Some ground-hugging yellow wildflowers had been crushed, and there were faint boot prints in the dirt. I looked for a cigarette butt, and didn't find one, but I did find a flashlight carefully placed under a creosote bush. It had been stashed there, not cast aside, which meant the culprit was planning to return. I wanted to stick a rattlesnake under there, but it wouldn't stay, and would probably end up in my house. I placed the flashlight into an evidence bag to send to the crime lab.

At the office I called the Ford dealer in Odessa and spoke with a salesman who confirmed that Fernando Rodriguez (Chapo) had made a cash down-payment of ten thousand dollars on his new pick-up.

Later, my mother and I waited in a restaurant while the sheriff, a deputy from Alpine, and Barney executed a search warrant for her house and grounds. She was calmer than I would've been with people going through my things.

After about an hour and a half, Barney came across the restaurant in great strides, and leaned down to me. "Come with me right now," he whispered.

I stood. "We're coming."

I looked down at my mother, who seemed shocked by Barney's tone. He might as well have screamed YOU'RE GOING DOWN. "We found the knife, and a bloody shirt," he said.

"What knife?" asked my mother. "I don't know anything about a knife, and there is no bloody shirt at my house."

"Listen," interrupted Barney, "don't say anything, either one of you. I talked the sheriff into letting me come and bring you from the restaurant so you can be arrested at home, in private."

"I'm being arrested?"

Barney grimaced. "Please don't say anything more. The sheriff will explain."

Sheriff Ben and Lonnie Richardson, one of the aggravating deputies from Alpine, were standing by the sheriff's truck in Mom's driveway. Evidence bags were lying on the hood in silent accusation.

The sheriff walked purposefully towards us. "Dr. Ricos," he said, "you're under arrest for the murder of Norma Bates. Deputy Richardson, please recite her rights."

I was so surprised I didn't speak. I heard the words I'd memorized but seldom used. Mom nodded and said that she understood.

Sheriff Ben came up beside her. "I won't cuff you," he said, "because I expect full cooperation. Don't disappoint me."

He guided her into the rear seat of his truck. Deputy Richardson stepped up into the front and sat there stone-faced, as if to guard the dangerous prisoner. I stood numb in my tracks while they were preparing to take away my mother.

"Deputy Ricos," said the sheriff, "I have to follow protocol on this. I'm officially removing you from the case, but I won't keep you in the dark."

He removed the bags from the hood. I wanted to grab them away from him and—do what? Destroy the evidence? It was late for that.

"Yes sir, but may I look at those?"

"No, right now you may not. This evidence is going to the Midland Crime Lab. When they've done the tests, you can look at it all you want."

"There's too much blood on the shirt," I said, craning towards it, angry with the sheriff and angry in general. "Somebody soaked it with blood."

"Deputy Ricos, you are no longer on this case."

"But you don't even know if that's Norma's blood."

"That's why we use a crime lab."

"I don't see how you can arrest my mother on such bogus evidence. Someone—"

"Deputy Ricos," said the sheriff, "Step over here with me." He gave me no choice since he took me by the arm and tugged me along next to him.

In a low voice he said, "If you want to stay in the loop on this, I'd appreciate it if you'd keep your comments to yourself. I'm doing my job, which is difficult enough when I have to arrest someone I know and respect. The lab will tell us the facts. What we need here are facts, Deputy."

His look was stern but his eyes were kind. "I know how upsetting this must be for you. I don't want to take your mother to jail, but understand that her hair was at the crime scene, a bloody knife has been found on her property, and a blood-stained shirt was hidden in her closet. In addition, we have a note in her own hand indicating a clear desire to kill Norma. Now let me do what I have to do without making it as difficult as you possibly can."

"Yes sir, I know you're right."

"I'm going to question your mother this afternoon and you may be there if you wish. Now buck up, your mom needs you to be strong."

He patted my shoulder and turned away, nodding at Barney. Then he climbed into his truck and started it.

"I'll call an attorney," I said to Mom.

"I don't need an attorney."

"You should have an attorney present during questioning," said the sheriff. "I strongly recommend it."

"I'm calling," I said with authority. "You'll change your mind." Then I hissed at her, not meaning to sound so harsh, "This is serious, Mom."

She said nothing, but her grim expression told me she knew it was. I reached out and touched her trembling hand, feeling guilty for jumping on her and ineffective as hell. What now, Super Deputy?

Then, like you see in the movies, the sheriff and his deputy rode off in a cloud of dust with the criminal. Only problem was, they had my mother.

I turned to Barney. "Where did you find the knife? And what's with that shirt?"

"The knife was in the brick planter out front, buried about four inches deep. The shirt was in her closet at the bottom of a storage container full of winter clothes. Somebody is trying to frame your mother, Ricos. We have to figure out who that is."

My mind ran off in all directions. When I didn't speak he continued. "Think about it, if she killed Norma, don't you think she would've thrown the knife away in a mine shaft or buried it somewhere out in the desert? Only an idiot would bury it in their own front yard."

"It happens all the time and you know it. Besides, even if it is a frame job, the sheriff bought it."

"No he didn't. He's following protocol, like he said. The murder weapon was found in her yard and a bloody shirt was hidden in her closet, so he has to take her in for questioning."

"He arrested her, Barney, and took her to jail."

"Okay, Ricos, I get it that you're freaked. You have to calm down so we can think rationally about this. Your mom will be out by tomorrow, I'm sure."

"My mother can't spend the night in jail!"

"Let's get going. The sheriff expects us and we have questions for him, too."

I stood there silently, thinking dark thoughts.

"Take heart, Ricos," said Barney. "You know the evidence will tell the true story. It always does. Sheriff knows that, too."

"There's too much blood on that shirt."

"We'll figure it out."

* * *

My mom was seated at a heavy metal table in a small, drab interrogation room. There was a cold bottle of water sitting in front of her, making a sweat circle on the table. Barney and I were watching through a one-sided glass window. I had seen this scenario before, but it looked wrong with my mother in it.

The attorney I called earlier was there, too. His name was Lloyd Preston and he was slightly younger than Mom and dressed in a three-piece suit and expensive-looking shoes. It always surprised me to see suits. Even attorneys in court in Alpine seldom wear them. Sport coats and blue jeans are usually the mode of dress for the good ol' boys of the west Texas legal system.

"Are you comfortable, Ms. Ricos?" The sheriff asked in his gentlemanly way.

"Yes, I'm fine."

"Let's talk first about 'Killing for Health.' As you know, we have a paper on which you'd written that Norma was the first to go. I've heard a recording of a conversation you had with Deputy George and in it you claim this was a tongue-in-cheek expression used by yourself and a few others."

"That's what it was," said my mother, more defensively than I would've liked. I wanted her be cool, detached—yeah, right. She was the *accused* and even I took it personally.

"'Killing for Health' was an expression used by Sylvia and me when we encountered people who thought it was wrong to take medical care into Mexico using resources mostly from the U.S., or people who stood in our way of helping anybody."

"Could you give me an example?"

"Well, sure. Sylvia told me about someone saying that donated American money shouldn't be used to help people on the other side of the river. I made the comment that people like that shouldn't be allowed to live. Sylvia would say 'Killing for Health' under her breath. Or we'd see some other outrage or unfair thing and we'd look at each other and say 'Killing for Health'. It was a motto, a promise to each other that we were going to do all we could for people who needed medical care and either couldn't reach it or afford it. That's all—it wasn't a real threat to anyone. I could give you hundreds of examples, but it would only bore you."

"How did that phrase get started?"

"We were at Sylvia's restaurant talking about my idea of a volunteer force of doctors that would treat patients along the border. As you probably know, the border is underserved, no matter which side you're standing on. Sylvia got on her high horse about the Border Patrol not letting her help the people in La Linda. We complained about the unfairness and then she said something like, 'if people can kill for money or vengeance or hatred, or even for Jesus, why not kill for the right to good health?' In the next breath she said, 'killing for health'. We've used that phrase ever since."

"Were you involved in helping people in La Linda?"

"Yes, I went over there at her insistence. There were people with untreated high blood pressure and diabetes, and a child with severe asthma. After that, Sylvia more or less adopted the pueblito and would make deliveries of medicine, and things like aspirin, Kleenex, bandages—things those people didn't have access to. She took the kids school supplies and little toys and yes, both of us knew what we were doing was technically illegal, but it was humanitarian outreach, not terrorism."

The sheriff changed the subject. "Do you own a hunting knife, Ms. Ricos?"

Barney and I looked at each other. Norma had been killed with a smooth-edged kitchen type of knife, not a hunting knife.

"You saw the one in the evidence bag. Did you recognize it?"

"Well, I couldn't see it very well, but I don't own a hunting knife or anything like a hunting knife."

"Would anyone else in your household own one?"

"No. I live alone and I'm not a hunter."

"What about your ex-husband?"

"He might have one but he wouldn't have killed her. He—"

"Yes ma'am. I'm only trying to determine if you could've gotten access to one."

"I can get anything I want," she said with attitude, "but why would I want a hunting knife? Someone else put that knife in my yard."

"You think someone set you up? Who would do that?"

"Someone who knows I'd come under suspicion, I guess. It would have to be someone who knows of the hard feelings between Norma and me. That would be just about anybody in the community."

"So you knew you'd be a suspect?"

"Yes, I knew. I had said I would kill her."

The sheriff watched her. Finally she said, "I threatened long ago that I would pay some guys to work her over, but it was just talk. I was so, so angry with her."

"And why was that?"

"She tried to destroy me both professionally and personally. She took a good thing I did and cast suspicions on it and accused me of—"

"I will let you tell me more about that in just a moment," Sheriff Ben interrupted her. "First, I want to ask you about something a witness said. He quotes you as saying, 'I'd like to hit her until her face is mushy and she's unrecognizable. Then I would stab her, and maybe shoot her, too.' Did you say that?"

Lloyd started to say something, but Mom held up her hand. "Yes, I said that and lots of ugly things. I don't deny it."

She paused and took a drink of water. "I thought seeing her face smashed against a brick wall would be satisfying, but I got past all that."

The sheriff tapped the table with a finger, thinking. "What about the shirt?" he asked at last. "Do you deny it's yours? It was found in a storage container in your closet among other clothes."

"The shirt is mine but I don't wear it because it doesn't fit me. And I don't keep it in a storage container. It hangs in my closet with my other clothes because I like to see it there. It has sentimental value to me."

"How so?"

"It was given to me by a friend when we were in Mazatlán together, years ago, before Margarita was born."

"So you're saying the shirt is yours but you can't wear it. Yet you keep it."

"I can't button it! Don't you think that maybe someone came into my closet and grabbed a pretty shirt, not knowing I haven't worn it since before I was pregnant?"

So that was the shirt.

"It's all wrong," I said to Barney. "If my mom was going to kill someone she would never wear that shirt even if it fit her. Her best friend Benny bought it for her in Mazatlán a long time ago."

Barney placed a hand on my back. "Stay cool, Ricos."

The shirt was made was of soft crinkly cotton and had several colorful parrots embroidered on it. I had seen it but had never seen her wear it. It was true what she said about the reason she kept it. She always said Benny bought it for her back in the day when she was skinny from all the running around they did together. She treasured it because her friend, now dead, gave it to her in a gesture of love.

The shirt was surely ruined, and from the look on Mom's face I could see she was thinking the same thought. Her eyes filled with tears and she was struggling to maintain her composure.

Lloyd turned to Mom. "You're sure the shirt doesn't fit?"

She gave him a look. "I'm sure."

"I believe you," he said, but sounded unconvinced.

There was a short break during which Marcy escorted Mom to the bathroom. Marcy and I are the only women deputies. We think we need more women; the men disagree, but not to our faces. It's an ongoing, non-violent dispute, like a cold war.

Barney and I took a break while we could, used the bathroom, and got something to drink. I caught the sheriff in the hall as he headed back to the interrogation room.

"May I speak with you a moment, sir?"

"Well, I'm busy. Is it relative to what I'm doing right now?"

"Yes sir, I have information that you don't have."

"Come into my office. Barney, you come too."

We went in and he shut the door. "What do you know that I need to know?"

"The earring found at the scene belongs to my mother, Sheriff. I didn't mean to withhold this information. I thought the lab would show that, but they didn't."

"Are you certain?"

"Yes sir. She has the matching one on her dresser. She doesn't know I was sneaking around in her house so please don't tell her."

"So you did an illegal search of your mother's house?"

"She's my mother. I'm in her house all the time. I grew up there."

"Yes, but you just asked me not to tell her. Your mother has the same rights as anyone else."

"I know that but, well, look—the more important thing is that I found her at the scene yesterday."

"Your mother was at the crime scene? Inside the house?"

"She was on the back porch crying. She hadn't been inside, but had gone there with that intention. The blood on the floor stopped her. I asked her why she wanted to go in and she told me that Norma had been blackmailing her but she wouldn't tell me why. I feel like I'm giving her up but I don't know what else to do. And there's something wrong with the evidence you gathered at her house, sir."

The sheriff glared at me, but then Barney spoke. "According to the autopsy, Norma was stabbed with a smooth-bladed kitchen knife. Maybe you didn't notice that on the report, Sheriff. So the hunting knife doesn't fit. Norma's blood might be on it but she wasn't stabbed with it."

Sheriff Ben looked like we'd slapped him. "What in the hell is going on here?" He stood and began to pace. "Maybe the blood belongs to someone else. We won't know that until the crime lab tests it." He looked like a madman running his hands through his hair. "I jumped to conclusions because of the Bates woman's murder. But no one else has been murdered."

"Not that we know of," Barney said. "For all we know it's animal blood."

"How do you explain the shirt?"

"The thing you have to know about the shirt is that even if my mom was going to kill someone, she would never wear that shirt, even if it fit her, which it doesn't. The shirt has significant sentimental value to her, Sheriff."

Another bloody shirt drifted by in my brain, but I shoved the thought aside; one bloody shirt at a time.

"Something is wrong," said the sheriff, "but I've no idea what."

I was trying hard to make sense of it. If someone had set up my mother, then she couldn't have killed Norma. That should have given me comfort, but like the sheriff said, there was something wrong—we just didn't know what it was.

Chapter 22

"Now," the Sheriff said as he seated himself again, "I would like to hear from you exactly what happened to make you want to harm Norma Bates."

Lloyd started to give my mom advice but she quieted him with a look. She had that look down, and it stopped him cold.

"I'd like to do that," she said, then glanced at her poor attorney, who evidently wasn't going to try to stop her again.

"Good," said the sheriff, smiling at her. "Just start whenever you're ready."

Mom took a deep breath before she began. "Norma got on our board of directors under false pretenses. She talked like she knew everything about boards and said she had years of experience serving on them. But then, a lot of the things she said were not true. She was a silver-tongued devil."

Barney and I laughed at that expression.

"Lil Munch came onto our board before Norma did, and we were trying to add more members. We needed people who would be committed to doing the work it was going to take to make a success of the organization. At first, none of us knew what we were doing board-wise, so nobody noticed that Norma lied her way in. She was not what you could call a great leader, but she tried. We thought her heart was in it. She spent time with me learning about the details of the operation of Doctores Fronterizos, and the history of how I got it started. She admired my dedication and complimented me on various things, and it seemed sincere at the time. Only my daughter had reservations about her and warned me repeatedly not to take her into my confidence."

"Good job, Ricos!" Barney slapped me so hard on the back I stumbled into the glass window. He grabbed my arm to steady me. "Sorry," he mumbled, and drew me back to where I'd been standing.

My mom was moving on in her story. It wasn't like I didn't know every bit of it, but I wanted to hear exactly what she told the sheriff.

"Lil's husband was killed in a construction accident and she was distraught and unable to cope with her job as treasurer. She begged the board not to replace her, said she'd be back when she could get it together. Of course we all went along with it. We felt terrible for her. In the meantime, it was decided that I would do her job because I knew the most about the operation, since I was the one who started it and the only one who had run it.

"Norma had insisted I be put on the bank account months earlier. I believe that was step one of setting me up. I was responsible for paying the bills and entered everything into the computer program and then made the treasurer's report. Sometimes Lil would look at it and deliver it herself. More often I gave it because Lil was not present at meetings. Not one board member ever questioned the reports or asked me any questions about them, or seemed to care about them."

Mom took a deep breath and kept going. "I was being paid as director, but it was very little and only when there was money. Most months we barely paid the minimum bills and we only did that because we did a lot of local fundraisers. I was writing grant proposals, but the problem with getting grants when you're a new organization is that nobody wants to take a chance on you. Meanwhile I had run through my savings so things were sometimes shaky."

The sheriff and her attorney watched her intently.

"I'm not complaining," she added. "I knew what I was doing and did it willingly. I really wanted this for my community, which to me includes the other side of the Rio Grande. I believed it would eventually get funding and the tough days would be behind us. I was right, too, only I had Hell to go through first." Mom paused and finished the bottle of water.

"Would you like another?" the sheriff asked. She said yes and he went to get it.

Lloyd leaned over and said something to her in a low voice and she nodded but didn't say anything to him as far as we could tell.

The sheriff came back with another bottle, and after she thanked him, Mom continued. "Everything was going along well, as far as I knew. We were serving more patients, garnering more community support, and plans were underway to build a clinic near the river. Imagine my surprise when I left on a short vacation and came back to find I was under suspicion. The board met while I was gone, and Norma and Lil told them there were discrepancies in the books and that I was stealing money. There was no money to steal!"

Mom was so angry I thought she'd start throwing things. These were memories best left behind, not sifted through now and again to see if they still stung.

She continued. "I don't steal. That's not who I am. I'm a doctor. I saw a need for an organization of this type. Many people here are poor and don't seek medical advice. What occupied my mind was how I could get the operation better funded, and how we could serve more people who needed us. Believe me when I say if I'd wanted to get rich, I would've started a business and not a non-profit organization. I have a medical degree and could have opened a for-profit practice." The way she said it no thinking person would argue with her.

"So," she continued, "there were a lot of other similar false accusations. In short, I was set up to take a fall by two women who had their own agenda and it wasn't about helping people. I think Norma wanted to take over so she could get credit. She was all about being a hero but didn't want to put forth much effort. Someone with a degree in medicine needed to head it up. And it had to be someone who spoke Spanish and knew rural Mexico. Norma wanted there to be a crisis so she could swoop in and save the day. The only way she could do that was to discredit me."

"And Lil Munch?" asked the sheriff. "What would she get out of the takeover?"

Mom didn't hesitate before she replied. "Lil is just stupid. She's easily led and she bought into Norma's lies and went along with her. I don't think she's ever had an independent thought in her life. But she was all puffed up with importance as Chief Financial Officer.

"Also, I don't think Lil understood the concept of someone doing something good for someone else with no thought of personal gain. She was always on my back about why I'd be willing to work for low pay since I have a medical degree. She wondered out loud why I would sink my own money into the project, and so on. I felt sorry for her, even then, because she has such a restricted view of things. She's suspicious and narrow-minded and lacks heart."

"That pretty well describes Lil Ass-Munch," I said.

"She's a bitch," spit Barney. "And did I mention what a whiner she is?"

"I think you did."

"World class."

"Right."

Mom was still telling her story. "Norma began calling various community leaders and asking who they'd recommend for director. When they expressed surprise that I wasn't continuing, she told them I was on administrative leave, and hinted about the grievous wrongdoings. I was not on any kind of leave except vacation.

"Lil and Norma held an illegal board meeting and put me on leave. They also stole the checkbook and took the money out of the bank account so it couldn't be stolen or misappropriated, and of course that left us with no operating cash.

"What neither of them counted on was my longtime reputation in the community. Most people blew Norma off. She was known as weird and cruel. I am known as The Doc. The truth of the matter is that Norma did what she did with no remorse, no feelings. She didn't care who she hurt as long as she got her way."

The sheriff shifted in his chair, trying to find a comfortable position. He scrutinized Mom for what seemed like a long time.

"I'm getting a clear picture of why you'd think that woman's face would look good smashed up against a brick wall," he said, glancing over at Lloyd.

"She made up lies about me, tried to ruin my reputation, attempted to close down Doctores Fronterizos, sued to oust the other members of the board, sued to stop all expenditures of money—I could go on. Really, I thought killing was too good for her, too easy and painless. The thing I thought about most was slapping that smugness off her face—not a lady-like slap. What I'm talking about is more of a punch than a slap."

Mom took a long drink of water. "When the lawsuit went to mediation, Maude, our secretary, kept us on goal by reminding us that we were about helping people in need and the sooner we finished mediation, the sooner we'd get back to doing that. During the middle of it, she said something I'll never forget. Some of us were distraught that we were going to get no money restitution or public apologies, but her wise words kept us on track."

"What did she say?"

"She said, 'The best revenge is living well' and we heard the truth of it."

"Actually," said Lloyd, gathering the guts to speak, "it's from the Talmud. The actual quote is: Live well. It is the greatest revenge."

"Yes, well, we'd been told once the lawsuit was settled we'd be approved for a large grant from a national organization, and that's what our side wanted more than anything. That was going to put us on the map, so to speak. To us, it did seem like the best revenge."

The sheriff nodded in understanding, then leaned back in his chair. "Ms. Ricos, the thing you haven't mentioned is that you were being blackmailed by Norma Bates. How could you fail to tell me something so important to this case?"

"Well I—I—"

My mother knew I'd given her up. I felt like the biggest traitor on the planet. Who gives up their own mother?

She sighed and drank water again, stalling. "I don't know anything about that, Sheriff Duncan."

I was speechless.

"Is that so?" The sheriff seemed stunned.

"I think you're mistaken."

"I don't believe I'm mistaken."

"With all due respect," my mother said, "I think you are."

"You didn't tell your daughter yesterday that you were being blackmailed by Norma Bates?"

"I did speak with my daughter yesterday, but I think she may have misunderstood what I said."

Barney and I stared at each other in disbelief.

"Well, Ms. Ricos, you're going to have plenty of time to think about this because I'm not going to let you go until I receive all of the crime lab reports. Is there anything else you wish to tell me before Marcy takes you back to the jail?"

"No sir."

"I'll get Marcy then." He rose and left the room.

I watched in shocked silence as Marcy came in, took my mother by the arm, and led her away. I couldn't believe my mother was going to jail. On the other hand, I was thinking she belonged there.

I went to see her after she'd been processed in and was sitting alone in a cell. She was crying and wouldn't look at me.

"Mom, please tell me the truth. Whatever it is I'll help you. I love you, Mom. You have to let me help."

"You really don't get it, do you? You always were the most hard-headed girl."

"Don't get what?"

"This is all about you. It's you I have to protect." That's all she would say, no matter how much I begged her.

The depression I had felt for over a year got a little worse.

* * *

My mom was going to be in jail until the reports from the lab were ready and could be studied by the sheriff and the district attorney. That would be at least a week, probably. The sheriff was going to try to wear her down about the blackmail. My mother though, is more hard-headed than I am. Still, the sheriff said to leave it with him. I thought maybe he could charm the truth out of her.

Presuming my mom was innocent, which I wanted desperately to believe, I thought I should continue my pursuit of other leads. I was officially off the case, but it couldn't hurt to nose around unofficially.

Anyway, on a hunch I called Dr. Estrada's office and asked if I could see her for ten or fifteen minutes about a murder case. She was the psychiatrist recommended to me by Sheriff Ben. Her secretary told me to come on, the doctor was in.

Dr. Estrada is a tiny Latina and was impeccably dressed in a three-piece suit and death-defying high heels. I guessed she was in her early fifties, around the age of my mother. I liked her immediately because of her warm smile.

"How can I help you, Deputy Ricos?"

"I'm working on a murder case, and I thought if I understood the victim better I could understand her killer, and that might give me a lead I don't have now."

"I commend your thinking. I believe that's probably true in most murders."

I proceeded to describe Norma Bates as fairly and accurately as I could, not calling her names or trashing her any more than necessary, but also not leaving out the terrible things she had done.

"Among other things," I said, "she seemed without conscience and didn't care who she hurt. Even her husband said she was a cold woman who didn't love him but wanted to live with him and raise their children."

"Sounds like a sociopath," Dr. Estrada said when I'd told her what I could. "A sociopath is said to have Antisocial Personality Disorder. Individuals with this disorder have little regard for the feelings and welfare of other people. They mimic the emotions of others but they don't truly share those emotions."

She recited a list of APD general symptoms and wrote them down for me as she spoke. When she handed me the list she added, "People with this disorder may exhibit criminal behavior. They often don't work, or if they do, they're frequently absent or quit suddenly. They don't consider other people's wishes, welfare, or rights. They can be manipulative and may lie to gain personal pleasure or profit."

"That sounds like her. Almost everything you've said sounds like her."

"Impulsiveness, aggressiveness, irritability, irresponsibility, and a reckless disregard for their own safety and the safety of others are traits of an antisocial personality, too."

"Do you think my victim had Antisocial Personality Disorder?"

"I think it's likely, yes, but I hesitate to try to diagnose her since there is no way I can meet her. Based solely on what you've told me, and for your purposes, let's say she did have APD. Your killer will be someone who was harmed by her. Normal people expect others to feel remorse over the bad things they do. An APD personality has no idea about remorse, which the rest of us find frustrating. I have a print-out here somewhere that lists characteristics and a more detailed explanation." She was digging in a file drawer in her desk and eventually handed me a list of the common characteristics of sociopaths. I skim-read it, but wanted to take it and read it carefully.

"In addition to persons harmed by your murder victim," Dr. Estrada said, "you might look for her accomplices."

Lil Munch.

"These are people who think they're friends with the APD person. For instance, your victim might have taken a so-called friend into her confidence, and that person went along with her plan for a while. Eventually though, an accomplice will become a victim because an APD doesn't have friends, can't form friendships, and will have to have everything their way. Does that make sense?"

"Yes, it does."

"And if things don't go exactly as planned," Dr. Estrada continued, "the APD will blame their so-called friend and can make their life miserable. They tend to raise the kind of emotions that can lead to murder."

Lil Munch had been an accomplice to a sociopath. Had she then become her victim? And had she struck back?

For a while we talked about law enforcement work. Before I left I said, "I have a friend whose husband was killed in a gruesome accident. She loved him very much and can't believe he's gone. She has bad dreams, wants to drink, holds onto the clothes he was wearing when he died, and is nearly always sad. She wants to move on, but isn't doing very well with that. Do you think you could help her?"

Dr. Estrada leaned back in her chair and seemed to be contemplating what I had said. "Yes, Deputy Ricos," she finally confirmed, "I believe I could help you."

Chapter 23

I wanted to hang around Alpine because my mother was there. I wanted to go home and pursue other serious suspects. I wanted my mother to have been framed—or whatever it took for her to be innocent. I wanted to drink. Badly. What I decided I wanted most was a good strong dose of Austin Williams. So instead of going home I got a motel room, called Austin, and told him I needed him. He made me feel like that made his day, and my spirits lifted.

"Can you meet me at the rodeo arena?" he asked. "I'm just finishing up work." Austin worked at the university's stables.

I told him I'd be there in ten minutes. When I arrived I saw that a student/ local cowboy competition was going on. Not a real rodeo. Still, my heart sank. I avoided rodeos—real or not—and everything associated with them. I told myself not to be a baby. I would go in, hold my head up, and bring Austin out. Maybe there wouldn't be any bulls. It couldn't get bad unless I thought about Kevin riding and winning for the same club when he was in college. I wouldn't think of it—the answer was simple.

When I went in the side entrance, there was a clown riding a donkey into the middle of the arena. The donkey stopped and wouldn't budge no matter what the clown said or which antic he tried.

I heard Austin's laughter before I saw him. He was leaning against the cattle fencing that separated the arena and the stalls. When I spotted him I felt my heart fill up and spill over. I should have come to see him long before now. His love was a salve on my wounds.

Austin loved everything about rodeo. I hated everything about it. He especially liked bull riding, which I especially hated. He was a member of the Rodeo Club, but rarely attended its meetings or events now because of repeated trouble with another member, Gil Young.

Austin was one of many members who supported the sport of rodeo but didn't compete. He was around the animals a lot and was paid by the university to muck the stalls, and help feed and water the horses and other animals in the corrals there. He used to hang around and watch when the rodeo team was practicing.

Once, after he and Gil had words at a club meeting, Austin was watching the practice. Gil was showing off on his horse. He noticed Austin and didn't like it, even though he was only leaning against the fence to observe, not bothering anybody. Gil yelled, "What are you looking at, retard?"

Unused to such treatment, Austin looked around, searching for someone else, not understanding that Gil would say such a terrible thing to him. This caused laughter among onlookers, and Austin ran and hid in the stalls.

This rough treatment of a handicapped man did not sit well with some of the other team members and they had a loud argument with Gil. After that practice, when nearly everyone had gone, Gil physically assaulted Austin, sending him flying into a fresh pile of horse manure that Austin had recently shoveled from the stalls. Gil and his followers laughed and sauntered off. Austin had not been physically hurt, but his pride and self-confidence were wounded. It took a long time for him to recover from that incident.

Gil was a senior who competed and took rodeo and himself seriously. He believed club members who didn't compete were 'pussies' and liked to announce it loudly.

He found Austin's excited outbursts irritating; his inability to express himself as clearly and quickly as others was intolerable to Gil. Several times, he'd shoved Austin hard into the arena fencing, intimidating him, and calling him Rodeo Pussy and similar names. He always managed to do those things when there were no witnesses except some of his witless redneck followers.

Now Austin went to great lengths to avoid the bully and his sidekicks. He worked when he figured they were in classes, and had mostly given up bull riding and barrel racing, events he loved.

I came up behind Austin and put my arms around him. "Hey, Big Guy."

"Margarita!" His pleasure was so instant it sent my spirits soaring. When he turned around and gave me a tight hug, I didn't want to let him go.

"I was just watching the clown," he said.

I couldn't help but notice a bull waiting in a chute to my right. "Are you through here?" I asked, even though I knew he'd want to stay.

"Yeah, but let's sit in the stands. We shouldn't leave yet." Austin started to move in that direction.

"Let's get something to eat," I said.

We could have made a clean getaway, but I wasn't quick enough. Suddenly a bull burst out of the chute. Austin grabbed the fence, enthralled. I grabbed it too, sick to my stomach.

The bull bucked the cowboy to the ground and I had to look away. A woman was singing *I Wanna Be a Cowboy's Sweetheart* over the loudspeaker. It sounded like a good idea that could go wrong in eight seconds or less.

Gil was up next. He was sitting tall, cocky as hell, waiting for the gate to open. A few people were cheering him on, attention he seemed to crave. As the bull rushed forward, leaping wildly, Gil was thrown from the animal and landed face down in a pile of wet manure. He hadn't made it five seconds, let alone eight. Austin laughed out loud; one of his noisy, unmistakable snorting laughs. Gil rose, took the handkerchief the clown offered, and began wiping his face. He searched for Austin in the crowd, his eyes full of fire.

"He fell in the bullshit," Austin said loudly, still laughing. "The bull threw him in it! Did you see that, Margarita? He fell right into the shit!"

Gil found us quickly, his look murderous. That was bad; Austin would be in danger now for sure.

"Let's go, Austin."

"But it's not over," he wailed.

"I have to go." I began pulling on him.

"Gosh," he said, thinking I was angry. "Gosh."

I tried to assure him everything was okay as we hurried out of the arena into the parking lot. "Let's go have a beer."

Austin loved to go out for a beer and I badly needed one. We headed for a country-western bar he liked because of the music. When I was in college, he and I would visit The Wrangler bar and grill. If anyone in the group knew Austin, he'd be invited to sing. His voice enhanced any band, even weak ones, and he could sing anything. Country was his favorite, but I'd heard him sing blues, pop, hymns, and tunes from musicals.

Once we settled at a table with beers and nachos, I tried to explain to Austin why we left the rodeo so suddenly. I didn't want to scare him, but I wanted him to be wary of Gil Young. I didn't know if Gil would seriously hurt Austin, but I'd rather he never had the chance. Austin seemed to understand.

"You're very sad," he said. It wasn't a question.

"Yes." There was no point in lying to him. He saw right through to my soul.

"Is it because of the murder, or because of Kevin?"

"It's because of the murder of Kevin."

"Kevin wasn't murdered, Margarita. It was an accident."

"Same outcome."

"It wasn't the bull's fault. It wasn't anyone's fault. Sometimes bad things happen and nobody knows why."

Austin watched me with clear green eyes. I smiled at him. He smiled back. Finally I said, "It helps me to blame the bull."

"No it doesn't. It keeps you from going on. It keeps you from living again." *Man.*

After a while we danced. Then, as I thought would happen, Austin was asked to sing. He stood on stage, looking serious and nervous. A few people always laugh when they see him go onstage, but when he opens his mouth things change.

I clapped hard when the song was over. He was asked to stay for one more and agreed.

Austin sang,

I want to ride to the ridge where the West commences
Gaze at the moon until I lose my senses
I can't look at hovels and I can't stand fences
Don't fence me in.

It was beautiful, better than Gene Autry did it or anybody since him.

When that set ended, Austin came back to the booth with two beers.

"You sounded great, Austin."

"Thanks. They wanted me to stay but I want to talk to you."

* * *

After about twenty minutes the band asked Austin to sing again.

"Go on, Austin, it's okay."

"Are you sure?"

"I love to hear you sing."

Towards the end of the set, when Austin was really into the singing, in walked Gil and his faithful few with some bronco betties in tow. Bullies always act worse in front of their women, more macho and belligerent. Gil coming in was not good. Austin was in the spotlight and couldn't see who was watching him. There was no way I could make an escape without leaving him behind.

"Well, I'll be damned," said Gil to his entourage. "The fucking retard can really sing." I was sure he already knew that but was showing off for the girls. What kind of girls would be impressed by Gil, I wondered.

"May I have a word with you, Gil?" I asked politely.

Gil Young is a tall drink of water—cowboy talk for long and lean. He has wavy brown hair that touches the collar of his western shirt. His eyes are dark and sit in a handsome, chiseled face made less attractive by his personality. To know him is to think he's really not all that hot. He thinks he is though, and I realized that because I was looking him over, he assumed I was coming on to him. Crap.

The entourage turned to look when I spoke.

"'Bout what?" Gil said casually, making sure I got the impression he couldn't care less what I had to say. I had his attention, though.

On stage, Austin was singing *My Shoes Keep Walking Back to You* to a now-clapping and cheering crowd. I had to move closer to Gil to be heard.

"I want to talk to you about Austin Williams," I said.

"The retard?"

This caused one of the women to giggle. I glared at her and the laugh stopped almost as abruptly as if I'd slapped her in the face, which I would've enjoyed.

"He has a name," I said.

"It's Retard," said one of Gil's followers who was wearing super-tight jeans—jeans so tight I could see the outline of his entire package. Not that I was looking. He was also wearing cowboy boots with shiny spurs, but I had the feeling he never participated in rodeo. He pushed his sweat-soiled hat back on his head to get a better look at me, and started to take a cigarette from the torn pocket of his western shirt.

"I'd be careful about name-calling," I said.

"Aw, you jealous? You want your own special name?"

I turned from the bogus cowboy to face Gil. "Please let me have a word with you over at the bar."

I chose the bar because Mike, the owner of the joint, was standing there listening to Austin, and was one of Austin's biggest fans. He also liked me, and

I knew if Gil started something, he'd throw him out without hesitation. Also, Mike was built for bouncing, with well-developed arms and a thick neck. He worked out and looked like it. He was a man I wanted on my side when the cowboys stampeded.

Suddenly Gil turned gentlemanly. "What are you drinking?" He eyed me like I might want to get it on with him and he didn't want to miss the opportunity.

"Corona," I said, and he indicated to the bartender that we'd have two of them.

"So what about the retard? You say he's a friend of yours. You aren't screwing him, are you? Now that'd be kinky as all get-out."

I held up my hand. "Whoa there."

"She's gay," said a man sitting on the stool next to mine. "Aren't you?" He leered at me. He had seen me there before with Vic and Morgan, my lesbian friends. We had been dancing and drinking and he had assumed whatever he wanted to.

I ignored him and said to Gil, "Look, I want to tell you that Austin has Down syndrome. He was born with an extra chromosome that causes certain attributes. Yes, he's somewhat retarded in ways, advanced in others. He can understand all the meanness you heap on him, and he gets his feelings hurt just like anyone else."

"I don't like him," he said, end of argument.

"That's your prerogative."

"Damn right it is."

"Couldn't you be kinder? He just wants to be around the animals. It seems like that's something the two of you have in common."

"We don't have anything in common," he sneered. He took a long drink of beer, studying me. "I think you're fucking him. Is a big dick one of his special attributes?"

"Will you get off that? He's like a brother to me."

"I'm telling you she's a dyke," said my shit-faced friend on the next stool, still leering at me. "Shame," he added.

"I have a big dick," said Gil, absently touching his crotch. "Wanna see it?"

"She don't like dick," insisted the drunk.

It was a comedy routine gone wrong. Mike had caught wind of the conversation and moved closer. He was ready for trouble, his powerful arms folded over his chest.

"All I'm asking," I continued, "is that you treat him like a person. He has feelings like everyone else. He's not some cartoon character for you to poke fun at."

I knew I was pleading and hated it, but I desperately wanted him to leave Austin alone. I desperately want to kick his ass too, but I didn't have much hope of doing it with his crew spread out around the bar, waiting for trouble. Also, I realized, I was still in Sheriff Ben's county, and I couldn't be caught drinking beer and making a scene.

"You are fucking him," Gil whispered, "you really are."

I felt sure my drunken neighbor was starting to say something so I turned towards him. "Just save it, will you?"

"I'm saving it for you, honey," he said, and waved a hand in the general direction of his crotch.

"Okay," said Gil, standing closer. "I'll never bother him again if you'll go out to my truck with me. I want to feel those sexy lips on my di—"

"That's it," roared Mike. He leaned across the bar into Gil's face. "I've heard enough. This is not a brothel. I've told you this before, Gil. Now shape up or get out and do one thing or the other right now!"

"I was just leaving," Gil said, then to me, "My truck, Sweet Lips?"

"In your dreams."

"I'm telling you she's a—"

"Yeah, yeah, I know. She's a dyke." Gil stood, smoothing his jeans and looking me up and down slowly. "If she's a dyke I'll suck your dick right here."

"Get on your knees," said the drunk, beginning to fumble with his zipper.

"OUT!" screamed Mike.

Gil headed for the door followed by his groupies, the cowboys and would-be cowboys and betties, who had mostly missed all the fun.

"Better put your pants back on," Mike said to the drunk. He didn't seem to get the joke.

When Austin finished that set we left. I took him by his house so he could get some things and he came to the motel with me. We showered, changed into pajamas, and then sat on the bed laughing, drinking sodas, and watching old movies. At nearly midnight we ordered pizza and stuffed ourselves. For a while we dozed, bloated and exhausted. When I opened my eyes, Austin was looking at me.

"I love you, Austin."

"I love you, Margarita. I want you to be happy again."

"You make me happy."

"That's not how it works," said the man Gil called retarded. "You have to make yourself happy."

"Okay, true, what I mean to say is that you make that easy when I'm with you."

Austin put his arms around me and pulled me close. "Tell me why you're not better."

He was always doing that to me, getting right to the heart of things. Austin was never afraid to approach things head-on. In fact, it was the only way he knew. If you ask Austin how he is he'll tell you. You can take it to the bank.

I laid my head against his broad chest and cried. He smelled clean, and slightly of soap. Austin said nothing, but his love covered me like a warm blanket.

Maybe I was thinking of cowboys. I don't know what made me say it, but after a long time I said, "I guess Kevin is off somewhere riding the wind."

"I don't think so," Austin said softly. "He's in the wind."

I spilled my heart to my best friend. "I told him I didn't care if he ever came home from Amarillo," I sobbed.

"What do you mean?"

"Those were the last words I ever said to him."

"He knew you didn't mean it."

"Maybe he didn't come home because I said that."

"No. He wanted to come home. It was an accident, Margarita. It wasn't Kevin's fault—or your fault. It wasn't anybody's fault."

"I think it was my fault, that's why I blame the bull."

"It wasn't. Kevin probably laughed because he knew you loved him. Anybody who saw you together knew you were in love. Everybody says angry things sometimes." Austin spoke slowly, thinking things through, but his words were clear and came from his pure heart. My heart heard them.

Whenever I insulted Kevin he would laugh and walk away. It was so irritating. I once called him a shit-kicker, a term that angered him, but he laughed and walked off, and came back later to make love to me like it would be our last chance. I'd called him all kinds of things I didn't mean, and he always laughed. *God, you have a mouth on you*, he had said more than once.

I realized, in a moment of clarity that came in spite of the late hour, that what Austin said was true. Kevin had known my heart. If he could have chosen he would have chosen to come home. I felt the weight of a hundred bulls lift off my heart and I slept like a baby, cuddled against the best man I knew, apart from Kevin.

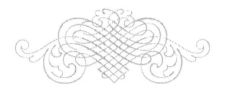

Chapter 24

Before I headed home, I tried again to get my mother to confide in me. It was impossible for me to believe that she wouldn't, but she didn't. She was angry about being in the county jail and I was angry, too. Her situation wasn't likely to change soon unless she came clean with the sheriff.

"I want you to be innocent," I said when I was saying good-bye. Mom said she loved me and that I should take care of myself. She said a lot of things, but she never said she was innocent.

On the way home, I had to pass the subdivision where Lil had bought a fancy new home after her husband's death. I turned in there, wondering about a few things. As I drove up the cottonwood tree-lined lane, I thought that if I had her money I would've bought a place with an awe-inspiring view, but maybe things like scenery and the beauty of the natural world didn't matter to a woman like Lil.

As Norma had been only about Norma, Lil was all about Lil. After speaking with Dr. Estrada I was convinced they had never even been about each other, which was what was causing me to do the wondering.

When Lil opened the door, her displeasure at seeing me was so obvious it was comical.

"Hello, Lil," I said, and removed my hat. "May I speak to you a moment?"

I'd picked up a fresh uniform at the cleaner's and knew I looked as sharp as the knife that ended Norma's miserable life. When I went anywhere I liked to look good, but when I was preparing to face an enemy I made an extra effort.

"I suppose you want to come in," she said with a sigh.

I stepped inside. "Thank you for the hospitality."

Her house was new and still smelled of fresh lumber. It was a pleasant odor, but under that was something that wasn't. The living room was beautifully decorated with expensive things, but I thought it was an unhappy little woman's attempt to make herself seem as normal and worthwhile as the next person. I found that sad but didn't dwell on it. I sat on the edge of a beige sofa, where Lil indicated I should.

"I hope this won't take long," she said.

"I just have a few questions."

"More questions? Couldn't you gather them up and ask them all at once instead of constantly bothering people?"

"It would be nice if investigating worked that way, but it doesn't." I didn't bother to try to explain it.

"What do you want to know now?"

"Do you know a man named Chapo Rodriguez?"

An odd look passed over her face. "No. Who is he?"

"Well, perhaps it doesn't matter. If you don't know him then it doesn't." Except I thought she did.

"You said that you and Norma were still close. Didn't you say that?"

She sighed. "Yes, that's what I said."

"Stanner says you weren't. He told me Norma had pulled away from you because she blamed you for the mess at Doctores Fronterizos. He said you never saw each other much after that."

Lil's eyes filled with tears and she looked away from me. "That's not true. Stanner didn't know anything about our friendship, or about what Norma did when she wasn't with him."

Lil stood and began to rearrange the books and magazines on the coffee table. I thought it was odd and it left me fairly speechless. After they were perfectly stacked, largest on the bottom and in order from largest to smallest, she made sure the edges came together just right. Then she moved to some attractive bookshelves nearby and began to rearrange the framed photos there. She checked all the books, running one finger over the spines. Everything looked perfectly in order to me, but she didn't seem satisfied. She glanced over her shoulder at me once with a furtive look. I wasn't sure what I should do. Did it mean something besides the general strangeness I'd always associated with Lil? I wondered what the sheriff would do.

"My husband's been dead two years," she said suddenly to a question I hadn't asked or even thought of.

"I know, Lil. I'm sorry."

"I was thinking of your husband," she said, really surprising me. "He was very young and handsome, wasn't he?"

"Yes, he was."

"Do you miss him?"

"So much." *All the time, every minute of every day and night.*

I wondered if I would become as obsessive as Lil. Suddenly my heart softened towards her. She had lost a husband, too. I didn't want her to be guilty of buying a murder—another thing I was wondering about. I wanted to leave her alone with her craziness and her memories. I wanted to get the hell out of her house and be alone to obsess on my own memories. I would run my finger along them like Lil did her books.

"Lil—"

"I know. I should do this later." She sat back down, just like that.

"I assume you didn't see Norma as often as you did when you were coming south for board meetings?"

"That's true but we were still friends, I don't care what Stanner thought. We would email and talk on the phone. Whenever she came to Alpine we'd go to lunch."

The emailing and phoning could be checked out with a warrant, not that I had much hope of getting one from our judge. Then I thought of another way to check her story. I stood and thanked Lil for her time.

She took the hand I offered. "I'm sorry about your husband," she said. "I mean it sincerely—even *you* didn't deserve that."

Huh. She had managed to stroke and slap me at the same time, typical Lil.

I roared back towards Terlingua with a lot of things dancing through my brain. My mother was acting squirrelly. Lil was pure squirrel. Roger Lockey had lied about the dogs being out. Chapo was up to something. Stanner was finally free of Norma. Alibi or not, with Norma out of his way, Gabe Stanton could now get custody of his son Joey, like he wanted. All of them appeared guilty—but of murder?

Was there someone else I was overlooking? That had to be it.

As I came off the hill onto the flats that stretched for miles towards the mountains of South County, a strong gust of wind shook the Explorer. I thought about Kevin being in the wind. If he was in the wind, then it stood to reason he was also in the mountains and the river, and the wide blue sky. He was in me and

I was in him and it would always be like that. I thought most likely that was all I was ever going to understand about it.

* * *

Barney looked up from his desk. "You look fantastic."

"Thanks. I feel—good. I haven't felt this good in a long time."

"You're coming back."

"Yes, I think I am."

"That's good, Ricos. I feel like hugging you."

"Do it then."

He came around his desk and gave me a bear hug. Afterwards he sat. "Did your mother give up her secrets?"

I took my usual place in front of his desk. "No. She refuses to talk to me. I'm going to talk to my dad and see if he knows anything."

"Sheriff Ben released the crime scene and it was cleaned up this morning by some of the maids from the Big Bend Motor Inn. The Bates family is back at home."

"That's great because I need to go back there and I was dreading that smell."

"Why are you going there again?"

"I want to look at Norma's computer. In fact, if Stanner will let me, I'm going to bring it here."

"What do you have in mind?"

"On the way back I stopped at Lil's. She insists that she and Norma were still friends and were emailing each other and phoning back and forth. She's lying and I think I can prove it."

"What's your point?"

"What if Lil stabbed her or paid Chapo to do it?"

"I think you're grasping at straws."

"Well, I have to grasp at something."

I told him about my talk with Dr. Estrada, which seemed to only mildly interest him, even when I showed him the papers she gave me. I couldn't get the *accomplices who become victims* idea out of my head.

"What about your mother?" he asked.

"I don't want her to be guilty."

He gave me a look, but was gracious enough not to say anything.

* * *

Stanner is a small man, not much taller than me. He always seemed serious, but when he opened the door he seemed smaller and sadder than I had ever seen him. His eyes were red, his clothes disheveled, and he needed a shave. When he shook my hand he looked like he would cry. It was hard to imagine him as a killer. He had always impressed me as kind and soft-spoken, the opposite of his abrasive wife.

"Are you all right, Stanner?"

"I'm fine. It's just hard without Norma, and the kids miss her so much."

"I apologize for not coming before to tell you how sorry I am."

"I know you're busy trying to find her killer."

"Yes, I am. May I look at your computer, Stanner?"

"Well, sure. You can take it if you need to. I barely know how to use it. Just bring it back when you're through with it. The kids play on it sometimes."

"I won't need it long."

"Do you think her killer was emailing her?"

"I don't know. I thought her emails might tell me something I don't know now. May I look at your long distance phone records, too?"

"Sure, if it helps you find Norma's killer, look at anything you like."

He took me to a desk and went through files until he came to phone records. The last phone call Norma made to Lil was six months after the Doctores Fronterizos lawsuit ended. That didn't mean Lil hadn't called her but I thought it was unlikely. With Stanner's records, I could get a court order for Lil's if I needed one, but I left them with him for the time being.

Norma's computer might have told me a lot if I was a genius with a computer but I'm not. Still, I could check her Sent Mail folder. It told the same story as the phone records, but in more detail.

The last email she sent to Lil read: *Please don't continue to contact me. You brought all this on yourself by being stupid and I have wasted a great deal of my time. I can't continue to be friends with you under any circumstance. Norma Bates.*

What a sweetheart.

I continued to nose around and found five emails she sent Lil about paying someone to do something. By putting all five together, I figured out that the two of them had been conspiring to have my mother killed. That was before the lawsuit and mediation, when they were still trying to get her to step down from her position.

Dr. Estrada had said it was Antisocial Personality Disorder. I thought Norma had been a remorseless bitch. I wondered where she had gone. I didn't believe in Hell, but I didn't think she was in the wind, either.

* * *

I was running back down my road. Darkness was settling on the land I loved and a sliver of moon was already up and alert, ready for what the night would bring. Ahead, in the last of the dying light, I could see my father's truck in front of my house. How convenient since he was on my list—inconvenient because I was wearing the shorts he kept forbidding me to wear.

He didn't seem to notice how I was dressed and that worried me. Something big was on his mind. I pulled on sweatpants, got us each a glass of water, and settled myself in a rocker in front of him.

"Qué pasa, Papi?"

"Mija," he said and didn't continue. I realized there were tears in his eyes.

"What's wrong?"

"I have to tell you something I had hoped never to have to tell you. It will be hard to hear, but it's much harder to tell." He took a deep breath and swiped one of his hands across his eyes. "Your mother was being blackmailed by that Bates woman and I think she may have killed her."

This was bad. If Papi thought Mom might be guilty, it was practically a death sentence. I was astounded. I waited quietly until he continued.

"A long time ago," he began, then stopped and started again. "Your mother can be a very difficult woman. She was always a little on the wild side and didn't want to settle down. The first time I saw her I fell in love with her. I took her to a few dances but couldn't get her to—couldn't get close to her, except for kissing."

In the dim light spilling from my house, I could see that my dad had gotten red. He never talked of these things with me.

"I soon found out she was sleeping with another man, which I took hard since she said she loved me and she wasn't sleeping with me. I don't like telling you this, Mija, but I have to."

"It's okay, Papi. I'm a grown woman."

"Yes, but you can still be hurt."

I thought that was an odd comment, but I knew he would get to the point eventually if I could be patient.

"I asked your mother to marry me and she said she couldn't because she was pregnant. I was young enough—and crazy about her—and I thought we could make it work in the way young people always think things will work. She was pregnant with the other man's child, you see."

"Papi, what does this have to do with me?"

"She was pregnant with you, Margarita."

I stared at my father. It was so ridiculous I could have laughed out loud except the suffering on his face was real and brutally etched there. I went the route of least resistance, which of course was denial.

"No," I said, as if the word could change it.

"Yes, Mija, I'm not your biological father. I love you as my own. It'd be impossible for me to love you more than I do."

"But how can I look so much like you?"

"I always thought that was a miracle. The first time I saw your face, I had the same question. It seemed like it was God's way of telling me I'd done the right thing. I've never regretted it."

"But couldn't you be mistaken? Maybe I really am yours."

"Mija, of course you're mine." He touched his hand to his heart. "In here you're mine and I'm yours. Eventually I stopped making the distinction between your real father and me because I was your real father in every way that counted."

I sat in stunned silence, staring at the man who had always been my father and always would be.

"We meant to tell you but we just never did. Years passed, and the longer we waited, the less necessary it seemed. I'm sorry we didn't tell you, but I don't think you would've loved me any less and I hope you won't love me less now."

"I'm just so surprised, Papi. Of course I love you the same. You never treated me like anything but your daughter. It's just hard to believe, that's all. I can't take it in."

"When Norma started blackmailing your mother, it was after Kevin died and we wanted to tell you, but it seemed too cruel. It still seems cruel and I didn't want to tell you at all, but you need to know. Your mother will go to prison before she'll do anything to hurt you."

"How could Norma Bates possibly know anything about this? She didn't even live here then."

"Your father came into quite a lot of money and he wanted to set up a will that included you. He called me and said he'd never done anything for you and wanted to do that much. I had no objection."

"Please don't call him my father. He must have a first name. Call him by that."

"His name is Ezekiél, but he's called Zeke." My father looked pained, like the mention of the name was hurtful.

"Go on, Papi," I said softly.

"Zeke went to an attorney where he lived, near Austin, and that attorney turned out to be Norma Bates' brother. He must have mentioned to Norma that someone in Terlingua stood to inherit a fortune, and he told her Zeke's story. When she found out it was you, she thought of a way to hurt your mother."

"If my mother said she loved you, why was sleeping with Zeke?"

"I don't know, Mija. Your mom was confused."

"My mother's behavior was unforgivable."

"No, don't be hard on her. Once you were born she settled down and was a good mother. Eventually she fell in love with me. She grew up and became a good wife and we never looked back. We set about raising you and loving each other and neither of us has any regrets about any of it."

Papi sighed as if he bore the weight of the world. "She's going to be furious that I told you, but it's the only way you can help her. Whether she killed Norma or not, you need to know why she's acting like she is. She wants to protect you at all costs."

"What was Zeke like?"

"He was a good man, a very fine-looking man. Like your mother, he hadn't really grown up. He was irresponsible but not a bad guy." Papi sighed. "I was responsible enough for everybody."

"I love you, Papi."

"I love you too, more than anything."

"It wasn't a mistake that we were put together."

"No, it wasn't."

"Thank you for being responsible."

He smiled at me, a smile so full of love I felt knocked down by it. I thought I should be mad, but how could I be mad at a man who had loved and taken responsibility for me before I was even born? He was eight years younger than my mom. Shouldn't she have been the more responsible one?

I pictured him carrying me around on his shoulders with me holding him by the hair. He took me rafting, and taught me to ride, rope, and track. When I begged to know how to shoot a gun, he'd taught me that, too. He would run boys away from the house late at night when they'd come around asking me to party. He taught more things of value than I could ever count. He had always been there for me, since my earliest memories, and continued to be. No, if I was angry, it was with my mother. What had she been thinking, and why hadn't she told me this herself?

My dad was headed down my porch steps when he turned back. "There's one more thing I should tell you."

I didn't think my heart could take another thing so soon, but I couldn't speak to tell him that.

He began to pass his hat back and forth nervously. "I told you Kevin died instantly and that wasn't completely true."

Oh God.

"Mitch and I ran out to him. He was barely conscious, but I don't think he was feeling any pain. Mitch and I agree on that. We knelt beside him and I took his hand. He murmured, "Margarita," and then he was gone. I thought you should know that. I think he meant to tell me he loved you. I know he did, and his last thought was of you. I couldn't tell you before because—I couldn't. Mitch wanted to, but he couldn't do it, either. It was so hard, being there."

My eyes had filled with tears so that I could barely see him. "I know, Papi. I thank you for being there, and for telling me."

Chapter 25

The following morning I ran past Cimarron Mountain, barely noticing it, my mind on other things. Today was my first appointment with the psychiatrist. It seemed like I had more to tell her than could fit into an hour-long appointment. And she probably wouldn't believe a word of it anyway. My life had begun to sound like a country song.

Ahead, on my left, were steep sandstone bluffs rising abruptly out of the desert, and as I got closer, I saw a dirt road winding up them. It looked like a vehicle hadn't passed that way in a long time. Grasses, weeds, and low-growing wildflowers had claimed the deep ruts. I ran along the edge of the old road, going steadily uphill, pushing myself.

By the time I reached the top, I was out of breath. I dropped to my knees, gasping. Sheriff Ben had said to get on my knees whether I believed in God or not. I didn't, not really, and yet when I surveyed the scenery I had to believe that something huge and powerful was in charge. If all I ever saw was Cimarron Mountain I would know that. But there were other mountains, lots of them, and deep, magnificent canyons, the Rio Grande, the colorful clay hills of the badlands—too many things to name. It was all perfect and would stay that way unless a human messed with it.

"It's so beautiful," I said aloud, not really a prayer, but a sort of thanksgiving. "I'm going to be okay," I added, and realized I meant it.

A passing raven cawed at me. I didn't know if he was agreeing with or challenging me. I laughed and noticed how great it felt.

When my knees began complaining I sat on the edge of the cliff with my feet dangling. I looked out over the landscape, which was even more awesome from this height.

Across from me was another sandstone bluff with sides deeply cut and scarred by rain runoff. I was sitting over Ben's Hole Canyon and an arroyo which, when it ran, emptied into Terlingua Creek. That went several miles, eventually dumping into the Rio Grande. Around here, everything goes to the river, and from my perch I could see several now-empty tributaries, large and small. The Rio was to my right, not far, but I couldn't see it because of the mesas and mountains between us.

To my left was Cimarron, so close I could look into one of its canyons and clearly see a cluster of mesquite trees and other green growth. I could see our office building and Cactus Hill. It looked less tall from here, but no less captivating.

What I needed to solve the murder was perspective. If it could all be laid out like the scenery, perhaps it would make sense. I began to skim through the things I knew and quickly came to the so-called evidence found at my mother's house. If someone had planted evidence, then my mother was innocent; that was the best part.

Assuming my mother was not guilty of some undisclosed murder, then someone else, as in the real murderer, had set her up—or someone who wanted Mom to be found guilty—a person who hated her.

Lil Munch.

I was back to her. Lil had already proved that she would go to great lengths to hurt my mother. She and Norma were planning to have her killed. I couldn't rule her out because she had lost her husband—that only made me not hate her. Of my group of suspects, only Lil and Norma had shown themselves as potential murderers. Norma was dead, leaving Lil.

If I let my imagination stretch out to where the desert meets the Chisos Mountains, then it seemed possible that Lil had killed Norma—or had her killed— and then set up my mom to take the fall. Stretching that far, I thought Chapo Rodriguez was in it, too. He had sudden money, and a lot of it. Lil had plenty of money, and she was cold and calculating. She would think buying the death of her former friend was okay if she didn't get her own hands dirty. Her soul was safe if Chapo got blood on his hands and all hers did was cross his palm with money.

I had no proof about Chapo. A cigarette butt and a crumpled wrapper didn't mean he'd done anything as wrong as murder. And until that Coke can was processed, I wouldn't know if those two things had even belonged to him.

In the five emails Norma and Lil sent back and forth, they never mentioned a name but had referred to "him." In one, Lil had called him 'That Creepy Man.' Was Chapo that man?

I had to get one of them to talk. That seemed about as likely as touching the sun. Still, I had to try.

* * *

I pictured myself lying prone on a couch and Dr. Estrada sitting near me with a pad and pen. She would be peering at me over bifocals, and asking me tortuous questions. A phone would be nearby in case she needed to call for reinforcements.

The reality was quite different. I sat in a comfortable leather chair across from her desk. I never lay down. She wore no glasses, had a pen and pad, but only doodled on it. She asked permission to record our conversation, saying it was for her own use only and couldn't be heard by anyone else without a court order. I agreed to it.

"Just begin when you're ready," she said. "Talk to me about the things on your mind as if I were your trusted friend. Eventually you'll see I am just that."

"My husband Kevin was killed in a bull riding accident a little over a year ago and I haven't been functioning very well." I almost laughed at that gross understatement. "I've been so angry and sad—more sad than angry. So I drink a lot and can't sleep and I think about him all the time. I miss him so much it seems like there's a knife in my heart. Sometimes I can't breathe. People say it's been over a year, like I should get over it and move on."

She nodded. "And you don't feel you're getting over it quickly enough?"

"No, it's not that. I think it takes a long time and I want other people to leave me alone about it."

For forty minutes I spoke about Kevin, drinking, running, and even told her about the bloody shirt. Dr. Estrada didn't seem horrified that I still had Kevin's bloody shirt, or even surprised. She'd probably heard worse. Maybe if I'd told her that I sometimes slept with it, maybe that would have raised her eyebrow, but I didn't mention that. I only admitted to holding, touching, smelling, and loving it, as I had the man who had died in it.

During the last twenty minutes, I told her the startling news about my father. She even took that in stride. If she thought we belonged on "Jerry Springer," she had the decency not to say it. I thought she was incredibly calm about everything. Maybe if it had been her life she would have stood up and screamed *Holy Shit!*

I was whining about my parents' lies when she asked, "Have you never lied to them?"

"Yes, I've lied to them, but that's not the same."

"How is it different?"

"They're my parents. Parents aren't supposed to lie to their kids, especially not about important things."

"So you can have human shortcomings but not your parents."

I wanted to say *Damn Right*, but thought that might sound unfair. I supposed it was.

"I think this doesn't upset you as much as you think it should," she said, surprising me. "You obviously feel secure in your papi's love and nothing has changed between you. He's done a respectable thing raising another man's child as his own."

"He has nothing to be ashamed of, but my mother was a tramp!"

"A tramp or a young woman so full of life it was hard for her to settle down?"

Crap. She made it sound like my mother had legitimate reasons for her behavior.

"I guess it's hard for me to picture my parents as young."

"Most peoples' kids have trouble with that. Each generation thinks it invented sex and all the wonders and problems associated with it."

"I can't think about sex as it relates to my parents." *I can't think about it as it relates to me, either.*

"I think the most important thing here is that your parents made it work and raised you so successfully you never suspected a thing. You've never doubted your mother before, why start now? Try to imagine a mistake you made when you were young coming back to bite you. Surely you've made a few."

"Of course I have."

"I can't tell you what to do, but I imagine I'm about your mom's age. I'm just thankful the mistakes I made don't have to be scrutinized by my children. They'd be horrified. We were young once, your mother and I."

What Dr. Estrada said made sense, but I needed to be angry with somebody. She said we would speak about anger issues our next visit.

"Meanwhile," she said, "Keep running. It's as effective as therapy."

* * *

I went by to see Sheriff Ben, assuming he'd let me see my mom. It wasn't visiting day, but surely deputies got special consideration.

"The crime lab just faxed me some things that will interest you, Deputy," the Sheriff said. "Whoever discarded the Coke can is the same person who smoked the cigarette you picked up at the scene. The fingerprints from the can match the ones on the Rojos packet. His name came up because he's been arrested before. Fernando Rodriguez. Is he a serious suspect?"

"I'm starting to think so, Sheriff. We're watching him."

"He's done mostly petty stuff."

"He's better known as 'Chapo,' remember? He's been in trouble a lot. We're always watching him."

"What would he have against Norma Bates?"

"I don't know that, but when I figure it out, I'll let you know."

The sheriff shuffled some papers. "The report on the condom came back, too. It contained Wayne Dooley's semen but no trace of Mandy."

"That won't matter will it, since we have solid witnesses and photographs—and the other evidence I collected at the scene?"

"No, I don't believe it will. The D. A. thinks he has a solid case without the condom. Everett Dooley continues to claim that we set up his son, but his argument is losing steam in face of the evidence. What would be our motive?"

"I don't know. We have enough to do without setting up people."

"It sounds like Dooley is going to step down as county judge, if courthouse scuttle butt is halfway true."

"That would be good, wouldn't it?"

"Yes, I think it would...what we get next might be worse, though."

"Would you let me see my mother?"

"Well of course. I'll get her and bring her to the interrogation room. I haven't been able to get her to budge. She still says you misunderstood."

I didn't want to tell him what I knew until I had spoken with her.

On the way to the room I said, "I'm going to hang out at La Kiva tomorrow night."

He stopped and stared at me, his mouth slightly open.

"I need to watch Chapo. Sometimes he gets drunk and brags about things he's done. I want to be there for that."

He started to say something, but didn't. That was good, because I didn't need another lecture.

When he brought my mother she looked old and defenseless, and like she'd been crying. My heart melted immediately. I hugged her and held on a long time. The sheriff stepped out of the room and shut the door.

"I spoke with Dad and he told me the truth you've been hiding."

I had never seen a look like the one on Mom's face. I couldn't read it. Was it remorse? Guilt? Sadness? Relief? Maybe it was all of it together.

"It's okay, Mom. I understand why you didn't tell me. It was a shock, but it hasn't changed how I feel about Papi—or about you, either."

She had her hand at her heart and her eyes were full of tears. "I tried so hard to protect you, Margarita."

"I know, Mom. You did protect me. I've never felt anything but love from the two of you. If you made a mistake in your youth, well, I guess everyone does."

She was crying and didn't speak.

"Had you gone to Norma's to talk to her about the blackmail?"

"Yes, but she wouldn't be reasonable. After she died, I went back to look for those photos and letters. That was when you saw me."

"I understand how Norma found out about Zeke, but how did she get photos and letters?"

"Zeke took the attorney a file box of things, I guess as proof that you were his daughter. I can't know what he was thinking, but he was called away suddenly and left the box there. Of course he thought his things would be safe with an attorney. I guess Norma's brother was about as ethical as Norma."

"Why didn't you sue him?"

"I tried to, but he was already in jail on other charges and had lost his practice."

"When were you in Norma's house?"

"I went there the day before she died. I'm sorry I lied to you, but I didn't want you to know about the blackmail for obvious reasons."

"I understand, Mom. Someday I would like to hear about Zeke, but not right now. First I have to get used to the idea that there is a Zeke."

She sniffed and blew her nose. "I'll tell you whenever you ask. But you have to ask because I'm never going to bring it up."

"I'll ask, Mom, just not today."

"As far as Miguel is concerned, you're his daughter."

"As far as I'm concerned I am, too."

I drove back to Terlingua thinking about Zeke and trying not to. I wanted to know about him—and didn't.

At the office Barney's first words were, "Do you know that the sheriff fired Jimmy Joe?"

"Yes, he told me."

"Shoots came here demanding to see you."

"What happened?"

"He told me he knows you spent the night with 'that retard.'"

"How would he know that? And don't call Austin a retard."

"Those are Jimmy Joe's words, not mine."

"How does he know I spent the night with him?"

"He followed you. He said he was awake all night agonizing about it because he loves you and his heart hurts and on and on."

"Oh my God, he had no right to follow me."

"Well, he did. When he left here, I followed him to your house. I arrested him and the sheriff already sent a deputy to get him."

"Maybe it was him sneaking into my house all along, Barney."

"That's what I'm thinking."

"At first I was terrified it was a rapist, and then I thought it might have been Chapo. That freaked me out, but Jimmy Joe—that's somehow worse."

Chapter 26

Friday afternoon my mother was released from jail and my dad went to get her. Sheriff Ben indicated we should keep looking for a murderer and figure it out pronto. I was back on the case and just in time, since I was still working it.

The District Attorney didn't want to try to prosecute on the evidence he had. One hair being at the scene when she was there the day before didn't concern him, or the earring. And he believed my mother's story about why she had gone to see Norma. He seemed to dismiss the fact that blackmail often led to murder. Maybe he didn't read as many mystery novels as I did.

He dismissed the 'Killing for Health' paper for what Mom had said it was: random wishful thoughts put on paper. He accepted Sylvia's statement and Mom's similar statement in her interview with the sheriff. She had a very solid reputation in our community, and based on that, they let her go. It wasn't like she was going to run away.

Also on Friday, Jimmy Joe Blanks was released by the judge. He swore in court that he would stay away from me but was given a restraining order anyway. If he violated it he would go back to jail. I wondered if that would stop him.

Saturday morning I ran. I was finding running infinitely more satisfying than drinking. Afterward, even though it was Saturday, I called Lil and asked to visit with her. She moaned and groaned and finally said she was coming to Terlingua anyway and would meet me in the office. I hated to get dressed in my uniform on the weekend but I didn't think shorts would present the professional or intimidating image I hoped to project. I intended to force some truth out of that little woman.

After cleaning my house I went to meet Lil. She kept me waiting, of course. I entertained myself by staring at Cactus Hill and trying to imagine naked men running around out there.

I heard the door open but didn't rush to meet her.

"Is anybody here?"

"Have a seat. I'll be right there." *Soon as these guys put their clothes back on.*

"Hello, Lil." I shook her cold, limp hand and then sat as tall as I could at Barney's desk. It'd be great to be as large and intimidating as him.

"I have plans, you know," she said, snooty as ever.

"So do I, so I'll get right to the point. When I saw you recently at your house you said that you and Norma were still close, and were phoning and emailing each other."

"That's right." She looked me right in the eyes and lied to me. I don't know why that was a surprise.

"That's not true. I recently checked Norma's phone bills, and the last call she made to you was about six months after the mediation of the lawsuit. The same is true for emails. You haven't heard from Norma in months."

Lil hesitated a long time. "I suppose it has been a while," she finally admitted.

"Why were you lying to me?"

"I don't like you and I don't like it that you're so nosy about my personal business. It's none of your concern who I talk to and when."

I sat back in the chair and gave her the Barney frown. "I'm trying to conduct a murder investigation, Lil. Personally I don't care what you do or to whom but——"

"And because you hate me you want to pin it on me."

"That's unfair and you're wrong. I sincerely hope you had nothing to do with the murder of Norma Bates."

"Then what is your problem?"

"My problem is that when I ask people simple questions and they lie, I get suspicious. If you're innocent then please give me straight answers. Otherwise, you're wasting my time and I'm wasting yours. I'll keep bothering you until I feel satisfied."

"But what does my friendship with Norma have to do with her murder?"

"For one thing, I have to eliminate you as a suspect. For another, it seems like you'd want to help us find her murderer if you were her best friend as you say."

"I do want you to find whoever did it."

"Once again I ask if you were still friends after the Doctores Fronterizos crisis ended."

"Yes, at first. Then Norma decided the whole thing was my fault and she got ugly about it. She said I was stupid to have ever trusted Stephanie in the first place just because she was my friend. How was I supposed to know she'd steal?"

"Lil, do you really believe my mother did all that thieving and mismanaging of the organization she started and still loves?"

"Well Norma said—"

"I know what Norma said. I want to know what you think."

"I thought it was true at first, and it really hurt me, but later I saw the proof that Stephanie didn't steal and I got confused. I asked Norma, and she said it wasn't really proof, just trumped-up facts and more lying on Stephanie's part."

It's hard to argue with that kind of logic.

"I see, so back to my original question. Your friendship with Norma had cooled off by the time she was murdered?"

"Yes."

I took a deep breath. "Let's talk about trying to buy the murder of my mother."

Lil couldn't have looked any more shocked if I'd stood up and done a slow bump and grind out of my uniform.

"What are you talking about?"

"I'm talking about five emails I have in which Norma was corresponding with you about hiring a man to kill my mother when she wouldn't move out of your way."

"I don't know anything about that."

"I have proof you knew all about it, Lil."

"Okay, look, there was a time when Norma was so upset she did talk to a man about getting rid of Stephanie."

"You spoke with him, too."

"Yes, I went with her, but I didn't even know his name. And we dropped the idea. We're not murderers."

"What did he look like?"

"I don't know. It was dark and I couldn't see him well."

"Lil—"

"He was short, dark, and Mexican. He came across the river to meet us. He barely spoke any English. He wore a ball cap pulled low and had shifty eyes."

"That tells me nothing."

"I'm sorry, but there was nothing remarkable about him."

"You don't remember even a first name?"

"No. I have no idea."

"I guess that's all for now then."

You little liar.

"If you want my opinion, I still think your mother is the most likely suspect and I guess the sheriff thinks so too, because he took her to jail, didn't he?"

"Yes he did. I don't think she's the person we're looking for, though."

"Well of course you wouldn't. You're her daughter." Lil stood, preparing to leave.

"That reminds me of one more thing," I said.

"What is it?"

"Were you aware that Norma was blackmailing my mom?"

Lil sat down hard. She blinked at me. I could tell she hadn't known about it. "You're making that up."

"No, it's true."

"How would she be blackmailing her? What could Norma have had on your mother? Maybe she'd found solid proof about her stealing."

"Don't go there, Lil. It wasn't about that."

"Had she had an affair with Stanner?"

"Of course not. Quit speculating because you won't figure it out and I'm not going to tell you."

"Well, whatever. But there's your proof, Margarita. Stephanie killed Norma to shut her up. Doesn't that make sense to you? Surely you must know that already."

"Things are not always so cut and dried, Lil."

She stood and looked down her nose at me. "You just don't want her to be guilty because she's your mother."

"That's the truth."

Her mouth gaped again, but she left without saying anything more.

Since I had on my uniform anyway, I decided to speak with Roger Lockey about the dogs. It was a loose end, and I wanted to eliminate as many people as I could and see who was left.

Lockey jerked his door open and glared. At that moment I hoped he was the one that stabbed Norma.

"You got a thing for me, or what?"

I nearly choked myself trying not to laugh. "No sir, I'm here about the murder."

"I suppose you want to come in." He turned and headed into his house, leaving the door standing open. I wondered if he'd been drinking. He waved his hand at the same chair I'd occupied previously, and I sat.

"When I was here before you said you'd gone to see Norma about her dogs."

"That's right."

"When Barney came to the scene immediately after your call, the dogs were not running loose."

"No, they weren't. I couldn't believe it. I'd heard dogs in my yard while I was making coffee, and I just assumed it was those sons-a-bitches, 'cause it usually was. But when I got to Norma's I saw that her dogs had been put away. I didn't know if she had just put them up or if it hadn't been her dogs in my yard. I was going to ask her, but she wasn't talking, and you know why."

"I see."

"You still working with that big ol' lug?"

"Yes sir."

"You ever get intimidated by him?"

"Well, no, he treats me well."

"'Course he would, you bein' so pretty."

I stood. "Well, Mr. Lockey, thank you for your time."

"You be careful around that big lug. Come back any time."

On the way home I tried to punch a hole in his story, but I thought it was true. He was a strange, grumpy old man, but that didn't make him a murderer. That loose end wasn't tied as neatly as I would've liked, but it would have to do for now. I turned my attention to Chapo Rodriguez.

* * *

There was a local band playing on the patio at La Kiva. My heart thundered as I went down the steps, dressed up for the first time since Kevin's funeral. It felt good, but I was nervous as a teenager on her first date and I didn't have a date. Or want one.

I was wearing a long, straight, denim western skit and a purple, crinkle cotton Mexican blouse worn low on the shoulder, and leather sandals. I'd taken great pains with my hair, although it was short and I didn't have a lot of options.

When I came up to the bar, Phil stopped speaking in mid-sentence and mouthed, *Wow* at me.

I smiled at him and slipped onto a stool. I didn't see Chapo anywhere, but the bar was packed. I hadn't looked around much as I entered because people were staring at me.

Phil came and stood in front of me. He seemed confused about what to do.

"I'd like a Coke please, with a slice of lime," I said.

"I saw you running the other day."

My head went instantly to my father and what he'd said about the shorts. I felt panicky.

Phil set the drink in front of me. "I take it running is working for you?"

"I love it."

"You look beautiful, Margarita. You stop a man's heart."

"Thank you, Phil."

He looked good himself in tan cargo shorts and a Hawaiian print shirt open nearly to his waist. I tried not to notice what a muscled chest he had—years of rowing. Still rowing. Big, muscular arms. *Row, row, row your boat...*

"Will you dance with me when I get a break?"

"Okay."

He had to move on to serve other customers, but I thought he looked surprised. I'd never agreed to dance before, and wondered if I was making a mistake.

Now that I was here, I questioned how I would overhear anything from Chapo without getting close to him. That was out of the question. Even if I did get close he wouldn't be likely to blab everything. It wasn't like he didn't know I was a deputy.

A high school friend came up next to me and put his hand on my arm.

"Hi Margarita."

"Hi Erik." *What a coincidence. Just a few hours ago you were running around naked on Cactus Hill.*

"Want to dance? The band is great."

"Not right now."

"I remember that you're a really good dancer."

I wasn't sure what to say. I hadn't needed to make small talk with a man in too long. I'd never been good at it, and a year in hiding hadn't helped hone my social skills. Eventually he went off to hit on more accommodating women. There were plenty of them.

Several other locals came up to speak with me, and then Phil was standing beside me, holding out his hand. "Shall we?"

I took his hand like it was a dangerous thing. Most likely it was. Once my hand was in his, it felt okay. Nice, even. We weaved our way through people standing around and then Phil slid open the patio door and held it for me. The music was louder and I remembered suddenly how much I loved to dance.

The band was a group of gringos, but they play Mexican music as well as most of the Mexican bands I'd heard. Phil and I joined the crowd twirling around the dance floor. Dancing felt good and I tried to forget everything except the music, the breeze, and the brilliant stars. There was the sweet scent of a flowering vine that covered a fence on one side of the patio. And there was Phil, who smelled faintly of Axe cologne and something nice but indefinable. I couldn't think about bulls or husbands who'd never come home, rape, or murder. It all seemed to fade with dancing and the beauty of the night.

When the pace slowed Phil pulled me closer. "I wish I wasn't working. I'd like to spend the rest of the evening dancing with you."

"This is nice."

"You seem like you're doing a lot better."

"I have to keep going, Phil. Running is helping and I thank you for suggesting it. It's taken me places I haven't been, literally and figuratively."

Someone tried to cut in. "I only have a fifteen minute break," Phil said. "I'm not giving her up."

The guy backed away as if Phil had pulled a gun.

"I haven't seen you in a skirt in a long time, Margarita."

"I seldom wear them."

"Well, you should."

When the band started into a waltz, he said, "Want to stand on my feet?"

I laughed. "I wouldn't do that to you now."

"I wouldn't mind."

"I came here to spy on someone, but I don't think that's going to work the way I thought."

"I was hoping you'd come here to dance with me."

"That, too."

"Does your spying have anything to do with the murder?"

"I honestly don't know. I only suspect it. Maybe. It's frustrating to work hard at something and still have zip."

"Yes," he said softly. "I know how that feels."

"Dancing isn't zip, Phil." I hoped I hadn't misunderstood him. "I have to take it slowly. Dancing is something I couldn't have done a week ago."

"I didn't mean anything. You're right that dancing is a big first step."

I was going to say this was probably never going to go where he hoped, but I remembered enough about dating not to cut a man off at the knees. Especially if he had nice legs. And I was right up against his chest, which made me feel kind of weak and fluttery. It was erotic to be so close to a man and irritating to feel it so intensely.

The band was back to Mexican polka but we were still slow-dancing. Phil brought my hand up against his chest and held it there. His fingers smelled like the limes he constantly sliced. I tried to be in the moment, instead of a step ahead of it, or worse, looking back at other moments. I was enjoying myself and it surprised the hell out of me. I was sorry when Phil had to return to the bar, because I didn't want to dance with anyone else. I was figuring out how to get back in the water, but if I moved too fast, I was sure I'd drown.

Just when I thought I wouldn't dance with anyone else, a man touched me on the shoulder. I turned to see my father. He was dressed so sharply I nearly did a double-take. He was even wearing what looked like a new Stetson. Women were watching him.

He beamed at me and swept me onto the dance floor without asking. I'd been dancing with him since my first memories. Sometimes he and my mother and I would dance together, with me held between them. How would a kid feel safer than that? In a way, they were still holding me between them, and I was still safe.

"Aren't you going to dance with some of these single women giving you the eye?" I asked after we'd been dancing a while.

"Sure, but I always dance with the most beautiful woman in the room first, if she'll let me. That's how I met your mom."

"And you didn't learn a lesson from that?"

He laughed.

I leaned my head against his chest. "I love you so much, Papi."

He squeezed me so tightly I could barely breathe. "It's good to see you out, Mija."

"It's good to be out."

"Be careful of Phil."

"Why?"

"He was a river guide."

I laughed at that. "Don't you think he might have changed in fifteen years?

"He's still a man."

"Are you saying not to trust men?"

"No, I can't say that. A father just worries about his daughter, that's all. I'm sure you'll do the right thing."

Later we walked to the bar together. "We'll have two of whatever Margarita is drinking," he said to Phil.

"You're very trusting," I said.

"I can tell by looking at you that you've given it up." That's all he ever said on the subject.

After a while, a woman came and asked my father to dance and he went off with her. Another man touched my shoulder. I turned to stare into the face of Chapo.

"Let's dance," he ordered. "I saw you dancing."

"That was my father."

"I know that. I know your father."

"I don't want to dance, except with him."

"And Phil. I was watching you dance with Phil." Chapo was not a man you'd want watching you. And I didn't like his tone.

"I've known Phil since I was a little girl."

"You don't want to dance with me."

"That's right."

My father suddenly appeared. "Let's go, Mija." He gave Chapo a steely glare and he backed away.

Papi paid Phil.

"I'll see you later, Phil," I said.

"Thanks for the dancing. Please come back, Margarita."

"I will. I enjoyed it."

Papi escorted me away from there by the arm. As we were going up the stairs, he said, "Let's get in my truck a minute. I want to tell you something."

Before he said anything, he started the motor and moved the truck onto the highway. I stayed quiet because I knew he'd speak when he was ready.

"I think Chapo killed someone for money and I don't want you around him."

My heart went into my throat.

"You know I don't repeat gossip," he said, "so I wouldn't be saying anything if I didn't think what I heard was true."

"What did you hear?"

"I was going out to tell the guys I was shutting down the pool hall."

My dad had his old mechanic shop set up with a pool table, and every night there would be at least a few guys hanging out. Sometimes the place was packed. They called it the pool hall.

"I went by the window and heard Chapo talking, so I waited there. He was falling-down drunk and telling a couple of equally drunk men than he'd knocked off an old gringa bitch for a large amount of money." My father rolled down his window and lit a Marlboro. "You know how he is, Mija. I went in and challenged him on it. I said *you didn't do any such thing. You'd never do something like that.* He went ballistic. Then he called me a fucker, in English, and said if I didn't believe it I could ask Ramon Rodriguez, his cousin. I don't know what to think, Mija, but you should be careful. Don't go around those men, and if you have to go, take Barney. Don't go alone."

"Do you think he's just bragging? Would he have actually done it?"

"He has a lot of sudden cash. You pointed that out."

"I still need proof."

"Well, think about it. I'm sure you'll think of some way to get it."

"I'm new at this stuff, Papi."

"You're smart, and you could do anything in the world you put your mind to." Spoken like a true father. "Want to come to my house? I'll make us some enchiladas."

I smiled at him. "When have you ever known me to turn down your enchiladas?"

"Don't start now," he said.

Later I sat on my porch without anything bloody on my lap. I thought of Chapo and wondered how to trap him—and who had paid him and why.

Mostly I stared at Cimarron's dark outline against a star-studded sky. I thought about my father, the one who had always been there for me, and how he was as dependable and strong, and every bit as beautiful as my mountain.

Chapter 27

Monday afternoon Barney left the office to deliver a deposition in a civil case. I was staring at my hill and thinking about the murder when Mitch walked in. It seemed like we avoided each other since Kevin died. Mitch is head paramedic at Terlingua Fire and EMS, and so like Kevin in some ways, the opposite of him in others. He has black hair and blue eyes and Kevin was blond with hazel eyes. Kevin was tall and slender, while Mitch is shorter and stockier. They were rodeo buddies and served on each other's teams. Kevin was better at bronc and bull riding, Mitch is a champion roper. I didn't know if Mitch was still in rodeo after what happened. We rarely spoke and never about rodeo, bulls, roping, or even cowboys.

Mitch approached me warily. "Are you busy?"

I stood, hugged him, and sat at my desk so he could sit in the overstuffed chair. "I'm glad to see you, Mitch."

"Really?"

"Of course."

"I was afraid seeing me would make you sad."

"I'm doing better."

"Listen," he said, "I saw Austin. I had an ambulance run, and saw him at a convenience store. He told me what you said about your last conversation with Kevin." Mitch sighed and looked around, as if for an escape. "I've been meaning to talk to you, Rita, but it's so hard."

"I know."

"I wanted to tell you that when Kevin hung up the phone he laughed and said, 'That woman is crazy about me.' I agreed that you were. He said, 'Let's go do this thing, Mitch. All I can think about is the make-up sex.' He knew you loved him, Margarita, and I can't believe you question that."

"I do know it, but I wish I could take back what I said. I would never have let those be my last words to him."

"He knew that. He said something else right before his ride."

"What was that?"

"He said, 'Margarita thinks I'm crazy to ride bulls, but they're nothing compared to her. They don't scare me nearly as much.' The things he said about you made me jealous. I wanted to have a woman I thought half as much of as he thought of you."

"Thank you, Mitch."

"I hope this puts your mind at rest."

"There's still one thing I want to know."

"What's that?"

"I need to know about the accident, the details of it. I think what I imagine is worse. Anyway, maybe I can quit wondering if you'll tell me the truth."

"I don't want to."

"I know, but please tell me. I can take it, Mitch. I have to know the details."

"Margarita, it happened in seconds."

"Did the bull's hoof go through Kevin's chest?"

"No, but it crushed him." He let out a long sigh and seemed to be thinking it over. "Look, I'll try to tell you."

He struggled to compose himself. "Kevin drew the meanest bull there," he finally said, "but he was undaunted—well, you know how he was."

I nodded.

"He had a great ride, even went past eight seconds. But when he started to jump off I saw him jerk his boot and I realized he was caught in the strap. His attention was on that instead of the bull, and it tossed him off. It went wild, kicking and bucking, and it dragged him for a few seconds, trying to get away. Kevin fought to free himself because he knew it could kill him. I saw the panic on his face.

"I ran forward to help, and your dad was beside me, but as we got there the bull's hind leg came down on Kevin's chest. Then it broke free and ran off." Big tears rolled down Mitch's cheeks. He grabbed a tissue from the desk, wiped his face, and then handed me one.

"He was unconscious, Margarita. We bent over him and your dad kneeled down and took his hand. His eyes opened and he saw your father. He said, 'Margarita' with so much love... I can still hear him say it. I know he was trying to tell your dad to tell you he loved you."

I wiped my eyes and blew my nose. "Do you think he was in a lot of pain? Please tell me the truth."

"If he was, it was for seconds. I think he'd gone into shock and wasn't feeling anything. As a paramedic I know that's true. I swear it. The life had been crushed out of him. He was bleeding from his nose, mouth, and ears—and of course, his chest. His eyes opened and he spoke a last word, but those were final physical acts. After that he was gone."

"Thank you Mitch."

I came around the desk and we gave each other a long hug. In dealing with my own grief, I'd barely considered his loss, or my father's.

Mitch went out and pulled the door shut. I had a good hard cry but I thought the gruesome dreams would stop haunting me. I might have cried longer, but something so terrible happened it took my mind away from my grief and even the murder.

The phone began to ring, and when I answered it, the sheriff said, "Deputy Ricos, you should come to Alpine right now. Austin Williams is missing."

"What do you mean missing?"

"His mother can't find him. He went to feed the horses this morning, and said he'd only be gone about two hours. He didn't come back, and when he didn't show up for lunch her worry escalated into real fear."

"Oh no," I said, thinking of his ailing heart.

"I sent a couple of deputies to the stables and so far they've seen no sign of him. I thought you might want to come have a look or maybe you know where he is?"

"I don't have any idea where he'd be."

"His mom says sometimes he goes off by himself to think, but she's convinced he would be back by now if that were the case."

"I agree. He'd have contacted her. He knows she worries and he's considerate of her feelings. Not to mention he wouldn't miss lunch without telling her."

"That's what she said. She also said he likes to go to the city park by the high school and she drove over, but he wasn't there. She's becoming distraught, and I thought it might help if you came up here."

"I'll be there as soon as I can. Should I come to your office first?"

"No, you should speak to Mrs. Williams first, but stay in touch with me."

"I'll leave here in a few minutes."

I stripped out of my uniform and pulled on shorts and a shirt I kept at the office. If I was going to search for Austin, I didn't need restrictive clothing. I put the uniform into my Explorer in case I needed it, along with my Beretta and a small pistol I wore in an ankle holster. Now if I just had a mask and cape.

After I was roaring north towards Alpine I called Barney. He thought I needed his help, but I assured him I'd call when I knew something. Once I was off the phone, I eased the speed up to somewhere around the Explorer's maximum limit and flipped on the lights.

I had noticed Austin on campus before I ever met him. One day I went to the university's stables to ride because I needed to get away for a couple of hours. Besides, there was the chance that I might run into that long-legged rodeo cowboy, Kevin Madison. Instead I met another blond, Austin, who was there feeding the horses and singing. At first I thought it was the radio, but there was no music, just a clear, strong voice. He was singing *San Antonio Rose* and I'd never heard it sung so beautifully. I walked over and saw that there was no radio, only a short, stocky man with Down syndrome who sang like an angel.

When he saw me watching, he blushed but kept singing. He smiled an engaging, heartfelt smile. I smiled back, and our friendship began. When he'd finished singing, I clapped and told him how incredible his voice was. He blushed a deeper red, and said, "Gosh!" several times. He asked if I was going to ride, and then said he'd seen me at the student center and in the library. He was shy, testing the waters to see if I'd keep talking to him.

I saddled a huge mare named Maybelle that I'd ridden before, and he came to help. He commented that he would love to ride, but didn't know how. I invited him to go with me and explained I wasn't going far, just needed to get my head away from studies for a while. He seemed astounded to be invited and said "Gosh!" about a dozen times before I convinced him it would be okay.

He punched out at the time clock and I helped him get on behind me. At first he held onto me in a grip of terror, but as we rode away from the stables, he began to relax. He didn't talk non-stop as I'd feared he might. After he laughed and said he thought being on the horse was great, not so scary after all, he got quiet. He seemed sensitive to the fact that I wanted some quiet time.

When we stopped to rest near a jumble of boulders, he didn't speak until I asked him about his studies. He said he liked college but was having a hard time with biology. Biology? I couldn't believe he was taking something so hard. He said he loved learning new things but had trouble remembering important stuff. Didn't we all?

I graduated from the Law Enforcement Academy first in my class, and I owe that to Austin. I saw how he struggled and refused to give up. He spent hours in the library studying, and I began to join him. I felt guilty that he put so much effort into everything he did when I was lazy and wasted my talents. Austin wanted to learn, and worked so hard at it, that I was shamed into being the best I could be.

Every single day he meets challenge after challenge in college, and in his personal life, but he continues believing in himself. He has a positive attitude and a sense of humor that carries him through hard times. I was in awe of him then, and still.

Nearly everything Austin does is a challenge, except singing. Once we were talking about how hard it is to be different and he said, "I know other people are smarter, but I wouldn't trade. If I had to choose between being smart and singing, I would sing."

I couldn't bear the thought of Austin hurt and alone. I wondered if his heart had failed him and he'd dropped wherever he was at the time. But where would he be?

My radio crackled. "Base to unit 6," the sheriff said.

"Unit 6. Come in."

"Nothing yet."

"10-4, Sheriff." I sped up a little more, terrified of being too late.

When I was about ten miles from Alpine I called Austin's mother. She hadn't heard from him and was frantic. She encouraged me to look for him, not waste time coming by her house. She said she had called his friends and none of them had seen him. She added that she'd been to or called all the stores in Alpine, and had driven to the park several times and to the public library. The sheriff had the college searching for him on campus but so far nothing had turned up.

My cell phone rang and when I answered, Barney said, "If I know you, Ricos, you're going over one hundred miles per hour with your lights on and your XM blaring."

I laughed. "I guess you know me pretty well."

"You probably have the whole problem figured out already since you're such an overachiever superhero type."

"I haven't figured out anything and I'm worried sick."

"Any word?"

"Not yet. The sheriff and Austin's mom haven't left much for me to cover."

"Do you have a plan?"

"Not much of one. I'm going to find that cowboy and make him sweat."

"You think Gil's behind this?"

"That would be my guess. If he's hurt him, Barney I don't know what I'll do. I've been thinking violent thoughts."

"Stay cool, Ricos. Make the law work for you."

"The law's too slow to suit me."

"You'll do the right thing," he said. "Call me when you know something, okay?"

I parked the Explorer on a side street near Gil's house, and put my small pistol into the pocket of my cargo shorts. From there, I walked to his house, trying to calm myself. I didn't know why I felt the need to hide my professional identity, but I didn't want him to know yet that I was a deputy. How that would be to my advantage, I wasn't sure.

Gil lived in a small, white frame house not far from campus. There were several pick-ups in the driveway and on the street. Great—I was just in time for a cowboy meeting. My hand went to, and rested against, the pistol in my pocket for courage.

Someone yelled, "Come in!" when I knocked. There were four or five cowboy types drinking beer and hanging out. I didn't see Gil at first but he saw me, and stood up from a ragged recliner where he was sitting.

"Everybody out!" he yelled. "Now!"

They gave him looks but within seconds, they were gone. Gil came up way too close to me. "Did you come back to take me up on my offer?" he said softly. He was looking me over in a way I didn't like.

"No. I'm here about my friend Austin."

"What's the deal with him, sweetheart? I'm twice as good looking and a lot smarter—"

"And so humble," I said with a smile I could barely believe I was able to produce.

He spit a stream of dark brown chewing tobacco into a plastic cup. "Would you like a beer?"

"No, thanks, I'm looking for Austin because he's been missing since this morning."

"What makes you think I have him? I don't swing that way, and especially not with retards."

"That's exactly why I'm here. I suspect you because of your intolerance of him."

"Suspect me how?" He'd moved his face so close to mine I could smell the nasty combination of tobacco and beer on his breath.

"That you've done something to him."

"I don't have time to fool around with him," he said. He stepped away from me but was staring at my legs. "I got better sense than that."

"Really?"

"Why would I hurt him?" He made a pouty face. "Don't frown so, little dar-lin'. I could kiss you and make it better. Just one little warm-up kiss?"

I'd rather take my little pistol out and shoot myself in the mouth with it.

I began moving away from him. "You'd better not be lying to me about Austin," I said between clenched teeth.

"Or what, sweetness? Are you going to work me over with those sexy legs of yours? Maybe you would wrap them around my neck?"

I wanted to wrap something around his neck and twist his head off. "I don't know," I said, "but I promise you'll regret it," and headed towards the door.

He laughed loudly. "You don't know whether to kick my ass or kiss it."

I turned. My hand was already on the knob. "I guarantee I'll never kiss it."

I stepped onto the stoop, caught my breath, and began walking back to my vehicle. So, Super Deputy, a lot that proved. Now what?

A nagging feeling dragged me towards the stables. I knew the sheriff already sent deputies, but they didn't care about Austin like I did. Most likely they thought he was a retard that had wandered off and would turn up again. A second look couldn't hurt, and I didn't know what else to do.

I parked the Explorer, got out my evidence gathering kit, and began walking and looking for anything that looked wrong or out of place. I refused to acknowledge that I was going into a rodeo arena. Alone.

First, I perused the time cards, and saw that Austin's was punched in at 8:30 and had never been punched out. So that was wrong. He was meticulous about his time card. If he hadn't punched out, then he hadn't left, unless there was an emergency or he was taken away by someone. That was a frightening thought.

Next, I looked around the arena, and then the stalls. There was only one bull who stared at me with doleful eyes. I felt more sorry for him than horrified by him. My eyes swept the stall quickly and saw nothing out of order. Many of the others were empty except for a few with horses.

At first I didn't see the blood. It looked like part of the fresh manure, which was everywhere. One pile of manure looks pretty much like another. I'd been looking until I thought I would throw up from the smell.

I saw a piece of golden straw sticking out of a pile and the end was reddish-brown, like blood. I put on my gloves and touched it. Looked like blood but I couldn't be sure. Smelled like manure. It could be animal blood or it could be Austin's. My instincts screamed that it was Austin's.

I nosed around the stall and discovered a broken-off shovel handle that had been shoved under a stack of saddle blankets. There was a small amount of blood on the handle and a faint spray over the blankets. I called the Sheriff's Office for help, wishing it would be Barney that came.

I kept looking around, moving faster. I was shoving back panic while checking the tack rooms, storage closets, and the office. Nothing. I walked around the building, looking for any sign of Austin, until I found an intermittent trail of blood drops that led towards a shed that was usually locked. The lock was gone. That was another thing wrong. The hinges creaked as I forced the door open.

Inside was worse than a cave. It took a moment for my eyes to adjust. I stood still, listening, and heard ragged, labored breathing. I forced the door open as wide as it would go, letting in some light. At the back of the shed Austin was lying on his stomach in a crumpled heap.

"Austin!"

With one hand I dialed 911, with the other I was feeling for his pulse. "Austin, Austin, can you wake up? Please wake up, Austin."

I can't lose you, too.

He groaned but didn't move. "Austin, can you hear me? It's Margarita. I'm here."

No response.

"It's okay, the ambulance is coming, just rest." I kept talking to him and eventually sat down beside him and held one of his hands in mine. "Help is coming, Austin."

After what seemed like an eternity, I heard the sirens and stepped outside to wave them over. An ambulance screeched in, along with a Sheriff's Office truck which I recognized immediately as Sheriff Ben's.

"I see you found him," said the sheriff as he jumped down. "Is it bad?" His brow was furrowed as he watched the medics get a stretcher out of the ambulance. "I didn't get a full report. The dispatcher only said that Deputy Ricos had found Austin Williams."

"He's non-responsive except for occasional groans. I found some evidence, Sheriff. It looks like he was beaten with the handle of a shovel. Blood in one of the stalls got my attention, and then I noticed a handle sticking out from the saddle blankets. There's blood spray on the blankets."

"Good lord," said the sheriff, rubbing his forehead. "Why would someone do this? What could he have done?"

"He hasn't done anything. It's Gil. I know it is."

The sheriff laid a hand on my shoulder. "Try to stay calm."

"He hates him because he's not a macho rodeo cowboy. Gil sees him only as a retard. Austin is easily upset by Gil's meanness, so Gil bullies him."

The medics brought Austin into the light to get a better idea of his injuries before transporting him. They set the stretcher down gently and began looking him over. The bruising was hideous; ugly purplish-black splotches covered his arms and face. There was a large lump oozing blood on the side of his head. Both eyes were swollen shut, and one looked much worse than the other. Fury boiled inside me.

"I taped the stall where I found the blood," I said to the sheriff with a shaky voice. "The evidence is in my kit."

"I'll take it from here," he said. "Don't worry."

Austin groaned. I couldn't tell if he was awake, but I wanted him to be.

"Austin," I said, kneeling beside him. "Are you waking up?"

There was no response. Did he have serious head injuries? What had all this stress done to his already-jeopardized heart?

"We're taking you to the hospital," I said. "You're going to be fine."

That had to be true. I thought calmly, however insanely, that if he wasn't fine, I was going to kill Gil Young.

In the emergency room, Austin was hooked up to a heart monitor that showed his heart to be stable. Still, he was in critical condition and for the moment, his prognosis was grim. The doctor said it was "wait and see."

"What in God's name are we dealing with?" the sheriff wondered.

"He hates him, but there's nothing about Austin to hate."

"I saw your uniform in your vehicle, and brought it with me. I want you to get deputied up and go with me to talk to suspects."

I wanted to drink; needed it more than I ever had. Drinking would dull my senses. All of this would go away. Sheriff Ben would never take me drinking.

I splashed cold water on my face.

After I dressed, I studied myself in the mirror. There was a small, haunted thing looking back at me. It looked swallowed up by a professional uniform.

I laughed at myself. "Super Deputy," I whispered, "you look like Hell."

Chapter 28

Gil's house seemed sinister and dark even though it was painted white. Nobody came to the door, so we went by the Wrangler. His dark blue Dodge Ram pickup was there, parked in the lot with many others. They all had gun racks or hat racks, many with roping gear hanging from them. Gil's had a bumper sticker that read: *Ropers need love, too!*

The sheriff called the bar. "Mike, this is Sheriff Duncan. How many guys are in there with Gil?" He waited while Mike spoke. "Oh, we assumed it would be him driving it." He turned to me. "Gil's not there."

He listened to Mike a few seconds. "Yes, we found him. He's in bad shape over at the hospital." Pause. "Right, Deputy Ricos and I are coming in now to question those cowboys."

Sheriff Ben flipped his phone shut. "There are three cowboys seated in back near the stage. Mike says they're part of Gil's group. We'll go in and find out what they know." He took a deep breath and let it out slowly before he moved.

When we entered the dark bar, we didn't see them at first, and they didn't notice us either. As we moved towards the back, we saw three cowboys seated at a table, drinking beer and having a huddle about something. I would've been willing to bet my paycheck I could name that something.

One of them saw us and stood up so suddenly he knocked over the bottle of beer that had been sitting in front of him.

"Well I—" he said, and didn't say anything else.

"Let's take all of them in," said the sheriff out of the side of his mouth. He called base for a deputy to bring another vehicle, then said to the guys, "Everybody stay where you are. We're gonna take a ride to my office."

"Where's Gil?" I demanded.

The wannabe who wore super-tight jeans spoke first. "How would we know that?"

"You're driving his truck—or one of you is."

"What is your name, young man?" barked Sheriff Ben.

"Rocky Hill."

"Which of you is driving Gil Young's truck?"

"I am," admitted Rocky. "My truck broke down."

"Where is Gil?"

"We don't know where he is."

So we waited. One of them started to say something to the sheriff but thought better of it. From the corner of my eye I noticed Mike, not far away, standing with his arms folded across his chest in a typical Mike stance.

When the other deputy arrived, Rocky Hill said, "I'd like to call my attorney."

Sheriff Ben frowned. "You'll be allowed to do that, but you're not under arrest yet."

After we transported them, the suspects waited in a room, guarded by a deputy, while the sheriff and I spoke in the interrogation room.

"I want you to bring in Gil Young," he said, "but first let's see if we can get one of these cowboys to tell us where he is."

I agreed that at least one of them would know.

The sheriff went out and came back with a young man who said he was Jess Whitman, nineteen years old, a member of the rodeo team. We told him about the vicious beating Austin Williams had endured and that we strongly suspected his friend Gil. At first Jess feigned ignorance, but wasn't convincing.

The sheriff talked about how serious assault charges are and how much trouble they were in. He recounted that our judge took a dim view of violent crime in general, but especially when it involved the abuse of handicapped people.

"I didn't have nothin' to do with it," Jess finally said, "but I was there this morning."

"Go on."

"That retarded fella, he was there too, and I could see trouble coming. I went and got in my truck and left. I swear it. I don't beat up people. I went over to the bowling alley. I work there part-time. You can call them if you don't believe me."

"Describe to us what was happening when you got disgusted and left."

"Well, we were gonna ride, but that fella was there feeding the horses and Gil started in on him."

"Started in on him how?" I asked.

"It was his usual meanness. He said he was a little pest and he didn't want him looking at us. He called him a 'shit-shoveling pussy.' We all saw the meanness come over Gil and I could see the man was scared of him. In fact, he begged Gil not to start something. He was just doing his job."

"Keep talking," ordered the sheriff.

"Well, the fella picked up a shovel handle to defend himself. He's brave if you ask me, standing up to Gil like he did."

"Had he said anything to Gil before Gil started harassing him?"

"No, nothing. At first he was feeding the horses and trying to pretend he didn't see us. When Gil started in, he tried to make a run for it, but Gil blocked the doorway to the stall. That was when I left."

The sheriff leaned towards him and spoke in a confidential tone. "Listen, I'm going to let you go. But I don't want you talking to anyone. Your friend Gil is in a lot of trouble and you don't need that hassle what with college and work and all."

"No, sir."

"Do you know where Gil Young is?" I asked.

"No I don't, but if he's done something wrong he's probably hiding."

"You're going to stay quiet," the sheriff said, "and I'm going to call if I need more information from you, okay?"

"Sure. Okay."

"So go!" The sheriff got up to bring in another cowboy.

Deputy Hansen, who had been watching through the one-way glass, was instructed to call the bowling alley about Jess's alibi before he had a chance to arrange anything with them. The owner was surprised for the Sheriff's Office to be calling, but confirmed that Jess Whitman had been there when he said he was.

"Wonders never cease," said Sheriff Ben when he got that news.

Next the sheriff brought in Rocky Hill. He was dressed like a cowboy, but still didn't impress me as being one. He admitted that he didn't make the rodeo team this year. Then, when I pressed him, he admitted he'd never been on the team but was an avid supporter. So was Austin, but Gil shoved him around and called him a rodeo pussy.

Rocky was twenty, attended the university, and belonged to the rodeo club. Yes, he knew Austin. Yes, he knew there'd been trouble between Gil and Austin.

No, he didn't go to the arena or stalls. He hadn't been since he failed to make the team.

"You're sure of that?" asked the sheriff, "because if our evidence shows otherwise it will go hard for you."

"I wasn't there!" He raised his voice to the sheriff but fixed his beady eyes on me. I stared back at him. He was shorter than the other three men. There was something about him I didn't like. Maybe it was the fat lip where he'd stashed a wad of chewing tobacco, and his general attitude.

"Where were you today?" asked the sheriff.

"Just hanging around, here, there, can you account for every minute of your day?" He spit a disgusting brown stream into a Styrofoam coffee cup.

"Pretty much," answered the sheriff without hesitation, "but I guess it's like that when you work."

"If you were there this morning," I said, "and you know anything about this, you'd better speak up now or you'll be an accessory to murder later, at the least. Do you understand?"

"I get it," he said angrily. Nobody spoke. "Okay, I was there," he finally said, "but I never touched the little freak. Gil had words with him." He shrugged his shoulders like it was no big deal. "Then we left."

The sheriff and I exchanged a look. His face was red with fury. "So that's your story? If you and Gil didn't assault Austin, who did?"

"How the hell would I know?"

"I expect you know because you were there."

"I swear, man, we didn't. Maybe it was that other guy."

"What other guy?"

"There was a man there when we got there. He acted kind of weird when Gil saw him. You should ask Gil."

"We have a few questions for Gil. It would help if you'd tell us where he is."

"I don't know where he is."

Rocky and I stared at each other. "Better to tell the truth now," I finally said.

"I am telling the truth!"

The sheriff stood. "Well, young man, I'm going to hold you until we locate Gil Young. You're under arrest for assault."

"But I didn't assault nobody."

"At the least," I said, "you're an accessory. You'd better hope Austin doesn't die."

The sheriff glowered at the suspect. "Deputy Hansen will recite your rights."

Rocky slammed his fists down so hard the table shuddered. "I didn't do anything!"

"So we're going with the mysterious stranger theory," I said. "Was he a one-armed man in a hooded sweatshirt?"

"I don't care what you say, I didn't touch him. And there was a man there. If you're arresting me, I want to call my attorney."

"What did the stranger look like?" I asked.

"I didn't take much notice. He was tall and he was wearing a brown ball cap. I had the impression he was dark, not black or Mexican, but dark for a white guy—like he had a tan. I think he had blond hair. Or maybe it wasn't exactly blond."

"Maybe it was purple or green. You're making him up, aren't you?"

He glared at me. "No, there was a man there, I'm telling you."

"Where is Gil?" I tried once more as the sheriff cuffed him.

"I told you I don't know where he is."

Sheriff Ben handed him over to another deputy who appeared when the door opened. "Book him," he said. "If you have any questions about the charges, talk to Deputy Hansen. And the prisoner wants to call his attorney."

"Yes sir." I heard the deputy reciting his rights as he led him away.

The sheriff shut the door again and sat down next to me. I couldn't tell what he was thinking. "Shall I bring in another liar?" he asked.

"We're all here. I guess you might as well."

The next young man was dressed in the same cowboy style as the others but he seemed less redneck, more like a regular college student. He came from money, I finally realized. That was the subtle difference.

His name was Robert Devers and he was twenty-one years old, a senior. He was well-mannered and well-spoken. I still didn't like him. He was hanging out with the creeps, so how great could he be? I thought the sheriff was thinking the same thing.

He said his friends called him 'Devers' and that he had met the guys at the stables and was going to go riding with them.

"What do you know about the assault of Austin Williams?" the sheriff asked.

"Assault?"

"Don't pretend you don't know about it," I said heatedly.

"I don't know anything about an assault."

"Tell us what you do know," demanded Sheriff Ben.

"I need to call my lawyer."

The sheriff combed his hair with his fingers. I could feel mine going white. Brewster County crime was taking its toll.

"You need to tell us what you know," said the sheriff. "There's no need for an attorney unless you're going to incriminate yourself. We're only asking questions."

"I—I left, Sheriff, I swear it on the Holy Bible."

Sheriff Ben gave me a look that would've been funny under other circumstances. "None of you boys seem to understand how serious this is."

The sheriff excused himself and came back with three bottles of water. In his absence nothing was said, although I had a few comments that I held back.

He handed each of us a bottle. "Do you know that Gil often harasses Austin and has shoved him around before?"

"Yes sir, I do know that."

"What happened this morning?"

"Gil had words with him, but then we left. Gil and Rocky were getting into Gil's truck when I left. Maybe it was that other man."

"Describe this other man," commanded the sheriff.

"I barely noticed him. He was tall, seems like, and had a black ball cap. He was wearing blue jeans and a red t-shirt, I think. I didn't know him but he could've been a friend of Austin's. I think he was waiting to talk to him."

"Was he a Mexican man?"

"Definitely not—he was white and had freckles."

"He wasn't tan?"

"No."

"What color was his hair?"

"I couldn't say—he was wearing a cap. On second thought, maybe his hair was reddish."

The sheriff let Devers go, but instructed him not to leave town.

Once we were alone, Sheriff Ben asked, "Do you think Gil might have come back alone and assaulted Austin?"

"I don't think it was the tall, dark or maybe white, blond, red-headed, black-haired stranger with freckles wearing a black or brown ball cap."

He chuckled. "No, that seems unlikely."

I couldn't wait to get my hands on Gil Young.

* * *

The sheriff took me to pick up my Explorer and I headed for the hospital. Austin had been moved from ICU to a private room, but he was still hooked to various machines. I spoke to him while I checked the safety on Bad Berretta and put it and the holster in a drawer of a built-into-the-wall dresser.

I realized I had nothing to sleep in. A passing nurse gave me a backless hospital gown; better than nothing, but not much. After a shower, I got the gown on, and crawled into bed next to Austin. I had to burrow my way under various tubes, and I thought the nurses might make me leave, but I was too tired to worry about it. Austin needed to know I was there. If it were me, I'd want to know I wasn't alone.

"Margarita?" Austin said groggily when I was nearly asleep.

"Austin, I'm here."

The next sound was only a groan. I wanted to put my arm around him, but he was so battered I thought it would hurt him if I did.

"Margarita?"

"I'm here, Austin. Do you need the nurse?"

"No."

"Do you remember what happened?"

"No."

"Don't worry, just rest."

I called the nurse anyway, to tell her he was awake. She thought I should move to the other bed, but Austin became so distraught she let me stay.

Later, when Austin was sleeping again, I lay awake staring at the ceiling, trying to process brain overload. I thought for a while about Kevin, and longed to spend just one more night with him. That would never work because then I would want one more, then another. I had to push those thoughts away or let them make me insane.

I managed to sleep a short while before a different nurse came in to check on Austin. It's hard to get decent sleep in a hospital. Everybody says to rest, but nobody lets you do it.

Chapter 29

"Get up, Good-Looking," I said when Austin stirred. "These nurses can't seem to leave you alone."

"Gosh," he said. One of his green eyes sparkled at me out of puffy, blue-black flesh.

His bruises were darker, and the other swollen shiner was oozing gunk. He looked even worse, but he was awake.

The nurse said his vitals looked good and the doctor would be in a bit later.

"Looking good," he said with typical good humor, but it was groaned more than said.

"You're in a lot of pain, aren't you?"

"I'm okay."

"Are you hungry?"

There was no hesitation. "Pizza," he said.

I knew then that he would recover.

"It's time for breakfast, not pizza."

"Pizza, Margarita," he said with effort, "anytime."

Obviously, speaking was painful. Probably breathing was too, but he didn't complain.

When I came back from the bathroom, Austin said, "I saw your ass," like a little kid.

"Well, I hope you're not too upset."

"Nah, looking good," he said happily.

* * *

I thought Rocky Hill was likely to know where Gil was since he had Gil's truck. I brought him into the interrogation room, cuffed and resentful. I seated him at the table and sat across from him.

"Bitch," he mumbled several times.

"I want you to tell me where Gil is."

He glared at me and I glared back.

After a while I tried again. "Where is Gil Young?"

"I don't know. I told you that already."

"You have his truck."

"So?"

"So you let him off somewhere yesterday and kept the truck."

"I borrowed it because my truck broke down."

I thought about that a long, silent moment. "I think we're failing to communicate, so let me put it this way." He watched me with a condescending smirk. "The county jail is a comfortable place to be, usually. You can watch television, read, and meals are served on time. You'll be allowed outside for a couple of hours every day. I can make sure you have none of those privileges—not one—while you're here." It was a total bluff, but it worked.

Rocky's smirk gradually turned into a glare. "You're such a bitch."

"You haven't seen bitch yet, but you will if you don't tell me Gil's location."

I had more threats in mind, but before I had to use them he considered, sighed heavily, and said, "I left him at the university stables yesterday."

"He was going to ride somewhere?"

"Yeah, he was going to an old line shack on the eastern side of the Sunshine Ranch. We go there sometimes and camp out."

Sunshine Ranch borders the university's land to the south.

"How far away is the shack?"

"It's about a three-hour ride, more or less."

"You're sure he's there?"

"That's where he said he was going."

"What did he think he would accomplish by running away?"

Rocky shrugged. "He thought it would blow over and he could come back in a few days."

"This isn't going to blow over."

"But we didn't do anything."

"Then why is Gil running?"

"I guess because he hit that retard."

"You call Austin names but he's more of a man than any of you. And Gil didn't hit him. He beat him viciously."

I took the prisoner back to his cell and tried to slip away, but Sheriff Ben was waiting in the hall outside the cells.

"Are you going to bring Gil in?"

"Yes sir."

"I'm going to send another deputy with you."

"I can't wait, Sheriff. I'll phone you if I have trouble."

"You are most certainly going to wait. This will only take a minute."

"Someone else will slow me down. I can ride and shoot. You don't need to send a man."

"Well I would never think that. I—"

"I don't want to wait."

"Deputy Ricos—"

"Will you arrange for me to take a horse? Meanwhile I'm going to go saddle one."

"Saddle two because Deputy White is going to go with you. And you had better wait for him. That's a direct order."

I didn't like waiting, or going with Deputy White, but the sheriff was the boss.

I saddled a bay gelding whose stall had no name posted. I called him Desperado because we were going after one. He was docile and cooperative and seemed glad to see me, so saddling him was easy. I put water, apples, and granola bars into a saddle bag. I was adjusting the saddle on a mare named Millie for Deputy White when he showed up.

He was one of the deputies that had looked for Austin without results. That was irritating, but he was usually an okay guy to work with.

"What's the plan?" he asked, hitching up his uniform pants by the gun belt. "The sheriff says you're the primary on this one."

I pictured Sheriff Ben delivering that news to a senior, male deputy, and tried not to laugh.

"Can you ride?" I asked.

"Of course."

"Then the plan is to ride in, grab the perp, and bring him out. You can finish saddling your horse while I find some boots that fit."

I went into the tack room and borrowed a pair of pink cowboy boots with a swirly turquoise design. They were heavy on girly—but the only size sixes in the group.

Deputy White, whose nickname is 'Red,' gawked at my boots, but had the sense to keep his mouth shut.

I mounted Desperado. "Okay, boy, let's go get that sonofabitch." He seemed enthusiastic about the prospect of it. Red and Millie seemed less so.

We walked around the perimeter of a large corral until I saw the unmistakable tracks of a horse heading south. To Desperado's delight, we began to gallop. Gil's path was easy to follow because the only other tracks were old ones left by cattle.

After a mile we stopped for Red and Millie to catch up.

"I didn't say I was a great rider," he whined. "I haven't ridden in a long time."

"We'll slow down."

It was a sparkling day with a cool breeze. Alpine is at a higher elevation than Terlingua, which means more rain and cooler temperatures. That equals less desert and more grassland. The mountains are greener, more covered with small trees and native grasses, and therefore not as stark and stunning as the mountains to the south.

The tracks became more confusing when there began to be others. I had to get down and study the ground.

"We've lost them," Red sighed.

"Not yet," I said, and thought of my papi, who had taught me to track when I was a kid and continued to challenge me with tracking dilemmas as I grew up. I once helped him track a runaway cow into Big Bend National Park, where having livestock was a serious offense. It had escaped the fencing at our ranch, and at times the hoof prints were non-existent. Not to Papi. He showed me how to figure it out.

Eventually the tracks became those of a single horse again. We stopped at a tiny copse of juniper and ash trees near a spring to let the horses drink. We rested and ate granola bars and talked about nothing worth repeating.

Before I got back in the saddle, I checked my Beretta. I prayed I wouldn't need it, but criminals are impossible to second-guess. Someone who would viciously beat a handicapped man without provocation wouldn't think twice about hurting a couple of deputies. Maybe it was better I wasn't going in alone.

Red patted his weapon. "This baby is always ready."

"Mine too, but I like to check it."

About the time three hours had passed, the tracks changed from a running gait to a walking one, which might mean nothing—or could mean we were nearing the shack. I didn't want Gil to see us before we got the lay of the place, so I slowed, but didn't dismount. We rounded a bend, and in a little valley ahead we saw it. There was a horse tied to a stately cottonwood that shaded the building. There was no sign of Gil, but we couldn't assume he wouldn't see us.

I studied the scene with binoculars, but saw nothing except the animal, its tail swishing calmly. When I handed the binocs to Red, he agreed.

We tied our mounts to some sturdy brush and took off on foot, up a rise to the left, planning an approach from the rear.

It took about half an hour to make our way to a promontory at the back of the shack. There were no windows in the rear wall. A line shack is only used occasionally by cowboys when weather becomes suddenly inclement or they have to be away overnight. They are not built for comfort or looks, and are not used much now that trucks often replace horses in fence line work. There were no roads leading to this shack though, and no tire tracks that I could see.

I hesitated a moment, then took out my Beretta and slowly approached. Red did the same, following so close that if I stopped he would slam into me. We were nearly there when an explosion blasted the silence and a bullet whizzed by our heads. It came from behind—and higher up—but it missed or I wouldn't be telling this story. It embedded itself in the wooden wall of the building and another followed. The second one hit Red. His weapon tumbled out of his hand. He cried out and stumbled forward, grasping his arm.

"Red!"

"I'm okay," came out in a groan.

"Stop or you're dead," yelled a voice I might not have recognized, except that it had to be Gil Young. "Don't move or I'll shoot again."

I didn't move. He was the type to shoot a woman in the back.

"Put your hands up," the voice commanded, coming steadily closer.

"I need to call for help," I said, but I put them up. My heart was pounding so hard I wondered if a twenty-five-year-old could drop dead of a heart attack.

Footsteps crunched behind me. "Turn around, and do it slowly."

When I did, I saw Red eying his fallen pistol. I hoped he could get it before Gil thought of taking it.

Once I faced Gil, he whistled low. "You failed to mention you're a lawman, Sweet Lips. You left that out on purpose, didn't you?" His tone was playful, flirty even, but his eyes were angry. "Drop your weapon right now."

I didn't want to put my beautiful Beretta into the dirt but didn't see a way out of it. When I let it fall, he moved the tip of the rifle to my breasts.

"Don't get any big ideas, amigo," he said to Red, and yanked up the fallen weapon.

Damn.

"Take that shirt off," Gil said to me.

"No."

"I'll shoot you."

"Go ahead. I'm not taking my shirt off."

"Margarita, you better do what he says," Red advised.

Desperado whinnied. I didn't know if his advice was to comply with the asshole or if it was an 'atta girl.' Anyway, I wasn't about to comply.

"I want to look at your titties."

"No."

I wanted him to move closer.

"I have the gun, sweetheart. I could just take it off you."

"Well, I'm not going to take it off."

"We could have some serious fun." He ran the rifle across my breasts, barely touching them. "You like that, don't you?"

No, I didn't. I willed him to come closer.

He took another step, still not close enough. "You want me so bad you came all this way looking for me."

The man was delusional.

"You've shot an officer of the law," I reminded him.

He appeared unconcerned. "Yeah, I guess I have, but he won't die."

"He needs medical attention."

Gil barely glanced at Red and then turned back to me. "We'll send him back on the horse he rode in on."

"That's not funny, Gil. You're in serious trouble and it will only get worse if you don't let me call for help."

He reddened in anger and stepped towards me, but still not close enough. It was hard to be patient.

"If you hurt me—"

"Shut up, Sweet Lips."

When he came still closer, and put his hand in the front of my shirt to rip it away, I brought my knee into his groin with all my strength. He groaned, dropped the rifle, and doubled over, taking the front of my shirt with him. I was finally exposed, but he had lost interest in my anatomy because of pressing problems with his own.

I yanked my pistol from the ground, picked up his rifle, took Red's Beretta from Gil's pocket, and watched Gil writhe in the dirt.

"We should get back." I wanted to say more, but none of it was kind, or professional.

Up on the ridge, Desperado seemed to be cutting loose with a whole string of the things I couldn't say.

"Why do I have to go with you? I swear, Sweet Lips, I think you're stalking me. If you want to have sex, you shouldn't knee a man in his privates."

"You're under arrest for assaulting a deputy."

"What gives you the right to come here in the first place?"

"We came to take you in for questioning."

"About?"

"You tried to beat Austin Williams to death."

"I did not."

"He's in the hospital in critical condition."

"You're insane. Just my luck, you're an insane fucking stalker bitch."

Lately I didn't seem to be making any friends in the cowboy sector.

I unclipped handcuffs from my belt. "You're under arrest."

"Hold on there, Deputy Do-Right. I hit him once with a shovel handle. I admit to that, but it wasn't assault, and when I left he was fine."

"Let's go."

"You're such a bitch."

"Now you're just being redundant."

"You're a heartless bitch."

"I'm a mean, heartless bitch. We still have to go." I flipped open my cell phone and called the dispatcher. He would send an ambulance as far as it could get and would also notify the sheriff. I told him we'd proceed towards the stables on horseback.

I cuffed Gil and recited his rights while he called me a lot of things—heartless bitch was the least aggravating. We walked with his horse until we reached mine. He made our progress as difficult as he could.

I brought Millie down for Red but I wasn't sure how I would get him onto her. His shirtsleeve was soaked with blood, but when I ripped the material away the bleeding had mostly stopped. It appeared he had a through and through.

"I can get on if you just give me a hand when I say," he said.

With less struggle than I would've thought, we got him on and headed back to where Gil waited against his will.

"There's no need for these handcuffs," the prisoner yelled as we approached.

"I'm not going to take them off."

"How will I ride with my hands cuffed together?"

"I'll show you how."

"I wouldn't really have hurt you, Sweet Lips."

He had a shirt that wasn't ripped and I needed it. I had all the weapons.

"I'm going to remove these cuffs so you can take your shirt off—slowly—and set it on the ground. One false move and I'll shoot you."

"You wouldn't shoot me."

"Try me."

"Oh, I get it. You want to see me naked."

I didn't bother to set him straight.

As he took off his shirt he said, "Next, it'll be my pants."

"If you take off your pants, I *will* shoot you."

Red chuckled at that but reserved comment.

When Gil was re-cuffed, I put his shirt on over my ruined one.

"Aw, Sweet Lips, you want to kill all the fun."

I ignored him and finally got him into the saddle while he protested and called me creative combinations of derogatory names.

We had to move slowly because of Red's injury. The rodeo cowboy wasn't doing so well either. He was not a horseman, only a two-second bull rider.

At one stop I heard hoof beats thundering towards us and pulled out my weapon, expecting more bad boys. It was Sheriff Ben. I was so relieved to see him I could've cried, except I was in my tough lawman role. In all those old cowboy movies Austin and I loved to watch, I'd never seen any sheriff or deputy cry.

After he greeted us, he said, "I thought I should come myself. You okay, Red?"

"Yes sir."

"The ambulance had to stop after the first pasture, but they're waiting."

"She's a bitch," spit Gil.

"Hmm," said the sheriff.

"I'm not kidding," he insisted.

"Hmm," said Sheriff Ben again. Then he rode up close to Gil. "Do you understand that you have the right to remain silent?"

"Yeah, she told me."

"I would advise you to exercise that right."

Gil didn't say another word for a long time.

We were nearly back when he spoke. "I didn't assault that retarded man, Sheriff."

"Then who did?"

"I don't know, I swear."

"We'll talk back at the office."

By the time we were in the home stretch, the sun was setting. It was making its usual spectacular display in the west, oblivious to the challenges faced by sheriffs and their deputies. The soft colors made the grasses and other plants in the pasture look golden, and even the air seemed filled with flecks of gold.

Red was hustled into the ambulance and the rest of us rode to the stables. Sheriff Ben's big truck was parked at the barn. He got Gil down and put him into the back seat, then walked over to me. I was still sitting on Desperado.

"Will you put these horses away, Margarita?"

"Yes sir."

"Then come to the office."

"Did you come for us because I'm a woman?"

The sheriff pushed his hat back and zeroed in on me. "I came for you because you were deputies in trouble. The two of you had gone after a man suspected of nearly beating another man to death. When I heard that Gil had shot Red I couldn't sit still. If it had been Barney, I would've still come. Does that answer your question, Deputy?"

"I don't want to be treated differently because I'm a woman."

"Yes, I know that about you. I knew that from day one."

"Okay, then."

"What happened to your shirt?" he asked.

"Gil tore it off me, before I subdued him."

"I see." His attention moved to my feet. "Are those your boots, Deputy Ricos?"

"You don't like them?"

The sheriff blushed. "Oh, I like them fine. They just don't look like you."

"They're definitely not me."

"I don't think you should let Barney see you in those."

"No sir, I won't."

He grinned, tipped his hat, and got into his truck.

* * *

When I returned to the office, I got an extra uniform shirt from my locker and took myself and Gil's shirt into the sheriff's office. I was glad to get the fake-cowboy-sweaty- criminal smell of him away from me.

"He admitted to hitting him once with the shovel," the sheriff said when I walked in. "But he swears Austin was conscious and walking when he left. Gil tells a similar story to the others, about another man being there."

"The tall, silent, one-armed stranger."

"I want you to talk to Austin and see if he remembers something else now. Maybe there was another man. Before you go, I need to tell you that the flashlight we sent to the lab had the prints of Jimmy Joe Blanks."

"So he was at my house." *Looking into my bedroom with a flashlight.*

"Are you surprised?"

"Well, no—and it explains a few things." A thought came that practically made my hair stand on end. "Sheriff, what if Jimmy Joe assaulted Austin?"

"Why would he do that?"

"He saw me with him and didn't like it. He can't understand that Austin is like a brother to me. He told Barney I'd broken his heart by sleeping with a retarded man."

"Jimmy Joe might be the tall stranger those guys saw hanging around. I'm going to get another deputy and go to his apartment. I'll call you when I know something."

Chapter 30

Austin was sleeping when I got there, and it took him a while to come around, but he looked much better.

He spoke with effort. "Let's order pizza. I could eat two, and we need lots of soda."

I nearly burst into tears at the normalcy of that. He was still an awful combination of colors, but he seemed more like himself. His eye had opened enough to see green. He looked much better with both of his eyes.

After I ordered the pizza I sat on the edge of his bed.

"Austin, is there any way another man could've hurt you? Gil says he hit you once and that there was another man there."

"That's right. Gil hit me once." Austin's words were strained, but he seemed to be thinking clearly. "When he left, the other man came up to me and said *she's mine you can't have her*. I didn't know what he meant."

My cell phone rang. When I snapped it open, Sheriff Ben said, "Jimmy Joe is not here but you should see his place. It's a shrine to Margarita Ricos. He—um—has some of your things. There is a life-size photo of you running towards a mountain, and others. You would be horrified."

"I am, Sheriff. I don't know what to say."

"The man is more ill than we realized. I've got every deputy looking for him except you. Barney is keeping his eyes open down south. Were you able to get anything from Austin?"

"Yes, he says Gil hit him once. When Gil left another man came up to him. It was Jimmy Joe Blanks, Sheriff."

"Tell Austin not to worry. We'll find him."

I related what I knew to Austin, who took it in stride.

"I'm so sorry, Austin. The man had been bothering me but I never had a reason to think he would hurt you."

Austin lifted one hand with difficulty and placed it on mine. "It isn't your fault. Stop now or I'll have to kick your ass."

I laughed and lay down next to him.

The man the cowboys called "The Retard" said, "You think you control everything, bulls and bull riders and rodeo cowboys and your friends."

I stared at him, speechless.

"Do you control the weather, too? Sometimes I don't like it."

That made us laugh, although his was stopped abruptly by pain.

"You expect sunny and seventy-two every day, don't you?" I said.

"Yes, if you were any good at controlling it, that's how it'd be."

I could see how he hurt. "Are the pain meds working?" I asked. "Do you need a stronger dose?"

"Don't talk about pain. Talk about something else."

"But Austin——"

"I'm okay. Better. Talk about something else."

"What did you do today while I was out messing up the weather?"

"I mostly slept. Sheriff Ben came by. I like him."

"I like him, too."

"I hope they hurry up with that pizza."

"I can't believe you want to eat pizza. Didn't they serve you dinner?"

"Sure, but a man can't eat too much pizza," he said. "Why don't we watch an old cowboy movie?"

I intended to watch the movie with him, but I was asleep before the pizza arrived, nestled safely against his warmth. Well, it felt safe then.

During the night I felt a sharp sting on my neck, the kind of quick jab a scorpion gives. I swiped at the imaginary creature and the room spun. Before I could say or do anything, I passed out.

* * *

I awoke disoriented and nauseated, lying on my side facing a metal wall, with my wrists tightly bound. My shoulders and arms ached. I didn't know where I was, but remembered the sudden sting and that I had been sleeping next to Austin. Then it came back in a jumble of vivid mental images, some comforting, like Austin, but most of them frightening.

The hospital gown had been replaced with black lace panties and bra, which meant that someone had undressed and re-dressed me. I didn't think I'd been raped, but before my mind began conjuring all the horrible things that can be done to a woman, a metal door squealed open and footsteps came towards me.

Jimmy Joe Blanks stood over me. "I'm glad to see you're awake," he said, as if I was a willing houseguest and he, my cordial host. Then he lifted me and set me on a straight-backed wooden chair.

"What am I doing here, Jimmy Joe?"

"I'm going to feed you some breakfast and we'll talk."

I didn't complain because I'd missed lunch and dinner the day before. I needed strength, and time to think about how to get away from this lunatic. I wasn't sure how to play the situation, so I kept my mouth shut and occupied myself by looking around the room. We were in a small barn-like structure made of metal and divided into a bedroom, kitchen, and living area by theme rather than walls. The theme in the bedroom was the same as the one in his apartment: Margarita. I was everywhere. There was a poster made from a photo of me running in the shorts Papi had said would bring me trouble. Jimmy Joe had been in Terlingua more than once, and had watched and followed me and been through my things. It was past terrifying and made me afraid for my life. There was only one door I could see, and I prayed to get through it unharmed.

The smell of bacon frying was tortuous and made it difficult to concentrate.

I wanted to berate Jimmy Joe and demand he untie me but I was alone God-knew-where with a perp who had tried to beat a man to death. He was cruel and insane and I kept reminding myself of that so I wouldn't run my big mouth.

"I hope you like pancakes and bacon," he said, playing the gentleman. For all I knew, he thought he really was one.

"I like them, but could you untie me Jimmy Joe? I'm in a lot of pain."

He set down the spatula he was holding and came to me and began rubbing my shoulders. I would've felt safer with a rattlesnake draped around my neck.

"Please untie me, Jimmy Joe."

"We haven't begun the lessons yet."

"What lessons?"

"I'm going to teach you how to treat a man who loves you."

"If you love me then you won't hurt me," I said as if sure of it.

"I won't hurt you unless you force me to. I think these lessons might come hard for you, Margarita."

No shit.

"I'll untie you when we eat," he promised. "I hope you won't try anything because I'll be forced to cause you pain if you do that."

"I won't try anything." *Unless I get half a chance.*

"I wish I could believe you but unfortunately, I don't. You've already demonstrated how hard-headed you are." He caressed my face lovingly, but his reptile eyes held nothing like love. I tried to show no revulsion.

"Everything is okay, my precious girl," he crooned. "I like a woman with spirit. You're sexy as hell."

A bit later, when he was flipping pancakes he said, "I think we'll be very happy together from here on out."

I managed to stay quiet on the subject and wondered if anyone was looking for me and how they would find me and if it would be too late when they did. If Sheriff Ben realized I was missing, he would search, and Barney, he'd come and kick ass if he could, and my papi—my papi was likely to bust down every door in Alpine looking for me, but I didn't even know if I was still in Alpine. My spirits sunk so low I was terrified I would cry in front of Jimmy Joe, and I didn't know how that would affect his behavior. I swallowed back hysteria.

"I would like some clothes, Jimmy Joe," I said when he moved me to a small metal café-style table for two. "I can't eat like this."

"Why not? You do it at home." That shut me up.

Then he said, "Let me see what I have," as if he was a reasonable man, and went into the bedroom area. Out of a wooden trunk he pulled some of my clothes, running shorts, a couple of t-shirts, a sheer violet teddy, and a lacy white negligee set Kevin gave me. It was beautiful and it infuriated me for Jimmy Joe Blanks to touch anything that came from my husband. How dare he take personal things of mine? But stealing was the least of his sins.

He held each item up against himself, as if to model it. He looked freaking ridiculous and I wanted to tell him he turned my stomach and that I felt like killing him for what he did to Austin, but instead I said, "I'd like to wear the shorts and a t-shirt, please."

He brought the teddy instead. "I prefer this."

I wanted to kick his teeth out and serve them to him on a plate.

"That's for sleeping," I said. "Please let me wear the shorts."

"You sleep naked, I happen to know. This thing is for sex. We'll get to that later."

I thought: *over my dead body*, but my next thought was that this adventure could end that way and I didn't want it to. I had to keep myself alive.

He finally brought me the shorts. Then he untied my wrists and let me dress, but he watched. Then he let me go to the bathroom while he guarded the door. I hoped for a window but there wasn't one. There were only two windows in the whole place and those held air conditioners. There was no way to see out of them, much less crawl through one of them.

When we sat at the table, Jimmy Joe laid a firearm on the table next to his plate. It was a Beretta similar to mine. He said nothing and didn't need to. I understood the message.

I ate in silence, listening to Jimmy Joe chatter as if we were a contented couple and one of us wasn't under house arrest. I was like a cat waiting in tall grass for a bird. If he moved from the table, I was going to spring for the Beretta and shoot him. I asked for more food, and later, more water, for the express purpose of getting him to leave the pistol on the table. Great plan, but it didn't work.

Suddenly he said, "I was trying to teach that retard a lesson about sleeping with my woman and he bit me."

What the hell?

"What do you mean?"

"I tried to make him suck my dick, but the little fucker bit me."

Way to go, Austin!

"I think the goddamn bite is infected."

"You should get medical help," I suggested sweetly.

After eating we sat in the living area. If he hadn't had the Beretta pointing at me, I would have kicked him hard in the crotch and taken it away. I waited for any chance to do that, but Jimmy Joe Blanks was as wary as he was demented. I sat on a sofa he indicated and willed him to sit next to me, but that didn't work either.

He began to talk about sex and what a great lover he was. I watched as impassively as I could, nearly biting through my lip to keep from commenting on his damaged equipment. I was cold with terror that he'd rape me with an assortment of unspeakable items. All attempts to reign in my imagination were futile.

I tried to steer the conversation away from sex by asking where we were and how long we'd been here. I didn't see how we could just live in a metal building forever and wanted a feel for how far from reality Jimmy Joe had slipped. He gave me no clue, except for his ramblings about sex and how much I'd enjoy it with him. That was pretty far from reality.

A tiny glimmer of hope surfaced when Jimmy Joe tied me so he could go to the bathroom. He handcuffed my wrists and then attached them to the bathroom door. Within seconds of entering, I heard him groan pitiably. That was where hope came in. I thought hard about kicking him with all my strength when he came out, but didn't know if it would be hard enough—or what he would do to me later. Patience would be best. Just have patience.

Jimmy Joe was in the bathroom a long time. When he came out he looked pale and sweaty and was breathing heavily. I resisted the urge to speak. He unhooked me from the door and led me to the bedroom.

"I need to rest," he said, "and I want you with me."

I lay down on the bed only because he insisted. I didn't want him to touch me or even be in the same state with me. He removed the handcuffs and tied me to the bedpost using the violet teddy and a pair of lacy white bikini underpants that didn't look up to the job. I knew if he would go to sleep I could free myself. My mind held to that happy thought while he touched my breasts. Mercifully for me, his pain was bad enough that his fondling didn't last long. Sweat stood on his forehead, even though the room felt cold enough to hang meat.

"I need a doctor," he said after lying still a while. "I'm sick."

"Do you have a phone? I'll call EMS."

"Nice try."

"You said you needed a doctor."

"I wasn't talking to you."

I didn't dare ask to whom he was speaking. I lay quietly, held captive by my own lingerie and had the irrational urge to laugh hysterically. They never talked about anything like my predicament in the law enforcement academy. I wondered if any other deputies had been tied up with their underwear and then hoped that none of my colleagues would ever have to know anything about it. I could live down throwing up at a crime scene, but I thought I'd never live down lying in bed with a man who had an infected bite on his penis, while tied with my own intimate apparel.

When I ventured to look at him after ten minutes or so, I saw that my captor had closed his eyes. He held the Beretta in his right hand, against his chest. I could feel the heat coming from him and wondered what his temperature was, but on the other hand, didn't care if his brain boiled.

When Jimmy Joe began to snore softly, I started working my right hand free of the wispy panties. To my surprise, they held on a long time before they began to give way. The lace made a tiny ripping sound and each time it tore I checked Jimmy Joe for a reaction. He cried out once, nearly stopping my heart, but continued to sleep, and after a few more minutes I pulled one hand free. I flexed it and then moved it slowly to the other one and undid the knotted teddy. My heart was pounding so hard I was sure it would wake Jimmy Joe so I lay still, trying to calm myself.

I was terrified to rise from the bed and risk waking him, but I thought it was just as risky to try to grab the gun from a prone position. The barrel of it faced me when I raised myself onto one elbow. He was on my left, so I was raised on my left elbow and since I'm left-handed it made it all the more awkward. If I panicked him, he could put a bullet into my chest without aiming.

Lying there passive, waiting for the lunatic to wake up wasn't an option, so inch by inch I moved myself to the floor. If he sighed or moved or cried out I froze in place. I've never done anything that required so much patience. By the time I reached the floor, he was breathing deeply and steadily. My weight was off the bed and he hadn't noticed, so if I was ever going to get my hands on his gun now was the time.

At a rate a crippled turtle could have beaten, I crawled around the bed. In one movement I stood and grabbed. Jimmy Joe turned fitfully in his sleep and my heart stopped. I didn't want to shoot a sick man lying down, but I was prepared to. In the process of removing the weapon, my fingers grazed his skin and I realized how ill he was. His skin was hot, hotter than human skin should be, but I wasn't going to stand around wringing my hands over him. I began backing towards the door.

It was locked by a serious contraption, similar to the kind used in a bank safe, and it required a combination. I wasn't going to be able to open it and if I shot at it, the door wouldn't open, and I'd probably be killed by a ricochet. Disheartened, I began looking for a cell phone—or any phone. I found one, but wherever I was, there were no bars. Finally I ran across Jimmy Joe's service radio still hooked to uniform pants that were in a jumbled heap on the bathroom floor. It was sheer luck that he had failed to turn in the radio to the sheriff.

I shut and locked the door, picked up the radio, and said, "Sheriff Ben." It was going to be an entertaining day for the police scanner eavesdroppers.

His response was nearly instant. "Margarita!"

"I need help," I whispered, "but I don't know where I am."

"I know where you are. Where's JJB?"

"Sleeping, I have his weapon."

"Will you be safe if I pull the door out?"

"I might have to shoot the subject."

"Do what you have to. I'm coming."

When I came out of the bathroom, Jimmy Joe jumped me and drove a knife into my side before I could shoot him. It was a surprise attack from a man who should've been too ill to plan it—too ill to move. The Beretta skittered across the floor like a live thing. I believe Jimmy Joe would've picked it up and shot me if two things hadn't happened at once. The winch on Sheriff Ben's gigantic Ford truck pulled the door away from the structure holding it. There was an alarming amount of noise that I barely noted because of the fire searing my side. The second thing that kept Jimmy Joe Blanks from killing me was that he passed out cold, or in his case, hot.

The sheriff was suddenly beside me, his pistol drawn.

"Don't move," he said to Jimmy Joe, but they were wasted words.

There was a knife handle sticking out of me, and I could feel the warmth of my blood flowing around my fingers where I held my side. I'd had enough emergency medical training to know not to remove it or I'd risk bleeding to death.

I was leaning against the wall and about the time my knees started to go, Sheriff Ben took hold of me.

"The ambulance is right behind me," he said. "I was afraid he'd hurt you, so I asked them to follow."

He was an amazing, larger-than-life superhero. I wanted to ask him how he knew where to find me but right then it didn't matter. The point was that he had.

Chapter 31

As it turned out, Austin had saved me by remembering that Jimmy Joe Blanks spoke to him once at a rodeo, and in the course of conversation, mentioned that he liked to take girls to his ranch. Austin called Sheriff Ben, the sheriff knew where the ranch was, and the rest you know.

Officially, Austin was released from the hospital two days before I was. He didn't leave my side and slept curled around me the same way I'd slept with him. We felt safe because a deputy was guarding Jimmy Joe Blanks, whose room was down the hall from mine. Jimmy Joe was being treated for "a really wicked bite wound"—Sheriff's words. After that he would be transported to the county jail.

Rocky Hill and Gil Young had been released on bail, but Gil would still have to face the judge, who would kick his ass for attacking a handicapped man.

I had quite a few visitors, including my parents. My mother insisted on checking my wound herself. She declared that it was healing nicely but if Jimmy Joe hadn't had a deputy guarding him, one or both of my parents would have made his life even more miserable. At one point my mom caressed my hot face with her cool hands like she had when I was little, declared that I had fever, and went to give instructions to my doctor.

In spite of visitors I still had time to think about the murder and was sure I knew what had happened.

I left the hospital walking gingerly, but I was going to be fine. There were stitches in my side, and I was full of antibiotics and pain pills. After I let Austin off at his house, I sat in my Explorer and called Barney.

"You realize you're the hot topic dontcha?" was the first thing he said. "The sheriff has forbidden the deputies from talking about it."

"Good, then you shouldn't."

"A lot of the details have been in the Alpine paper."

I groaned. "Please don't tell me anything else."

"Are you all right, Ricos?"

"I'll live, but I may not want to when the deputies get hold of me. Anyway, let's don't talk about them. I want to talk to you about the murder."

"Well, if you insist."

"I'm sure Lil Munch paid Chapo Rodriguez to kill Norma."

"Dígame," he said. Tell me.

"We know Chapo's been up to something. Lil knows that Norma lied to her and used her. After the lawsuit was over, she turned against Lil and told her it was her fault, because of course, Norma couldn't accept blame about anything."

"Right."

"Lil thought Norma was her friend, but Norma was incapable of real friendship. You know what the list says about sociopaths being charming, yet covertly hostile?"

"Yeah, I remember."

"It also says, and I quote, "Instead of friends, they have victims and accomplices that end up as victims." Lil started out as a friend, and became Norma's accomplice. But then when things didn't go Norma's way, and the case was mediated, Norma didn't need Lil and Lil became her victim."

"Makes sense so far."

"I'm thinking Lil didn't take that well. She's a how-dare-they type, the type that burns to get even. And she has little man syndrome, even though she's a woman."

We had a laugh about that then I pressed on. "She was in Houston, and that took us off her scent at first. Her alibi seems airtight, and it is. She stayed with her cousin and paid pathetic, stupid Chapo to do her dirty work. Then, because she knew Mom was sure to come under suspicion, she decided to set her up with falsely planted evidence."

"I see where you're going, Ricos."

"Setting up Mom is Lil's style, and it wouldn't be the first time. She watched Norma do it before, and was her willing accomplice."

"So Lil had motive," he said.

"She's the only suspect we know about who makes sense. And Chapo has been bragging that he killed an old gringa. We've only got the one dead gringa."

"You have something here."

"Lil has money, so she could buy a hit. And like my mom said, she lacks heart. And she and Norma had already spoken to someone about killing my mother, so all Lil did was turn the tables. I'm sure she thinks she's clever."

"It's so cold."

"They were the coldest ever. Norma was like a deep freeze. Lil was Deep Freeze, Junior."

"How are we going to get them?"

"I think you should go see Lil and put some pressure on her," I said. "Make her admit it, then——"

"Whoa there, John Wayne. I think you're getting ahead of yourself. How will I make her admit anything?"

"Let me finish. I was going to say that while you do that, I'll talk to Chapo and tell him Lil gave him up. He'll either crumble or be forced to tell me what he's really up to. You can tell Lil that Chapo is talking. She's easy to read and she'll freak."

Barney drummed a pencil against the desk. "I think your plan is good but I should talk to Chapo and you should talk to Lil. For one thing, you're already up there. For another, she's afraid of you."

"She knows I hate her guts."

"You just don't want to see her again."

"That's true."

"You'd rather hang out with Chapo?"

"Okay, I get your point. I suppose I'd choose Lil. What a crappy choice. "

"No kidding. It's like choosing between shit and vomit."

I laughed even though it hurt.

"Should we do it at the same time?" he asked.

"No, let me talk to Lil first, because if she admits to it, then you can go arrest Chapo and you won't be in so much danger."

"How do you figure?"

"I don't know—I guess it's dangerous no matter how it goes. I was thinking you could slam him over the head with a beer bottle when he's drunk, cuff him while he's out cold, and drag him in."

"Oh sure, Sheriff Ben will love that approach."

"Let's do it today."

"Are you sure you feel up to it? How are you really?"

"I feel as up to it as I'll ever be. My side hurts like fire, but working will keep my mind off it. I want to get this murder off our plate."

"Me too, Ricos."

"I have to say, it'd make me happy to see Lil's smug ass go to prison."

"You forgot former Deputy Blanks, poor ol' Shoots."

"Don't start. It's really not funny. He's a sick man."

"I know it, Ricos. I don't know how you're keeping it together."

"My husband is dead. My father isn't really my father. My mother lied to me about my birth and lied to the sheriff about being blackmailed. I've been stabbed in the side by a raving maniac who made shrines to a woman he never knew. My best friend, the kindest man in the world, was viciously beaten. What else is going to happen, Barney? What the fuck else?"

"I don't know, but when you use the F-word—well, I've never heard you use it. It won't do anybody any good if you go off the deep end. We don't want you bein' 'flicted, too."

He made me laugh, and that seemed to dispel the dark cloud hanging over my head.

"I guess you're going to go see Lil today," he said, "because you're such an over-achieving superhero type."

"I just need a mask and cape, Batman."

"No you don't."

"Austin thinks the superpowers are in the uniform, but lately it's failing me."

"The superpowers are in *you*, Ricos. Wake up, smell the bat cave, Batgirl."

I laughed at that even though the movement pained me.

"If we solve the murder," Barney said, "do you think people will treat us with more respect?"

"I doubt it. Nobody cares much about Norma's death. And nobody in Terlingua trusts law enforcement. If we come down on them we're macho hard-asses and if we don't we're a couple of stupid pussies."

He laughed. "Well it might at least shut a few people up."

"I'm all for that, and it'll impress the sheriff."

"Ricos, the sheriff thinks you hung the moon."

"He does not."

"Does too. Well anyway, good luck," he said. "Call me the minute you can."

I was in no mood to face Lil. I needed to run a few miles just to calm myself, but any movement pained me too much. I thought a frosty longneck would be good instead. But no, longnecks paled next to running. Besides, running made me feel alive. Drinking made me wish I was dead. There wasn't even a contest.

* * *

I took a deep breath and flung off my seatbelt, dreading what I had to do. Lil threw open the front door when I was about halfway up the path to her house. She stopped in mid-motion, staring in disbelief.

"Good morning, Lil."

"You're just hassling me because you don't know what else to do." She looked like she was going to start stomping her foot like a two-year-old. Then she said, "Come on in," with civility. Go figure. I followed her inside, slowly, holding my side, and we sat.

"What happened to you, anyway?" she wondered.

"I was stabbed working a case."

She smirked. "I guess your work is more dangerous than I would've thought."

It was horrible being with her again.

"I just have a few questions for you," I said in my solemn law enforcement voice. It's good to wear a professional uniform and look serious and spiffy when you have to keep a straight face and do unpleasant work.

"I'm sure I don't have anything to add to what I've already said a hundred times."

"Lil, I'm finding it hard to believe you don't know Chapo Rodriguez." I was trying to stare her down. "I believe you do know him."

"Well you're mistaken. I don't."

"I think you paid him to kill Norma."

Lil stared at me with her mouth open. She started twice to speak. Finally she said, "What the hell? You've lost your mind."

So much for the direct surprise attack. What had I expected? To see guilt on her face? For Lil to cut and run? For her to pour out her heart about the wicked thing she'd done? She was staring at me, probably expecting me to say something. I wanted to cut and run.

"You're going to sit there and tell me that isn't true?" I asked.

Of course she was. And I couldn't see one drop of guilt or anything else on her face.

"You want so badly for it to be me that now you're making shit up. Does the sheriff know what you're doing?"

"The sheriff expects me to find the murderer."

"Well, I'm not it." She began compulsively smoothing her cotton slacks, running her hands down her thighs to just past her knees, over and over. There had to be something to that. But maybe she was only crazy, not guilty of murder.

"Why can't we just admit we're enemies and you go your way and I'll go mine?" she said, still smoothing her pants.

I took a deep breath. "Chapo told me he was the one you and Norma spoke with about killing my mom."

"You're lying!"

I was following a hunch.

"No, Lil. He's also been telling people that he got a new truck because he killed someone for money."

Lil stood and began checking the books and magazines on the coffee table, even though they looked perfectly aligned to my eye.

"If someone paid Chapo to kill Norma, it must've been Stanner." She was busy, and not looking at me.

"Why do you say that?"

"Well who else would it be if it wasn't your mother? He had plenty of reasons to get rid of her."

"What reasons?"

"Maybe he wanted Norma out of the way so he could be with his girlfriend. I imagine Norma was hard to live with. I think your mother is most likely, though. I couldn't believe it when they put her in jail and then let her go."

"There wasn't enough evidence to keep her."

Lil turned to me, incredulous. "A bloody knife and shirt found on her property wasn't enough? What kind of shoddy crap is it that you people call investigating?"

The bloody shirt had never been mentioned in the news of the arrest and Mom's subsequent release. There was no way Lil could know about it unless she had something to do with placing it there. Finally, I was getting somewhere.

"It appeared the evidence had been placed by someone wanting to implicate Mom. Some things about it were wrong. It was a weak attempt by an amateur."

A look of fury passed over Lil's face. "Your mother hated Norma. She seems obvious as her killer."

"Yes, you've said that already and frankly, Lil, she hates you, too. Why would she murder only one of you?" I stared at her with open dislike, the way you look at dog poop you just tracked onto new white carpet.

My side throbbed and my gut screamed to get away from there.

Lil came back, sat, and was smoothing her pants again.

Suddenly she sighed. "All of the people I trusted let me down."

"How so?"

"Stephanie let me down by stealing—I don't care what receipts she produced, I know she was stealing. And Norma blamed everything on me and it wasn't my fault. She told me we'd get control of the organization, that Steph would step down, that she'd be shamed into it. She said the other board members didn't know anything or care about financial things. She didn't think they would back up Stephanie. She was wrong about everything, and then she blamed me."

She looked at me and clasped her hands together. "Really, I have things to do and I've already been interviewed three or four times. I have a busy day today."

"Lil, did you plant the evidence at my mother's house?"

She slowly flushed scarlet. I thought she was going to go for my wound any time.

"My God, you just won't give up, will you? Of course I didn't do any such thing. I wouldn't go near that woman's house."

"You had someone plant it for you?"

"No. I had nothing to do with it."

"Then how can you know there was a shirt? That detail wasn't made public." I could see I'd shocked her. "I guess I heard it somewhere," she finally said.

"You had it put there," I said, pressing my luck.

She turned to face me. "I want you to get out of my house right now!"

"I'll leave, but this isn't over."

"Don't you ever come back here," she growled. "GET OUT!"

I stood. "I'm leaving, but Chapo is talking, Lil, so it's just a matter of time."

I headed back to my Explorer. She was ranting about reporting me to the sheriff. *Fine.* If I came back, she said, she would shoot me. *Go for it.*

We were close to solving Norma's murder; we just had to work out the details.

I called Barney. "I shouldn't have done it today," I said. "I'm not thinking clearly. I barely got any sleep last night and I have a lot of things on my mind."

"I don't think the way you did it matters. The point is you stirred things up."

"She just didn't react the way I thought she would."

"She's in deep, Ricos. That's the point."

We agreed that Lil had either murdered Norma, paid to have it done, or knew something she didn't want to share.

"I'm going to look for Chapo," Barney said.

"Be careful, Barney. Don't forget he's most likely a killer."

"I would assume that man has killed someone, even if it wasn't Norma."

"Yeah, well don't forget it."

I hung up and sat there picturing Cimarron Mountain standing alone in the hot morning sun. I longed to be running towards it.

Chapter 32

I was parked near Highway 118, and if it hadn't been for that, I would've missed Lil. She screeched onto the pavement in her small Honda SUV without stopping to check for traffic coming either way. So she failed to see a Sheriff's Office Explorer sitting there, off the road, but in plain view. Lil took off in the direction of Terlingua, leaving behind a cloud of dust. I felt compelled to follow her.

Soon after I pulled onto the highway I called Barney.

"Are you still in the office?"

"Why are you checking on me?"

"I'm following Lil because she's headed that way. I'm calling to ask you to wait to look for Chapo. Maybe I can catch them together."

"What makes you think she's coming here?"

"A gut feeling, and she hasn't pulled off the highway, and she's going ninety. She's hauling ass to get to Chapo before we do. My guess is she's going to kill him."

Barney was uncharacteristically quiet a moment. "That would shut him up, wouldn't it?"

"No silence like death." *I've been hearing it for over a year.*

"Be careful, Ricos. Stay in touch with me."

"I'll touch base when I get closer to Terlingua. I'd like for you to join me."

"I'll be standing by," he said.

We were coming out of the mountains that stand between north and south Brewster County, Lil in front, and me a safe distance behind. We flew past the picnic area at Elephant Mountain, where Sheriff Ben had a stern talk with me what seemed like an eternity ago.

When we reached the top of Halfway Hill and the long road stretched for miles towards the mountains of South County, I knew that I was nearing the end of my own long road back. I had loved with all my heart and been loved back the same way. I would never forget Kevin, but I would love again because loving and living are in my nature. A peaceful feeling settled over me that even chasing a murderer couldn't remove.

In the distance, the rugged mountains I adore stood sure and serene in the dazzling sunlight.

* * *

When we reached the flats, Lil eased her speed up to one hundred miles per hour. I wondered if she noticed a vehicle far behind, going as fast as she was. No matter her speed, I stayed the same distance from her. I doubted if she had thought about it. I believed she had murder on her mind, and not much else.

Finally we were passing Cimarron. It forms the right side of the broad hill that slopes down to Terlingua. The Chisos Mountains stand to the left, protecting the national park, but are further away than Cimarron.

I flipped open my cell phone, and when Barney answered I said, "I'm here."

"Where's she heading?"

"It looks like she's checking for him at the café."

"I'm going to my Explorer. Don't hang up. I'm with you."

"Thanks, Barn." I heard him start the vehicle. "He's not at work—or at least his truck isn't there, but she's parking in front anyway."

"Where are you?"

"I'm next door at the motel, behind the sign. I don't think she'll notice me. It looks like she's talking on her cell phone."

"She's making arrangements to meet him, don't you think?"

"Yes, that's exactly what I think."

"I'm going to pull up near the highway and sit there until you say to move."

"Good idea."

"What are you thinking, Batgirl?" he asked after a few seconds.

"She sure is long-winded."

"Maybe she hasn't been able to reach him yet."

"That's possible. Surely she wouldn't be talking to him so long. Then again, she might be lecturing him. I told her he'd been talking."

Suddenly Barney laughed.

"What?"

"I was just thinking I'd like to see that little woman back Chapo into a corner."

"Maybe they'll kill each other."

"That would save us a lot of effort."

"I don't think it'll be that easy," I said.

"Of course not, it never is. Ricos, do you think Austin will be able to get over it?"

"Yes, he most likely will. He's a loving and forgiving man. And he's happy from within and believes in himself. But I doubt if he'll ever be as innocent and trusting as he was. I'd like to kill Jimmy Joe for destroying that."

"Yeah, I know what you mean."

I saw that Lil had started her SUV.

"She's moving Barney, heading your way. My guess is she's going to Chapo's house. When I pass you, follow me."

"10-4."

I pulled onto the highway far enough behind Lil that I didn't think she'd notice. When I passed the road to our office, Barney pulled in behind me.

"Tailing," he said.

"If she's going to his house we can't just follow her."

"What do you have in mind?"

"When we start to get close, let's pull off and approach on foot. We'll run across the desert and come in the back way to his place. She'll be going in the front."

Lil surprised both of us by not turning where we thought she would. She stayed on the highway, heading west, and was picking up speed.

"I bet she's meeting him at the river," I said.

"He must be there already."

"That would be my guess."

Before long we passed the Ghost Town on the right and then Reed's Plateau on the left. I thought that would be a good place to run. There was also Long Draw, an arroyo that crossed the highway in three places. It went off into a valley to the right that was surrounded by steep cliffs. That would be a good place for running, too. I realized, with a profound sense of gratitude, that there were more beautiful places to run where I lived than I'd ever have time to explore in one lifetime.

"Maybe he was drinking beer over in Paso Lajitas," Barney said, drawing me back to the job at hand.

"Probably, it must be his day off."

"How's your side holding up?"

"I'm okay."

Lil slowed slightly as she entered the resort town of Lajitas but flew right through it, passed the river crossing just west of there, and the stone wall where I'd overheard the conversation of the Mexican cowboys.

"Do you think she's going to Presidio?"

"No," I said. "I think she's going to the old movie set."

"What makes you think so?"

"It would be private and a good place to kill somebody. It could be a long time before his body is discovered."

"Have you given a lot of thought to killing somebody at the movie set?"

"I'm just trying to imagine where I'd take a guy I was planning to eliminate, and it seems like a good place."

In the 1980's a movie was filmed near Lajitas and a set was constructed on the bank of the river a few miles upriver from there. It pretended to be a tiny piece of a Mexican town in the movie, and the scenes were shot from Mexico looking back into the U.S. You can't believe anything you see onscreen. It is now part of Big Bend Ranch State Park and the buildings have been preserved as part of the area's history.

"If she doesn't stop there, then it would be anybody's guess what she's doing," I said. "Maybe I'm completely wrong about everything."

"I highly doubt it," said my partner. "What are the chances you'd leave her house and she'd get a sudden uncontrollable urge to look at the Rio Grande?"

"Well, she's a bit on the crazy side."

Because the road went constantly into dips and curves, it was impossible to tell that Lil had stopped until I was all but on top of her. I flipped on my lights. "She's stopping," I said. "Our only chance is to speed by like we've been called to an accident upriver. I'm going to floor it."

"I'm with you."

I glanced behind to see that his lights were flashing, too. We sped past in a blur. Lil was still sitting in her vehicle. I didn't see Chapo's truck, but didn't have much chance to look for it, either. Ahead there was a sharp curve and I pulled off the road, out of sight of the movie set. Barney pulled close behind, got out of the vehicle, and came towards me.

"We should approach from the river," I suggested. "We can go down that embankment on the other side of the highway and walk along the bank until we get there."

"You make it that sound like it'll be easy."

"If our jobs were easy everybody would want them."

"True enough. They don't talk about walking through the desert at the law enforcement academy—picking your way through cactus-covered terrain—"

"Are we going to go stop a murder or are you going to write a novel first?"

"Okay," he said, grinning and shrugging his massive shoulders. "Let's go."

We hurried across the highway in the direction of a sheer cliff that stands on the Mexican side. My injured side was screaming to slow down, but my gut told me to hurry up. Chapo was a slimy sort, and not someone I cared to be around, but I didn't think Lil had the right to end his life.

We picked our way down a steep embankment that was held in place by low-growing cacti and sharply pointed lechugilla plants. Falling would mean agony—and having someone pick the almost invisible cactus barbs out of your butt—nobody's idea of fun. At one point Barney reached up and took me by the arm to steady me. I smiled at him in gratitude.

The shore was uneven and rocky, but easier to negotiate than the incline. I breathed deeply of the comforting Rio Grande smell. It flowed lazily along, making a gurgling sound as it passed over tons of stones and pebbles, faithfully inching them downstream.

As we neared the movie set, we waited a second behind a sparse stand of salt cedar trees and mesquite bushes. Chapo's flashy red truck was parked on the highway behind Lil's vehicle. We didn't see any humans, but heard voices in one of the houses. We crept towards the sound.

Lil was ranting, to nobody's surprise.

"No tell nobuddy," Chapo insisted. "Me no tell."

"Deputy Ricos told me you've been bragging about the money and saying you were doing a job for a gringa."

"Liar! Her liar. Me no tell nobuddy."

"I paid you good money," she whined.

Barney and I looked at each other. I don't know what he was thinking, but I wasn't sure what to do. I had no proof that Lil was armed, but also a burning suspicion that she was. I didn't want to pop in on her and get myself shot. If she had a weapon and the opportunity, she'd do it.

Barney took his pistol out of its holster and indicated wordlessly that I should do the same. With a hand motion he suggested I go around the building one way and he'd go the other. I nodded and then crept towards the open door.

I was about to peek in when the blast of a gunshot pierced the quiet. Lil had shot Chapo and was poised to put another in him when I shot the pistol out of her hand. I ran inside with Barney right behind me. He went to Lil and I went to Chapo, as if we'd coordinated our moves ahead of time.

Lil was shrieking about bleeding to death, about suing, about her fingers. As usual, everything was about her.

I knelt beside Chapo and saw that he was in pain but would live. He'd taken a bullet to the thigh. I called the 911 dispatcher to send the medics and pressed a handkerchief against his wound.

"Me duele, me duele," he said pitifully, telling me it hurt.

"I know, but I'm trying to stop the bleeding."

I glanced at Barney who was trying to stop the flow of Lil's blood, too.

"I had to shoot her," I said. "She was going to shoot Chapo again."

Lil yelled, "You did NOT have to shoot me!"

"I know that, Ricos." To Lil Barney said, "She had to stop you somehow. She could just as easily have killed you. You might not know that Deputy Ricos is a sharpshooter."

I don't think Lil was impressed.

"I didn't kill that gringa," Chapo said.

"Just rest, don't talk." I didn't want to listen to him. My side was not going to be ignored and was making my life miserable. Lil was ranting on and on. I should've shot her tongue off.

"I have to tell you about this," Chapo whined.

"It can wait."

"No can wait," he said, reverting back to bad English. "See, she pays me twenny tousan dollahs to kill woman. I go do but no, she dead. Somebuddy kill for me."

"WHAT?!" screeched Lil.

"Stop it, Lil," Barney said. "If you can't be quiet I'll put a gag in your mouth."

"That's police brutality," she said snootily.

"It would be self-defense," he said.

"Necesitan escucharme," Chapo whined, back to Spanish. You need to listen.

I just wanted everyone to shut up. I could feel the blood pulsing in my side like the steady stabs of a knife. I sat down next to Chapo with my back against the wall.

"I'm trying to tell you something important," Chapo said in Spanish.

"I'm listening," I said and I was, but only halfway. I had to listen first to my injury because it was even more irritating than Lil or Chapo and just as insistent.

"I got to her house and she was dead on the floor."

"Right, Chapo," said Barney.

"I'm not bullshitting you, man."

"I believe every word you say."

"Nobody ever listens to me."

"Chapo," I said, "you can make a statement when we get to Alpine. The sheriff will come to your hospital room and you can tell him everything."

"I don't want to tell the sheriff. I want to tell you."

"Please Chapo, give me a break. My side hurts so badly I can't think."

"I insist you find my fingers," Lil whined to Barney.

"I don't see them," he said without looking.

I wanted to laugh but I was in too much pain. Lil launched into another rant about suing and brutality. She'd never seen brutality, except perhaps in the things she and Norma had done.

Chapo was finally resting with his eyes closed. Barney's uniform shirt was under his head. We weren't heartless. As I watched my partner ministering to Lil, I wondered how many x's there were in front of the 'XL' on the tag on his t-shirt.

Finally we heard a siren approaching. I got up and went outside to stand by the river. The muddy water swirled around the heavy rocks it couldn't move out of the way. In the stiller areas along the bank, where slender reeds grow, shiny silver minnows dart, glinting as they pass through rays of sunlight. Across the wide expanse of water, a wild burro approached timidly to take a drink. As the ambulance siren grew louder, he scampered away, kicking up his heels in protest. By the time it parked, he was gone.

Mitch ran up and gave me a quick hug, then ducked into the building. I heard him talking to Barney. He came out with Lil and her fingers. I guess it was gruesome but I didn't apologize—or even regret it. I had my mind on other things.

Mitch and another medic, Joe, brought a stretcher and loaded Chapo onto it. When the medics passed me with Chapo, Mitch said, "You're going to ride with us, aren't you? Aren't these people criminals?"

"Yes, they are. Barney's going with you."

"You should go," said Barney, coming up next to me. "You can check on Austin."

"I can't go yet. I'll be up later."

He gave me a questioning look but didn't argue.

"Mitch, can you give me a ride to my Explorer? It's not far."

He indicated I should get in.

Chapo began to insist again, using butchered English, that he hadn't killed Norma; had planned to, but she was already dead when he got there.

Lil started to chastise him, but Barney held up one of his handkerchiefs. "If you don't want this in your mouth, I suggest you close it right now."

She did.

"I mean it, Margarita, I swear it. She was dead. Her blood was all over the floor."

At my vehicle I hopped down. "I believe you, Chapo."

"You can book them on conspiracy to commit murder," I said to Barney. "They'll do time the same as for murder."

"What? What are you talking about, Ricos?"

"I'm going to bring in the murderer of Norma Bates," I said.

I got into my Explorer, my heart hurting about as much as it ever had.

Chapter 33

"It was an accident," my mother said. "I never meant to kill her, Margarita, even though she hurt me so much and in so many ways."

I hadn't said one word. This was the *what the fuck else*.

Mom was standing in the kitchen in the house where I'd grown up, her hands in the sink. The kitchen had always been a comfort-filled place with her in it. It was the place where she'd set me on the butcher block island to look at my various injuries, usually cuts and scrapes on my knees. I was hard on my knees. She would clean me with a cool cloth, apply a band-aid, and lots of kisses. Her kisses were magic and she made my world happy and secure.

My mom is a healer, not a killer. I couldn't see her that way and I suppose that's why I hadn't wanted to face the truth I had known all along. As I'd thought the day I found her on Norma's porch, one of my parents had made a terrible mistake.

"Why couldn't you have told me the truth?"

"I panicked. When I didn't tell you first thing it became harder and harder to tell you. I didn't think anyone would understand."

"I have to take you in, Mom."

"I know, Missy. I'm ready."

"Does Papi know?"

"No."

That was a relief. One of my parents hadn't lied to me—about the death of Norma Bates, anyway.

My mother sat in the back seat, not cuffed. Stephanie Ricos wasn't dangerous, and especially not to me. This happened because of her desire to protect me. I thought I'd cry about that later, but at the moment I had no tears. It was like I was too sad and disappointed to cry.

Mom didn't talk and I was okay with that. What was there to say? I thought about how she used to sing to me when she thought I was asleep. Most often she sang *Rock-a-bye Baby* but with her own words:

Rock-a-bye Rita, in the tree top
You're the best baby ever did drop
Out of the sky, you came one day
My own little angel came down to play

Corny, yes, but it was full of her love and I adored it. Man, I couldn't believe I remembered that. There was another verse, but it didn't come to mind.

We were passing Cimarron Mountain when she finally spoke. "Should I tell you what happened?"

"Mom, I should tell you that you have the right to remain silent. Anything you say can be used against you in a court of law. You have the right to have an attorney present during questioning. If you cannot afford an attorney, one will be appointed for you. Do you understand these rights?"

"Yes, Missy."

"Okay, then tell me what happened if you want to."

"I went to Norma's to try to talk some sense into her. That was on Saturday afternoon. She wouldn't budge. If I didn't make a public statement that I'd stolen funds from Doctores Fronterizos and that I'd lied about everything, and even lied in court, then she was going to show you and everybody else the letters and photos."

"What happened?"

"Well, we were at an impasse. I wasn't about to do that, and she was waving the photos around. I left very angry, and didn't have a clue what to do. I honestly didn't think about killing her. I never thought about that in a serious way, even after all she did. If I was ever going to kill her it would've been when she was trashing me in the community. But you know I'm not a killer, Margarita."

"Yes, Mom, I know."

"So I went to talk to your father who always had better sense than me. He thought we should tell you and I knew, I guess, that he was right."

She took a breath and let out a long, shuddering sigh. "I didn't want to add to your suffering. Your dad and I saw how you were still agonizing over the death of Kevin and we didn't want to add to your burden."

She was quiet a few minutes and so was I. Finally she spoke. "On Saturday night Norma called at eight o'clock and said she'd rethought her position and wanted to talk to me. I should come for coffee. I was wary but I went. There was no coffee made but she invited me in and said she'd make it. She was standing at the sink, and then the next minute she was attacking me, calling me a bitch and other, worse names. She lost it completely.

"I told her I'd decided to tell you the truth about everything, and that I was never going to cave to her ridiculous demands. She could shame me in front of the whole community. As long as you knew, I didn't care. Well, I was feeling badly for Papi, but he knows who he is, and he had faith all along that the truth would not change the relationship you two have. People would talk but so what? After a while they'd move on to someone else. Old scandal is not nearly as enticing as new scandal.

"Now I know what a real cat fight is. I've never fought like that with anyone. She kicked me and slapped me and gave me the black eye and she started throwing things at me and then she was coming at me and she was *growling*, Margarita. It's the only way I can describe it and I grabbed the handiest thing from the counter to fend her off." She sucked in a breath but barely slowed. Her next statement was said all at once with no breaks. "It was a knife but I wasn't thinking about that I didn't care what it was and I stabbed it at her but all I was thinking was to get her away from me and I thought she'd jump back but instead she was coming at me again and I couldn't believe I'd done it and there she was with all that blood going everywhere and she was dead."

She took in a few breaths, calmed a little, and began to speak more slowly. "I grabbed the letters and photos she'd laid out but there were others, worse ones she had hidden away. Those are the ones I went back for."

"How did she get those personal things?"

"I was told that Zeke left a file with his attorney for safekeeping. I suppose he forgot the nature of some of the things. The attorney was supposed to get a bank box and organize his will and personal papers. I guess he thought it was odd to have a client with connections in Terlingua and unfortunately, he spoke with his sister Norma about it. One thing led to another, and she got her hands on the things no one was ever meant to see except Zeke and me."

"When did this happen?"

"It was a few months after the mediation."

"So my biological father knows about me?"

"Yes, Missy, he knows. He has stayed away because Miguel took responsibility for you before you were born, before Zeke settled down, and he didn't want to interfere. He felt he'd lost all rights to you, but he wants to leave you money when he dies."

"So you have a photo of this Zeke Somebody?"

"Zeke Pacheco. Yes, in my purse. Do you want to see it?"

"Yes."

She handed the photo over the seat. I stuck it into my shirt pocket without looking.

"I thought you wanted to see him," she said.

"I do. I'll look at it later, when I'm not driving."

I didn't want to see Zeke for the first time with my mother looking on. I wasn't even one hundred percent sure I wanted to see him at all. I would have to think about it. I thought one father was all any girl needed, and especially when he was such a good one. Then I had the thought that I had already seen Zeke. He was the man in the crumpled, ripped photograph with the stars in his eyes. That was the man who had fathered me. Norma had the photo and my mom was trying to take it from her. It was my mother that had an affair with him, not Norma. Norma had only tried to use him against my family. I think killing is wrong, but I felt glad she was gone.

"Margarita, I hope one day you can understand that I was young and stupid twenty-five years ago," my mom said. "I was older than you are now, but not nearly as responsible as you. I got pregnant by accident, but I hope you know I never regretted it. I wouldn't trade you for anything."

"I know that, Mom. You always treated me like I was planned and you'd been waiting on me."

"You weren't planned, but when I saw your little face I did feel as though I'd been waiting for you. I knew you were exactly the right daughter for me. I don't believe God makes mistakes."

"Mom, what did you do with the knife?"

"I buried it out in the desert. I could show you if you need it."

"I'll tell the sheriff," I said, feeling no desire to see it.

After a while she said, "What will happen to me? Will I get the needle?"

"No, Mom. What you've described is self-defense. I think the District Attorney and the judge will consider it that. It'd be better if you'd come forward at the beginning, but I don't think it'll go hard on you."

"I'm sorry, Margarita, so, so sorry."

"I know, Mom. I hope you know I love you no matter what."
"I love you, too," she said in a voice breaking with emotion.

* * *

That night I stayed with Austin in a motel. My mother stayed in the county jail. It pained me, but there was nothing to be done about it until the judge had his say.

Austin and I spent the first half-hour crying in each other's arms. Then we watched old movies, ordered pizza, and laughed until we were sick. We finally exhausted ourselves and fell asleep together like little kids. I woke up once during the night with Austin's silky hair against my cheek and realized that he was the brother I had chosen for myself.

* * *

On the way home from Alpine I stopped at the picnic area, sat up on one of the tables, and stared at the mountain a long time. The shadows of fast-moving clouds were skittering over it, making constantly changing patterns of light and dark. Elephant Mountain is beautiful, with valleys and ridges, similar to Cimarron, but not as rugged. One deep canyon faced me and I could see it was full of green trees, but it was impossible to tell what kind from the distance between us.

After a while, I got out the photograph of Zeke Pacheco at age twenty-six and stared at that. It was hard to grasp that he was my father. The photo was of the same handsome man as the ripped one I found at the crime scene. I saw my resemblance to him in coloring—golden skin, dark hair and eyes, but I didn't want to see anything else. I wanted to look like my papi.

Zeke had a wide, rugged face and a beautiful smile. I couldn't find anything wrong with him, and remembered that my father, the one I'd grown up with, said he was a fine-looking man and a good one. I thought Zeke had nothing on Papi, either in looks or in goodness. I finally put the photo back in my pocket, got back in the Explorer, and headed home.

* * *

A few days later Mom was freed. The District Attorney declined to press charges after he heard from a variety of Terlingua residents about Norma's erratic and often violent behavior. Everything he heard backed up Mom's story of self-defense.

When we were standing before the judge, I looked over at her and remembered the second verse of *Rock-a-Bye Rita*. It went:

When the wind blows, you won't even cry.
You'll know you're a gift to Daddy and I.

I was smiling and the judge was looking at me like I'd lost my mind, but he did right by my mother. She was going to walk away because she'd gone to Norma's with the intention of settling their problems, not killing her. Mom had acted in good faith, typical of her, and Norma had acted in bad faith, also typical.

Mom killed her in self-defense, with no malice aforethought and in fact, it had been an accident. Norma ran forward with the intention of doing harm to Mom and had run into a knife. There were also extenuating circumstances in the form of blackmail and cruel harassment.

Lil Munch and Chapo Rodriguez were likely to serve time for conspiracy to commit murder even though Mom had been the one to end Norma's life. Conspiring to murder is a Capital Offense, in the same category as actual murder, and is a first degree felony with a prison term of five to ninety-nine years, same as first degree murder. I thought that was the way it should be. Those two had done a terrible thing; my mother had only made a terrible mistake.

Jimmy Joe Blanks was in jail, awaiting a hearing. His competence had yet to be proven one way or the other.

Austin was healing and had returned to classes but not to the stables job. The university offered him a position as an intern with the music professor, a job for which he was perfectly suited. It didn't pay much, but neither had the other one.

Austin turned his attention from love of rodeo to his love of music and people. Among other responsibilities, he would work with the chorus.

My friend would have a long journey back to mental and physical health; one that included an upcoming heart operation, but he had an indomitable spirit and a heart as big as Texas. Whenever I look into those bright green eyes, I know that he is the hero, not me.

* * *

"Well," said my big ol' partner with a sigh of relief, "that's done." He rubbed his huge hands against his blue-jeaned thighs. He was sweating profusely and had streaks of dirt on his face and some in his hair. He looked like a giant-sized boy that had been playing all day in the dirt.

We had just buried Kevin's bloody clothes under a sprawling cottonwood tree in my back yard. I stuck a note in the pocket of the shirt, telling Kevin I would never have said those awful words if I'd known they'd be my last. I tried to express my great love for him and said how much I missed him and that I would never forget him. I knew Kevin wouldn't see it but I needed to write it. And what if he somehow could see it? Nothing in this world could be ruled out and really, we don't understand much, or in some cases, anything.

At the last minute, I wanted to hold back the Stetson. Barney studied me a long time. Finally he said, "It's dented, dirty, and has drops of blood. Put it in the hole, Ricos."

I knew he was right. I held it a while and then put it with the other things. He covered them for me, and we marked the spot with colorful stones I'd gathered from the base of Cimarron Mountain.

For a while Barney and I sat in companionable silence on my front porch, drinking iced tea and watching the colors of sunset in the sky and on the mountains. For a few minutes Cimarron looked fiery red, purple, then golden, and the day began to fade.

"You never told me why Roger Lockey dislikes you so much."

"Well, for one thing, I beat him at pool."

"Tell me the truth, that's not the reason."

"No, I suppose it isn't."

"Come on. Give it up before I have to get rough with you."

He laughed at that. "Well, I did a stupid thing. I had a date with this divorced woman—this was before I met Julia—and I said some things about her to Lockey when we were drinking beer and playing pool. And not very complimentary things, like she was a 'sleazy skank' and you know, guy talk. She lived in Alpine, so how would I know she was Old Man Lockey's daughter?"

"Uh-oh."

"Yeah. I was new in the Sheriff's Office then, and he tried to get me fired."

"It must irritate the crap out of him that you're down here now."

"No shit, Batgirl."

We were quiet a long time.

"I have a brother," announced Barney suddenly.

"Oh yeah? Is he as big as you?"

"Naw, he's a little guy—only six four."

"What happened? He didn't get enough to eat when he was growing up or what? I bet you hogged all the food."

"He's better looking than I am and he's single."

"Your point?"

"My point is that you're single and he's single and I think you'd like each other."

"Please don't do this. Let me find my own man."

"Are you even going to look?"

"No. Not like you'll think I should, probably. The right man will cross my path and I'll know it when the time comes."

He crossed his amazing blue eyes at me.

"Don't do that," I said. "You look positively 'flicted."

He winked. "I'm lost as a goose in a snowstorm."

About the author

Elizabeth A. Garcia has lived for more than thirty years in the Big Bend country of far west Texas. She has hiked, rafted, explored, and earned a living in this wild desert-mountain land near the Rio Grande, on the border of the United States and Mexico. It was experiencing the deep canyons, creosote-covered *bajadas*, and stark, jagged mountains; the wide-open spaces and dark, starry nights that eventually brought her to writing.

One Bloody Shirt at a Time is her first novel, but not her first written story. It is the first of many Deputy Ricos tales.

Beth lives with her cat, Bubs, who watches intently from his sovereign space on the desk next to her computer—when he isn't napping or critiquing her work.

Visit www.deputyricos.com or email the author: deputyricos@yahoo.com

Made in the USA
San Bernardino, CA
29 July 2016